THE HERALD OF HELL

THE HERALD
OF HELL

Paul Doherty

CRÈME de la CRIME

This first world edition published 2015
in Great Britain and in the USA by
Crème de la Crime, an imprint of
SEVERN HOUSE PUBLISHERS LTD of
19 Cedar Road, Sutton, Surrey, England, SM2 5DA.
Trade paperback edition first published 2016
in Great Britain and the USA by
SEVERN HOUSE PUBLISHERS LTD.

Doherty, P. C. author.
  The Herald of Hell. – (The Brother Athelstan mysteries)
  1. Athelstan, Brother (Fictitious character)–Fiction.
  2. Murder–Investigation–Fiction. 3. Tyler's
  Insurrection, 1381–Fiction. 4. Great Britain–History–
  Richard II, 1377-1399–Fiction. 5. Detective and mystery
  stories.
  I. Title II. Series
  813.6-dc23

ISBN-13: 978-1-78029-079-9 (cased)
ISBN-13: 978-1-78029-563-3 (trade paper)
ISBN-13: 978-1-78010-710-3 (e-book)

All Severn House titles are printed on acid-free paper.

Severn House Publishers support the Forest Stewardship Council™ [FSC™],
the leading international forest certification organisation. All our titles that
are printed on FSC certified paper carry the FSC logo.

Typeset by Palimpsest Book Production Ltd.,
Falkirk, Stirlingshire, Scotland.
Printed and bound in Great Britain by
TJ International, Padstow, Cornwall.

*To our second beloved grandson: Aaron Paul Abrahams ('Mr CC'),
with all our love*

HISTORICAL NOTE

By the early summer of 1381 England was teetering on the brink of bloody mayhem and murder. The fourteen-year-old king, Richard II, exercised the rights of the Crown but real power was firmly in the grasp of Richard's paternal uncle, John of Gaunt, head of the house of Lancaster. The glory days of Crécy and Poitiers were over. England had been driven from most of its conquests in France and now found it difficult to combat French influence, be it in the Narrow Seas or even attacks along England's southern coastline. At home discontent seethed, especially in London and the surrounding shires. The peasants fiercely resented the new poll taxes as well as attempts to keep them chained to the soil through legal chicanery. Revolt was being furiously plotted and the peasants' battle chant was rising to a thunderous roar:

'When Adam delved and Eve span
Who was then the gentleman?'

PROLOGUE

'Et Tenebrae Facta – *And Darkness Fell*'

Thibault wished the night was not so black. The rain had ceased but a dense fog had now descended, swiftly falling over both the river and city, creeping along the alleyways, lurking in the narrow yards, drooping from the gables and eaves of houses to clog the eyes and pinch the skin. Nevertheless, the regent's Master of Secrets conceded to himself, the fog also provided a cover for subtle intrigue and tortuous treason which, if discovered, could send him to the scaffold on Tower Hill. He wiped his face and sat back against the stern of the narrow boat. He could only dimly make out the snow-white hair, creamy skin and milky blue eyes of his henchman, Albinus, who was straining at the oars. The man had become his soul-sharer, his father confessor, comforter and counsellor. If their treason failed he too would join Thibault on the scaffold. Albinus lifted his head and smiled through the murk at his master.

'We must be careful,' Thibault murmured, 'ever so careful and prudent.' Albinus just nodded and went back to pulling at the oars, holding the boat steady against the swell of the river. Thibault hitched his cloak closer about him and returned to his thoughts. He and Albinus were committed to the task set them by John of Gaunt. The King's uncle and self-styled regent had taken Thibault to a secret chamber in the heart of his magnificent palace, an ideal place to plot the deadliest treason. No windows. The one and only door was thick and heavy, fashioned out of the purest oak. The walls of the chamber were covered in quilted tapestries displaying all the colours of Gaunt's royal claims: the lions rampant of England, the silver fleur-de-lis of France and the golden crowns of Castile. A truly ambitious man, Gaunt nursed dreams of founding a dynasty which would span the kingdoms of Europe. He faced only one obstacle: his nephew Richard, the boy king of England.

In that secret chamber, lit only by a three-spigot candelabra, with no one else present and the room secured against any eaves-dropper or court spy, Gaunt had whispered the most dangerous treason. One hand on Thibault's shoulder, the other on his pearl-encrusted dagger in its purple-gold sheath, Gaunt had asked Thibault if he too could drink from the chalice being offered? Thibault had replied, without hesitation, that he would drain such a goblet to its dregs and lick the cup clean. Gaunt had smiled with that dazzling look of friendship which always captivated Thibault's soul. Gaunt's fingers fell away from the dagger whilst the hand on Thibault's shoulder became an embrace. Both men were joined in a conspiracy which could end in royal splendour, or in the most excruciating execution. Thibault had witnessed men, naked except for a loin cloth, being tied to a sled and dragged at the tail of a ragged horse through the Lion Gate and up the rocky path to the soaring gallows on Tower Hill, the hangman's nooses dangling like loathsome garlands against the sky. If discovered, Thibault could expect no mercy. The executioners would paint red lines on his naked torso to show where they would cut, before he would be half hanged, his belly split open, his entrails plucked out even as he breathed . . .

The strident cry of a gull startled the Master of Secrets from his hellish reverie. He breathed in sharply, coughing on the cold, salty, fish-tinged river air. Gaunt had shown him the true path their plotting would open – a glorious path, he reminded himself. A veritable highway leading to manor lands, rich pastures, profit-able licences and lordships. Thibault's heart, to quote the psalmist, had leapt like a stag. He, a lord! He, the offspring of a common whore and some wandering scholar, to be clothed in silk and ermine, to have his arms emblazoned on a banner carried before him by a herald, to sit in splendour close to the throne of a king who would exalt him even higher. All he had to do was keep faith with Gaunt, do his bidding and help spin a web which would entangle the kingdom. Of course, as now, danger threatened with many a potential slip between cup and lip. Thibault had, however, been most prudent as that web began to spread. The Master of Secrets played with the chancery ring beneath his gloved finger. He suspected his own clerk, Amaury Whitfield, had begun to realize how far this web stretched and what it entailed. Nevertheless, Whitfield could be controlled and, if necessary, dispensed with. Until then, the clerk had to be watched. Thibault moved restlessly. Whitfield had absented himself from the secret chancery, he and his minion, the scrivener Oliver Lebarge. They had both pleaded for boon days so as to attend the Festival of Cokayne at the Golden Oliphant, the tavern brothel run by that queen of whores, Elizabeth Cheyne.

Thibault glanced up as a horn blew, ringing through the bank of fog rolling across the surface of the river. Albinus rested on his oars and Thibault watched the bobbing light of a passing barge disappear into the blackness of the night. Albinus returned to his rowing and Thibault to his ruminations. Cheyne was a whore amongst whores. She reminded Thibault of his own mother, and that made him feel sick to his stomach. He loathed doing business with Cheyne yet at times he had no choice. The whore mistress, like all her kind, was a snapper-up of trifles which might contain real nuggets of political intrigue. Whitfield and Lebarge would be with her now, celebrating a world turned upside down, a bacchanalian feast where all kinds of filthy practices took place. Not that Whitfield would have joined them to the full. If the whispered gossip was truth, Amaury Whitfield, clerk of the secret chancery, was a veritable gelding in bed. Whatever, Thibault reflected, let him wallow in his sty. Soon Whitfield would have to return to the chancery and concentrate on that secret cipher. The document had been seized from the Upright Men, the leaders of the Great Community of the Realm who were plotting furiously to bring about violent revolution to topple both Church and Crown. Thibault hugged his arms close. He was playing a dangerous game, plotting against the Upright Men even as he journeyed secretly to meet one of their most prominent leaders. They both sought to foment rebellion and revolution, but to different ends. The Master of Secrets wondered how much he would learn tonight, both directly and indirectly. Would he discover more about the cipher seized from Reynard, the Upright Men's wily courier, who was now reflecting on his sins in the grim fastness of Newgate prison? Or perhaps he would glean something about the Herald of Hell, the mysterious envoy of the Upright Men who appeared at night, all over the city, to warn those judged to be opponents of the Great Community of the

Realm. Whitfield and Lebarge had been visited in their chamber in Fairlop Lane. The Herald had delivered his grim warning and disappeared, leaving Whitfield and Lebarge frightened out of their wits. Thibault had granted both men leave. Perhaps the charms of Mistress Cheyne and her moppets would soothe their humours, then Whitfield could return refreshed to the study of that mysterious document.

'Master?' Albinus leaned forward. 'Master, we are almost there.'

Thibault steadied himself as Albinus pulled once more and the keel of the boat crunched on the gravel and silt surrounding the Black Vale, a small, desolate island close to the south bank of the Thames. The boat rocked slightly, embedded in the shale. Thibault rose and, once Albinus had secured the boat, followed his henchman up from the riverside. He felt the dagger in its sheath on his warbelt, on the other side a small hand-held arbalest with its quiver of barbed quarrels. At the top of the slight rise they paused and stared into the darkness. The fog had thinned. Thibault could make out the ruins which peppered this gloomy islet: jagged walls, the carcasses of ruined cottages. A bleak wilderness of dark, shiny pools, sluggish ditches and heaps of mud which fed the coarse grass, rank weeds and stunted trees which grew there.

'An ugly place,' Albinus whispered, 'with an even uglier reputation. Master, we must be prudent.'

'As always,' Thibault hissed. 'You have the lantern, the tinder?'

'Yes.'

'Then spark the flame.'

Albinus crouched and opened his leather sack. Thibault heard the tinder strike then Albinus lifted the shuttered lantern against the night.

'Make the signal.'

Albinus obeyed; three times the shutter on the lantern clattered up and down. Thibault stared into the darkness, oblivious now to the raw fog nipping his skin.

'There,' he breathed, pointing into the night. 'Look, Albinus.'

Their signal had been answered by three sharp bursts of pinprick light. 'We wait.' Thibault walked a few paces forward. 'Keep the lantern light turned towards them but stay behind me, Albinus. Prime your crossbow. At the first sign of trickery, loose.'

Albinus stepped back into the darkness as Thibault watched the bobbing light approach. A figure emerged out of the murk, cowled and cloaked. The stranger walked purposefully, the lantern swinging in his right hand, and in his left Thibault glimpsed a small crossbow, probably primed and ready. The figure stopped about a yard from Thibault and lifted the lantern. The Master of Secrets glimpsed an oval face, clean-shaven, a hairlip mouth and beetle brows: this fitted the description Gaunt had given him. Thibault pushed back his own cowl for the stranger to glimpse his face.

'You choose a peculiar place to do business, Master Thibault, nothing more than blighted heathland with old charcoal burnings. They say the soot still falls like snowflakes garbed in mourning.'

Thibault recognized the prearranged greeting. 'Safe enough,' he replied in kind, 'for men swept up in a carnival of bloodshed. You are what you call yourself, Master Tyler, Wat Tyler?'

'I am Wat Tyler, I am Jack Straw, I am every man and I am no man.'

'Yet you are leader of the Upright Men?'

'One of a few.'

'How do I know that this is not a device to trap me?'

'Fear not, Master Thibault, except that you are here and so am I. In the darkness beyond you Albinus waits ready. Behind me stands my escort with his warbow, also primed.'

Thibault nodded in agreement.

'Then let us do business, Master Thibault. Tonight, at this witching hour, you can call me Tyler, for that is what I am. My true name and identity will only be revealed when we end this game together.'

'And the game you propose?'

'Master Thibault, I am a leader amongst the Upright Men, a chief in the Great Community of the Realm which plots to topple prince and prelate and build a New Jerusalem here in London, you know that. We conspire against you, you and your master reply in kind. We despatched the Herald of Hell to haunt your adherents in the city; who he is and where he comes from is my business, not yours. If you caught him you would cut his heart out at Smithfield just as you intend a similar death for our courier, Reynard, seized by you and lodged in Newgate until he hangs.'

'Or confesses and throws himself on our mercy.' Thibault
regretted the words as soon as they were out of his mouth. He
could almost see Tyler smile through the dark. 'Whatever the
case,' Thibault added hastily, 'we have your cipher, and my clerk
Whitfield, a peritus, skilled in cryptic writing, will break it to
reveal the truth.'

'Will he now?' Tyler mocked.

'And Reynard will hang for the murder of Edmund Lacy, bell
clerk at St Mary Le Bow.'

'And he deserves to,' Tyler jibed. 'He allowed himself to be
caught. Reynard can rot in Newgate or dance in the air at Tyburn
for all I care.'

'We are not here for him,' Thibault declared sharply, eager to
gain control of this midnight meeting.

'No, we certainly are not, Master Thibault. We are here as the
deadliest of opponents. The Great Community of the Realm,
the Upright Men and our soldiers the Earthworms, hunt you as
you do them. Our all-seeing eye watches you as you watch us.
Let us face the facts, the revolt is coming. You cannot prevent it
and neither can I. The peasant armies will march. London will
be stormed, its bridge seized and the Tower besieged. The
Earthworms intend to burn Newgate and drag out its keepers by
the hair of their heads. Men will die barbarously. I must make
sure that I do not, and you too should take great care that you
are not swept up in the great slaughter.' Tyler paused. 'And your
daughter, Isabella. I understand you will lodge her with Athelstan,
the Dominican priest at St Erconwald's . . .?'

'He has promised to protect Isabella. We rarely mention it,
but he has given his word. I believe he will be her safest refuge.'

'The Upright Men are strong in St Erconwald's. You know
that, Master of Secrets, you have your own spy there.' Tyler
laughed softly as Thibault abruptly stiffened. 'Do not worry,
Master Thibault, we know there is one, but not his or her identity
or name. Fret not, the priest Athelstan and your daughter have
nothing to fear. Both will be protected most closely by our
representative, someone who sits very high in the Council of the
Upright Men.'

'Enough,' Thibault snapped. 'What are our conclusions?'

'You know what they are. The revolt will occur but its outcome can and will be controlled by you, your master and myself. To achieve that, certain conditions must be met, yes?'

'My Lord of Gaunt, together with his elder son, Henry, is about to leave for the Scottish March,' Thibault declared. 'He will take with him a host of mailed men, mounted and on foot, engines of war and an array of bowmen and hobelars. And for yourself, have you chosen the day?'

'Very close,' Tyler replied. 'As for you, Master Thibault, you must remain ensconced in the Tower along with that bitch of a Queen Mother, Princess Joan. She and her whelp must be kept there whilst we – I – must be allowed entry to their gilded cages.' Tyler let his words hang in the air. Thibault, even though he was committed to this, felt a chill of deep fear.

'In storming those cages,' Tyler continued evenly, 'certain men will and must die. Make sure you are not one of these. You and I cannot control events, only their outcome. Once this has been achieved, all will be well. The path will be cleared. Gaunt can come hurrying south with his army. Meetings can be arranged, councils held, punishments meted out and pardons proclaimed.'

'And does the cipher we have seized have any bearing on this?'

'Master Thibault, until certain conclusions are reached, the war between us continues. The cipher is the work of Grindcobbe and others. I am party to it but I have no control over it. Only a few know its secrets. I am one of these, and to betray it would only deepen suspicions.'

'About what?'

'Divisions are already appearing amongst the Upright Men over what we intend, what we hope will happen once the revolt has occurred and the kingdom been shaken. Some of us talk of a republic like those in Northern Italy, others of a commonwealth like the cities along the Rhine, whilst we, Master Thibault, dream of a realm purified, purged and under the strong leadership of a new royal house.'

'And for you personally, Master Tyler?'

'Why, Master Thibault, like you I have dreams of power, lordship and dominion, a free and complete pardon from my Lord of Gaunt so like you I can sit high in his councils. No need then to meet along muddy marshes or beside squalid ditches full of filth with the fog curling in about us. However, until then we must shake the dice from the hazard cup and see how it falls. Master Thibault, I bid you adieu.'

Gaunt's Master of Secrets watched Tyler walk away into the gathering gloom. He strained his eyes, certain that he detected a second figure following him.

'Master?'

'A good evening's work, Albinus. Now there goes a man who thinks he controls the game but doesn't.'

'Master?'

'My Lord of Gaunt and his eldest son Henry of Lancaster will go north. If the rebels are defeated he will turn swiftly south to be in for the kill. If the rebels succeed, he will then sit, wait and watch. If Master Tyler's plot comes to fruition, my Lord of Gaunt will be the only royal prince with a standing army behind him. If Tyler's plot fails, my Lord of Gaunt will return to crush all flickers of rebellion. In the end, our master will be safely removed from the season of slaughter and be free to plot and take action as he thinks appropriate. So yes, Albinus, in all an excellent night's work.'

'And the cipher?'

'I want to unravel that for my own reasons, apart from my nagging curiosity. For that we need Whitfield, once he has finished wallowing in the squalid pleasures of the Golden Oliphant.'

Sir Everard Camoys, mercer and leading banker in Cheapside, was dreaming. He was locked in a nightmare about boiling the flesh from the corpse of his former comrade, Simon Penchen, killed whilst fighting alongside the Teutonic Knights against Slav intruders on the eastern marches of the Holy Roman Empire. Sir Everard, and more especially his brother Reginald, had been determined to bring their comrade's remains home for a proper burial in St Mary Le Bow. They would not leave Simon's corpse out on those frozen plains dotted with dark, sinister-looking forests: a desolate landscape, a Hell on earth, where the spirits of the departed, in their own dead flesh, roamed the countryside with their coffins held aloft. Such monstrosities could only be despatched by being dug up and decapitated, their rotten hearts roasted until they cracked open and the evil angel which had animated them, fled in the form of a crow. This malignant spirit would join the other demons yelling in the air: grotesques with flames dancing in their eyes, their mouths crammed with noxious fumes. Fighting alongside the Teutonic Knights, Sir Everard and Reginald had learnt all about the living dead, which had made them even more determined not to leave Simon's mortal remains in that ghastly land.

They had dressed Simon's cadaver in an ancient chapel which also served as the treasure house for the Teutonic Knights. At the time Sir Everard should have realized something was dreadfully amiss, and that Reginald was bent on committing heinous sacrilege. Satan, unbeknown to Sir Everard, had been there sticking out his tongue whilst holding his fork in the crook of his arm, with Death sidling beside him, his quiver full of fiery arrows. Satan had certainly struck. Oh, Reginald had always been hungry for riches, determined to return and strut the streets of London, garbed in a puffed tunic bounded by a belt with precious studs to match the gold and black of his sheath and hose, a bejewelled chaperon on his head. Reginald, a self-proclaimed artist, was always taken with any exquisitely precious object, be it a ring, a brooch or, as in this case, a holy relic. Sir Everard wished he had paid greater heed to one of the wall paintings in that ancient chapel. The fresco depicted a man in a blue gown and red hose, seated on a flesh-coloured chair, a harp with golden strings resting on his lap. At first glance a picture of serenity, except, in the bottom corner, lurked Death in the guise of a skeleton, drawing his bow fashioned out of bone and taking careful aim at the harpist. Of course, Reginald would have ignored any warnings, as well as the advice scrawled beneath the painting: that any violator of that hallowed place would have his body consumed by furry rats. Reginald was never a man to be warned . . .

Sir Everard jerked awake from his half-sleep and pulled himself up against the feather-filled bolsters. They had eventually brought Penchen's corpse back for burial in St Mary's, then he and Reginald had gone their separate ways. Sir Everard had joined the Goldsmiths' Guild and soon prospered. As for Reginald . . . Sir Everard sighed. His brother had become involved with the whore Elizabeth Cheyne.

Only years after they had returned from Prussia did Reginald confess that he had stolen the precious relic, the Cross of Lothar, with its antique cameo of the Emperor Augustus, a miniature but exquisitely carved cross, carved and decorated with gold, gems, pearls and precious enamels. Reginald had cheerfully admitted, rogue that he was, that he had filched the relic from the treasury in the ancient chapel of the Teutonic Knights not simply for profit, but because he truly lusted after the cross's delicate beauty and its links with an ancient past. Reginald also viewed the cross as part reparation for the death of his comrade Simon. He had refused adamantly to restore it and had taken the secret of the relic's whereabouts to his grave. Did the whore Elizabeth Cheyne now possess it? That might explain why she seemed to have little or no interest in where it could be. And it might be the real reason why Sir Everard's own scapegrace son Matthias frequented that brothel, especially now with its Festival of Cokayne. Sir Everard snorted with annoyance – Cokayne! Why were they celebrating at a time when London teetered on the abyss, with the threat of revolt growing ever more imminent? Out in the surrounding shires, the Commonwealth of the Peasants plotted furiously under their leaders like the hedge priest, John Ball, who warned that God's wrath would envelop them all.

Sir Everard thanked God that heaven had taken his beloved Eleanor to itself: his wife would not witness the bloody mayhem which would soon drench the city. Cheapside turned into a corpse-strewn battleground. Pitched battles outside the Tower. The rebels storming across London Bridge, seizing the Gatehouse and forti-fications which, if their doggerel proclamation proved prophetic, would be swiftly decorated with the severed heads of their oppo-nents, especially that of John of Gaunt, self-styled protector, uncle and regent of the boy king, Richard II. Others would soon join him, such as Master Thibault, Gaunt's Master of Secrets who now huddled with his henchmen behind the grim fortifica-tions of the Tower. Already many of the court party were preparing to flee; even members of Master Thibault's own household were drawing their gold and silver from the bankers of Cheapside and slipping into the night, well away from London and the doom which threatened.

Fiery preachers, garbed in horse- and goatskin, stalked the

streets warning citizens that the iron seats of judgement had been set up amidst a swarm of serpents. The skulls of London's citizens would be split and, with the parting of the sutures, their souls would fly out to mingle with a host of spirits in the air. A dark, dank yet glittering mist would encase the city like a funeral shroud, and through this would prowl all the demons of Hell. The preachers, undoubtedly sent by the Upright Men, foretold that London would undergo the blood-splattered pangs of rebirth to emerge as the New Jerusalem with silver ramparts and gold-encrusted doorways fashioned out of pure white crystal and blue marble. Gaunt had hanged a few of these self-proclaimed prophets on moveable four-branched gallows, pushed up and down Cheapside so all could gaze on the strangled remains of his enemies. However, terror piled upon terror did nothing to curb the fear creeping across the city like a thick river mist which swirled and curled its way through everything.

Sir Everard pushed back the thick woollen rug and crisp linen under-sheets. He glimpsed the early dawn of this late May morning piercing the gaps between the shutters, shimmering in the light of the polished floorboards. He gazed round his bedchamber with its empty cloth poles hanging from the ceiling, the polished aumbry with cleared shelves, the great chestnut coffer now stripped of its contents: the high-backed settle before the hearth bereft of cushions, the empty spaces on the walls where paintings, triptychs and coloured cloths had been taken down. Gathering up his cloak from a stool, he dragged the candle-table closer. He took some comfort in the fact that he had removed all the costly items as well as his great iron-bound coffers with their triple locks. A former comrade in arms, now Constable of Leeds Castle, had indentured to protect all of Sir Everard's movables. The goldsmith wondered whether he should also leave, but he was not sure if Matthias would accompany him. And what would happen if the revolt was crushed, its leaders torn to pieces, their dead flesh hacked into bloody chunks to decorate the spikes of London Bridge and the Lion Gate at the Tower: would Gaunt and Master Thibault then begin to sift amongst those who had fled? Would they adopt the line from scripture, that whoever was not with them was against them? Sir Everard let his vein-streaked legs dangle over the side of the bed, then lowered his feet and felt

the crushed herbs which dusted the floor planks. He wondered if
Matthias had returned home from his roistering or if he was still
at the Golden Oliphant, searching for the Cross of Lothar. Then
his heart skipped a beat at the sound of a horn braying outside.
He sat, the breath catching in his throat, as he waited for what he
knew was coming. One blast, two, followed by a third. The Herald
of Hell was outside this house! Pierced by a dart of chilling fear,
Sir Everard crumpled on to the bed as he heard the voice, powerful
and carrying, like a blast from a hollow trumpet:

'Lord Camoys and all who with you dwell,
Harken to this warning from the Herald of Hell,
Judgement is coming, it will not be late,
Vengeance already knocks on your gate.'

The same doggerel threat which, he knew, had been proclaimed
throughout the city. He had hoped to be spared. The goldsmith
drew a deep breath, his courage returning, angry that he had been
so frightened. He lurched to his feet, hearing noises coming from
below as servants hurried to find out what was happening.

Sir Everard pulled back the oxhide draught excluder and
opened the door window with its glazed, painted glass. He stared
out, but Acre Street lay empty, not even a wandering dog or cat.
He wrinkled his nose at the foul smell from the sewer which ran
along the centre of the street, then sniffed at his linen bedrobe,
sprinkled with Provins Roses.

'Who's there?' he shouted, leaning out of the window. Other
windows along the street were being opened. The ward watchman
came into view, staff in one hand, lantern horn in the other.

'Is that you, Poulter?' Camoys bellowed. 'Did you hear that?
Did you see anything?'

'Nothing, Sir Everard.' The watchman pulled down the folds
of his heavy cloak. 'I heard the proclamation and I came round
the corner out of Spindle alleyway. But,' he shrugged, 'I saw
nothing at all.' Poulter pointed in the direction of the front door.
'I think you'd best see this for yourself.'

Camoys grabbed his cloak, slipped on his sandals and hurried
down, pushing aside the few frightened servant maids who still
worked in the house. By the Angelus bell most of these would

have slipped away on this excuse or that pretext. Shepherd, Sir Everard's steward, had already gone to visit an allegedly ailing mother in Dorset. The goldsmith pulled back the bolts and turned the heavy key, then swung open the door and stared down at the beaker of blood containing two stalks, each bearing a small onion, a macabre imitation of heads poled in blood above London Bridge. The Upright Men had sent both him and his son Matthias a warning of their possible fate. Now beside himself with anger, Camoys kicked over the beaker even as he wondered who had bellowed that proclamation. Despite an obvious attempt to disguise the voice, the Goldsmith was certain he recognized it, but that would have to wait. The Herald of Hell, whoever he was, had issued his dire summons and Sir Everard realized that he faced as great a threat as any he had confronted on the eerie borderlands of the Holy Roman Empire.

The Herald of Hell watched Sir Everard close the door to his gilded mansion. He continued to lurk in the shadowy recess further along the street, waiting until all the excitement had died down. The neighbours who had been roused now doused their candles; doors, shutters and gates were locked and bolted. Poulter, the ward bailiff, a lonely, doleful figure, rubbed his face with one hand and beat the end of his staff furiously against the ground in frustration. Then the watchman straightened up and trudged away, muttering to himself. The Herald waited for a while before crossing to an empty laystall and filling his sack with what was hidden there. He then slipped into the thinning dark, hastening along the alleyways, flitting like a shadow, one hand grasping the sack, the other on the hilt of his dagger. No one would accost him, and if they did, he had warrants to explain his presence on the streets of Cheapside long before dawn fully broke. The Herald turned a corner and, keeping to the shadows, crept along to the old ironmonger's shop which stood on the corner of an alleyway halfway down Fairlop Lane. The Herald placed the sack on the ground, then drew his dagger to prise open the lock on the door of the narrow house belonging to the chancery clerk, Amaury Whitfield. To his surprise, the door was off its catch and creaked open. The Herald of Hell stiffened with fear. He recalled a wall painting in his church of goggle-eyed Hell hounds slipping

through the murk, watching a spirit of the damned fall into the
deathly salamanderembrace of a hairy-mouthed fiend. An
unspeakable horror! Did such grotesque terrors lie beyond this
door which should have been firmly locked?

He pushed it open and stepped into the darkness which hung
like a thick, stifling pall, reeking of musty damp. He started at
the cry of some night bird further along the street, followed by the
shrill scream of a hunting cat and the bark of a dog howling at
the lightening sky. The Herald drew a deep breath and closed the
door behind him. A rat scurried across the floor, a scampering,
startling sound which only sharpened his anxiety. The Herald
paused, leaning against the wall. He had been instructed to come
here just before the Jesus bell tolled the approaching hour for
the first Mass of the day. An Earthworm, one of the street warriors
of the Upright Men, had delivered the message detailing what
the Herald should do and where he should go. He had expected
someone to meet him outside Whitfield's house but there had
been no one, yet he was not at all sure that he was alone. He
could feel a cold sweat prickling his back and he fought to control
his breathing. Was this a trap? He did not want to be seized,
taken up and lodged in Newgate like Reynard, put to the torture
until he broke and confessed everything. Yet the Earthworm
messenger had shown him the all-seeing eye, the mark of the
Upright Men. The Herald caught his breath as a faint sound
echoed further down this hellishly dark passageway. Again the
sound, and abruptly a lanternhorn, light glowing like a beacon,
shone through the gloom.

'Approach, Herald,' a voice mockingly called. 'Step into the
pool of light so I can see your face clearly.'

Curbing his rising panic, the Herald obeyed, walking slowly,
boots slithering on the greasy paving stones.

'Who – who are you?' The Herald couldn't keep the tremor
out of his voice.

'Simon Grindcobbe.'

The Herald relaxed at the name of one of the most senior
captains of the Upright Men.

'How do I know?' he stuttered.

'Lift the lantern,' the voice mocked, 'and turn around. Quickly
now, the hour is passing. Take the lantern.'

The Herald did so and started at a sound behind him. He lifted the lantern, turned and stared in horror at a devilishly garbed figure who must have followed him in from the street. An Earthworm, hair spiked with grease, his face hidden behind a feathery raven's mask. This grotesquely attired figure carried an arbalest, primed and ready, the brightly barbed quarrel pointing directly at the Herald.

'Now, now,' Grindcobbe's voice soothed, 'no need to fear, put the lantern down. Good. Just a few questions then we shall be gone. Reynard is taken up, he failed to deliver the cipher. Master Thibault, Gaunt's creature, now has it but not the key. I suspect Reynard must still hold that on his person.'

'I don't know,' the Herald mumbled. 'I was just waiting for orders.'

'True, that is now our concern, not yours. So, to other business. Sir Everard Camoys received a visitor tonight?'

'Yes, he did. I saw . . .'

'Good, good,' Grindcobbe broke in. 'Camoys is a merchant banker. It's well to terrify the likes of him. He needs to be gone from this city and take his feckless son with him. We do not need Matthias Camoys haunting the church of St Mary Le Bow, do we, with his stupid questions and hunger for the Cross of St Lothar? God knows what he might stumble on to.'

'He could be disposed of.'

'No, no.' Grindcobbe's voice turned hard. 'There has been enough dancing around the maypole with the killing of Edmund Lacy the bell clerk. Matthias Camoys' death would only attract unwanted interest. No. Let's hope we can frighten both father and son out of London. After all,' Grindcobbe laughed softly, 'it would be the best for everyone, including themselves. So,' he continued briskly, 'we are here. I asked you to come for two reasons. First, I have been across to Southwark. I was supposed to meet Amaury Whitfield regarding the cipher taken from Reynard but he failed to appear. I wonder why. Have those ladies of the night, those moppets of the moon at the Golden Oliphant, sapped his strength? Has Whitfield drunk too deeply of Mistress Cheyne's best Bordeaux . . .?'

'What has that to do with me?'

'Oh, everything, Master Herald. Gaunt's henchmen regard you

as the leader of the Upright Men in London, but you are not. You are only our faithful servant, one who has been richly rewarded for his work. Anyway, I was supposed to meet Whitfield tonight whilst you were ordered to search this property. However, nothing runs smoothly in this valley of sorrows we call life. Whitfield, as I have said, did not appear. So I hastened across here with my friends, one of whom, Brother Raven,' Grindcobbe chuckled, 'now guards your back. We did your task for you, Master Herald. We have searched this house both here and above, only to find nothing. Swept clean, it is, bare as a poor widow's pantry. Strange, is it not?'

'Again, sir, I know nothing of that.'

'But you are prepared?' Grindcobbe snapped. The Herald peered into the darkness, but all he could make out was a shadowy outline moving slightly against the poor light. 'You are prepared,' Grindcobbe repeated, 'for the day of the great slaughter?'

'Of course. All is ready, but Whitfield . . .' The Herald's curiosity was now pricked. 'He appears to have fled. My warning must have . . .'

'So it would appear,' Grindcobbe replied. 'In the circumstances this is a little unfortunate, but I suspect that our clerk, like so many at the Tower and Westminster, fears for the future. Your warning may have simply spurred him on his way. Whitfield,' Grindcobbe added almost as an afterthought, 'has a great deal to fear from so many quarters.'

The Herald's unease deepened in the ominous silence, broken only by the sound of his own breathing and the slither of footfall as Brother Raven moved behind him.

'If Whitfield has stripped this place . . .'

'He and his friend, Lebarge,' Grindcobbe interrupted sharply. 'Yes, apparently they have got busy on their own affairs, as you have been, Master Herald?'

'Of course . . .'

'Busy in particular tenements not far from here, buying warbows and quivers crammed with yard shafts, everything a master bowman needs? You have left these in certain chambers overlooking Cheapside?'

'Of course,' the Herald rushed to answer. 'I was instructed to.'

'By whom?'

'By the Upright Men. I have been visited by another of your great captains. He meets me, as you do, deep in the shadows. He shows his warrant and . . .' The Herald fell silent as Brother Raven pushed the sharp barb of the crossbow quarrel against the nape of his neck. The Herald tried to quieten his panic. 'Was I not supposed to do that?' he gabbled, his stomach pitching with fear. He fell silent as the sharp barb again brushed his skin. He had heard rumours about how serious divisions were appearing amongst the captains who sat high on the Council of the Upright Men. 'I did,' the Herald stammered, 'what I was told. The warbows and arrows are stored. Why, do you want me . . .'

'Never mind,' Grindcobbe snapped. 'You must be ready for the signal which will come soon enough.'

The dark shape moved through the murk. The lantern was lifted, its shutter pulled down, and the darkness returned.

'Go,' Grindcobbe ordered. 'Master Herald, you may leave. Brother Raven will show you out.'

Grindcobbe watched the Herald stumble back up the passageway and through the door into the street. The Upright Man closed his eyes and reflected on what he knew to be the truth. He and his confederates had planned to build a new Sion, a holy city here in London where pauper and prince would be equal before God and the law. A return to the harmony of the Garden of Eden where no predator swaggered or heralded knight rode arrogantly on his warhorse. A new beginning was what they had planned, but now demons had invaded their carefully constructed paradise, snaking in amongst its trees. Divisions had appeared. The tapestry of interwoven ideals and dreams was rent. Disunity had emerged here, there and everywhere. Rumours swarmed like loathsome spiders and mistrust, like the croaking of some foulsome toad, could be clearly heard in certain voices of the Upright Men.

'Master, what now?'

'God knows.' Grindcobbe opened his eyes and stared at Brother Raven. 'Whitfield appears to have fled. He may or not be at the Golden Oliphant, or so drunk he's incapable of movement.' Grindcobbe drew in a deep breath. 'Master Thibault has the cipher. More importantly, he has Reynard locked up in Newgate and our messenger may still carry the key to that cipher. If so . . .'

'Can Reynard be trusted?' Brother Raven's voice echoed dully from behind the grotesque feathery mask.

'No, he certainly can't be. I suspect that Master Thibault may well offer him a pardon, an amnesty in return for everything Reynard can reveal, but that must not happen. So,' Grindcobbe rubbed his hands together, 'we have brothers in Newgate?'

'Hydrus, Wyvern and the madcap Benedict Bedlam, all ripe for hanging.'

'And I am sure,' Grindcobbe murmured, 'that Reynard is determined not to join their dance in the air above Tyburn stream. Get messages to our followers amongst the Newgate turnkeys. What has to be done should be done swiftly, eh?'

'And the matter of longbows and arrows left in those chambers along Cheapside?'

'It's too late and far too dangerous to do anything about that,' Grindcobbe retorted. 'Leave it for the moment. Get messages to our friends at the Golden Oliphant. I want to know what has happened to Whitfield. Keep that brothel under close watch.'

'And you, Master?'

Grindcobbe rose to his feet. 'I think it's best to say as little as possible. I intend to return to Southwark and visit our friends at St Erconwald's.'

'Master, be careful. Rumours abound that the parish houses one of Thibault's spies, a traitor to our cause.'

'I have heard the same,' Grindcobbe murmured. 'I will be careful, but I need you to get messages to our captains there. Swiftly now.'

Brother Raven left. Grindcobbe sat back on the stool. He tried to control his sense of urgency, yet time was now the most precious commodity. He had received messages from Kent and Essex; banners were about to unfurl and the season of slaughter was closer than ever.

PART ONE

'Oliphant: a curved, ornately embellished drinking horn.'

B rother Athelstan, Dominican friar and parish priest of St Erconwald's in Southwark, sat on the sanctuary chair placed in the entrance to the rood screen of his church. He stared in utter disbelief at the pageant being staged before him. Judith, once a member of the travelling players, 'The Straw Men', who had now settled in the parish, had been persuaded by his council, led by Watkin the Dung Collector and Pike the Ditcher, to prepare a play for midsummer. They had chosen the translation of a famous French masque, *La Demoiselle de la Tour* – 'The Lady of the Tower'. The principal role had of course been given, despite the best efforts of the parish wives led by Imelda Pike's hard-faced spouse, to Cecily the Courtesan with her sister Clarissa as her lady in waiting. Both madams had risen to the occasion, their gold-spun hair a glorious mass of curls framing pretty faces, their gowns cut deliberately low so, as Athelstan secretly reflected, they literally carried all before them.

Athelstan had risen before dawn and recited his office in the chantry chapel of St Erconwald's. Bonaventure, the great, one-eyed tom cat who had adopted the friar as his closest friend, had been his only companion. Athelstan had then celebrated the Jesus Mass with this most faithful of gospel greeters amongst his parishioners. Afterwards the friar had broken his fast in the priest's house and then returned to convene the parish council, where Mauger the bell clerk had taken careful note of the decisions about repairs that Crispin the Carpenter insisted must be done to the tower and its beacon light. According to Crispin, these needed to be carried out urgently. In fact, Crispin argued, until these essential repairs were completed, he would be grateful if their parish priest did not use the tower for his star-gazing at night. Once Athelstan had agreed, to the murmured approval of his parish council, Judith had insisted that their priest remain to

see part of their mummer's masque. The friar could only sit and
stare in quiet wonderment.

Cecily and Clarissa were hiding in the tower chamber whilst
outside in the nave ranged their defenders led by Ranulf the
Rat-catcher, Hig the Pigman, Mauger, Moleskin the boatman and
a host of others. These would protect the ladies against the coven
of the evil black knight – Watkin, ably assisted by Pike and their
followers. Athelstan's gaze was caught by a miniature painting
executed on one of the drum-like pillars which separated the
nave from the chancel, the work of their parish artist, Giles of
Sempringham, also known as the Hangman of Rochester.
Athelstan stared at this depiction of the death of Dives, the rich
man in the gospels, damned and ready for burial deep in the fiery
bowels of Hell. The hangman had caught the dramatic scene so
accurately that Athelstan could almost feel the symptoms of
approaching death which now plagued Dives: the misty eyes, the
drooping skin, the furry tongue thrust through blackened lips and
the rigid feet. Athelstan wondered what the hangman was doing
now – carrying out executions at Smithfield or above Tyburn
Stream? Would the Hangman know anything about what had
happened at the Golden Oliphant, Southwark's most notorious
brothel, from which one of his 'enforced guests' had so recently
fled?

Athelstan turned in his chair and peered across the sanctuary
at the mercy enclave, where fugitives from the law could remain
unmolested once they had grasped the altar horn and demanded
the church's protection. The recess now housed two such guests.
The first was Oliver Lebarge, a slender, mouse-faced man dressed
in drab fustian, his grey hair unkempt, a scrivener, obviously,
from the inkstains on his fingers. Lebarge had walked quietly
into St Erconwald's just after Mass, touched the corner of the
altar, demanded sanctuary and allowed Athelstan to usher him
into the mercy enclave. He had given his name almost in a
whisper. Lebarge refused to declare what he had done except
that he had fled from the Golden Oliphant, where a violent death
had occurred so he feared for his own life and safety. Lebarge had
surrendered his dagger to Athelstan in accordance with the law
and allowed the friar to search his person, but the Dominican
had found nothing else. Lebarge had remained taciturn, sullen

and withdrawn. Appearing highly nervous, the scrivener had informed Athelstan that he would only eat and drink what the parish provided and that he would wait for justice. Athelstan shrugged, blessed him and walked away. Benedicta the widow woman, together with Crim the altar boy, had later taken the fugitive some bread, meat and ale. Once Lebarge had established who they were and the origin of the food, he reluctantly accepted it, and now sat huddled, lost in his own thoughts.

The second fugitive next to Lebarge made Athelstan grin. Radegund the Relic Seller! This cunning charlatan now lay stretched out, head resting against his 'Holy Satchel' as he called his bag of religious artefacts. Athelstan had never really decided whether he should indulge in limitless admiration for Radegund's persuasive patter or sheer pity for the relic seller's many victims: men and women who blithely bought a scrap of Jesus' napkin, nails pared from the Virgin Mary, hair from St Joseph's beard, a feather from Gabriel's wing, straw from the manger, a loaf from the Last Supper, Salome's bracelet, or even dung from the donkey in the stable at Bethlehem! Radegund sold these ridiculous forgeries yet people kept coming back for more – except for now. Apparently Radegund had been busy selling a bloodstained tunic purportedly worn by one of the Holy Innocents slaughtered by Herod to some court notable. Unfortunately, the tunic was recognized by a flesher's wife who, in a voice as brazen as the last trump, accosted Radegund, boldly proclaiming that the tunic had been stolen from her washing line and steeped in a vat of blood near her husband's stall. Radegund had tried to defend himself, or so he said, claiming the clothing was almost 1,400 years old. However, when the relic seller held up a bloodstained hand in protest, the crowd had decided against him, so Radegund had fled here for sanctuary. As usual Radegund would lie low for a while and, when the time was opportune, slip back to his usual mischief.

'Brother! Brother!'

Athelstan turned back. The masque of 'The Lady of the Tower' had descended into chaos, with Judith shouting at everyone that this was a parish play, not a time of misrule.

'Brother!' Athelstan glanced up. Tiptoft, messenger of Sir John Cranston, Lord High Coroner of London, stood smiling down at

him. Athelstan narrowed his eyes at this most eccentric of
retainers, garbed in Lincoln green like some forest verderer, his
flame-red hair spiked with nard.

'Brother Athelstan, I am sorry to intrude, but Sir John Cranston
needs you immediately at the Golden Oliphant.'

'Yes, yes,' Athelstan murmured, staring across at Lebarge, 'I
did wonder . . .'

Athelstan crossed himself and went into the sacristy to collect
his chancery satchel. He stopped and beckoned Benedicta to
join him. Once inside, he half closed the sacristy door.

'Benedicta, I must leave. Sir John awaits.' He indicated with his
head. 'Let Judith deal with the mummers. Try to persuade our
sanctuary man Lebarge to take comfort from where he is. Reassure
him that only you or Crim will bring his food from my house
and oh,' Athelstan tapped the side of his head, 'did you know
that Pike the Ditcher has a cousin, Sister Matilda, a nun, one of
the Poor Clares?'

'No, Brother.' Benedicta laughed. 'Pike, of all people!'

'Well, apparently she is passing through Southwark later today.
Pike has asked to meet her here in the sacristy about the third hour
after midday. He says he needs a little privacy. I can see no diffi-
culty in that.' Athelstan grinned. 'I just wish I could meet her.'
The friar paused as the widow woman quickly turned and went
back to the half-opened sacristy door and peered out. 'Benedicta?'

'My apologies, Brother.' She smiled. 'I must be hearing things.'
She handed him the chancery satchel. 'Go, Brother, all will be
well here, whilst Sir John must surely be fretting . . .'

The Golden Oliphant was in uproar when Athelstan reached it just
before the bells of Southwark tolled the noon day Angelus. The
brothel was ringed by Cheshire archers from the Tower sporting
the young king's personal insignia of the White Hart Couchant
with a crown and chain around its elegant neck. Athelstan knew
from Sir John that both Gaunt and his Master of Secrets, Thibault,
depended more and more on these skilled and loyal bowmen with
a personal allegiance to the popular young king. The Cheshires
also enjoyed a reputation of being ruthless zealots: they had already
taken over the brothel, frightening its occupants into corners. Sir
John, cloaked in bottle green, a beaver hat clamped on his thick

white hair, beard and moustache freshly trimmed, stamped his booted feet on the cobbles of the stable-yard. Master Thibault, along with his faithful shadow Albinus, stood opposing him. Gaunt's principal henchman was dressed in dark robes with his blonde hair neatly crimped, his genial face shaven and oiled. He looked like some jovial Benedictine monk, the refectorian or cellar man. Athelstan knew different. Despite the ever genial smile, the pretty gestures and the soft voice, Thibault was a killer to the bone, a ruthless street fighter totally dedicated to his royal master John of Gaunt. This morning, however, the mask had truly slipped. Thibault was beside himself with fury, icy blue eyes popping in anger, bejewelled fingers clawing the air as he gestured at a group of women, amongst whom Athelstan recognized Elizabeth Cheyne, the mistress of the brothel.

Athelstan sensed the pressing threat and danger. Thibault was yelling at the whores whilst Albinus was preparing a makeshift scaffold. He had looped a noose over a wall bracket, removing the lantern hung there, and pushed a handcart beneath. Two Cheshire archers were shoving a young, blonde-haired prostitute on to the cart, one binding her hands behind her whilst the other looped a noose around her neck. Thibault shouted imprecations as the whore's frightened screams pierced the air. Cranston, uncertain about what was happening, fingered the hilt of his sword as he acknowledged Athelstan's arrival with a curt wave of his hand. Athelstan realized the tension was about to tip into hideous violence. Whatever had happened, Thibault, in a dancing rage, was determined to make someone pay for it. The shouting and screaming grew more intense. The archers had now seized the poles of the handcart, ready to push it away and let the whore dangle in the air. A mastiff, lips curled in a snarl, burst out of an outhouse and lunged at one of the archers, who drew his dagger and thrust it into the dog's exposed throat. The animal collapsed, whimpering in a welter of blood. The chaos deepened. Horses in the stables overlooking the yard smelt the blood and grew increasingly restless. From inside the brothel echoed shouts and the barking of dogs. Cranston had now drawn his sword. Some of the archers were stringing their bows.

Athelstan hurried forward. He pushed his way through, climbed on to the swaying handcart, lifted the noose from the young whore's neck and, with a dramatic gesture, placed it around his own. Silence immediately descended. Cranston raised his sword in salute and resheathed it. Thibault turned away, hands on hips, and walked back to the entrance of the brothel. The archers released their captive. Athelstan slipped off the noose, climbed down from the cart and exchanged the osculum pacis – the kiss of peace – with Cranston. The coroner's bristling moustache and beard tickled Athelstan's face as Sir John clasped him close.

'Be careful, little friar. Thibault is in a murderous rage. His chancery clerk, Amaury Whitfield, attending the Festival of Cokayne here has been found hanged . . .'

'And his scrivener, Oliver Lebarge, fled.' Athelstan smiled as he freed himself from Cranston's embrace. 'He has taken sanctuary in St Erconwald's.'

'Sir John, Brother Athelstan!' a voice interrupted.

'Our master summons us,' Cranston whispered. 'Remember, watch your tongue!'

They entered the Golden Hall, the great taproom of the brothel: a dark, sombre chamber where guests could sit at tables and be served from the food bench close to the kitchen, the doors to which were now flung open. The air was savoury with cooking fragrances from the bread ovens either side of the mantled hearth, carved in the shape of a gaping dragon's mouth. Athelstan noticed how the fire irons hanging close by were priapic in shape, a motif repeated in the torch brackets and candle-spigots around the hall. Here and there were replicas of the huge sign hanging outside, a golden Oliphant, or a curved drinking horn, encased in precious metal, the actual cup covered by a lid surmounted by a bejewelled cross. The 'Oliphant' was a subtle title for a brothel, the horn symbolizing good wine, cheer and all the pleasures of both bed and board. The friar had learnt from his parishioners how the word 'horn', *cornu* in Latin, was a priapic symbol often used to describe the penis.

The Golden Oliphant undoubtedly did a prosperous trade: its taproom walls were strangely bare but its floor was of waxed, scented wood with rope matting placed to catch the slops. They passed through this into the heart of the brothel: a sumptuously decorated parlour with its adjoining 'betrothal chamber' as it was called, where guests could meet the ladies of their choice and negotiate what they wanted and how much they would pay. Rooms ranged either side of the grand gallery, similar accommodation being on offer above stairs. Mistress Elizabeth Cheyne, along with her hard-faced assistant Joycelina, walked in front, leading Athelstan, Cranston and Thibault and his escort up an extremely steep staircase and on to the top gallery. Narrower, its ceiling rather low, this gallery contained only two chambers, their doors set back in a slight recess. One of these lay open, the door, wrenched off its leather hinges, resting against the inside wall. A bleak, low-ceilinged room, with a broad bed of stuffed straw supporting a thick mattress, the starched, homespun linen sheets thrown back. Nevertheless, all the chamber's meagre comfort was shattered by the corpse swinging slightly from the oiled hempen rope which had been lashed to a lantern hook on the ceiling beam. Nearby lay an overturned stool. Thibault ignored the corpse. He went and stood at the door window, all its shutters pulled back, staring at the oiled pigskin covering which allowed in a yellowish light. Athelstan gazed swiftly round at the elmwood coffer and cloth poles, the chancery satchel and saddle bags heaped in the corner. The air smelt foul and Athelstan glimpsed a half-covered chamber pot beneath the table close to the bed.

Albinus, Thibault's henchman, drew his dagger and moved to saw at the hempen rope. Athelstan told him to stop. Albinus half smiled and glanced in the direction of his master, who weakly raised his hand as a sign to let Athelstan have his way. The friar stared up at the corpse. Amaury Whitfield's plump face was a hideously mottled hue under a mop of reddish hair, a stout man, his belly bulging out. Athelstan wrinkled his nose; the dead man's bowels and bladder must have emptied as he died his choking death. The friar swiftly blessed the corpse and whispered words of absolution followed by the requiem before returning to his study. He noted Amaury's bulging, watery eyes, the swollen tongue twisted through bloodless lips, the dried saliva on the corner of the gaping mouth. Athelstan pulled back the cuffs of the dead man's dark green jerkin; he could find no marks to the wrists. Athelstan picked up the stool and placed it beneath the dangling feet, allowing the soft-soled boots to brush against it. He took this away and his gaze was caught by the scarlet gown and blonde wig hanging on a wall hook. He walked across, took these down and glanced at Mistress Cheyne standing in the doorway.

'The Festival of Cokayne,' she declared, her harsh face betraying a smile.

'Ah, yes, Cokayne,' Athelstan replied, 'the world turned topsy-turvy! Where hares hunt hounds, males become female, piglets roast themselves and birds land on your plate fully cooked.' Keeping a watchful eye on Thibault, who was still standing with his back to him, Athelstan gestured at the gown and wig. 'Master Amaury's?' he queried. Mistress Cheyne nodded. Athelstan walked slowly around the chamber, observing the different items: an old sack full of clothing, a jerkin of dark murrey which bore the fading insignia of the royal chancery, a finely stitched leather belt with Amaury's name etched on it and other items.

'He dressed for death,' Athelstan murmured. He pointed to the sack bulging with clothing. 'And why were these kept separate from the rest? And what's this?'

He knelt and opened a chancery satchel, filled with writing materials including a pumice stone, ink horn, quills, wax and rolls of parchment. Athelstan shook his head and continued his scrutiny. He picked up an empty wine goblet from a dusty wall ledge, swilled the dregs and sniffed, but he could only detect the rich tang of Bordeaux. He walked back to the corpse, the rope creaking, boots toed down as if even in death Whitfield was desperate to secure a foothold.

'What do you see, friar?' Thibault still stood at the window.

'Master,' Mistress Cheyne broke in, 'I have other business to . . .'

'Get out!' Thibault screamed over his shoulder. 'Leave us, you painted bitches, you false-faced whores!'

Mistress Cheyne and Joycelina scurried off, their footsteps echoing down the stairs. Thibault was breathing noisily and Athelstan recalled stories of how this lord of intrigue loathed prostitutes with a passion beyond understanding. How once he had left here, Thibault would strip and cleanse himself, an act of purification more suitable to an ascetic than Gaunt's master of mischief.

'Why are you really here, Master Thibault?' Athelstan asked softly. 'Why have you graced this place?'

Thibault half turned and thrust a piece of parchment at Athelstan. In colour and texture this was very similar to that in the dead man's chancery satchel. Athelstan held it up to the light and read the elegant, courtly hand. Its message was stark and brutal. 'All is lost. The Herald of Hell has called my name, better to die in peace than live in terror. Pray for my soul on its journey, God have mercy on me and all of us.' It was signed, 'Magister Amaury Whitfield, *clericus* – clerk.'

'Did Master Amaury Whitfield kill himself,' Athelstan asked, 'because of this Herald of Hell? I have heard rumours about him.'

'A mysterious figure,' Albinus said, his voice hardly above a whisper, 'an envoy of the traitorous Upright Men. He appears at all hours of night outside the lodgings of loyal servants to the crown. He threatens them with doggerel verse and leaves a pot brimming with blood and stalks, onions on their tips, like heads spiked above London Bridge.'

'And he visited Whitfield?'

'About a week ago,' Albinus confirmed. 'Whitfield reported it the following morning in the chancery chambers at the Tower.'

'Was he frightened?' Cranston asked, sipping swiftly from the miraculous wineskin he deftly hid beneath his cloak.

Athelstan studied his great friend's usually jovial face. Cranston looked thinner, the icy blue eyes no longer crinkled in merriment. The friar also glimpsed the light coat of Milanese mail beneath the coroner's bottle-green cloak. Athelstan glanced at Thibault and Albinus; he suspected both wore the same. The terrors were closing in. The Upright Men and their soldiers the Earthworms openly roamed the city, waiting for the day of the Great Slaughter to begin, for the strongholds to fall, for the blood to stream along Cheapside like wine pumped through a conduit. Citizens were fleeing the city. Cranston's wife, Lady Maude, together with their two sons, the Poppets, their steward, dogs and other members of the coroner's household had joined the great exodus, disappearing into the green fastness of the countryside against the violence about to engulf the city.

'He was terrified!' Thibault declared.

'So did he commit suicide?' Athelstan wondered aloud.

'Why, Brother,' Albinus exclaimed, 'do you suspect murder?'

Athelstan shook his head and turned back to the corpse to scrutinize it more carefully. He then felt the pockets in the cloak and jerkin, which were slightly twisted. He found a few coins and the same in the unbuttoned belt wallet. Athelstan suspected someone had already searched the corpse.

'Master Thibault, where did you find Amaury's last letter?'

'On the bed.'

'Though you didn't come here just to mourn your clerk?' Athelstan retorted. 'You have already searched his corpse, haven't you? You sent someone up from the yard, that's when you really found his last letter.' Athelstan pointed at Thibault. 'You crossed into Southwark to visit a brothel, a place you deeply detest. You took a risk. You are a marked man, my friend,' Athelstan added gently. 'The Upright Men must know you are here and,' the friar pointed at the window covered with oiled pigskin, 'I would not stand so close to that. Now, what are you really here for? What were you hoping to find?'

'A document,' Albinus answered. 'A manuscript holding a great secret which Master Amaury was striving to decipher. We have not found it.'

Athelstan gestured at the corpse. 'Cut it down.'

Albinus hurried to obey, helped by the Captain of Archers who held the swaying corpse. Albinus severed the rope and they both lowered Whitfield's mortal remains to the floor. Athelstan knelt down and, taking the phial of holy oils from his own satchel, swiftly anointed the corpse. He scrutinized it again for any mark of violence but, apart from the purplish mark around the throat caused by the noose as tight as any snare, he could detect nothing untoward.

'A manuscript?' Athelstan glanced at Thibault, who now sat on a stool well away from the window.

'A manuscript,' Thibault mockingly replied.

Athelstan searched the dead man's clothing for any secret pocket. He was about to give up when he recalled how his own order, the Dominicans, conveyed important messages. He drew off the dead man's boots and smiled as he searched the inside of the left and felt the secret pocket sewn into the woollen lining. He deftly opened this and drew out two scrolls of parchment. The first was greasy, worn and slightly tattered, the second the costliest any chancery could buy. Athelstan, ignoring Thibault's exclamations, insisted on studying both. The first was simply an array of signs and symbols, numbers and letters. Some of these were from the Greek alphabet, a common device used in secret ciphers. The second was a triangle with a broad base, alongside it a litany of saints with a second triangle inverted so the apex of each met. Athelstan studied the litany of names. He could not recall seeing the likes before: St Alphege, St Giles, St Andrew and others. He curbed his temper as Thibault greedily plucked the parchments from his hand.

'It makes no sense!' the Master of Secrets whispered hoarsely. 'I will . . .' Thibault whirled around as a crossbow bolt shattered the pigskin-covered window and slammed into the opposite wall.

Athelstan leapt forward, dragging Thibault to the floor as a second bolt thudded against the window frame, followed by a third which whirled through to sink deep into the broken chamber door. Athelstan crawled across as if to open the window and peer out. Cranston roared at him to lie still. The coroner, despite his bulk, crept swiftly towards the door, bellowing at the Cheshires, now alarmed by Thibault's cries, to remain outside. One of the archers opened the door to the adjoining chamber. Athelstan heard the coroner shout, yells echoed from the garden below followed by the clatter of armour and the braying of horns as the alarm was raised to shouts of, 'Harrow! Harrow!'

Athelstan lay face down next to the corpse, staring at Whitfield's swollen, mottled features all hideous in death. Did the dead speak to the living? Athelstan suppressed a shiver at the half-open, sightless, glassy eyes. Had Amaury Whitfield written that despairing letter and, his wits turned by fear and wine, taken his own life here in this chamber? Athelstan turned and stared across at the far corner where the fire rope lay half coiled. Whitfield must have cut some of this off to fashion a noose. He'd then stood on the stool and lashed the other end over a beam hook before stepping off into judgement. Or so it seemed. Nevertheless, Athelstan nursed a growing suspicion that Whitfield's suicide was not so simple or so clear. Had fear of the coming revolt truly turned his wits? Certainly the Master of Secrets was marked down for destruction by the Upright Men, yet Whitfield had lived with that fear for months, even years, so why now? And why had Master Whitfield apparently brought all his possessions to this brothel – baggage, chancery satchel and other objects – only to commit suicide?

'They are gone.' Cranston strolled back into the room. 'I suspect the Upright Men. They entered the garden and must have escaped the same way.'

'Who told them which chamber Master Thibault was in?' Athelstan asked, getting to his feet.

'Brother,' Cranston shrugged, 'the Upright Men's spies are as thick as lice on a Newgate cloak. They know Master Thibault's here and the reason for it: their assassins must throng in and around this blessed place.'

'More like the sty of a filthy sow,' Thibault retorted, sitting down on the bed. The Master of Secrets began to brush his clothes and whisper to Albinus. Athelstan walked to the door window. There were shutters both within and without. These had now been flung open, the bar to the inside one lying on the floor; the window was narrow but big enough for a slender man to enter. Athelstan stepped closer to continue his scrutiny. The pigskin covering, now in tatters, had been stretched out and fastened over small hooks. The hinges of the door window were of the hardest leather, the wood and paint tarred against the elements, and the handle was a clasp which fitted neatly into a metal socket on the frame. The window looked stout and in good repair except for the damage done by the crossbow bolt.

Athelstan pressed on the latch and pushed; the door window swung open on the outside. He peered down at the sheer drop to a well-cultivated flower bed, rich with spring flowers and ripening roses. Revelling in the fresh, breezy air, sweetened with fragrant garden smells, Athelstan turned his head to catch the strengthening sunlight and closed his eyes. This reminded the friar of his father's farm and the sheer delight of a summer's morning. Athelstan was convinced that such beauty could not be matched in any other kingdom, even in this place of ill-repute! He opened his eyes. The brothel was a wealthy house and its garden reflected this: the vegetable plots with sorrel, cabbage, spinach, lettuce, peas and broad beans; the numerous herb beds which undoubtedly produced marjoram, sage, snakeweed and rosemary amongst others. He glimpsed gooseberry and raspberry bushes as well as cherry, plum and apple trees. The garden was dissected by high walls against which black, wooden-trellis fencing was in the process of being fixed: long, narrow poles, the horizontal and vertical creating squares across which vines and rambling rose bushes would grow. Athelstan watched the soldiers move carefully through the garden, swordsmen first, a line of archers behind, the shouts of their officers clear on the morning air.

'Brother Athelstan?' He turned away from the window.

'Do you think my clerk committed suicide?'

'At a guess, Magister,' Athelstan replied swiftly, 'I would say not.'

Thibault gave a loud sigh. Albinus walked to the door to shoo away the guards. Cranston moved to the window as Athelstan took a stool before Thibault, who was still sitting on the edge of the bed.

The Master of Secrets leaned forward. 'Begin, Brother.'

'No.' Athelstan pointed at Thibault. 'You tell me, Magister. First, Amaury Whitfield?'

'A graduate from the schools of Cambridge, a scholar skilled in the Quadrivium and Trivium. A shrewd clerk who trained himself in cipher, secret alphabets and other chancery matters. He was highly skilled.'

'Loyal?'

'Undoubtedly.' Thibault's face turned more cherubic as he smiled to himself.

'Magister?'

'I have my spies, Brother. I call them my sparrowhawks and I loose them along the lanes and runnels of London. Naturally they collected information about Whitfield, a bachelor with comfortable lodgings in Fairlop Lane near the Great Conduit in Cheapside. A clerk who liked games of hazard and the soft flesh of whores. Oliver Lebarge was his scrivener, who lodged with Whitfield and shared his pleasures. They were both constant visitors here. Mistress Cheyne proclaimed that the Golden Oliphant would hold the Festival of Cokayne, so, naturally, Whitfield and Lebarge were included. I understand they arrived three days ago.'

'He was missed at the Chancery?'

'Of course, but, according to the indenture he sealed with me, Whitfield was granted Saturdays and Sundays as boon-free along with other such days in each quarter.'

'You suspected nothing wrong?'

'Nothing,' Albinus replied, moving to sit beside his master.

'Nothing?' Athelstan demanded. 'Except the summons from the so-called Herald of Hell that frightened him, yes?'

'We thought he had taken his boon days to recover,' Albinus pulled a face, 'to wallow in his filthy pleasures and so forget all threats and menaces.'

'You have visited his chambers in Fairlop Lane?'

'No, not yet.'

'Do not,' Athelstan declared. 'If you want me and Sir John to investigate this matter, then we need the truth as we find it. Yes?' Thibault just shrugged.

'The recent attack,' Athelstan gestured at the window, 'nothing or no one was found?'

'If they had been,' Albinus jibed, 'they would have met the same swift fate as Whitfield.'

'And the other guests?' Athelstan asked.

'Cheshire archers now ring the Golden Oliphant. No one is allowed in or out without permission.'

'Good,' Athelstan breathed. 'I need to question Mistress Cheyne, her servants and the guests, as well as study those manuscripts. What are their origins?'

Thibault rubbed his hands. 'Thank you, Brother, for finding them. As for their provenance, the Upright Men have a messenger who calls himself Reynard. God knows his true name; some claim he is a defrocked friar of the Order of the Sack.'

'Reynard the Fox?' Cranston interrupted. 'Leading emissary of the Great Community of the Realm, a true miscreant who prides himself on slipping in and out of the city as easily as a fox does a hen coop?'

'Well, this time he was trapped and caught,' Thibault snapped. 'Reynard murdered the bell clerk of St Mary Le Bow, Edmund Lacy, and fled. He was recognized and caught in the Hall of Hell – a disreputable tavern.'

'A veritable mummer's castle,' Cranston agreed. 'Deep in that filthy maze of streets around Whitefriars.'

'Anyway,' Thibault hurried on, 'Reynard was arrested and lodged in Newgate, where he was searched and interrogated. We discovered the cipher on his person but not the alphabet to go with it. Under torture Reynard admitted he was to meet a leader of the Upright Men in London who styles himself the Herald of Hell.'

'And where is Reynard now?'

'Recovering in Newgate, he, ah . . .' Thibault pulled a face. Athelstan held his gaze. Reynard, or whoever he truly was, would have been harshly tortured, probably crushed beneath an iron door until he began to plead. Thibault's cruelty was a byword in the city.

'Master Thibault has shown great compassion,' Albinus lisped. 'The traitor Reynard could have been immediately condemned, hanged, drawn and quartered.'

'Great compassion indeed!' Cranston murmured drily.

'Reynard,' Albinus continued, 'has been given the opportunity to reflect and mend his ways.'

'By helping to decipher that message?' Athelstan intervened.

'As well as informing us of other secret matters affecting the Crown and its business.'

Athelstan studied this precious pair. Thibault and his eerie henchman were royal officials who could expect no mercy if the Upright Men stormed London and assumed power. The punishments threatened to Reynard would be nothing compared to what the Earthworms would inflict on both these men at Smithfield or Tyburn.

'And now?' Athelstan asked.

'Reynard is still reflecting. We await his answer by Vespers tomorrow evening, Brother Athelstan.' Thibault thrust both documents back into the friar's hands. 'Sir John will be officially commissioned to investigate the mysteries here at the Golden Oliphant. We expect you to assist with this *secreta negotia* – secret business – and, in doing so, win the approval of the Crown, not to mention its undying gratitude.'

'Of course, what could be more pleasing?' Athelstan murmured. Thibault smiled with his eyes.

'We also ask you, as we know you are peritus – skilled in these matters – to unlock the secret of the cipher and so tell us the messages being carried to this Herald of Hell.' Thibault wagged a finger. 'I suspect the other manuscript, displaying the triangles and saints' names, represents Whitfield's workings before he died, but what they mean . . .' Thibault shrugged. 'In the end that cipher, I am sure, refers to matters which are most important, crucial to the rebels when they raise the black banner of treason against our sovereign lord . . .'

'And that includes yourself and His Grace, my Lord of Gaunt?'

'But more especially the person of our young king Richard,' Cranston intervened swiftly, fearful that this little friar might provoke Thibault too far.

'Traitors, Brother Athelstan,' Thibault hissed, 'thrive on their dunghills. I have, and will leave alone, those who burrow deep in certain parts of Southwark.' He shrugged. 'What difference does it make now? Why hunt sparrows when more dangerous birds of prey circle overhead?' He abruptly recalled himself. 'Unlock the cipher, Brother Athelstan, and you will have my usual gratitude.'

Athelstan held Thibault's gaze. The Master of Secrets had raised this matter before and, to be fair to him, had kept his word. St Erconwald's had its own coven of Upright Men – Watkin, Pike and the other miscreants – and, though Thibault knew this, none of them had suffered some violent raid on their dwellings in the dead of night. No mailed horsemen had clattered into yards, damaging property, seizing goods whilst none of the parish's young men had been seized and hustled away to rot in the Bocardo, Southwark's filthy prison or those other hellish pits in Newgate, the Fleet or the Tower.

'Good, good.' Thibault clapped his hands like a child, rocking backwards and forwards on the bed. Athelstan glanced quickly at Albinus and was surprised. Thibault's henchman was gazing sadly at him with those pink-rimmed, glass-coloured eyes, then he winked slowly and pulled a face. Athelstan went cold. Albinus, for his own private reasons, was warning him that Thibault may well leave the parish of St Erconwald's alone because he did not need to bother himself. Thibault already knew what the Upright Men were plotting there, which meant that the Master of Secrets had a traitor, someone deep in the parish. Shocked and yet certain of the warning given, Athelstan abruptly rose to his feet and walked across to the window. He leaned against the ledge, watching the tattered pigskin flutter in the breeze as he recalled Albinus' warning. Athelstan knew Thibault's henchman was most amicable towards him: the friar had done good work for Gaunt and never indulged in the cheap insults others directed Albinus' way, either about his strange looks or sinister status. Nevertheless the possibility of a spy in St Erconwald's would have to wait. Other matters demanded his attention.

'I will need to question this Reynard,' Athelstan pushed himself away from the ledge, 'as I do Oliver Lebarge, Whitfield's scrivener who fled from here this morning to seek sanctuary at St Erconwald's.'

'So he is definitely there,' Thibault murmured, glancing swiftly at Albinus. 'We wondered why he should shelter in your church. According to Mistress Cheyne, Lebarge fled as soon as Whitfield's corpse was discovered. He had the chamber next to this.'

'And his possessions?' Athelstan asked.

'Also gone. Why, Brother, you look surprised.'

'Because Lebarge came with nothing, Master Thibault, a true fugitive. No possessions except for the clothes on his back. What do you know about the man?'

'Amaury Whitfield's one and only friend,' Albinus whispered. 'Both bachelors with no close kinsmen. Lebarge and Whitfield occupied the same lodgings in an old ironmonger's shop in Fairlop Lane. Whitfield was a senior clerk; he would deal with *secreta negotia* – secret business. Lebarge was his personal scrivener, skilled in his own right.'

Albinus paused as the captain of archers entered the room and bowed.

'Master Thibault, we have searched the brothel, its outhouses and gardens. We've found no trace whatsoever of the attackers. I understand three bolts were found, which means,' the man scratched his bearded face, 'a trained archer, perhaps one of the Earthworms who might have followed us here, or someone sheltering in the brothel itself. But,' he held up a leather-mittened hand, 'we have no proof of that. The Golden Oliphant is now ringed with archers. Sir John, your chief bailiff Flaxwith and others have arrived. They too have taken up position.' The captain coughed apologetically. 'Oh, Sir John . . .?'

'Yes?'

'Your bailiff Flaxwith is accompanied by the ugliest mastiff I have ever seen!'

'Keen-eyed, you are,' Cranston grinned, 'and, what is worse, the ugly bugger thinks I am his bosom comrade.'

The captain left, chuckling to himself as he clattered down the stairs.

'So,' Athelstan resumed, 'Whitfield and Lebarge, two bachelors, came here to participate in the Festival of Cokayne, the topsy-turvy world, a stark contrast to the rigours and the discipline of the royal chancery at Westminster on the Tower. Then the festival turns fatal . . .'

Athelstan took a set of Ave beads from his pocket and threaded them through his fingers, a common gesture which always reminded him of other realities hidden from the human eye.

'And you suspect murder?' Thibault demanded, getting to his feet.

'Yes, but I could be wrong.' Athelstan pointed at the corpse. 'Whitfield's remains will begin to swell and stink: his cadaver should be taken to Brother Philippe in St Bartholomew's at Smithfield. He must perform the most scrupulous search of the corpse and report his conclusions to me and the coroner as soon as possible. In the meantime, Master Thibault, Sir John, nobody must leave this tavern. I will need to meet the guests who resided here yesterday evening. Though,' Athelstan pulled a face, 'I am sure they are now as eager to depart this place as Lebarge was.'

The friar walked over and stared down at the corpse. 'And this Herald of Hell?' he asked. 'What do we know of him?'

'Nothing more than a title,' Thibault replied. 'Whether he truly exists or not cannot be proved. My sparrowhawks have skimmed the streets and shelter under the eaves and gables. They report that the leader of the Upright Men in London has assumed such a title. The only fact that I do know is that this herald mysteriously appears outside the dwellings of God-fearing citizens to deliver his warnings.'

'But never here?'

'Why should he, Brother? Though this house has its own mysteries. It was once owned by Sir Reginald Camoys. I believe his brother, Sir Everard, is a former shield companion of yours, Sir John? Sir Everard has recently been visited by the Herald of Hell but, as for the Golden Oliphant, all I can say is that this is a strange house with an even stranger history. Who knows, Sir John, you may even find Lothar's Cross here. Now,' Thibault beckoned at Albinus, 'we must be gone.' And both men swept from the room, Thibault shouting for his entourage to be ready.

Athelstan waited until the clatter on the stairs faded. Cranston moved across to the bed. He took out the miraculous wineskin, drank a generous mouthful and offered it to Athelstan, who shook his head. The coroner sat cradling the wineskin in his arms, staring moodily at the damaged door.

'Thibault did not really tell us much,' he remarked. 'But, there again, Gaunt's henchman never opens his soul to anyone.'

'Sir John, you are quiet, withdrawn, querulous?'

'I always am when Thibault is within spitting distance. I don't trust him or his royal master John of Gaunt, our dear king's loving uncle. I am sure Gaunt nurses a deep ambition to be king. Richard is only a boy, a mere child. Gaunt wouldn't really mourn if his nephew died without an heir, leaving only him and the House of Lancaster to occupy St Edward's throne and wear his sacred crown.' He glanced quickly at Athelstan, 'The preacher is correct: *Vae regno ubi rex est puer.*'

'Woe to the kingdom whose king is a child!' Athelstan translated. He paused as a clerk of archers came up the stairs and into the chamber, accompanied by four Tower guards carrying a makeshift stretcher. They waited whilst Athelstan once again searched the corpse, but he could find nothing. The clerk lit a candle, took a sheet from the bed and used it as a shroud, sealing the linen cloth with blobs of wax from his writing satchel so the corpse and other items could not be interfered with. Whitfield's baggage was then scrupulously searched. Athelstan declared himself satisfied that he had overlooked nothing and repeated his instructions: Whitfield's remains and all his possessions were to be taken to Master Philippe at St Bartholomew's for further scrutiny and examination. The busy-eyed clerk of archers promised all would be done and, with a little help from both Cranston and Athelstan, the corpse and the other impedimenta were taken out on to the gallery.

'So bleak and empty.' Athelstan gestured around.

'Why, little monk, what did you expect?' Cranston teased.

'Pictures, paintings depicting love, lust and all the other fascinating things and, by the way, Sir John, I am a friar, not a monk.'

'And one apparently acquainted with brothels?'

Cranston, his face all curious, came over and gently poked the Dominican in the chest.

'Oh, yes,' Athelstan smiled, 'I visited one in Perugia, Italy. I was studying at Pavia but, in the summer months, I journeyed round the northern cities. One glorious afternoon, I was walking across a sun-washed piazza in Perugia. The square was a sea of brilliant colour. Beautiful young men and women dressed in multi-coloured silks and taffeta milled back and forth. Children were selling the freshest fruits. Open air, portable stoves cooked the most appetizing food: cheese and herbs on flat savoury bread with strips of quail and other meats grilled to perfection. A group of musicians played heart-plucking melodies. Anyway, I was there, all agog, when a beautiful nun, her face framed by a wimple, approached me and grasped my hand. She had the most brilliant smile. Although I could not understand her, she talked so softly, so prettily; she pulled at my hand, urging me to come with her.' Athelstan paused. Cranston was now sitting on the stool, face in his hands, shoulders shaking. 'She took me across the square to what she called her *Domus*, her convent.' Athelstan ignored Cranston's snort of laughter. 'A truly exquisite place. The outside stone was honey coloured, the walls within covered in rich paintings, a shimmering black and white tiled floor reflected the light. Only when I entered what I thought was the convent parlour did I suddenly realize that something was very wrong.' Cranston was now sobbing with laughter. 'There was a painting of a young man, supposed to be Adonis, attended by two graceful young ladies, naked as when they were born . . .'

Athelstan smiled as Cranston, shaking with laughter, his eyes brimming with tears, rose and clapped him on the shoulders.

'Oh, little monk!'

'Friar, Sir John!'

'What did you do then?'

'I explained that she had me wrong. I was there to see the sights . . .'

Cranston threw his head back and roared with laughter.

'I asked if she would like to accompany me, did she wish to be shriven? I . . .'

Sir John turned away and slumped back on the stool.

'She became very angry.' Athelstan drew a deep breath. 'So I thought it best to leave.' He went and stood over Cranston.

'I often think of her, Sir John, her exquisitely decorated chamber, the bed with its snow-white sheets . . .'

'Have you ever been with a woman,' Cranston asked, 'having lain with one?'

Athelstan coloured and turned away. 'I know what it is to love, Sir John, to love and lose and nurse a broken heart. As for the sex act, strange to say, my good friend, and you can ask many a priest, it's not the coitus, the little death of the bed which haunts your soul. No, being celibate, remaining chaste bites deeper than that. It's the loneliness, Sir John, the yawning, empty solitude. Bonaventure, not my cat but the great Franciscan theologian, had it correct. He claimed the greatest friendship in the world should be that between husband and wife.'

'And the good Lord does not fill that emptiness, Brother?'

'We worship a hidden God, Sir John, an elusive one. We search for him, the hidden beauty, and that search can lead us down many strange paths. In the village where I was born an old widow woman lived in a well-furnished cottage surrounded by a garden overlooked by a small rose window filled with coloured glass. Turtle doves nested beneath this. Now the old woman lived by herself. Her husband had left an eternity ago to fight in Normandy. He promised he would return: the first she would know about it was when he tapped at that rose window. He never came back, killed by a crossbow bolt at Crécy. Nevertheless, every evening that old lady, just as dusk fell, waited for the turtle dove to begin its passionate pattering against the darkening glass. Love, Sir John, manifests itself in so many strange ways. The human heart is a hungry hunter; it starves for love, for acceptance and deep friendship, and the road it follows twists and turns. Sometimes it can bring you to a place like this. They say a man who knocks on the door of a brothel really wants to knock on the door of God. He is searching for that hidden beauty and joy.'

'You are a strange one, friar.'

'Then I am in good company, Sir John.'

'You deal with sin but never commit one?'

'I did not say that, my portly friend. Yes, I sit in the shriving chair and listen to souls pattering their sins. However, the more you listen, the more you realize that you and your penitent have so much in common.' Athelstan laughed. 'They often confess what you would love to do yourself, which, Sir John, brings us back to Perugia and what I saw there compared to what we have here, a stark bareness, which is not what I expected.'

'Brother, any house openly proclaiming itself a brothel would be condemned, raided and closed. So the Golden Oliphant masquerades as a wealthy tavern.'

'Where other appetites are discreetly served?'

'Precisely, little friar. Now we should go down and meet those other guests.'

'They will wait, they have to,' Athelstan murmured. 'It's good for their souls. Rest assured, Sir John, The Golden Oliphant now houses the deep, curdling mystery of Whitfield's death. Logically therefore it also holds the solution which, I suspect, is already known to one or more of its occupants. So, let us get the measure of this place.'

Athelstan crossed to the door then came back.

'Thibault claimed there was a story to this house. He mentioned an old comrade of yours, Sir Everard Camoys, his brother Reginald and the Cross of Lothar. I have heard of the latter; an exquisitely beautiful, bejewelled cross of great antiquity. Come, Sir John, there is a story behind the Golden Oliphant?'

The friar gazed expectantly at the coroner, who just stared back. You are, Cranston thought, a little ferret, you gnaw away at a problem until you reach the truth. The coroner half-cocked his head, listening to the sounds from below: the archers leaving, Whitfield's cadaver being loaded on to a sled, the clatter of pots, all drowned by the deep growling of dogs.

'What are those?' Athelstan asked.

'Hunting dogs, mastiffs, Mistress Cheyne lets them loose at night to roam the gardens. Well, there is one less now, thanks to Master Thibault.'

'So those mastiffs must have been prowling last night?'

Cranston raised his eyebrows. 'Brother, we should go down and begin the questioning.'

'In a while, Sir John. Thibault said that you have a story and, as I have said, I want to hear it. I need to capture the very essence of this place. We must summon up all our wit.'

'Why?'

'Because a very clever, subtle murder has been committed here.'

'You are sure of that?'

'Sir John, I feel it here.' Athelstan beat his breast. 'Something is very wrong and we must uncover the truth. We must listen, reflect and pray. Eventually that truth will emerge like light from a candle, the pool will spread and strengthen. So,' Athelstan spread his hands, 'the Golden Oliphant?'

'Many years ago,' the coroner began lugubriously, 'when I was young and handsome . . .'

'Sir John, you still are!'

'And my hair was golden, my body svelte. I was like all the others after our great victory at Crécy, we flew on eagle's wings, young warriors, Brother. English knights and English bowmen were needed here, there and everywhere. Many of my comrades hired themselves out to form companies and fight for this prince or that. Everard and Reginald Camoys, together with their bosom shield companion, Simon Penchen, were leaders amongst the Black Prince's eagles. They journeyed into Eastern Europe where they were hired by the Teutonic Knights to fight the Slavs. Everard was the real soldier; Reginald was a dreamer, an artist who valued beautiful objects. He and Everard were close but Reginald was totally devoted to his childhood friend, Simon Penchen. They had served as pages, squires and household knights in this noble retinue or that. Two young men who saw themselves as David and Jonathan from the Old Testament or Roland or Oliver at Roncesvalles.' Cranston paused to drink from his miraculous wineskin. Athelstan listened to the sounds of the tavern, dominated by the deep growling of those mastiffs. Another strand to this mystery, the friar reflected. If Whitfield was murdered, the assassin must have entered from the garden. The door to this chamber had not been forced, so the murderer must have used the window to get in and get out, but how? The chamber was at least eight yards up from the ground. What ladder, if any, could reach that height and, above all, those mastiffs would surely tear any intruder apart?

'Brother?'

'Ah, yes, Sir John: Simon Penchen and Reginald Camoys?'

'Two peas from the same pod. Penchen was killed fighting the Easterlings; Reginald Camoys was distraught. He had the mortal remains of his comrade embalmed and brought home and buried in a chantry chapel he founded at St Mary Le Bow. Later he erected an ornate table tomb for Penchen and eventually one for himself. Reginald died just a few years ago. Now listen, Brother,' Cranston wagged a finger, 'Reginald loved the beautiful, the work of skilled craftsmen. When he and his brother left the Teutonic Knights and hastily brought Penchen's corpse back to England, Reginald was so distraught that, to compensate himself for his grief, he stole a precious relic from the chapel where the Teutonic Knights had their treasury, the Cross of Lothar, a price- less precious object, only six inches high and about the same across. Nevertheless, it is fashioned out of pure gold and decorated with pearls, gems and precious enamels. At the centre of the cross piece is a medallion of the purest glass and ivory delineating the head of the Roman Emperor Augustus. A rare object indeed, Athelstan, blessed, sanctified and bestowed on the Teutonic Knights by the Emperor Lothar.'

'Did the knights pursue Reginald?'

'No, never. A few years after the brothers left, the Easterlings overran the garrison town. I think the Teutonic Knights had to move their treasury. Chaos ensued there . . .'

'And in England?'

'Sir Everard settled down to become a mercer, a prosperous goldsmith. He married, but his wife died giving birth to their scapegrace son Matthias.'

'And Reginald?'

'A painter. He embellished the chantry chapel at St Mary Le Bow, dedicating it to St Stephen. He also used his skill to become one of the finest sign writers in the city. Go down Cheapside, those magnificent shop signs, guild markings, escutcheons, heraldic devices are, in the main, the work of Reginald Camoys.'

'And he never married?'

'No. According to Everard, who served with me in France, Reginald returned a broken man. We talked of coitus, lying with a woman – in a word, Reginald became impotent.'

'Kyrie Eleison – Lord have mercy on him.'

'Yes,' Cranston smiled, 'the Lord certainly did have mercy on Reginald Camoys. He met Elizabeth Cheyne, our Mistress of the Moppets. Heaven knows her skills and devices, but she apparently cured Reginald of his impotence. He became deeply smitten with her – hardly surprising. He bought this tavern, the Golden Oliphant. When he died his will divided his wealth: one third to his brother and one third to the maintenance of the chantry chapel at St Mary Le Bow for the singing of requiems for the repose of his soul and Simon Penchen's.'

'And a third to Mistress Elizabeth Cheyne?'

'Yes, the tavern, all its moveables and the garden. Mistress Elizabeth found the maintenance of such an establishment, not to mention keeping herself in her accustomed luxury, beyond all income, so she decided to supplement her revenues with the most ancient trade available.'

'And the Cross of Lothar, did Reginald Camoys have that buried with him?'

'No, no . . .' Cranston paused as a young girl came breathlessly clattering up the stairs and into the chamber.

'Mistress Cheyne asks how long?'

'Tell Mistress Cheyne,' Athelstan replied, 'that we appreciate her patience and that of the others.' The girl stood chewing the corner of her lip.

'Tell your mistress,' Cranston declared, 'we will be down soon enough.'

'Oh, child?' Athelstan pointed to the window. 'If I climbed through that, is there a ladder long enough to take me down to the garden?'

The girl shook her head. Athelstan recalled the recent murders at the Candle-Flame tavern. 'Is there a cart high enough to place a ladder on and so lean it on the window ledge outside?' The girl stood, fingers to her mouth, then again shook her head and clattered off.

'You suspect the assassin used this window?'

'I don't know, Sir John, but to return to Lothar's Cross, what did happen to it?'

'It disappeared. Reginald always maintained that it would not be buried with him but displayed in a most appropriate place.

What that is, or where, no one knows. People still come here looking for it, pilgrims searching for a precious relic.'

'Or treasure hunters?'

'Yes, above all Reginald's own nephew, Matthias. I understand from Sir Everard that Matthias and the Golden Oliphant are almost inseparable. Sir Everard does not know if his son comes here for the delights of the ladies or for Lothar's Cross. Matthias also haunts St Mary Le Bow and the chantry chapel there.'

'And the relic has never been found?'

'No, but, come, little friar, the world and his wife await.'

'This chamber,' Athelstan walked over to the door, 'was definitely forced. Look, Sir John, the bolts at the top and bottom of the door have been roughly wrenched, the lock has bulged and snapped . . .'

'Surely it must be suicide?' Cranston whispered. 'Whitfield locked and bolted the door from within, he intended to die. Perhaps his wits had turned, that's why he was dressed: he was leaving and, in his own befuddled way, he was preparing to quit life.'

'Perhaps, Sir John. However, let's say it was murder. The assassin must have come by this window and yet he could not use the fire rope – that was impossible – so it would have to be a ladder if there was one long enough. Secondly, even if he used a ladder, how could he release the clasp on the outside shutters or lift the bar, or those inside? Only someone within could do that. Then there's the window itself – its handle can only be lifted by someone inside. No one could slip a hand through. I am sure the pigskin covering was intact until Thibault's would-be assassin loosed his crossbow quarrels.' Athelstan pulled up the latch, opened the window and glanced down.

'Be careful, Brother: you do not like heights.'

'I stand on the top of St Erconwald's tower to study the stars. Yes, heights can frighten me, but only if I let them, as I do on London Bridge. No, Sir John, anyone who used this window would need a long ladder and, even from here, I can see the garden below has not been disturbed. This window and its shutters only deepen the mystery around a possible intruder and, of course, there's those dogs.' Athelstan came away and stared down at the floor, tapping his feet. 'You're right, it's time we went below where, as always, we will have to sift the truth from the lies . . .'

'Newgate is truly the gateway to Hell.' So preached John Ball, hedge priest and leading captain of the Upright Men. 'The very antechamber of Satan and all his fallen angels, the deepest pit of brooding despair and the veritable anus of this wicked, filthy world . . .'

Reynard, principal courier to the Upright Men, could only agree. He had been lodged in Newgate three years ago over the question of a pyx stolen from a church. In the end he had managed to escape the gallows, though he had been branded as a suspect felon. He lifted his manacled hands and traced the outline of the 'F' burnt deep into his right cheek. Leaning against the slimy wall, he felt the flies and lice crumble between the stone and his back. He moved his bare feet and curled his bruised toes against the muddy mush of rotting straw, decaying food and the filthy contents of the common close-stool which had brimmed over to drench the floor with its slops. The air was thick with corruption. The stench would have offended a filthy sow, whilst the only light came from a needle-thin window high in the wall and the flickering cheap oil lights which exuded more foulness than light. Shapes lurched through the gloom to the clink and heavy scrape of chains. Other prisoners, groaning and cursing, were groping their way to the common hatch for their bowl of scraps and stoup of brackish water. Reynard could not be bothered. His entire being ached from the beatings he had received, the burn marks to his legs and the scalding to his arms where the Newgate gaolers had poured boiling water; his back was one open wound from being wedged under that heavy door in the press yard.

Reynard was now lodged in the condemned hold which lay at the very heart of the grim, battlemented, soaring mass of dark dwellings built into the ancient city wall and given the mocking title of Newgate. There was nothing new, clean or fresh about the prison. However, Reynard ruefully conceded, he would not be here for long. Master Thibault had given him a choice. He could stay and rot in the condemned hold until the Hangman of Rochester came with his execution cart for that last, grim journey to Smithfield or Tyburn. He would be dragged up the steps of

mourning into the chamber of the damned, where a priest would
offer to shrive him before being thrown into the execution cart.
Or . . . Master Thibault had made him another offer. Confess!
Confess to everything he knew. Well, he had been caught red-
handed over the slaying of Edmund Lacy, the bell clerk at St
Mary Le Bow, whose death the Upright Men had ordered for
their own secret purposes. Reynard had tried to discover what
these purposese might be, but found nothing. Lacy had to die
and Reynard had been instructed to make sure this happened.
He had done so, knifing Lacy in the Sun of Splendour tavern,
and had then fled to Whitefriars, only to be recognized there and
arrested. He had slipped whilst trying to escape; a filthy pool of
ale had brought him down! If this had happened to anyone else,
Reynard would have scoffed and jeered, but all he felt was shame
that the great Reynard, famed for his cunning and guile, had
been trapped so easily. And as for the documents he'd been
carrying, he'd been told to leave them at St Mary Le Bow within
a cleft in the window of the chantry chapel dedicated to St
Stephen, which housed the tombs of Sir Reginald Camoys and
Simon Penchen. He had failed to do so, being arrested before he
could complete his task. Reynard, despite his pain, smiled to
himself. Who, he wondered, were these documents for? Reynard
could not say, nor did he understand the cipher. He could read,
of course, educated in his previous life before he had fallen from
grace, never to rise again. Reynard, or Peter Simpkins as he had
been baptized, had been a friar at the Order of the Sack, but
now . . .

Reynard moved restlessly as one of the huge rats, a swarm of
which haunted this hideous place, slunk out of a congealed mass
of dirt and refuse. Nose twitching, its ears flat against its knobbly
head, back haunched as if ready to spring, the rat sloped across
a pool of light. One of the feral cats brought in to contain such
vermin as well as provide fresh meat for the prisoners, sprang
out from the dark. Reynard watched the life-and-death struggle
reach its inevitable bloody climax in a long drawn-out screech.
The cat loped away, prey in its teeth, and Reynard returned to
his reflections. What could he confess to? He could provide the
names of the leading Upright Men of Essex, yet Thibault knew
these already. Reynard had been asked for other names, including

the identity of the Herald of Hell. Reynard could not reply to that. All he could say was that the Herald was a will-o'-the-wisp with no true substance.

He glanced up at a shrill yell. Dark shapes milled around Benedict Bedlam, a hedgerow priest sentenced to hang for the murder of a doxy outside St Bartholomew's the Less. Bedlam was defending himself against Wyvern and Hydrus, wolfsheads hired by the Upright Men to attack a convoy of weaponry Thibault had organized at Queenshithe. Brutal scavengers, Wyvern and Hydrus had decided to take Benedict's bowl of filthy pottage. They had returned too late to the condemned hole to collect their own meagre meal after they had been taken to a separate chamber to be searched for any knife or dagger. Reynard looked away. Perhaps he could advise Thibault how wrong the Master of Secrets was about the timing of the impending revolt? Indeed, it was already beginning. The black and red banners of anarchy, along with longbows, quivers crammed with arrows, swords, clubs, maces and spears were being taken from their secret hiding places behind parish altars or dug up in village cemeteries. Soon, very soon according to John Ball, the Armies of God would be marching. Finally there was that scrap of parchment Reynard was still carrying, hidden in the stitching of his clothing. Was that the key to the cipher? Would it make the other document intelligible and so provide Thibault with valuable information? If it did, Reynard could buy his life and his freedom. He would receive the promised pardon, be escorted to the nearest port with food, weapons and licence to be taken across the Narrow Seas. Once there, like the fox he was, he'd lie low until the storm blew over.

'Brother! Brother!' Reynard glanced up. Hydrus and Wyvern were crouching on either side of him. In the gloom Reynard could not make out their ugly faces, yet a spurt of fear gripped his belly.

'Brother?' Hydrus leaned forward. 'The turnkeys who searched us support the Great Community.'

'Liars!' Reynard replied, his mouth turning dry, his tongue seeming to swell.

'They say you are here to reflect, that you have been offered a pardon by Thibault the turd.' Hydrus laughed at the crude joke. 'You wouldn't be thinking of leaving us, would you, Brother?'

'No, of course not.' Reynard pushed himself back against the wall.

'Look up to the hills, Reynard,' Hydrus exclaimed, 'from whence our salvation comes. Look up! Look up!' Reynard had no choice and Wyvern swiftly sliced his throat with the razor-edged dagger Benedict the Bedlam had slipped to him during their pretend quarrel.

Cranston and Athelstan left the death chamber. The friar was insistent on walking around the Golden Oliphant. They first visited the garden strip beneath Whitfield's bedchamber. Both of them scrutinized the black-soiled flower plot but could find nothing to suggest a ladder or anything else had been placed there, or that anyone, though God knows how, had slipped down from Whitfield's chamber. They then visited the kennels. Athelstan warily inspected the mastiffs, smooth-haired dogs with long legs, bulbous faces and powerful jaws: red-eyed with anger, the hounds threw themselves against the stout oaken palings, foam-flecked teeth snapping the air.

'In the dark, certainly,' Cranston murmured, 'they wouldn't distinguish friend from foe. Perhaps we should accept the obvious and the inevitable, Brother: Whitfield hanged himself.'

He grasped Athelstan's shoulder and made the Dominican face him. 'Why do you pursue this, little friar?'

'God's work, Sir John. God gives life and only God can take it away. The first sin committed outside Eden was Cain slaying his brother Abel. He then hurled the challenge which still echoes through all human existence, "Am I my brother's keeper?" And yes, Sir John, I am, you are, we are.' Athelstan paused, as if listening to the cooing from the dovecote. The dogs had fallen silent, so the birdsong carried strong and clear. 'I just feel here in my heart that something is very, very wrong. But what,' Athelstan sighed, 'I cannot say. We have a saying where I come from: "The whole world is strange except for thee and me, and even we are a little strange sometimes." So, just bear with me and let's continue our survey.'

They visited the stables. Athelstan glimpsed a magnificent destrier in its stall and wondered who the warhorse belonged to. They inspected the other outhouses and entered the kitchen block, where a sweaty-faced galopin or spit-turner informed the ever hungry Sir John that the previous evening they had served leek and venison pie and jugged hare, followed by fresh cheese tartlet. The coroner smacked his lips and took a serving of fresh waffles and a small cup of hippocras for 'refreshment's sake'. They continued their tour, oblivious to the messages from an increasingly agitated hostess. Athelstan was insistent on learning all he could about the Golden Oliphant, from the cellar with its barrels, casks, earthenware jars and baskets of dried fruit and vegetables to its wet storeroom, where fish were salted and brined and pâtés placed along the shelves in their strong crusts or 'coffins'.

Only then did Athelstan declare himself satisfied and moved into the spacious taproom where Mistress Elizabeth Cheyne, Joycelina, Foxley, the weasel-faced Master of Horse, and Griffin, Master of the Hall, were assembled along with others. Athelstan and Cranston's arrival was greeted with grumbles and dark looks, despite the free stoups of ale and platters of lait lardel – beaten eggs cooked with lardons and saffron – which had been served. Athelstan gathered that some of those present were guests, others servants – slatterns or, as Cranston tactfully described them, moppets of the bedchamber. Athelstan stood on a bench and, having apologized and delivered a special blessing, issued a spate of questions about what had happened the night before.

He soon established that it had rained. The mastiffs had been loose in the garden but, in the end, nothing remarkable had occurred, or so they said. Master Whitfield, along with his comrade Lebarge, had eaten and drunk deeply here in the taproom before going their separate ways. Lebarge stayed to converse with Hawisa, one of the moppets, whilst Whitfield had climbed the stairs to his chamber. Apparently, Mistress Cheyne pointed out, the Festival of Cokayne was over; the dinner parties and topsy-turvy chamber games had finished, and Whitfield was due to leave the following morning. Eventually the explanations and answers petered out. Athelstan continued to stand on the bench and stare around. He realized he could not detain them for long but insisted that, for the time being at least, all retainers of the Golden Oliphant, together with those who had participated in the Cokayne festivities, should stay lodged under pain of arrest and confinement in

Newgate. They could leave to do this or that but they had to return to the Golden Oliphant by nightfall.

Athelstan and Sir John then retired to what Mistress Cheyne called her 'Exchequer Chamber', where she kept accounts, a pleasant, wood-panelled room with a large window overlooking the sweet-smelling kitchen garden. The chamber boasted a chancery desk, chairs and stools all polished to gleaming like the waxed floorboards. Athelstan noticed, from the marks on both the wall and floor, that items such as pictures, painted cloths and carpets had been removed. He had observed the same elsewhere on his tour of the house.

Cranston sat behind the desk with Athelstan next to him on a high chancery stool. The friar opened his satchel while Cranston summoned in Elizabeth Cheyne and her principal maid, Joycelina. The two women sat together on the high-backed cushioned settle which Cranston had moved in front of what he called his 'judgement table'. Athelstan, under the pretext of laying out his writing instruments, closely studied these two ladies of the night. Elizabeh Cheyne, Mistress of the Moppets, was dressed in a dark blue gown fastened at the neck with a silver brooch carved in the shape of a leaping stag; her auburn hair was clamped with jewelled pins and hidden under a gauze veil. Despite her homely dress and head gear, she was harsh-faced and hard-eyed, her bloodless lips twisted into a sour pout. Nevertheless, Athelstan caught traces of her former beauty and grace: the way she sat and the delicate gestures of her long, snow-white fingers as she adjusted her headdress or the brooch on the neck of her gown. Joycelina, her principal maid, was equally demure in her light grey gown with white bands at cuff and neck; thin-faced and sly-eyed, Joycelina exuded the air of a woman very sure of both herself and her talents. She sat, legs crossed, skirts slightly hitched back; on her feet soft, red-gold buskins, well tied, with thickened soles.

'You have kept us waiting, Sir John. We all have lives, duties and tasks . . .'

'As I have mine, Mistress Elizabeth.' Cranston spread his hands. 'And principal amongst these is mysterious, violent death such as Master Amaury's in that chamber on the top gallery of your, some would say, notorious establishment.'

'Some say a great deal about you, Sir John.'

'Why did Whitfield hire a chamber on the very top gallery?' Athelstan asked brusquely.

'He was a customer, a guest, that's what he asked for. Perhaps he liked to be away from the sounds of the taproom to enjoy his games.'

'What games?'

'Brother, you are in the Golden Oliphant. During the last week of May we celebrate the ancient Festival of Cokayne.'

'And?'

'As the poem says.' Cheyne closed her eyes.

> *'We all make happy and dance to the sound*
> *of lovely women being taken and bound.*
> *Nothing to fear, nothing so tame,*
> *but pleasure and laughter without any blame.'*

She opened her eyes. 'You have never heard of such pleasure, Brother?'

'Oh, yes, it's common enough in confession when penitants come to be shrived.'

'But you are not a sinner, Friar?'

'Greater than you think and one who constantly stands in need of God's mercy.'

'Mistress Elizabeth,' Cranston interjected, 'you held festivities here not just to make the rafters ring with merriment but for good coin and plenty of custom. Some would claim you run a bawdy house, a place of ill-repute. You host a bevy of whores and prostitutes.'

'Then, Sir John, arrest me. Let Flaxwith and your bailiffs raid this house. I am sure,' she added drily, 'most of them, not to mention the justices I would appear before, will know all about what happens here.'

'And what is Cokayne here?' Athelstan insisted. 'Feasting, music, dancing? The Lord of Misrule and his festive games in a world that's gone topsy-turvy?'

Cheyne nodded, and Joycelina smirked behind a velvet-mittened hand.

'Including,' Athelstan continued, 'men dressing up as women

and women as men. Master Amaury did that, yes? We found a woman's robe and wig in his bedchamber.'

'Joycelina knows more about that.' Cheyne sniffed.

'I allowed Amaury to be what he wanted and do what he liked,' the maid murmured, eyes rounded in mock innocence. 'It brought him some satisfaction, eventually.'

Athelstan decided to change the thrust of his questioning. 'When did Master Whitfield arrive here?'

'Three days ago.'

'He died on his last night here?'

'Yes,' Cheyne agreed.

'How was he during his stay?'

'Deeply troubled, Brother. Highly anxious and greatly agitated. He talked, when sober, of the coming doom which hovers like a cloud of deep night over the city. He was terrified that when London was stormed, he would be hunted like a coney through the streets, caught, trapped, mocked and ridiculed before suffering the cruellest death, and what could we say?' Cheyne shrugged. 'He spoke the truth. Amaury Whitfield, in the eyes of the Great Community, was a tainted traitor worthy of death. He would have been hauled through the city on a sledge, barbarously executed, his head poled, his mouth stuffed with straw to face that of his dead master.'

'So he was frightened even until death and thought to immerse himself in the soft pleasures of this house?'

'In truth, Sir John.'

'Did he manifest or betray in any way a desire to take his own life?'

'Sir John, in his terror, in his fear, Whitfield might have, though he did relax. Joycelina took care of him.'

Athelstan glanced at the maid, who winked mischievously back. The friar smiled.

'And last night?' he asked.

'Everyone was tired, the festivities were over. Whitfield and Lebarge were to leave after breaking their fast this morning. Amaury went upstairs, Joycelina was with him.'

'And?' Athelstan glanced at the maid.

'He was tired. He pulled back the sheets of the bed and fondled me for a while. I do remember he made sure the shutters were closed and barred. He did the same for the window, ensuring the latch was firmly down. I asked him if he was fearful, and he replied, "Only of the sweating terrors of the night." I kissed him, said I would see him in the morning and left. I recall, very distinctly, him locking and bolting the door behind me. I came down immediately. Ask the others. I didn't tarry long.'

'And Lebarge?'

'He stayed below stairs conversing with some of the guests.'

'Who?' Cranston snapped.

'Odo Gray, Captain of the *Leaping Horse*, and the mailed clerk Adam Stretton.'

Elizabeth Cheyne paused as Cranston chortled with laughter, rocking backwards and forwards in his chair.

'Sir John?' Athelstan asked. 'You know these worthies?'

'Oh, Brother, I certainly do. Gray is a man involved in so many pies he has to use his toes as well as his fingers: pirate and smuggler, merchant and mercenary, he would sell his mother for any price.'

'And Stretton?'

'A mailed clerk, a graduate of St Paul's and the Halls of Oxford. A man of peace and war who has performed military service on land and sea; the destrier in the stables must belong to him. Stretton is the most trusted retainer of Fitzalan, Earl of Arundel.'

'John of Gaunt's great rival?'

'John of Gaunt's great enemy,' Cranston confirmed. 'So, this precious pair were also revellers?'

'Oh, yes, Sir John,' Cheyne replied. 'There were five in all: Whitfield, Lebarge, Stretton, Gray and, to a certain extent, Matthias Camoys.'

'To a certain extent?' Athelstan queried.

'Matthias comes here to drink and lust but he nourishes a great ambition to discover the whereabouts of the Cross of Lothar.' Cheyne rubbed her brow. 'He is so importunate with his questions. He believes the Golden Oliphant retains some subtle device or secret cipher which will reveal the whereabouts of Lothar's Cross. I thank God that he also believes the same is true of the chantry chapel at St Mary Le Bow, where my beloved Reginald lies buried. Matthias divides his time between both places.'

For a mere heartbeat Elizabeth Cheyne's face and voice softened. Athelstan glimpsed the great beauty which must have captivated Reginald Camoys.

'You never married?'

'No, Brother Athelstan, never. Reginald, well,' she smiled, 'Reginald was Reginald: irreligious, a true devotee of the world and the Land of Cokayne.'

'Yet he lies buried in a chantry chapel?'

'Reginald maintained, better there next to his shield comrade Penchen than anywhere else. If chanting masses would help his soul he would surely profit. However, if there was nothing but eternal night after death, then he'd lost nothing.'

'I have heard the same argument before,' Athelstan murmured. 'But to leave the Cross of Lothar for the moment. Do you know of anything during Whitfield's stay here which would explain his mysterious death?'

'Nothing.'

'He was well furnished with monies?'

'And still is,' Cheyne retorted. 'Brother, you will find nothing stolen or borrowed from Master Amaury's possessions, be it his chancery satchel or his purse. This house enjoys a reputation for honesty. We are not naps, foists or pickpockets. Any girl found stealing is handed over to the sheriff's bailiffs. Sir John, you know that, don't you?'

'Not from personal experience,' he quipped. 'But I know enough of your dealings, Mistress Cheyne.'

Athelstan caught the sarcasm in Cranston's voice. The coroner was well versed in the secret affairs of London's grim and gruesome underworld; the Halls of Hades and the Mansions of Midnight, as the coroner described the seedy twilight life of the city.

'Did Whitfield mention that he had been visited by the Herald of Hell?'

'Yes, both he and Lebarge referred to it. It apparently happened some days before they arrived here and, certainly, both men were terrified.'

'Did they know who it was?'

'No. Do you?'

'Has the Herald visited your establishment?'

'Of course not. Why should he?'

'Why should he indeed?' Cranston soothed. 'I am sure you pay the Upright Men as well as pass on any information you glean from this customer or that, juicy morsels the Great Community might find interesting and yet,' Cranston jabbed a finger, 'when it suits you, you're also of great assistance to Master Thibault. Is that not so?'

'Sir John,' Cheyne fluttered her eyelids, 'we live in a true vale of tears, in the very shadow of the Valley of Death. So, what can a poor wench do to survive, earn a crust for her belly and keep a roof over her head?'

'Whitfield brought a great deal of baggage here, didn't he?' Athelstan asked sharply. 'Clothes, possessions?'

Cheyne pulled a face. 'God knows,' she murmured.

'And the letter he wrote despairing of his life?'

'Again, Brother, God knows. Perhaps Amaury realized he was about to return to the Chancery in the Tower and all that entailed. Lebarge was no better, deep in his cups most of the time, furtive, withdrawn though he revelled merrily enough with some of the maids.'

'Did either describe a certain memorandum taken from a wolfshead, Reynard?'

'I have heard the name.' Joycelina spoke up quickly. 'A courier for the Upright Men. A travelling tinker who visited here declared how a certain Reynard had been taken up and thrown into Newgate.' She forced a smile. 'Brother Athelstan, with all due respect, men come here to forget their lives, their woes and tribulations. Master Amaury and Oliver Lebarge were no different.'

'Was Lebarge ever talkative?'

'No, he was taciturn, even in his cups, very much in the shadow of Master Amaury.'

'And whom did they talk to?'

'The other customers, the maids, the servants.' Joycelina waved her hands airily. 'But about what? You must ask them, not us. I suppose,' she added, 'they discussed the revels.'

'Which were?'

'Hodman's bluff, mummer's games, dances and masques, and,

of course,' Joycelina glanced slyly at her mistress, 'antics in the bedchamber. Some men like to partake with two, others like to watch.'

'To watch!' Athelstan exclaimed, ignoring Cranston's boot pressing on his foot.

'Yes, Brother, to watch,' Mistress Cheyne replied. 'Each of our chambers has a small eyehole; of course, it can be closed from the inside. This allows someone in the gallery outside to watch what is happening on the bed. In the end,' she sighed, 'we strive to please all our customers. Why, Brother, does it shock you?'

'No, I find it fascinating, I mean, man's absorption with all aspects of loving, including watching others . . .'

'Though who likes to watch whom?' Joycelina murmured coyly. 'Well, I just cannot comment.'

'In the end, what Joycelina and I are saying,' Mistress Cheyne added, 'is that we know about the revelry, but why Amaury hanged himself or Lebarge fled this house for sanctuary in your church, Brother Athelstan . . .'

'Who told you that?'

'Brother, it's common tittle-tattle in the taproom.'

'What intrigues me . . .' Cranston slurped from his miraculous wineskin and offered it to the ladies, who refused; Athelstan, hungry and thirsty, took a sip.

'Sir John?' Mistress Cheyne demanded.

'What I would like to know is why?' Cranston pushed the wine stopper back in. 'Yes, why should Amaury dress himself as if to leave before hanging himself? He was found booted and cloaked?'

'Yes, he was,' both women agreed.

'But Sir John,' Mistress Cheyne declared, 'as to why, I do not know. Perhaps some evil humour, some sickness of the night seized poor Amaury's soul? It defies all logic. If he was of sound mind and keen wit this might not have happened . . .' Her voice trailed off.

Athelstan moved restlessly on the chancery stool. He was about to enter the maze of murder, to take a path which might lead him to the truth; nevertheless, that path would twist and turn, be fraught with danger. He needed to reflect very keenly on the answers he and Cranston had received since they had arrived here. Athelstan's suspicions about Whitfield's death had been sharply honed. The friar was certain that the dead clerk had been terrified out of his wits, but why hang himself as he had, in this place and at that time?

'Joycelina,' Athelstan continued, 'you say you left Whitfield in his chamber, and he locked and bolted the door behind you.' She nodded. 'Did anything untoward happen during the night?'

Joycelina glanced at her mistress, who shook her head vigorously.

'Nothing,' Mistress Cheyne whispered, 'on my oath, ask the others.'

'And this morning?'

'Our guests were summoned to break their fast at eight. Griffin, Master of the Hall, rang the bell. He then went along the galleries knocking on each door. All came down except Whitfield. At the time, nothing untoward was heard or seen. Eventually we noticed Amaury was absent so I despatched Joycelina to rouse him.' She nudged her maid.

'I went upstairs,' Joycelina declared. 'I knocked on the door but I could tell when I leaned against it that it was securely locked and bolted. I called his name, I knocked again. I stared through the eyelet and the keyhole; both were blocked. I grew concerned, so I went downstairs. Mistress Cheyne was in the refectory we use for both our guests and the household.'

'Joycelina told me what had happened and I followed her up the stairs. Oh, no,' Mistress Cheyne's fingers flew to her lips, 'I first told Master Griffin to keep everyone at the table, not to alarm them. I took Foxley, our Master of Horse, with me. I sent Joycelina ahead to quieten the maids on the other galleries as I had already decided what to do.'

'What was that?'

'Brother Athelstan, in the Golden Oliphant men lock themselves in chambers with our young maids. Sometimes, rarely, matters of the bed get out of hand. We have a makeshift battering ram, a yule log with handles along its sides. I told Foxley to fetch that along with two of the labourers working on the trellis fencing in the garden.'

'And the mastiffs?'

'Dawn had broken, Foxley had secured them in their kennels. We went out into the garden and summoned two of the labourers – they are still out there. We went up to Amaury Whitfield's chamber. I knocked on the door – no answer. I looked through the eyelet and keyhole: both were sealed. Foxley did the same. I ordered the labourers to break down the door. Joycelina, who later joined us in the gallery after I shouted for her, was correct: the door was obviously locked, bolted at both top and bottom. Foxley supervised the labourers and at last the door broke away. The light in the chamber was very poor, almost pitch black. The candles had burnt out and the window was firmly shuttered. I told the labourers to take the ram back into the garden and instruct Master Griffin to keep everyone in the refectory. I had already glimpsed poor Amaury's body creaking on the end of that rope, head and neck all twisted. I ordered Foxley to cross and open the shutters. He did so, then the window. Joycelina and I entered the chamber. We waited until there was enough light. I wanted to . . .' Her voice faltered.

'We realized there was nothing we could do.' Joycelina took up the story. 'So we went downstairs. By then of course everyone was roused and fearful. Lebarge had apparently grown very frightened. He pushed past Master Griffin and fled the refectory. Foxley and I went back up the stairs. Lebarge was standing in the death chamber, just staring at his master's corpse. He was distraught, shoulders shaking. He left, hurrying down the stairs. By then the Golden Oliphant was in uproar. Mistress Elizabeth sent messengers to the Savoy Palace and the Tower to give Master Thibault the news.' She spread her hands. 'The rest you know.'

'And Lebarge?'

'In all the commotion,' Mistress Cheyne replied, 'he simply slipped out, disappeared. I didn't see him go but he definitely fled.'

'Yes, he certainly did,' Athelstan agreed. 'He arrived in St Erconwald's carrying nothing. No possessions except a knife and the clothes he was wearing.'

'Brother, I cannot explain it; he was here then he was gone. We thought he may have locked himself in his chamber or, consumed with grief, gone out into the garden. We were all distracted, especially when Master Thibault and his retinue

arrived. He was furious, spitting curses, blaming us and threatening to hang everyone until he had the truth. You arrived and
went up to the chamber; only then did the news trickle through
about how Lebarge had fled for sanctuary in St Erconwald's.'

'Why would he do that?'

'Sir John, he is in sanctuary, ask him yourself.'

'And his baggage is still in his chamber?'

'No, that's as empty as a widow's pantry.'

'So where is it?' Sir John asked.

'Ask Lebarge, we have nothing of his.'

'We certainly shall, but first we have others to question.'
Cranston tapped the table with his hands. 'Mistress Joycelina,
of your great kindness, ask Masters Griffin and Foxley, together
with those two labourers, to come in here.' The coroner smiled.
'Quickly now, then we will be gone and you can return to your
business.'

She hastened off. Cranston, to break the embarrassing silence,
began to question Mistress Cheyne about the Cross of Lothar but
she seemed reluctant to answer. Athelstan, whose attention had
been caught by the ornately carved mantel above the empty
fireplace, rose to inspect it more closely. He scrutinized the two
medallions on either end. The one on the left displayed carved
initials, 'IHSV', the letters wreathed with vine leaves; the one
on the right had a sun in splendour with the inscription 'Soli
Invicto' – to the Unconquerable Sun – carved beneath.

'Both of these inscriptions . . .' Athelstan scratched his head.
'I am sure I have seen them before.'

'Reginald's work,' Mistress Cheyne called, turning on the
settle. 'For the life of me I don't know what they signify. Reginald
refused to say. You will find the same in his chantry chapel at
St Mary Le Bow. Young Matthias has questioned me about them
often enough. I wish to God I could explain them, but I cannot.
Go around this tavern, Brother Athelstan, and you will find those
two roundels carved elsewhere, along with the Golden Oliphant.
Reginald loved nothing better than riddles and puzzles. He
claimed it reflected life . . .'

She broke off as the door opened and Foxley entered, a beanpole
of a man with a dark, pointed, stubbled face and greasy hair
hanging down to his shoulders. He was garbed in a leather jerkin,

leggings and boots. Athelstan caught the reek of the stables. Master Griffin, who accompanied him, was a squat tub of a man with deep-set eyes and a ruddy, bewhiskered face, clearly a person who loved his food: he kept smacking his lips and rubbing his swollen belly.

The two labourers reminded Athelstan of Watkin the Dung Collector in their muddy rags, leather aprons and cracked, shabby boots, though their bearded faces and dull-eyed looks were in stark contrast with Watkin's cunning wit, devious ways and mordant sense of humour. Both men, in deep, gruff accents, confirmed what Athelstan had already been told. Mistress Cheyne had come out into the garden with Master Foxley; they had collected the battering ram and climbed to the top gallery. It was dark and narrow, difficult to swing the ram, but they had succeeded. The door collapsed, their mistress told them to take the log downstairs and inform Master Griffin to confine all the guests to the refectory, though they understood Lebarge had already fled. Despite the poor light they had glimpsed the corpse dangling.

Throughout the labourers' blunt speech, Foxley and Griffin nodded like two wise men. The Master of the Hall then explained that he had stayed downstairs looking after those who were breaking their fast. They had heard the pounding but he had insisted, on Mistress Cheyne's instructions, that everyone remain at table.

'Except Lebarge,' he concluded. 'He pushed by me and went through the door.'

'And you, Master Foxley?' Athelstan turned to the Master of Horse.

'I was all troubled. I'd drunk deeply the night before. Anyway, I helped batter the door; it was securely locked and bolted. Eventually it collapsed. Mistress Cheyne ordered me into the room. It was very dark and smelly, all the candles and lamps had burnt out.' He drew a deep breath. 'Master Whitfield's corpse just hung like a black shadow. I was, I was,' he stumbled, shaking his head, 'deeply frightened.'

'Did you see anything else amiss in the chamber?' Athelstan asked.

'No, except that Master Whitfield looked not so fat in death.'

'Not so fat?'

'Slimmer, Brother Athelstan, his belly not so swollen, but, there again, that could have been a trick of the poor light.'

'And what next?'

'Mistress Cheyne asked me to open both shutters and window.'

'Did you notice anything wrong?'

'No, Brother Athelstan, the shutters, both within and without, were firmly closed. I had to remove the bar from the inside.'

'That's right,' one of the labourers broke in. 'Just before I left, I saw Master Foxley lift the bar and place it on the ground.'

'And the window itself?' Cranston asked.

'Securely latched.'

'And the pigskin covering?'

'Tightly in place.'

'When we took the battering ram back downstairs,' one of the labourers affirmed, 'we went outside and looked at the flower bed beneath the window, but nothing had been disturbed.'

'Why did you do that?' Cranston asked. 'I mean, if the window was shuttered and barred . . .'

'You don't recognize me, Sir John?' The burly labourer stepped closer. 'Until Master Foxley hired us, we worked in the Candle-Flame tavern, now in Master Thibault's hands. I remember the murders there.' He grinned. 'The way the window was breached. Everybody discussed how clever you were.' Cranston, flattered, nodded in agreement.

'So,' Athelstan asked, 'you, Master Foxley, opened both shutters and window and then what?'

'I turned away. Mistress Cheyne and Joycelina were standing in the room looking at poor Whitfield.' He spread his hands. 'Sir John, Brother Athelstan, that's what I saw.'

'And Lebarge?'

'Brother, by the time I had returned to the refectory he was gone. Joycelina and I went looking for him. Mistress Cheyne was concerned. We found him in Whitfield's chamber, all tearful and trembling.'

'He said nothing?'

'No, he pushed past us and left, that's the last I saw of him.'

Athelstan whispered to Sir John, who had the chamber cleared. Odo Gray was summoned next. The sea captain swaggered into the room. He was weatherbeaten, sloe-eyed under a mop of white hair, his hard-skinned face set in a cynical smile as if he knew the world and all it contained. Dressed in a cote-hardie which hung just above low-heeled boots, he bowed perfunctorily and sat on the settle before Cranston and Athelstan.

'Well, well, well.' The coroner rubbed his hands together. 'Odo Gray, Master of the *Leaping Horse*, a high-masted cog. Odo Gray, pirate, smuggler and merchant in all kinds of mischief.'

'Sir John, I am equally pleased to meet you.' Gray bowed sardonically at Athelstan. 'Greetings also to the noble Dominican of whom I have heard so much.'

'Have you now?' Athelstan smiled. 'And why is that?'

'Whispers, Brother Athelstan, amongst your parishioners. How, when the Great Revolt occurs, your little flock wish me to kidnap you and spirit you away from all the bloodletting.' He grinned as Athelstan gaped in surprise while Cranston swore beneath his breath.

'Oh yes, it's been mooted, Brother. Moleskin the Bargeman would call you away from your church, saying that the Lord High Coroner here wanted words with you. In truth you would be bundled aboard the *Leaping Horse* and taken out of harm's way.'

'And what came of this clever plan?'

'Brother, I pointed out that once the revolt breaks out . . .'

'The Thames will be sealed,' Cranston broke in. 'Thibault has already deployed fighting cogs, and he is hiring Breton galleys – wolves of the sea – to prowl the estuary and prevent all ships from leaving.'

'And you refused?' Athelstan asked.

'Of course, what was the use? The *Leaping Horse* is well known to harbour masters from the Thames to Berwick . . .'

'And with good cause,' Cranston retorted. 'You've sailed under the black flag of piracy.'

'Jealous rivals, Sir John.'

'And you are known to make landfall with tuns of Bordeaux which the customs collectors never stamp.'

'Fables, Sir John!'

'And you are reputed to excel at spiriting away any fugitives who can afford it, before the sheriff's men arrive.'

'Tittle-tattle fit for fools, Sir John.'

'So what were you doing at the Golden Oliphant?' Athelstan asked.

'Why, Brother, God forgive me, indulging in the Cokayne revelry. I am,' Odo crossed himself swiftly, 'a man of fleshly desires. Often away from hearth and home.'

'Which is where?'

'Barnstaple in Devon.'

'And you frequent this place often?'

'I am well known to Mistress Cheyne and her moppets in every sense of the word.'

'And Master Whitfield?'

'Oh, the clerk who hanged himself?' Gray shrugged. 'I talked to him, as I did other guests, but I hardly knew the man or his shadow, the scrivener Lebarge.'

'Do you know any reason why Whitfield should hang himself and Lebarge flee for sanctuary?'

'None.'

Athelstan gazed quickly at the hour candle under its metal cap on a stand in the far corner. Lebarge needed to be questioned as swiftly as possible to corroborate all of this. Athelstan was certain that the ship's master, this wily fox of the sea, was concealing something: his replies were too glib, and why inform Athelstan about some madcap scheme of his parishioners? Athelstan felt warmed by their deep affection, the determination that he would not be caught up in the coming violence. They had discussed what he should do and he had heard rumours about all kinds of stratagems and ploys to protect him. On reflection, what Odo Gray had told him was not so startling. Athelstan was now more intrigued as to why the captain had brought it up in the first place. To distract him, but from what?

'Brother?' Cranston's voice broke into Athelstan's thoughts. He turned and smiled at the coroner.

'Sir John, I believe Master Odo Gray is lying.' The sea captain's jovial demeanour promptly disappeared – the twinkling eye, the ready grin and the relaxed pose – almost as if the man's true soul had thrust its way through, aggressive and surly, fingers slipping to the hilt of his dagger. Cranston coughed and the hand fell away.

'Explain yourself, Brother.'

'Captain, I would love to but I cannot. I just believe you could tell us more about the nights of revelry, the conversations you had and the words you overheard. Perhaps also the real reason for you being here? So, Master Gray, Sir John here will ensure the harbour masters at the mouth of the Thames do not issue you with clear licence to dip your sails three times in honour of the Trinity and make a run for the open sea. You, like all the rest,' Athelstan got to his feet, 'will remain here until I am satisfied that we have the truth.'

PART TWO

*'Mithras: the Roman Sun-God beloved by the
Legions until the Emperor Constantine replaced
him with Christ's Cross.'*

Oliver Lebarge crouched on the mercy seat in the sanctuary enclave at St Erconwald's. The scrivener was in mortal fear for his life. The pillars of his humdrum existence had collapsed all about him with the mysterious and unexpected death of his patron, his magister, Amaury Whitfield. Teeth chattering, Lebarge pulled his cloak closer about him. He felt in the pockets of his grease-stained jerkin and fingered the dirty piece of parchment he had found close to the enclave. It was crumpled and stained, but Lebarge still recognized the threat it carried: a crude but clear drawing of a human eye and beneath it in doggerel Latin, the ominous words, '*Semper nos spectantes* – We are always watching.' Whitfield and he had received similar warnings at the Golden Oliphant, left on the bolsters of their beds or thrust beneath their chamber doors. Like those others, Lebarge would push this one down the jakes' hole. The scrivener wondered who was responsible, but, there again, that was a measure of his own stupidity. He had fled to St Erconwald's because its priest, the Dominican Athelstan, was regarded as a man of integrity, the secretarius of Sir John Cranston, who could also be trusted. However, the parishioners of St Erconwald's were another matter. The Upright Men had their adherents here, high-ranking ones, even captains of their companies. Lebarge had glimpsed different individuals slip through the rood screen and stare up at him. The scrivener picked up the tankard and sipped from it. He was grateful for the Dominican's kindness. Before the friar had left, Lebarge had begged him that only those whom the priest trusted should feed him, and this had been agreed. Victuals and drink had been brought by either the beautiful widow woman Benedicta, with her black hair and soulful eyes, or that tousle-haired urchin, the altar boy, Crim, who, like Benedicta, insisted on handing the tray of food and drink directly to him.

Lebarge did not trust anyone, not now. After Amaury had died in such a mysterious fashion, what was the use of going back to that narrow garret in Fairlop Lane, or worse, being dragged down to the dark dungeons of the Tower to be questioned by Thibault and his henchmen? He and Amaury had shaken the dust from their feet and drunk the cup to its dregs. No, it would be best, Lebarge reflected, if he sheltered here for the statutory forty days then allowed himself to be escorted to the nearest port and shipped to Dordrecht or some other port in Hainault or Flanders. Once there, he could offer his skill as a scrivener, settle down and begin a new life.

He drew comfort from such thoughts as he recalled what had happened at the Golden Oliphant. He could not truly understand it. Amaury had been so determined. They had discussed what to do after that mysterious figure, the Herald of Hell, had delivered his warning. They had stripped their chambers, made ready to leave, then both he and Amaury had joined the revelry of Cokayne at the brothel. Odo Gray had appeared and all was settled. He and Whitfield had both visited the Tavern of Lost Souls and completed their business. So why had Amaury allegedly killed himself? Or was it, as Lebarge suspected, murder? There had been no warning the previous evening. Lebarge had been in the taproom, the Golden Hall, roistering with the rest, whispering with Hawisa, Whitfield with Joycelina. Then Amaury, much the worse for wear, even though Lebarge suspected he had other secret business to attend to, had staggered upstairs with Joycelina, saying that he needed an early sleep. She had returned almost immediately, claiming Amaury was intent on sleep. Lebarge followed suit at least an hour after the chimes of midnight. He had tried Whitfield's door but it was secure, the eyelet sealed as was the keyhole when he peered through it. Lebarge had taken a goblet of wine up, drunk it and enjoyed a refreshing night's sleep until roused by Master Griffin announcing that victuals were being prepared in the kitchen. He needed no second invitation. Mistress Cheyne had promised him his favourites; simnel cakes, fresh and hot from the oven smeared with butter and honey. Lebarge had been feasting on these when he noticed Amaury had not appeared. Joycelina had left to rouse him and the night-mare had descended. He could not believe the dire news which trickled down. Even Hawisa could provide no comfort.

Lebarge shifted on the mercy seat and peered across the sanctuary, alert to the sounds beyond the rood screen. He started as a shadow flittered, only to sigh with relief: Bonaventure, the one-eyed tom cat, bosom friend of the Dominican Athelstan. The cat waged unceasing war on the vermin which apparently plagued this church, or so Radegund had informed him. Lebarge again supped from the tankard of light ale resting on the floor before him. In fact, where was Radegund? The relic seller had taken sanctuary, apparently fleeing from some irate customer. Radegund had proved to be a thoroughgoing nuisance, asking Lebarge a litany of questions, flitting like a bat around the sanctuary until two leading parishioners had appeared, Pike the Ditcher and Watkin the Dung Collector. From snatches of conversation which Lebarge overheard, Watkin, Pike and Radegund had been gleeful at the news that the relic seller's most recent victim had been one of John of Gaunt's household. They offered to shelter him and the relic seller, cloaked and cowled, had slipped out of sanctuary. As he left, Radegund had thrown dagger glances at Lebarge, and the scrivener now wondered why. He thought he would be safe here – after all, it was not far from Hawisa and the Golden Oliphant . . .

To distract himself, Lebarge rose and walked around the sanctuary, studying the different paintings. Some of these looked eerie in the half-light pouring through the lancet windows. Hellish scenes: the Garden of Eden after the fall with a giant mollusc shell ready to snap shut on Adam and Eve. A tainted paradise illuminated by the colour of dangling jewels, yet the gemstones were sharply spiked, whilst deep in the foliage berry-headed half-demons hunted a hawk-billed raven perched on a huge apple. Lebarge stared. He recalled a recent story from Annecy in France about an apple which emitted such strange and confused noises that people believed it was full of demons and belonged to a witch who had failed to give it to someone. Lebarge glanced away. He must keep his wits sharp and not allow his imagination to drag him deeper into fear.

He wandered over to peer through the lattice window of the

rood screen. Shapes and shadows moved around. He glimpsed Giles of Sempringham, better known as the Hangman of Rochester, deep in conversation with the tar-hooded Ranulf the Rat-Catcher and Moleskin the Bargeman. Lebarge shivered. A deep chill of ghostly fear gripped him. He had fled here to be safe, free from Thibault's questioning, protected from the nightmare of Amaury's corpse swinging by its neck, the pestering of Adam Stretton, the ominous warnings of the Upright Men. He recalled that greasy scrap of parchment with its horrid symbol of the all-seeing eye. Was he being watched by Thibault or the Upright Men? Would someone deal out sudden, brutal death to him, here in this holy place? Lebarge chewed on his nails and stared up at the sanctuary cross. Was it too late, he wondered, to pray for salvation in this world as well as the next . . .?

Adam Stretton swaggered into the Exchequer Chamber of the Golden Oliphant. Athelstan recognized the type immediately: the mailed clerk, the henchman, the professional killer, a seasoned soldier who could quote the Sentences of Aquinas as well as wield sword and dagger. Keen-eyed and swarthy faced, a little fleshy, his black hair cropped close on all sides to ease the war helmet he would don in battle. Clean-shaven and sharp in move- ment, Stretton peered at Athelstan from under heavy-lidded eyes as his be-ringed fingers fluttered above a warbelt with sword and dagger as well as a pouch for ink horn and quill. Stretton slouched down on the settle, flicking at the dust on his murrey- coloured jerkin and hose, moving now and again so the spurs on his high-heeled riding boots clinked noisily.

'Are you preparing to leave?' Cranston asked. 'In which case you are most mistaken.'

'My Lord of Arundel . . .'

'My Lord of Arundel.' Cranston smacked both hands down on the table. 'My Lord of Arundel,' he repeated, 'will have to wait. You, sir, shall not leave this brothel until we are satisfied as to the truth of what happened here.'

Stretton licked thin, almost bloodless lips, his slit of a mouth twisted in protest.

'Why are you here, Master Stretton?' Athelstan asked quietly. 'Just tell us.'

'For the Cokayne Festival.'

'For the delights of the flesh?' Athelstan queried. 'Master Stretton, I doubt that. I believe,' Athelstan lifted a hand, 'that you, a mailed clerk, the esteemed henchman of a great lord, did not come here just for revelry.' Athelstan paused. 'I wonder, I truly do.'

'What?' Stretton had lost some of his arrogant certainty.

'Well,' Athelstan glanced swiftly at Cranston. 'Master Thibault is Gaunt's henchman. Amaury Whitfield was Thibault's creature, his principal chancery clerk. My Lord of Arundel, by his own proclamation, is Gaunt's heart's blood opponent. True? Well?' Athelstan smiled at this arrogant clerk. 'Did you come here to meet Master Whitfield? To negotiate with him, to suborn him, to learn his master's secrets?' Athelstan sat back. He and Cranston had discussed this while they had broken their fast on some delicious simnel cake and a pot of ale. Cranston strongly believed that Stretton was a 'Master of Politic' and that it was no coincidence that he had lodged at a brothel along with Thibault's principal chancery clerk.

'Well?' Cranston barked. 'Master Stretton, I could put you on oath and, if you lie, indict you for perjury . . .'

'I came here,' Stretton made himself more comfortable on the settle, 'to revel, but also because I – we – learned that Whitfield also liked to attend such festivities. My Lord of Arundel felt it might be profitable to fish in troubled waters. I did keep Whitfield and his close-eyed scrivener Lebarge under sharp watch.' Stretton paused as if to collect his thoughts, determined to be prudent about what he said.

'Under sharp watch?' Cranston queried, taking a slurp from the miraculous wineskin. 'So, what did he do?'

'Revel, as did Lebarge, with the ladies of the night.'

'Who in particular?'

Stretton blew his cheeks out. 'Whitfield with Joycelina, Lebarge with one of the others. I forget now.'

'You forget so you can question her later?' Cranston tapped the table. 'I want her name.'

'Hawisa. I think it was Hawisa.'

'How did Whitfield appear?'

'Frightened and, despite the wine and wenching, he seemed to grow more cowed and withdrawn.'

'Why?'

'I do not know.'

'So why did you say that?'

'Whitfield drank a great deal,' Stretton replied. 'He was often by himself. He kept rubbing his stomach as if his belly was agitated. Sometimes he disappeared. He left the tavern, slipping out like a shadow and returning just as furtively. But, why and where he went?' Stretton gabbled quickly to fend off Athelstan's next question, 'I don't know.'

'Did he have any visitors?'

'None that I saw.'

'And he knew who you were?'

'Oh, yes,' Stretton conceded, 'Whitfield and I had met before. He recognized me for what I am . . .'

'Fitzalan of Arundel's man, body and soul,' Cranston intervened, 'in peace and war.'

'You have travelled the same road as I, Sir John. Arundel is my liege lord.'

'And Arundel is my Lord of Gaunt's arch-enemy,' Cranston jibed. 'We are correct, Stretton. You came here to suborn and subvert Whitfield.'

'And I failed; the man was too distracted.'

'And yesterday evening?' Cranston demanded.

'I was with the rest, in the taproom, what they ridiculously call the Golden Hall. Whitfield and Lebarge were present.' Stretton sniffed. 'Whitfield left for the stairs, Joycelina went with him, Lebarge continued drinking. Joycelina returned fairly swiftly.' Stretton's voice was now monotonous. 'I retired to bed. I was roused for the morning meal, I came down. Lebarge was already there feeding his face on simnel cake, for which he is so greedy. Eventually Lebarge asked where his master was. The Mistress of the Moppets sent up her chief whore.' Stretton did not hide the contempt in his voice. 'She came clattering back all breathless about not being able to rouse Whitfield. Cheyne told us to stay with Griffin; she and Joycelina left the kitchen. We later heard the banging, then those labourers came down.'

'And?'

'Oh, chaos ensued.'

'What about Lebarge?'

'He slipped away.'

'Did you go up to the death chamber?'

'Yes, I did, whilst waiting for Thibault and his coven of . . .' Stretton licked his lips and grinned, '. . . his henchmen to arrive. I glimpsed Whitfield, cloaked and booted, swinging like a felon at Tyburn.'

'Suicide, in your opinion?'

'Sir John,' Stretton wagged a finger, 'Whitfield did not commit suicide. Oh,' he sat back as if enjoying himself, 'I cannot tell you anything more – just a feeling. I stared at the corpse of a man dressed for leaving rather than a toper garbed in his nightshirt eager to die. But,' he shrugged, 'the full truth of it I cannot say. Am I done now?'

Cranston glanced at Athelstan, who nodded. Arundel's man rose, bowed and, with Cranston's shouted warning not to leave the Golden Oliphant ringing out behind him, sauntered out of the chamber.

Matthias Camoys came next. He was the opposite to Stretton, almost stumbling in to meet Cranston and Athelstan. He was pinch-faced and slender with a toper's flushed, swollen nose and constantly blinking eyes. His sandy hair, wispy moustache and beard did little to improve his appearance. The same could be said for his loose-fitting, ill-hung, ermine-lined scholar's gown. Matthias seemed more like a monk who'd donned a hair shirt, shoulders constantly twitching against some vexatious scratching. To Athelstan he appeared ill at ease in his own flesh: he kept fingering a small cross on a silver chain round his scrawny neck, his fingers all dirty, the nails close bitten. He sat himself down on the cushioned settle. Athelstan peered closer; he was sure the cross Matthias was wearing was a miniature replica of the Cross of Lothar. The questioning began. Matthias' answers were desultory, like a prisoner forced to admit certain facts. He confessed to enjoying the Cokayne revels, as well as being a frequent visitor to the Golden Oliphant and a patron of a number of what he called, 'the delicious Moppets'. A scholar from the halls of Oxford, he claimed he was here for the May festivals, though Athelstan suspected the masters of the university had sent him home for lack of study. It soon became obvious that yesterday evening Matthias Camoys had been deep in his cups and could remember very little except being helped up to his chamber by two doxies who had fumbled with him before he fell into a wine-soaked sleep.

'And this morning?' Cranston asked.

Matthias' reply was as banal as the rest. He had awoken all mawmsy and staggered down to the refectory. He confessed to being so inebriated that he'd failed to realize what was happening.

'Did you know Whitfield?'

'Oh, yes, Sir John. My father mentioned him and, of course, he often came to our house on his master's business. I also met him at festivities held in the Royal Chambers both at the Tower and Westminster. I recognized him as a skilled cipher clerk, that's the real reason I came here.'

'I beg your pardon?' Athelstan replied.

'Oh, yes, Brother. I like the wine, the sack, the roast, spice-laced pork and the ladies, but . . .' Now all animated, Matthias sprang to his feet and walked over to the mantelpiece and pointed at the carvings, 'IHSV' and the Sun in Splendour with its inscription, '*Soli Invicto*'. 'I have always been fascinated by these.' He drew a deep breath. 'When Uncle Reginald was alive, he showed me the Cross of Lothar. Brother, Sir John, believe me, I have never seen anything so beautiful. Beautiful,' he repeated, returning to the settle. 'Uncle promised . . .' The young man brushed the tears brimming in his eyes.

'What did he promise?' Athelstan demanded.

'He said he would bequeath it to me but I would have to strive and search for it. These riddles are the key, that's why I come here. I thought Amaury would decipher them. He promised he would, but . . .'

'But what?' Cranston asked.

'Amaury arrived all frightened and closeted himself against the world. He took part in the revelry but he was distracted. I asked him about the symbols my uncle had left. Amaury claimed he could decipher them but there were more pressing matters . . .'

'Did he say what?'

'He and Lebarge hid behind a cloak of secrecy.' Matthias thrummed his lips with dirty fingers. 'He left, I think, to go to the Tavern of Lost Souls.'

Athelstan glanced at Cranston. The Tavern of Lost Souls lay in the dingiest and darkest part of Southwark, close to the treacherous mud flats along the Thames, a place where, according to popular legend, anything could be bought or sold, including human souls.

'Why should he go there?'

Matthias scratched his head. 'I don't know, but what I find most strange is this. I pestered him about "Uncle's great mystery", as I called it. I told him about the insignia here where Reginald once lived and in his chantry chapel at St Mary Le Bow. I admit I drove Amaury to distraction. He kept fobbing me off and went to sit in a corner whispering with Lebarge whilst trying to avoid Stretton. He seemed very frightened, cautious. He was desperate to forget his fears immersing himself in the revelry, with bowls of wine and trysts with Joycelina.'

'Do you know why he should commit suicide?' Athelstan asked.

'No. I was very surprised.'

'Why?'

'He told me last night, before he supped, that he was leaving the Golden Oliphant today but that he would meet me at the Tavern of Lost Souls, just around vespers.'

'What?' Athelstan and Cranston chorused.

'That's what he said. He believed he could resolve the mystery of Lothar's Cross for me.' Matthias pulled a face. 'I confess, this morning I was muddled, still deep in my cups after last night.' He blinked. 'Nevertheless, Whitfield's death shocked me. I can't see why he should commit suicide . . .'

The execution ground next to Tyburn stream was crammed with all the denizens of the dark, mildewed tenants of the city. Ribaldry, debauchery, lewdness, drunkenness and flaunting vice were both master and mistress of the day. The executions had begun after the great bell of St Sepulchre had tolled ominously across the city, summoning the mob to converge on the muddy fields around Tyburn to watch the gruesome spectacle. The soaring execution platform, black against the sky, had already witnessed the grisly decapitation of a traitor. The yellow-and-red masked executioner, drunk and staggering, had held up the traitor's head but his hands, slippery with gore, had fumbled. He'd dropped the severed head and was immediately greeted with catcalls of derision and cries of 'Butterfingers!'

All the mummers and grotesques of the city flocked busily around; conjurers and cross-biters rubbed shoulders with Friars of the Sack and members of the Guild of the Hanged, who ministered to felons condemned to die. The air was rancid with the sweat of unwashed bodies and the different odours from the mobile stoves where meats of doubtful origin were grilled, stewed or roasted before being sold along with hard bread, beakers of wine and stale ale. Smoke billowed up from makeshift fires to mingle with the fragrance of incense streaming out of the censers belonging to the pious groups who attended execution day to offer spiritual comfort to anyone who needed it. Itinerant story tellers stood on makeshift platforms ready to pontificate on all matters, be it a horde of yellow-skinned warriors massing in the east under lurid dragon banners; the signs and portents seen recently in the sky over Rome; or that troop of devils prowling the lanes north of London. Friars of every order moved amongst the crowds chanting psalms, hymns and songs of mourning. Leeches and hedge-physicians offered the most miraculous cures, while relic sellers, hawkers, pedlars and costermongers pushed their barrows of tawdry items through the crowd. Puppet masters, stone-swallowers and fire-eaters had set up stalls. Prostitutes of every kind, garbed in their tawdry finery and heaped, dyed wigs, shoved and pushed their way through, fingers fluttering out, carmined lips mouthing the most solicitous offers.

This tumultuous assembly had already been entertained with stories about the execution of the traitor who, whilst the gore-stained, butter-fingered executioner was trying to disembowel him, had struggled up to strike his tormentor. Such gruesome detail only whetted the appetites of those who flocked here to witness and indulge in every form of mischief. This execution day, however, turned different.

The death carts came and went, delivering their condemned human cargo, men and women, roped and manacled, to be pushed up the narrow siege ladder to the waiting noose. The Hangman of Rochester from St Erconwald's parish had despatched at least eight felons. Now he was waiting for his last two final victims:

Wyvern and Hydrus, condemned felons who'd murdered a fellow inmate just before they had been seized and dragged from Newgate. The hangman watched the cart, drawn by two great dray horses, black plumes nodding between their ears, trundle ominously through the smoky clouds. Others, however, had also entered the execution ground: the Upright Men had arrived! Their foot soldiers, the Earthworms, were snaking through the mob, long lines of men, faces daubed black and red, greasy hair twisted up into demon horns. They were dressed in tawdry armour; ox hide shields in one hand, lances in the other. They were moving like stains through water towards the execution platform.

The hangman glanced at John Scarisbrick, Captain of the Tower archers, his bearded, sweaty face framed by a coif and almost hidden behind the broad nose guard of his conical helmet. Scarisbrick plucked nervously at his chainmail jacket as he stared out over the crowd, nose wrinkling at the disgusting stench and gruesome sights on the execution platform.

'They are intent on mischief!' the hangman shouted.

'But when?' Scarisbrick yelled. He walked towards the edge of the platform. The execution cart was drawing closer.

'They won't attack the cart,' he bellowed at his men. 'It is too high-sided and moving. Here!' Scarisbrick pointed to the steps and bellowed orders at his archers to fall back and gather there. The columns of Earthworms were moving faster through the throng. Scarisbrick sensed the trap: his archers dared not loose; innocents would be killed and the rifflers and the roaring boys would whip the crowd into a murderous riot. Scarisbrick screamed at his men to unstring their staves, push them under the execution platform and draw sword and dagger. They did so. The death cart arrived at the foot of the steps, its tailgate slammed down. The Newgate turnkeys almost threw Hydrus and Wyvern, ragged, dirty and bruised, out on to the ground. Once they were out, the tailgate was lifted, the gaolers eager to be gone. Archers pinioned the condemned men, now struggling in a rattle of chains. The Earthworms were closing in, the crowd breaking up like shoals of fish before them. Yells, catcalls and curses dinned the ear. Daggers and swords were drawn in a clatter of steel. Women screamed and clutched their children, desperate to escape the coming conflict. The breeze thickened. A billow of thick black smoke gusted from the braziers on the execution platform and swept the killing ground. The Earthworms attacked, throwing themselves at the screed of archers. Scarisbrick glanced at the hangman who had now come up behind him.

'I have my orders,' he yelled and hurried down the steps. Scarisbrick crossed himself, recalling Thibault's instructions that no prisoner should escape. The Earthworms were fighting their way forward beneath floating banners of scarlet and black, some displaying the crude device of the all-seeing eye. Scarisbrick reached the prisoners. He thrust his sword into Wyvern's neck then turned, slicing open Hydrus' stomach. Both prisoners, manacles clasped tight, collapsed in a welter of blood. Scarisbrick did not pause. More orders were screamed. The archers grasped the still juddering bodies of the prisoners, raised them as if they were sacks of flour and hurled them directly into the oncoming enemy. The attack faltered as the captains of the Earthworms realized what was happening. One of their number, his face disguised behind a black, feathery raven's mask, hurried forward. He knelt beside Wyvern and clasped the dying man's bruised, bloodied face between gauntleted hands. The prisoner, eyes glazing, shook his head, indicating his companion. The Raven turned to Hydrus who lay on his side, body twitching, and crouched, ear close to the mortally wounded man's mouth.

'My jerkin,' Hydrus spluttered bloodily. 'We found it on Reynard.' The Raven stripped off the dying man's tattered leather jerkin and hurried away, passing it swiftly to a Friar of the Sack who knelt on the muddy cobbles, Ave beads wreathed about his fingers.

'The stitching,' the Raven muttered. The friar bundled the jerkin beneath his robe, rose and pushed his way through the noisy throng into the darkness of a nearby tavern. Once inside, he sat on a corner stool and picked at the rough, loosened stitching on the inside of the jerkin. It gave way easily, and the friar plucked out the roll of yellowing parchment, opened it and smiled to himself. He glanced up, pushing back his cowl to reveal a face well known to Thibault, who had proclaimed the likeness of Simon Grindcobbe, leader of the Essex Upright Men, across all the shires of the kingdom. The manuscript was safe. Thibault might have the cipher and any notes Whitfield had made. Gaunt's henchman might even have passed these on to the Dominican Athelstan, but, Grindcobbe assured himself, he would take care of that very soon. All in all, a good morning's work. Even if Thibault had the cipher, he did not have its key; otherwise there would have been tumult throughout the city. Grindcobbe pulled back his cowl to cover both head and face; he still had business to do in Southwark.

'Yes, yes,' he whispered to himself, 'a chat with Brother Athelstan might be profitable in more ways than one.'

Cranston and Athelstan had instructed Matthias Camoys to withdraw whilst they, the coroner pithily declared, 'took a little refreshment'. Joycelina brought them chicken with brewis, a shin of beef generously garnished with onions, parsley and saffron, along with French toast and two blackjacks of ale from the local brewery. Athelstan blessed the food and, for a while, they sat and ate in silence.

'I wonder,' Cranston wiped his mouth with a napkin, 'I truly do.'

'What?'

'The attack on Thibault here. The Upright Men have taken a great oath. If Thibault or any of Gaunt's minions appear in public, each Upright Man has a sacred duty to kill them. We have learnt that from spies, and the evidence is clear to see with members of the Regent's coven being struck down in public. Some are now so cautious, they stay cowering in their castles or fortified manors.' Cranston grinned. 'For all his faults, Thibault is not frightened so easily. He is well protected and would consider himself safe in a brothel in Southwark in the early hours of the day, which means . . .' Cranston popped a piece of chicken in his mouth and chewed slowly.

'The Lord High Coroner is about to share his wisdom with his poor secretarius?'

'Impudent monk!'

'Impudent friar, Sir John.'

Cranston grabbed Athelstan's arm. 'First, friar, whatever Whitfield was working on must be of vital importance to Gaunt and Thibault, that's why our Master of Mischief appeared here. Remember he was livid with rage, fair dancing around the

maypole, mad as a March hare. Thibault was quite prepared, or
at least he pretended so, to have that wench hanged. Secondly,'
Cranston fingered the crumbs on his platter, 'the attack on
Thibault was sudden. True, the Upright Men may have followed
him here, but his soldiers surrounded the house, the attack came
from the garden, the guard dogs were locked away . . .'

'Only someone in the Golden Oliphant would be certain of
that,' Athelstan added. 'An attacker from outside would have to
get in then flee, a very dangerous task with Thibault's men
swarming all over the brothel. Finally the attacker knew exactly
which chamber Thibault and Albinus were in.'

'Which means, my little ferret of a friar, our mysterious
bowman is a member of this august household. He, she or they
must have seized an arbalest along with a belt box of quarrels,
hastened into the garden and chosen some concealed place.
Whoever it was realized they had little chance of striking a mortal
blow, but at least it demonstrated to Thibault and his kind that
they could never be safe. The Upright Men,' Cranston continued,
'have now assumed a new insignia, that of the all-seeing eye.
They intend to demonstrate that it's no idle boast. Anyway,
Brother, enough of this. Let's have Master Camoys back in again.'

Athelstan rose, crossed to the door, opened it and beckoned
Camoys into the chamber. The young man entered, slack-eyed
and shuffling from foot to foot like a scholar before his magister.
'Whitfield and Lebarge,' Athelstan asked, 'they liked the ladies,
did they?'

'Yes.' Cranston grinned.

'And they also liked to dress up as ladies?'

Matthias glanced away.

'Well?' Cranston barked.

'Yes, we all did, that's Cokayne,' Matthias mumbled. 'The
world turned upside down. Why, Brother?'

'They never left the Golden Oliphant disguised as such?'

'Not that I know of.'

'And Whitfield promised to meet you at the Tavern of Lost
Souls, when?'

'Around the time of vespers, I've told you that. He claimed
to have some idea about the cipher my uncle used, both here and
at St Mary Le Bow.'

Athelstan sensed that fear had made this young man more malleable. He beckoned him towards the settle as he winked at Cranston. 'Why should Whitfield visit the Tavern of Lost Souls?'

'Why does anyone?' Matthias stated nervously as Athelstan joined him on the settle, drawing as close as possible, whilst Cranston leaned across the table.

'I asked a question,' Athelstan murmured.

'The Tavern of Lost Souls buys and sells anything.' Matthias shrugged.

'And what would Whitfield be wishing to sell or buy?'

'Brother, I don't know why he was going there, he just told me he'd meet me as a favour.'

'A favour?'

'That's what he said, but I don't know what he meant.'

'You knew Whitfield already?'

'Father is a goldsmith. Thibault had business with him as he does with others. I have told you this. Whitfield visited our house. Perhaps he wished to please my father.' Matthias pulled a face. 'Many people do.'

'And he claimed he could help you resolve the mysterious carvings left by your dead uncle?'

'So I thought.'

'You haunt the Golden Oliphant,' Cranston interposed, 'but also St Mary Le Bow?'

'Yes, my uncle's tomb and that of his comrade: their chantry chapel is dedicated to St Stephen. I often visit it to study the same carvings found here.'

'Have you asked Mistress Cheyne about them?'

'Of course, Sir John, but she just laughs. She claims she never really understood my uncle's absorption with the Cross of Lothar. She does not care for it.'

'And St Mary Le Bow?' Athelstan held a hand up for silence as he recalled Thibault's remark about Reynard, the envoy of the Upright Men, who had been arrested for the slaying of Edmund Lacy, bell clerk at the same church.

'Brother?'

'Yes, Matthias.' Athelstan edged a little closer. 'St Mary Le Bow?'

'I go there when the church is empty. But,' Matthias pulled a face, 'it is haunted.'

'I know what you mean,' Cranston interjected. 'About a hundred years ago, when gang violence in the city was rife during the reign of Edward, ancestor of our present king, a murder took place in St Mary Le Bow.' Cranston sat back in his chair. 'I make reference to it in my magnum opus, my great work on the history of this city . . .'

Athelstan closed his eyes in exasperation. Sir John's absorption with the history of London was famous, and nothing could stop the coroner from delivering a long, unsolicited lecture on any aspect of city life. Cranston was already preparing himself with a swig from the miraculous wineskin, which he offered to Athelstan. The friar bluntly refused.

'Sir John, the hour passes. Time is short, pleasure is brief. I think I know . . .'

'Laurence Duket,' Cranston jabbed a finger at Athelstan, 'as I have said, about a hundred years ago he was a gang leader in London. He met his rival Ralph Crepyn in Cheapside and there was the usual dagger play. Anyway, Duket wounded Crepyn and fled for sanctuary in St Mary Le Bow. Yes, Master Matthias?' The young man, fascinated by Cranston, just nodded. 'The church was locked and sealed for the night,' Cranston continued blithely, 'yet when the priest opened the church the following morning, Duket was found hanging from a wall bracket. Of course, such a mystery swept the city. The King sent a royal clerk to investigate. The mystery was solved and ended up with a woman, Alice atte Bowe, being burned alive at Smithfield. Other members of the gang were hanged, either by the neck or the purse.'

'Duket's ghost is supposed to haunt St Mary Le Bow,' Matthias took up the story. 'I can well believe it. I go in when it falls quiet after the morning masses, when the market bell has sounded . . .'

'You said haunted?'

'Oh, I am sure, Brother, that the ghost of Laurence Duket glides the gloomy nave. The light is always dappled there, the shadows ever present, growing longer as the day dies.' Matthias paused. 'Strange sounds echo. You know the church is built over a Roman temple to a god called Mithras? I have been down into the crypt and seen some of the ancient ruins, but they don't concern me; my uncle's chantry chapel does. Duket's ghost,' Matthias shrugged, 'has probably been joined by that of Edmund Lacy, slain in a tavern brawl.'

'By the villain Reynard, who,' Cranston peered at the hour candle standing in the corner, 'should be meeting God above Tyburn stream. Now, young man, Whitfield and Lebarge – whom did they carouse with?'

Matthias scratched the side of his face. 'They revelled and drank deep in their cups. They had conversations with, well,' he shrugged, 'with everyone. Though, for the life of me, I cannot recall specific occasions.'

'And the wenches – whom did they favour?'

'Whitfield, Joycelina; Lebarge, Hawisa – a pert little doxy with a swan-like neck, sweet-faced and full-bosomed.' Matthias abruptly rose. 'If you are finished with me,' he stammered, 'can I go?'

'For the time being,' Athelstan replied, asking Matthias to fetch the two women he'd named.

Joycelina and Hawisa arrived, the former looking cold-eyed and solemn, though Hawisa, pretty as any spring maid, seemed eager to please; yet neither was forthcoming, claiming that they had entertained their clients and knew next to nothing about their business affairs. Exasperated, Athelstan dismissed them.

'You know more than what you have told us,' he declared. 'We will undoubtedly talk to you ladies again. So, until then.' He swung open the door and gestured them through, then closed it behind them and leaned against it. 'Sir John, we certainly do not have the truth about all this.'

'Murder, little friar?'

'Murder, Grand Coroner! Oh, yes! Murder has taken up residence here, along with a whole coven of mischief. Now, Sir John, let us return to . . .'

Athelstan stopped at a pounding at the door. It was flung open and Sir Everard Camoys, white beard and moustache bristling, stormed into the chamber.

'Why, my good friend . . .'

'Don't good friend me, Sir John.' Everard unclasped his cloak and threw it to the settle. 'My feckless son is here, in this den of iniquity, this haven of harlots. I . . .'

Cranston swept round the table and clasped Sir Everard's hand, drawing him into a full embrace before stepping away, grinning from ear to ear. 'Fiery as always, Everard, but we are not charging the French. I have business here and, I admit, so have you. Now come.' Cranston made the goldsmith sit down and served him a blackjack of fresh ale and a platter of bread and cheese. Athelstan introduced himself. Sir Everard, now slightly embarrassed, offered his apologies. Athelstan just smiled and sketched a cross in the air above the goldsmith's head.

'I am sorry,' Sir Everard repeated, 'but my waking hours were disturbed by the Herald of Hell. I sent you a message, Sir John.'

The coroner nodded.

'Tell me more about this Herald,' Athelstan said. 'I know . . .'

'Brother, a true will-o'-the-wisp, a night walker cloaked in the deepest dark. He appears, delivers his proclamation and vanishes.'

'What did he say?'

Everard closed his eyes. 'Lord Camoys,' he began,

'And all who with you dwell,
Harken to this warning from the Herald of Hell,
Judgement is coming, it will not be late,
Vengeance already knocks on your gate.'

Everard opened his eyes and took a deep breath. 'Doggerel verse! When I went down to investigate, out in the street, I could see no one. The watchman Poulter also reported the same, yet I heard that horn, those threats. I saw and held that beaker of blood with two sticks, small onions spiked on them like traitors' heads poled above London Bridge.'

'He is appearing all over the city,' Cranston declared. 'No one knows who he is or how he can come and go with such impunity.'

'And yet,' Sir Everard broke in, 'I am sure . . .'

'About what?' Athelstan asked.

'I recognized that voice, I am certain of it. Oh, I know they say the Herald of Hell is the leader of the Upright Men in London, and that he has the power to turn invisible and be in many places at the one time.' Everard shook his head. 'I am more a believer in human wickedness and cunning tricks. I recognized that voice but I cannot place it.' He turned toward Cranston. 'Remember, John, when we were in France? You and I were regularly despatched forward towards the enemy lines.'

'I remember.' Cranston smiled dreamily. 'Warm nights, the air rich with the fragrance of apples. Do you remember that night outside Crotoy?'

'Sir John,' Athelstan warned.

'Ah yes.' The coroner recollected himself.

'They used to call us the King's eyes and ears,' Everard declared. 'You with your sharp sight.'

'And you, my friend, with an ear for the faintest sound.'

'So you recognized the Herald's voice?'

'Yes, Brother, but, the angels be my witness, I cannot place it. I have done some searches. You are correct, Sir John. The Herald appears all over the city from Farringdon to Cripplegate.' The goldsmith shook his head. 'He knows where people live; he appears, then, like some will-o'-the-wisp, he vanishes into thin air.'

'And the Cross of Lothar?' Athelstan asked. 'We know its origins . . .'

'I am sure you do.' Sir Everard waved a hand. 'I could understand my brother's absorption with it. What I find difficult to accept is that he soaked my son's mind and soul with stories about that cross; the legends surrounding it, the richness of its jewellery, its dazzling appearance.'

'Why didn't Reginald just leave it to his nephew?'

Sir Everard sighed noisily. 'Oh, Reginald eventually realized what he had done. Matthias was totally obsessed by that cross.' The goldsmith blew his cheeks out. 'About the only thing Matthias was interested in, apart from wenching and drinking. Anyway, my brother decided he would not make it easy for his nephew. He would force Matthias to use his wits. After all, he is an intelligent scholar; he could discover its whereabouts for himself. Ah, well,' Sir Everard struggled to his feet. 'I came to rescue my son from this house of stews with its filthy fleshpots. Sir John, if that is acceptable?'

'As long as you stand guarantor for him. Matthias must not leave London and be ready to be questioned by us at any hour of the day. Everard, my old friend . . .' Cranston came round the table. 'One final question about the Cross of Lothar: do you have any idea of its whereabouts? Could it lie buried with your brother?'

'No, I am sure it is not. Matthias is correct. I would wager a pound of pure gold that the Lothar Cross lies hidden, either here or in St Mary Le Bow. But now I must go.'

'And so shall we.' Athelstan gathered up his chancery bag. 'Sir John, we must visit Whitfield's chamber.'

Everard turned, his hand on the door latch. 'Did Thibault's clerk commit suicide?'

Athelstan smiled faintly. 'For now, God only knows, but come, Sir John, I want Foxley, Mistress Cheyne and Joycelina to join us. Sir Everard, I bid you good day.'

They left, and Athelstan went ahead, up the steep, narrow stairs to the top gallery and what he now called 'The Murder Chamber'. He walked into the musty room and crossed to the window, noticing how the floorboards creaked. He scrutinized everything most carefully: the inner shutters, the window, the tattered oiled pigskin. He could detect nothing out of place except that the latch on the door window was rather stiff and creaked when moved. He opened it, leaned over and peered either side.

'Impossible,' he whispered. 'According to Foxley, this was all sealed and locked.' He tapped a sandalled foot against the floor. 'The window is big enough for someone to enter, but how could they?' He turned away. 'There is no ladder long enough to reach it, and even if there was, the guard dogs roaming the gardens below would have been alerted. The soil has not been disturbed, and anyone climbing up to this window on the top gallery could easily be noticed from any window overlooking the garden.' He paused. 'I wonder,' he whispered, 'why Whitfield, not the fittest of men, should have a chamber on the top gallery? Why not a more comfortable one below? So . . .' He moved over to the door propped against the wall and carefully inspected the dark stained oak, the bolts at top and bottom, both savagely ruptured, the torn hinges and the bulging, cracked lock with the key still twisted inside. He examined the lintel – slivers of wood had broken away – then stepped back into the chamber. The door was built into the wall with a recess on either side. He glanced to the left where robes and cloaks still hung on pegs and then to the right where the lavarium and hour candle stood. He walked around scrutinizing the floor, walls and ceilings, but the chamber was enclosed, with no traces of any secret door or passageway. He crossed himself and went to gaze at where Whitfield's corpse had hung so eerily, swaying slightly on the end of that tarred rope.

'Impossible,' Athelstan breathed, staring up at the beam. 'Did you commit suicide? Does your spirit still hover here? Has Satan appeared with his hellish mirror so that you can gaze forever on your immortal soul stained with sin, or has God sent this great angel of mercy to comfort you? I pray that he has . . .' He stopped as he heard a harsh clatter on the stairs and Sir John's booming voice assuring the ladies that they could soon return to their normal business.

The coroner led Mistress Cheyne, Joycelina and Foxley into the chamber. The Master of Horse looked a little tipsy, the two women rather anxious, the usual arrogance drained from their faces. Athelstan ushered them out to the gallery and asked them to repeat exactly what had happened earlier in the day when the door was forced. Mistress Cheyne immediately described how she had been busy in the refectory with guests and servants who were breaking their fast. Griffin had gone to rouse everybody, but Whitfield's absence was eventually noted and Joycelina despatched to fetch him. The maid then took up the story, explaining how she had knocked on the door, tried it, then peered through the eyelet, but this had been blocked, whilst the key had definitely been in the lock. She had then hurried down to the refectory to raise the alarm. Mistress Cheyne, now seated on one of the coffers, described how Foxley had gone out into the garden to bring the battering ram, along with the two labourers, whilst Joycelina had been despatched to tell the maids not to be disturbed by what they heard. The labourers had brought the ram; they had mounted the stairs and begun pounding the door, Foxley assisting them. The Master of Horse intervened and explained that he had also examined the door and found both eyelet and lock blocked. He had helped the labourers while Mistress Cheyne had shouted for Joycelina to join her, which she had done.

'So you are gathered here,' Athelstan declared, 'in this dark gallery, then what happened?'

'The door gave way, it collapsed. Immediately we saw

Whitfield's corpse swaying in the poor light.' Mistress Cheyne
wiped her mouth on the back of her hand. 'We were very frightened. I told Foxley to go in.'

'I entered,' the Master of Horse explained. 'I passed the corpse.
I was terrified. The shadows seemed to dance. I wondered if
pig-faced demons . . .'

'Yes, yes,' Cranston interrupted, 'then what happened?'

'You went straight to the window?' Athelstan gently insisted.
'And?'

'I lifted the bar on the inner shutters and pulled at the window
latch.'

'Was that easy?'

'No, it stuck a little, as if it had been clamped shut for some
time. I pushed the door window back and lifted the hooks on the
outer shutters.'

'Tell me,' Athelstan demanded, 'did you notice anything amiss
about either the shutters or the window?'

'No.'

Athelstan studied Foxley's face. 'You may not have told me
everything,' he murmured, 'or even the full truth behind other
matters, but I believe you are telling me the truth about this.' He
turned. 'Sir John, inform all those whom we have questioned to
make themselves readily available if we wish to question them
again.' Athelstan forced a smile. 'Or we shall have them put to
the horn as *utlegati* – outlaws . . .'

Athelstan and Cranston left the Golden Oliphant, pausing
beneath the huge, exquisitely painted sign to decide what to do
next. Athelstan stared up. With its hidden sexual connotations,
the curved, beautifully decorated drinking horn, its goblet sealed
by a cross, struck him as a most accurate depiction of the house
he was leaving. All fair in form, but what was its essence, the
very substance of the place? A house of murder. Pondering how
he could resolve the mysteries confronting him, the friar was
tempted to return immediately to St Erconwald's and question
Lebarge, yet he sensed Whitfield's scrivener would claim sanctuary
in all its rights and refuse to talk. Why had Lebarge fled there?
What was he so frightened of? Athelstan put these questions to
Cranston, who simply rubbed his face and stared up at the
gorgeously painted Oliphant.

'The day is passing quickly enough,' the coroner grunted. 'We have other places to visit before we cross the river. Let us leave Lebarge for a while and thread these murderous alleyways to a house of even greater ill-repute, the Tavern of Lost Souls.'

Cranston and Athelstan made their way along the narrow runnels heading towards the stews along the Thames. The coroner was correct. The day was passing and the strengthening sunshine had coaxed all the inhabitants of these grim slums out into the streets to mingle with those making their way up to London and the approaches to the riverside. Cranston was recognized and mocked, but his *comitatus* or retinue, led by the burly bailiff Flaxwith, his ugly mastiff Samson trotting aggressively beside him, kept the threats to nothing more than hurled curses and obscenities.

They entered what Cranston described as the 'footpaths of Hell', mere slits between decaying houses, so rotten and dilapidated they leaned in dizzyingly close to block out both light and air. These derelict shells were only kept from collapsing by struts and crutches shoved under each storey. All windows were blind, shuttered fast, whilst doorways were hidden behind rough sheets of oxhide doused in vinegar as a protection against fire. Rubbish heaps, so slimy they glistened, exuded rotten smells, a haven for the fast, slinking rats almost as big as the long-haired cats which watched from the shadows. Dogs on chains, ribs showing through their mangy hides, howled and threw themselves from their foul kennels. Flies moved in thick black clouds like a horde of demons above the refuse which lay ankle-deep, swilling in the filthy water seeping from cracked rain tubs. Figures moved, flitting shadows through the murk. Voices echoed eerily. Here and there a lantern-horn, lit by candles reeking of tallow fat, glowed through the gloom. Along these footpaths, the dead hour, the witching time for all forms of wickedness, lasted from dawn to dusk. Now and again this sanctuary of sin showed some life: a beggar woman crawled out to plead for her husband, whose wits, she screeched, had been stolen by fairies. Athelstan was appalled at the sheer ugliness of her raw-boned, one-eyed face, her scalp scratched bloodily bare of hair, her fingers thin and crooked like hooks. He hastily threw her a coin and sketched a blessing. Cranston quietly cursed and immediately ordered his bailiffs to ring them as a huge, barred door was speedily flung open. A gang of beggars, swathed in rags, swarmed out to pester this generous friar. Cranston's bailiffs drove them away as they hurried along the main thoroughfare leading down to the river.

Here the crowd was more busy about their own affairs. Athelstan, face hidden deep in his cowl, caught snatches of the teeming life around him. A wedding party: the groom, festooned with green leaves, a chaplet of roses on his head, led his merry guests in a spritely dance to the music of rebec, viol and harp. A knight, sombre in black and yellow livery, rode a powerful, roan-coloured destrier down to the tilt yards. He sat in the majestic, horned wooden saddle carrying lance and great shield; the caparison of his destrier matched his own colours, whilst before him a squire carried a decorated helmet with a leaping panther crest festooned with yellow and black feathers. Friars of many orders in robes of black, white, cream or muddy brown administered to the needs of funeral corteges, mourning parties or vigil fraternities. Traders and hucksters, their trays strapped round their necks, touted a range of goods, from threads to potions which could cure the plague. Leeches offered to bleed those too full of blood. Wild-eyed relic-sellers, who proclaimed they were fresh from Jerusalem or Rome, offered wares which included Delilah's hair or bloodsoaked soil from the Garden of Gethsemane.

The noise was constant: curses, yells, shouts of traders offering 'fresh mince', 'clear water', 'sweet grilled meals', or 'the fattest figs in a sugared sauce'. The night walkers and dark prowlers were also out with a keen eye for the loose purse or dangling wallet. The crowd surged and broke around funeral parties, pilgrim groups and the different fraternities who moved in clouds of incense and a blaze of colour to this church or that. The stink and stench proved too much for Athelstan, and he hastily bought two pomanders from a young girl, who also invited them over to a puppet show on a garishly decorated cart. Athelstan smiled and shook his head. They turned a corner on to a rutted trackway which swept down to a three-storey, lathe and plaster building with a purple-painted door approached by steep steps. Above this hung a sign proclaiming in red and gold-scrolled lettering: 'The Tavern of Lost Souls'.

'Undoubtedly the work of Reginald Camoys,' Cranston

declared, taking a swig from the miraculous wineskin. 'A work of art, eh, Athelstan? Red and gold against a snow-white background. Snow-white!' Cranston snorted. 'That certainly wouldn't be the description of what goes on behind that purple-painted door!'

'Which is?'

'Everything under the sun,' Flaxwith, standing behind them, lugubriously intoned. 'Buying and selling, cheating and cozening, where the Devil's pact is sworn over this soul or that and lives are marked down for ending. Whatever you want, Brother, Master Mephistopheles and his minions will arrange.'

'Mephistopheles? The devil himself?'

'The devil incarnate!' Cranston snorted. 'Come.'

They climbed the steps. Cranston brought the bronze clapper, carved in the shape of a grinning demon's face, down time and again. The door was flung open, and a man dressed in a grey robe bounded by a red cincture beckoned them into the most extraordinary taproom Athelstan had ever seen. A long hall stretched before them, well lit by catherine wheels lowered on chains. Candles crammed around each rim provided light, along with lanterns hooked on beams or pillars. The floor gleamed with polish, the air fragrant with the smell of beeswax and herb pots placed judiciously along the walls. There was no obvious furniture, but a long row of cubicles was set in the centre, each one carved out of shimmering oak with a door on either end. One of these hung open and Athelstan glimpsed a shiny table with cushioned benches on either side. The bright lighting meant that customers could view the extraordinary paintings which proclaimed the most frightening images of Hell: minstrels tortured by the very instruments they used to play; vain beauties forced to admire their own reflection in a mirror on the devil's arse; adulterers impaled by demon birds; gluttons devoured by a huge stomach on legs.

Halfway down the taproom they were told to wait. Athelstan could hear murmurs of conversation from the cubicles, but these were so cunningly contrived and placed, it was nigh impossible to hear what was actually being said. He walked across to study the frescoes more carefully. The entire row of paintings all displayed scenes from Hell: demons depicted as part animal, part human and part vegetable; devils with gauzy wings and fly faces; sinners who once frolicked in the pond of lust now stood blue-bodied next to a frozen lake where more of the damned floated and froze, their heads just above Hell's foul waters. The more he studied the paintings, the more Athelstan was convinced they were inspired by the teaching of the mystic Richard Rolle who proclaimed, 'As a war-like machine strikes the walls of a city, so shall hideously fanged frog-demons strike the bodies and souls of the damned.'

'You like our paintings, Brother Athelstan?' The Dominican turned. A man, dressed in the same way as the one who had opened the door, emerged out of the darkness at the far end of the taproom. He walked across the dancing pools of light, hands outstretched in greeting. Athelstan grasped them and the man introduced himself as 'Mephistopheles, Master of the Minions'.

'You were not called that over the baptismal font?' Athelstan enquired, stepping back.

'You mean when I, or those who sponsored me, rejected the Lord Satan and all his pomp and boasts?' Mephistopheles grinned in a display of white, shiny teeth. He drew closer and Athelstan caught the very cunning of this man. A shape-shifter, the friar thought, a man who could be all things to all men. Mephistopheles was quiet-voiced, his face cleanly shaven, his red, cropped hair shiny with oil. A pious face with regular features except for the slightly sardonic twist of his full lips and cynical eyes, as if the soul behind them contemplated the world and all who passed through it with the utmost mockery. Mephistopheles gestured at the paintings.

'We like to remind our customers that life is short, judgement imminent and punishment eternal; this concentrates the mind something wonderful.' He paused as Cranston strolled across, Flaxwith trailing behind him. 'My Lord Coroner, a great pleasure!'

'I wish I could return the compliment, Master Mephistopheles, but we must have words.'

'And so we shall.' Mephistopheles nodded towards Flaxwith. 'But first ask your bully boys to stand by the door; they make me nervous.'

Cranston looked as if he were about to refuse.

'Please,' Athelstan murmured.

Cranston assented and Mephistopheles led them across to one of the cubicles. He opened the door and grandly gestured them to sit on one side of the table whilst he took the bench opposite. He asked if they wanted refreshment. Cranston was about to agree when Athelstan pressed his sandalled foot hard on the toe of Cranston's boot. Mephistopheles grinned and rubbed white, fleshy hands together.

'Sir John?'

'Amaury Whitfield, Thibault's clerk, has been found hanging in his chamber at the Golden Oliphant.'

'So I have heard.'

'He visited you?'

'So it would appear; otherwise you wouldn't be visiting me!'

'Why did Whitfield come here and why did he intend to return this evening?'

'You are right that he intended to return.'

'What was his business?'

'His business.'

Swifter than any dagger man, Cranston whipped out his knife and pressed the blade against Mephistopheles' throat.

'You will slit me, Sir John?'

'Of course, defending myself, a royal officer, the King's own Coroner in the City of London against a notorious miscreant resisting arrest.'

'On what charge?' Mephistopheles held his head rigidly still.

'Oh, I can think of quite a few after Flaxwith and my bully boys, as you call them, have ransacked this house of ill-repute from cellar to garret. Now come, Master of the Minions, the truth.'

Mephistopheles nodded and Cranston resheathed his dagger.

'He came here yesterday,' Mephistopheles said carefully. 'He met me. He held certain goods he wished to trade and enquired if I would inspect them and offer a price.'

'What goods?'

'I don't know.' Mephistopheles rubbed his throat where Cranston's dagger had rested. 'But he seemed satisfied and said he would return here later today, towards the evening, but . . .' Mephistopheles spread his hands.

'Was he frightened?' Cranston asked.

'Certainly. He mumbled something about the Herald of Hell, the sinister doom threatening the city, and his desire to escape the coming fury.'

'Did he seem frightened enough to commit suicide?' Athelstan asked.

'Perhaps.'

'And Lebarge?'

'Oh, he came with him but remained as silent as a nun in vows.'

'And Master Camoys?'

Mephistopheles pulled a face.

'A callow youth whose uncle executed the sign outside. He has been here before to ask me what I knew about his dead uncle, which,' Mephistopheles sniffed, 'wasn't much.'

'Did you know why he should meet Whitfield here?'

'No, Sir John.' Mephistopheles leaned forward. 'But for the love of God, you know what is coming.' He indicated with his head. 'The river is not far from here. As soon as the revolt begins, I intend to flee; half of London will follow me.'

'So?'

'Whitfield was the same. He was a coney caught in a trap. He was Thibault's creature, marked down for capture, humiliation and a gruesome death.' Mephistopheles lowered his voice, a look of pity in those strange eyes. 'As you are, my portly friend . . .'

Cranston and Athelstan left the Tavern of Lost Souls. Mephistopheles had remained enigmatic and Cranston, as he informed Athelstan, had no real evidence of any wrongdoing by this most sinister of characters. They made their way along the busy runnels and alleyways towards the river. They were now in the heart of the stews of Southwark, where the bath houses and brothels did a thriving trade. Wandering food sellers pushed their moveable grills and ovens on barrows or pulled them on roughly made sleds. Water sellers, ale men and beer wives hovered close by, ever ready to sell drink to those who bought the rancid meats, their taste and smell carefully hidden beneath bitter spices and rich sauces. Whores, their heads and faces almost hidden by thick horse-hair wigs dyed orange or green, thronged in doorways and at the mouth of alleyways, or leaned from windows offering blandishments to all and sundry. Nearby their hooded, sharp-eyed pimps, needle-thin daggers pushed through rings on their tattered belts, kept an eye on business. Sailors, wharfmen and those who lived off the river thronged in to visit the stews and bath houses, taverns and ale cottages.

Cranston's party was given a wide berth by all of these as they swept down to the quayside, where the coroner, using his seal of office, managed to commandeer a royal barge which had just berthed. They clambered in, followed by Flaxwith and his bailiffs. Cranston roared his orders and the grinning bargemen, who knew the coroner of old, pushed away, turning their craft into the swell, oars rising and falling to the sing-song voice of their master. The barge, its pennants fluttering, ploughed into the slow moving river. Athelstan was relieved; they would have gentle passage. He sat under the leather canopy in the stern, clutching his chancery satchel. Feeling more relaxed, he closed his eyes and quietly recited a psalm from the office of the day. He felt the salty, fishy breeze catch his face. Athelstan opened his eyes and stared up at the blue sky; the sun was strong, the clouds mere white tendrils. He recalled the words of the poet, 'How nature mirrored the shimmering mind of God.' He murmured a prayer and turned to what he had seen, heard and felt that busy morning. Deep in his heart the friar realized that he and Cranston faced a truly cunning mystery. He thought again about Lebarge, sheltering in sanctuary. Had the scrivener fled the Golden Oliphant so precipitately because he feared that he also would die a mysterious death which would be depicted as an accident or a suicide? Athelstan turned and glimpsed a royal war cog in full-bellied sail making its way down to the estuary.

'Sir John?' He tapped the coroner's arm.

'Yes, Brother?'

'The *Leaping Horse*, Odo Gray's ship, is berthed at Queenshithe. Let us seek it out.' Cranston had a word with the master and the barge swung slightly and made its way past the ships moored close to the north bank of the Thames. The *Leaping Horse* came into view, its name scrolled on the high stern and gilded bow strip, a powerful, two-masted, big-bellied war cog. Cranston stood and peered up.

'It's ready for sea,' he murmured, 'on the evening tide. Wouldn't you say so, barge master?'

The fellow agreed, pointing out how the sails were loosened, and crew men were scurrying about the deck whilst others were busy in the rigging.

'Sir John, should we approach and board?'

'No, no.' The coroner shook his head. 'Interesting, however, isn't it, my floating friar? How Captain Odo Gray believed he would be up and away before this day was out? Well, he won't be, so let's continue.'

The barge master shouted at the oarsmen and the craft pulled away before turning to run alongside the landing place at Queen's Steps. Cranston told Flaxwith and his bailiffs that he no longer needed them before leading Athelstan up one of the alleyways into Cheapside. The afternoon was drawing on yet the heat in the narrow streets was stifling. Worthy burgesses pushed by, sweating heavily in their high-necked shirts, ermine-lined robes and fur-edged caps. Their wives were equally splendid in gorgeous coloured gowns and robes, faces almost hidden by the studded pomanders pressed to their noses against the ever pervasive stench. Traders and stall-holders, tinkers and costermongers shouted the cries of their trade. Nips, foists and other petty thieves slunk amongst the crowd looking for prey or plunder only to flee at the sight of Cranston. The dung carts were out, the self-important rakers shoving people aside so as to empty laystalls and cesspits. Tavern doors hung open, ale fumes and cooking smells wafting into the streets to mingle with the myriad of odours swirling about.

At the crossroads, close to the Standard, market bailiffs were lashing the naked buttocks of two ale traders found guilty of adulterating their product. Butchers stood in the stocks, heads and hands clasped, forced to smell the putrid reek of the mouldy meat they had been caught selling. Nearby a bailiff wailed on a set of bagpipes to attract attention as well as drown the groans of the convicted miscreants. Cranston took direction from a stall holder and led Athelstan along an alleyway and into Fairlop Lane. A quiet street, formerly lined by shops, it had now been converted into dwelling places, their doors flung open to catch any breeze or coolness. Athelstan glimpsed scenes as they passed: a fat man at table gnawing a bone; beside him, his even fatter wife with a dish of cold meats being importuned by a plump child, a soiled loincloth around its ankles. In the next house a man garbed in outside clothes dozed on a pillow before an empty stone fireplace. A yard winder and spindler with thread stood idly by as his young wife primped herself in a hand-held mirror, more interested in that than the rosary beads wrapped around her fingers. Cranston beckoned her serving girl to come out and, for a penny, she led them to Whitfield's chambers, a narrow, two-storey dwelling on the corner of an alleyway. The downstairs window, previously a shop front, was bricked and boarded up. She nodded at the door, loose off the latch.

'Others been here,' she said. 'They forced the lock, went in and came out.'

'Who?' Athelstan asked.

'King's men.' She patted her chest. 'They wore the White Hart.'

'Bowmen,' Cranston declared, 'Cheshire archers.'

'The same,' the girl smiled crookedly, 'led by a man with hair and face as white as snow.'

'Albinus,' Cranston whispered, 'with a company of archers. He ignored our request to leave things well alone. Oh dear!' He thanked the girl and pushed open the door. Inside the dingy dwelling, a flagstone passage, greasy underfoot, led them to different chambers: a bedroom and chancery office next to a shabby kitchen and scullery.

'Everything is bare,' Cranston murmured. They went up the stairs to what must have been Lebarge's chambers: a bed-loft and writing room with rickety furniture. The house seemed to have been swept clean, with little to show who actually lived there. They searched but found nothing except scraps of parchment, ragged remnants of clothes, discarded chancery items and an ancient, battered lanternhorn. The small walled garden at the rear of the house was no better: overgrown flower patches, herb plots with rubbish piled high. Athelstan glimpsed a broken money casket and two small coffers, their metal studs gleaming in the afternoon sunlight.

'Truly a wasteland,' he declared. 'Sir John, there is nothing here for us and, I suspect, Thibault's men found the same.'

They left the house and made their way up to St Mary Le Bow, standing at the heart of Cheapside. The crowds were now thinning as the day began to die. The breeze had turned cooler and stronger, blowing the saltpetre strewn in the streets to sting the eye and clog the throat. St Mary's loomed, a turreted, gabled mass against the fading blue sky, its steeple pointing like a warning finger towards heaven. On its steps stood a storyteller delivering a tale about a fairy king in Essex who had cleared a swampy place near a pool, long overgrown with briar to form a coven for foxes. All this had been pruned to build a pretty, timber banqueting-house now known as 'Pleasaunce-in-the-Marsh'.

Cranston and Athelstan brushed past him, as they did a wonder-teller proclaiming that he had seen a fleet of demons cross the Middle Sea. On the top step a public penitent, garbed completely in red, a mask covering his face with slits for eyes and mouth, brazenly declared, 'I have lived in the Devil's service with late suppers and even later risings. I must repent, otherwise after death my soul shall curse my body. I shall have demons for fellows, burn in fire and shiver on ice.' The penitent gestured at Athelstan. 'I'll give you a blessing for a coin.'

'And I will give you one for free,' Athelstan retorted: he turned and went back down the steps and studied the church carefully. He had a feeling, an instinct that something was not quite right, though he could not say why. He had no evidence, nothing at all to justify his unease, except he did wonder about the storyteller and the public penitent. Once, deep in his cups, Pike the Ditcher had confessed to Athelstan that such eccentrics were often the spies and watchmen of the Great Community of the Realm.

'It's the wrong time of day,' Athelstan murmured to himself. 'The church won't have many visitors now, so why tarry here?' He returned to his study of the church. St Mary Le Bow stood in its own ground behind a low stone wall, a little removed from the busy clamour of Cheapside. An eerie sadness hovered around the church: a touch of menace, of baleful watchfulness. Athelstan walked back up the steps and stared at the evil-looking gargoyles guarding the door. He glanced over his shoulder; the public penitent was watching him carefully. The friar shrugged, turned away and led a bemused Cranston into the gloomy nave. On a pillar near the baptismal font, a leaping figure of St Christopher caught Cranston's eye. The coroner wondered what was bothering the little friar but, as always, he'd let this sharp-minded ferret of a man have his way. They walked up the church. At the far end reared a huge rood screen dominated by a twisted figure of the crucified Christ. The light streaming through the windows, some of them filled with painted glass, was beginning to fade. Visitors scurried about, dark shapes in the gathering murk. Incense and candle smoke fragranced the air. On the left of the high altar, a host of tapers glowed before the Lady altar.

Athelstan led Cranston into the north transept, stretching beyond the drum-like pillars, which housed a number of small chantry chapels. Each of these was partitioned off by a polished, gleaming trellised screen. A small door led into a carpeted interior with a stained-glass window high in the outside wall, an altar on a slightly raised dais and a prie-dieu placed before it. Each chapel was adorned with statues, pictures and triptychs extolling the merits of the saint in whose name the chapel was dedicated. Some of the chantries contained tombs. Reginald Camoys', at the far end, dedicated to St Stephen, housed two: simple table tombs with a knight in armour as an effigy, a naked sword clasped in his folded hands, the carved face almost hidden by the chain-mail coif and nose guard of the conical war helmet. A sculptured frieze ran along the side of each tomb. Athelstan crouched down to examine these.

'Look, Sir John, they are virtually the same. This,' he traced the carving with his finger, 'must be the Cross of Lothar with a kneeling knight, paying devotion as he would before the Sacrament, and this, repeated twice, is the cipher or cryptic symbol "IHSV" beneath the rising sun, and the inscription to "The Unconquerable Sun", an allusion, I suspect, to the resurrected Christ. The stone is costly, possibly Purbeck marble, specially imported.'

Athelstan straightened up and stared at the window above Penchen's tomb. Filled with painted glass, it proclaimed the same message as the one found on the frieze. Reginald Camoys' tomb, built along the wooden trellis screen which separated the chapel from the one beyond, was almost identical. Athelstan stared around, a comfortable, well-furnished chantry with its elmwood altar, white cloths, silver-chased candlesticks and a cross which undoubtedly replicated that of Lothar. Athelstan picked this up and examined the imitation treasure with its green and gold paint, a cameo of a Roman emperor at its centrepiece.

'Can I help you?' a voice grated. A man stood in the doorway to the chantry chapel, tall and thin, with sparse black locks falling in wisps to his shoulders. The stranger's face was mere bone, the white skin stretched across tight and transparent. He stepped closer to meet Athelstan, his milky-blue eyes sunk deep in their sockets, his nose hooked like a hawk's, his thin-lipped mouth all pursed. He was dressed in a stained yellow jerkin and hose of the same colour. From his belt hung a naked dagger and a couple of tooth drawers; around his neck two rosaries fashioned out of human teeth.

'And who are you?' Cranston stepped out of the shadows. The stranger glimpsed the coroner's badge and hastily retreated.

'Well?' Athelstan asked.

'Raoul Malfort, bell clerk of St Mary Le Bow.'

'Ah yes, recently appointed following the murder of the previous office holder, Edmund Lacy, stabbed to death in a tavern by the villain Reynard now dangling at Tyburn.'

'Not so, not so.' The bell clerk shook his head. 'You've not heard the news?' He sniffed and abruptly changed the conversation. 'I am also a tooth-drawer. I still practise my trade.' He gestured with his head. 'I use the bell tower now Lacy has gone.'

'You disliked him?'

'Until he died he was the master,' Malfort declared. 'Now he has departed this vale of tears and I have taken over his position.' He beckoned. 'Do you want to see my chamber?'

'No, no,' Athelstan replied hastily, glimpsing a bloodied tooth on the macabre necklace. The friar smiled to himself. No wonder, he thought, Matthias Camoys believed this church was haunted with strange cries and sounds – it was no more than some poor soul losing a tooth! Nevertheless, Athelstan shivered. This eerie-looking bell clerk only deepened the apprehension he'd felt before entering this so-called hallowed place.

'You talked about news?' he demanded.

'Oh, yes, Reynard.' Malfort grinned in a show of yellowing, broken teeth. 'He did not dance in the air at Tyburn. Murdered, he was, in the death closet at Newgate, killed by two felons Hydrus and Wyvern. Now, when they reached Tyburn . . .' In brusque sentences, Malfort described the riot around the execution ground. Once he'd finished, Cranston whistled under his breath.

'Brother,' he gestured, 'we should leave and reflect on all that has happened.'

'True, true.'

Athelstan and Cranston left the chantry chapel accompanied by Malfort and crossed the church to the other transept. Athelstan walked through its shadows, stopped and pointed to a door at the far end.

'Where does that lead?'

'Down to the crypt. Nothing there except bones and ancient ruins.'

'I would like to visit it.'

Malfort shrugged and walked back to take a cresset from its wall niche.

'Brother?' Cranston asked. 'Why the curiosity?'

'Because I am curious,' Athelstan smiled, 'and I am curious because I am uneasy.' He rubbed his forehead. 'Perhaps I am growing tired, I just sense something's amiss. Anyway . . .' He paused as Malfort brought back the cresset, its flame dancing merrily in the draught.

The bell clerk led them to the crypt door and, taking out a bunch of keys, opened it and ushered them in. They went down mildewed, decaying steps into a spacious cavern, its floor covered in cracked white bones, scraps of skulls and decaying shards of wood and cloth. A truly ghostly place with its litter of battered bones and all the refuse thrown here when the parish cemetery was cleared of the dead to make room for more corpses. A shadow-filled, shape-dancing chamber where the darkness seemed to lurk in the cobwebbed recesses, ready to spring out. Athelstan took the torch and moved over to inspect a crumbling wall, obviously much more ancient than the crypt which enclosed it.

'Romans.' Malfort's voice echoed. 'They say they built a temple here, but, Brother, Sir John – it is the Lord High Coroner, with his secretarius Athelstan?'

'It certainly is,' Cranston's voice boomed.

'Sir, I have other tasks. I must ring the bell for evening prayer, trim the candles . . .'

'Yes, yes.' Athelstan walked back. 'Do you have many dealings with Matthias Camoys?'

'He often comes here asking questions and studying those

tombs, even coming down here to stare and search. That young man likes to haunt solitary places, his sleep broken by garish dreams as he pines to discover the whereabouts of the Cross of Lothar. But, gentlemen, if you have finished . . .'

Cranston and Athelstan left the church. They had reached the bottom step when there was a flurry of movement in the church porch behind them. Alarmed by the sudden patter of footsteps, Cranston turned nimble as a greyhound, pushing Athelstan behind him as he drew both sword and dagger. Their attackers paused, giving Cranston more time to ready himself into a half-crouch, sword and dagger out, moving to the left and right. The three hooded and masked assailants swirled in, then one of them screamed and staggered back, clutching his arm, at Cranston's sudden parry. His two companions immediately retreated, grabbed their wounded comrade and promptly disappeared, running across the steps, jumping down and vanishing into the alleyway running alongside the church.

'Well I never! Satan's tits!' Cranston murmured, gesturing away the curious bystanders who were now drifting over to view the effects of the brief but furious encounter. 'Well I never!' The coroner resheathed both sword and dagger.

Athelstan just stood clutching his chancery satchel, staring up at the tympanum of Christ in glory carved above the entrance to the church with its inscription sculptured around its edges: *Hic est locus terribilis, Domus Dei et Porta Caeli* – 'This is a terrifying place,' Athelstan translated, 'the House of God and the Gate of Heaven.' He patted Cranston's arm. 'Well, it certainly is! Why did they attack like that, Sir John? They came out of the church behind us; they let us pass and then they struck. I truly believe they did not mean to harm us. I suspect,' Athelstan stared up again at the tympanum, 'they wished to seize me.' He grinned. 'It would have taken more than three to hold you.'

'And?'

'I suggest they wanted this.' Athelstan held up his chancery satchel. 'I have no real proof for what I say, yet I am sure of it. Why else should they attack and then, as soon as you became Sir Galahad, flee like the wind?'

'And what *does* that chancery satchel hold? Of course,' Cranston answered his own question, 'the scraps of parchment

Thibault gave us at the Golden Oliphant. But why not wait until you are in your lonely priest's house at the dead of night?'

'I am protected there,' Athelstan grinned, 'and that's the paradox. The very people who keep an eye on me at St Erconwald's want this.'

'The Upright Men?' Cranston rehitched his warbelt. 'I would agree. They wanted those pieces of parchment before you had time to copy and memorize them.'

'Precisely, Sir John, which is what I suggest we do now.' Athelstan poked the coroner's generous stomach. 'My stalwart knight, you have done well. It's time to feed the inner man.'

Cranston needed no extra urging and led Athelstan at what the friar considered to be a charge through a maze of alleyways and into Sir John's favourite retreat, the Lamb of God in Cheapside. Mine Hostess, as always, came bustling across holding napkins and a jug of the finest Bordeaux with two deep-bowled goblets. Pleasantries were exchanged, kisses bestowed and compliments passed, before Cranston decided on chicken in white wine, a meat porridge, roast pork slices in caraway sauce and fresh white bread softened with herbal butter. Athelstan murmured he would eat what Sir John left.

No sooner had Mine Hostess hastened back to the kitchen, the odours of which were making the coroner's mouth water like a fountain, than Leif the one-eyed beggar and Rawbum, his constant companion, made their way into the tavern having 'espied', as both screeched like choirboys, the King's Lord High Coroner. Cranston groaned but patiently sat as he always did to listen to their half-mad gossip. Leif rested on a stool but Rawbum, ever since he'd sat on a pot of bubbling oil, stood nodding wisely as Leif ranted about various different signs and portents. How red rain as bitter as vinegar had fallen over Cripplegate, a sign, Leif assured Cranston, that the sun was about to turn black, the moon disappear and the stars fall from heaven, a sure prophecy that they were now living in the End of Times. Cranston politely thanked them. The coroner parted with two coins and both self-proclaimed prophets of doom merrily jigged out of the taproom.

Mine Hostess returned with the food and Cranston, cloak unhitched and warbelt looped over a wall hook, ate and drank as if there was no tomorrow. Athelstan put a little of the food on his platter and ate carefully and slowly, sipping occasionally from his goblet of wine. Once he'd finished he moved to a nearby table and took out the documents collected from the Golden Oliphant: Whitfield's despairing letter, the strange document depicting two triangles, their apexes meeting, and beside these, that puzzling litany of saints. The third document rendered in cipher remained unintelligible. Athelstan hid that deep in his chancery satchel and, whilst Cranston cleared the platters, carefully made copies of the other two and handed them to the now sated coroner for safekeeping.

'I agree with you, Friar.' Cranston deftly used his toothpick and sat back on the settle. 'Those attackers did not intend to hurt, maim or kill but to seize something, and logically the only item I – we – can think of is what we received at the Golden Oliphant. Now that cipher was originally taken from Reynard, the Upright Men's courier, so the Upright Men want it back. But what does it mean? Why is it so important?'

'Sir John, Brother Athelstan?' Mine Hostess came out of the kitchen with a scroll, a dark purple ribbon tied around it. Athelstan wiped his fingers and took it, then opened and read it.

'Brother Philippe,' he declared. 'He scrutinized Whitfield's corpse. He cannot account for some slightly reddish marks on the dead man's waist, though he said that this had nothing to do with Whitfield's death.'

'So what does?'

'Nothing, Sir John.'

Athelstan handed him the letter. 'According to Philippe, Whitfield hanged himself. He can find no other trace of violence on the corpse or any symptom of poison or any baleful potion.' Athelstan sat back in his seat. 'Nevertheless, Sir John, I suggest that Whitfield no more hanged himself than I did.'

'So, let's begin from the beginning – perhaps we will stumble on the truth.'

'In which case, shouldn't we leave immediately for St Erconwald's?' Athelstan asked. 'Lebarge must have the truth of it.'

'You can deal with him later,' Cranston replied brusquely. 'Let us concentrate on what we know, or think we know, little friar.'

Athelstan intoned his conclusions. 'Item: Amaury Whitfield,

Lebarge, Odo Gray, sea captain, Adam Stretton, Arundel's mailed clerk and Matthias Camoys gathered four days ago at the Golden Oliphant to celebrate the Festival of Cokayne, which salutes a world turned upside down, where male becomes female and so on . . . Really,' Athelstan shrugged, 'an excuse for licentiousness and bawdy humour. Item:' he continued, 'this revelry is held at the Golden Oliphant, a high-class, fairly sophisticated brothel owned by Mistress Elizabeth Cheyne, ably assisted by her troupe of moppets and maids, all available to anyone who pays for their services. She is also supported by leading members of her household: Joycelina, chief of the strumpets; Foxley, Master of Horse; and Griffin, Master of the Hall – in this case, the Golden Hall, the main taproom of that brothel-cum-tavern. Item: there is a history to this establishment. It was bought by Reginald Camoys for his doxy Elizabeth Cheyne. Reginald, a former knight and warrior, returned from the eastern marches. He and his brother Everard brought back the embalmed corpse of Reginald's bosom comrade, Simon Penchen. Reginald also secretly brought back a great treasure of the Teutonic Knights, his former patrons, the Cross of Lothar, an exquisitely beautiful and precious object. Reginald settled down into city life, thoroughly enjoying the charms of Mistress Cheyne, and he developed an undoubted skill as a sign writer, winning the favour of leading guilds in the city.' Athelstan paused as Cranston nodded in agreement, then raised a hand, beckoning a slattern to refill the jug of Bordeaux.

'Everard Camoys,' Athelstan continued, 'also settled down to emerge as a leading city mercer and goldsmith. Item: Reginald, lost in his own world, used his wealth to found that chantry chapel at St Mary Le Bow, to house his bosom friend's corpse as well as to prepare for his own mortal remains when God called him to judgement, which he eventually did.'

Athelstan paused. A tinker with a tray hung around his neck slipped through the door and went to sit on a corner stool at the far side of the taproom. The tinker's tray was crammed with geegaws and other petty items. The man's face was hidden deep in a dirty cowl, but the friar was sure he was looking in their direction. Athelstan breathed in slowly. Surely no tinker would have a tray so full at this late hour, and why hide his face and head? Was he a spy sent in by the Upright Men to keep himself and Cranston under close scrutiny?

'Item, dear friar?'

'Yes, yes, Sir John,' Athelstan whispered, 'but just keep an eye on our tinker friend over there. Anyway, item: Reginald, before he died, left mysterious and enigmatic messages which might reveal the whereabouts of the Cross of Lothar. No one is really concerned about this except Matthias Camoys, who haunts both the Golden Oliphant and St Mary Le Bow, the two places where the insignia are shown. Now, whether these ciphers do contain the truth about the whereabouts of the Cross of Lothar is just an educated guess. Matthias certainly believes they do. He joined the Cokayne Festival to sample the delights of the sisterhood and to drink deeply, but also to seek the help of a skilled cipher clerk, Whitfield, to resolve the riddles of his uncle's carvings. Whitfield may have offered his assistance, telling young Camoys to meet him at the Tavern of Lost Souls, a place he had already visited.' Athelstan scratched his head. 'But why there, why not the Golden Oliphant? And what was Whitfield's real business with Mephistopheles? Item: we know very little about what truly happened during those evenings of festivity at the Golden Oliphant. Whitfield was often deep in his cups. Was this because of the threats from the Herald of Hell? According to reports, both he and Lebarge were frightened and anxious. What else, dear coroner?'

'Reginald Camoys certainly loved to carve those symbols, wherever he could. What do the letters IHSV mean? And that salutation to "The Unconquerable Sun"? Why carve both on the tombs as well as at the Golden Oliphant?'

'For the moment, Sir John, let's leave the inscriptions. I have seen, or heard about them before, but I cannot place where or when. Anyway, item: Whitfield's mysterious death. Last night he left the revelry and went up to his chamber. Sometime in the following hours, or so it would seem, he locked and bolted his chamber door, closed the eyelet, turned the key and apparently sat down to write that final letter. Once finished, dressed to leave, he took the fire rope, fastened the noose to a rafter, moved that stool and,' Athelstan blew his cheeks out, 'the rest, God bless him, we know. Except,' he lifted a finger, 'Master Whitfield

intended to go to the Tavern of Lost Souls. He invited young
Matthias to join him there. So, why Whitfield's interest in meeting
Mephistopheles and his minions? Was it just the sale of objects
from his dwelling place? In which case, why have Matthias there
with him, eh?'

Cranston just shook his head.

'Item: that bundle of clothes lying on the floor of Whitfield's
chamber. Is that significant? And why did Whitfield, a fairly
prosperous man, hire a room on the top gallery? To protect
himself, to keep something safe and the curious at bay? Then
there's Foxley's offhand remark that Whitfield seemed slimmer
in death than he did in life: what did he mean by it? Why were
Whitfield's chambers in Fairlop Lane cleared of possessions? I
noticed something amiss there but I cannot recall it for the
moment. To continue. Item: where are Whitfield's chamber
possessions and Lebarge's baggage? The scrivener arrived in St
Erconwald's with little to show. Item: why is Lebarge sheltering
in sanctuary? What crime has he committed? If he is not careful
he could fall under suspicion, but, to return to my question, where
is the property of both Whitfield and Lebarge? The curtains, the
strongbox, the covers of damask, the candlesticks, the books –
the usual items owned by a prosperous clerk? Have they been
sold to Mephistopheles? Yet the Master of the Minions claims
that Whitfield only approached him about a possible sale.'

'What are you saying, little friar?'

'Amaury Whitfield did not kill himself; he was murdered before
he could leave, which explains why he was dressed. He was
going down to the Tavern of Lost Souls; he was definitely meeting
Matthias there. Nor must we forget Master Gray's ship, the *Leaping
Horse*, all ready for sea . . .'

'In other words, Brother, Whitfield was preparing to flee?'

'Patience, Sir John. Let us go back to the beginning and the
root cause of all that has happened.' Athelstan felt a glow inside
him, a sense of serenity as he moved towards a logical conclusion to a most vexatious problem. 'Whitfield and Lebarge worked
for Thibault, therefore both men would be marked down for
destruction when the Great Uprising occurs. Whitfield was
worried by the warning from the Herald of Hell and became
deeply anxious. He confided in his friend and scrivener Lebarge;

both decided to flee across the Narrow Seas and seek sanctuary elsewhere. They stripped their personal chambers in Fairlop Lane of valuable possessions and sold them to Mephistopheles at the Tavern of Lost Souls. I suspect they had other minor items which they would also wish to pawn or sell to that cunning miscreant. Whitfield was continuing these negotiations when he moved to the Golden Oliphant for the Cokayne Festival. He and Lebarge would use that as a pretext to cover their escapes. Both planned to sail from London on Odo Gray's ship, the *Leaping Horse*, and our sea captain attended as their guest, probably part of the bribe to take them across the seas.'

'And Thibault?'

'He will be furious that his chief chancery clerk was about to desert him.'

'And the cipher Whitfield was working on?'

'Oh, Whitfield wouldn't really care for that except,' Athelstan tapped the table, 'we know that the Golden Oliphant houses at least one member of the Upright Men. If so, they would have approached Whitfield to retrieve that cipher.' He pointed at Cranston. 'Apparently Reynard was murdered in Newgate, yes?'

'Yes.'

'I suspect that somewhere on his person Reynard still had the key to that cipher. He may have been mulling over the possibility of surrendering it to Thibault in return for a pardon. Instead, those two felons murdered him, they took it and gave it back to the Upright Men during that fatal affray around Tyburn scaffold.'

'If Whitfield was so engrossed in fleeing, why did he offer to help Matthias Camoys with his late uncle's cipher?'

'I can't say, Sir John, although I will reflect on that. Suffice to suggest that Whitfield and his scrivener plotted to cover their flight on the *Leaping Horse* with some accident or pretended suicide, hence that letter and the bundle of clothes separate from the rest which, I think, would have been found floating on the Thames.'

'And the Tavern of Lost Souls?'

'Mephistopheles – correct me if I am wrong – pawns goods. Whitfield went down to see to the last of his property, sell all those little objects he could not take with him, be it a candlestick, statue, book or painting, which explains why both Whitfield and Lebarge's chambers were empty. Mephistopheles would be a natural choice. Any other merchant might report Whitfield's trading back to Thibault; Mephistopheles certainly wouldn't. I would hazard a guess that for a few days before he moved to the Golden Oliphant, Whitfield was a fairly regular visitor to the Tavern of Lost Souls.'

'And so all his possessions are in Mephistopheles' safekeeping?'

'I suggest so, and the Master of the Minions will not be forth-coming, which is why the likes of Whitfield go to him in the first place.'

'Very well.' Cranston moved the goblet and platter aside and leaned across the table. 'Whitfield, witless with fear,' the coroner smiled at the play on words, 'plotted to finish the pawning of all his moveables and to arrange his own death by leaving a bundle of clothes floating on the river as if he had slipped, been pushed or took his own life. In truth, Whitfield was planning to disap-pear, and Lebarge with him. They were terrified at what is about to engulf this city.'

'In a word, yes, Sir John, but someone intervened – who, how and why I do not know. Whitfield was killed, Lebarge panics, hides whatever baggage he has and flees for sanctuary.' Athelstan laughed drily. 'Lebarge realizes that Whitfield's plan has been foiled. He thinks he is now in the safest place. Once forty days have passed, our scrivener will be compelled to leave sanctuary and seek shelter in the nearest port, which is down by the Thames. Who knows, he may still board Odo Gray's *Leaping Horse*. True?' Athelstan picked up his goblet. 'Lebarge cannot be convicted of any crime, he cannot be accused of involvement in Whitfield's death . . .'

'But he can declare that he is living in mortal fear for his own life,' Cranston added. 'And that he fled to protect himself. The sheriff's men would accept that, they have to. They would also arrange safe escort to the nearest port, which is what our scrivener wanted in the first place.' The coroner paused. 'Do you think Lebarge could have been involved in Whitfield's death?'

'I don't think so. True, he and Whitfield were master and servant, but they also seemed to be close friends. Lebarge fled because he thought he might be the next victim. He is, as you say, in mortal fear for his life.'

'Could Thibault have a hand in this?'

'For what reason, Sir John?' Athelstan pulled a face. 'If Thibault had suspected his trusted henchman was about to flee, he would simply have detained him. Thibault was beside himself with fury because Whitfield died without breaking that cipher.' Athelstan paused to collect his thoughts. 'We have three pieces of manuscript. The first is Whitfield's letter of desperation, hinting at suicide, an accident or whatever. What he was actually going to do, I don't know, and I don't think we ever will. Remember, what we see now are shadows, the way things might have been. Secondly, there is the cipher; close, cramped and secret with all sorts of symbols and signs. I have only given it a cursory glance, but it was enough to see that it is intricately locked. I doubt if I could break it. Thirdly, there is that drawing of the two triangles and the list of saints, which is probably Whitfield's work. He had begun to unravel the mystery; perhaps I might make sense of that. So, Sir John, there you have it. We see the truth but dimly as if in a mirror. We will have to work a little harder to make matters clearer.'

'Could Stretton, Arundel's man, be caught up in this murder?'

'Possibly. He may have learnt something and hoped to bribe, coax or threaten Whitfield into betraying Master Thibault's secrets. I truly don't know, Sir John, except a great deal of mischief occurred in that brothel before Whitfield's mysterious death.'

'And the Herald of Hell, Brother? This invisible creature who crawls out of the darkness to challenge and threaten – he too may be involved?'

'Your friend Everard Camoys believed he recognized the voice, yet this herald moves across the city like a will-o-the-wisp.' Athelstan shook his head. 'I do wonder if this so-called herald is no more than a figment of people's fevered imagination.'

'Brother, he exists! Sir Everard is a trusted friend and veteran soldier, he does not suffer from such imaginings.'

Athelstan sighed. 'I agree, but this herald appears here and there, never glimpsed, never caught. The Herald of Hell plays a game of mystery, just as mysterious as the Cross of Lothar.

Indeed, Sir John, I am truly intrigued why Mistress Cheyne is not interested in its whereabouts. Or perhaps she is, yet she seems almost to dismiss the relic as some cheap trinket, not worth bothering about. Matthias Camoys searches for it, she doesn't, and, despite her late paramour leaving enigmatic devices and signs for others to follow, she shows no interest whatsoever. I do wonder about that as I do about a terrified clerk like Whitfield offering to help Matthias Camoys discover the whereabouts of this precious treasure. I mean, at a time when Whitfield was fleeing for his life and couldn't give a fig about anything.' Athelstan paused as Mine Hostess, like a war cog in full sail, came charging out of the buttery. She came across and filled Sir John's goblet, but Athelstan put a hand over his as she offered a cup against what she called, 'the weariness of the day'. Cranston thanked her and toasted Athelstan with his brimming goblet.

'And all this,' the coroner murmured, 'shrouds what you truly suspect: that Whitfield did not commit suicide but was murdered. True,' he nodded, 'I can see the logic of your argument. Whitfield was dressed, ready to go, he had promised to meet young Matthias, and that's another mystery: Whitfield was to meet Camoys in the early evening, so why was he already dressed to go out before dawn even broke?' Cranston cradled his goblet. 'Satan's tits, Athelstan! We have overlooked something very important.'

'Which is?'

'If Whitfield and Lebarge cleared their chambers and later disappeared, leaving the possibility that Whitfield was dead due to an accident or possible suicide, Thibault would eventually discover the truth. He'd realize that Whitfield had fled or died trying to. Indeed he probably has. Albinus visited those chambers in Fairlop Lane; it would be obvious that those who'd lived there had left for good.'

'Sir John, Sir John,' Athelstan smiled bleakly, 'Whitfield didn't care about what might happen later: all he needed was a little time to throw Thibault off the pursuit, to block his master for a while.'

'Of course,' Cranston whispered. 'Whitfield knew a storm was imminent which would engulf Thibault, who would have other, more pressing matters to worry about. Whitfield expected that

Thibault would not survive. By then he would be long gone into hiding where he could lie quiet for many a day, begin a new life and even return to a London greatly changed from the city of today.'

'Exactly, Sir John, a London possibly with no Thibault, no secret chancery, no threat. Whitfield was gambling on that. All Whitfield wanted was to put as much distance between himself and London as possible until the season of slaughter came and went.'

'And yet, Brother, we need more evidence to justify our suspicions.'

'Sir John, I concede: all I nourish is a deep and jabbing suspicion. I also admit that the obstacles to a logical conclusion about Whitfield's death appear unsurmountable.' Athelstan spread his fingers to emphasize his points. '*Primo*: Joycelina reported the door was locked and bolted. We know from the testimony of others and the scrutiny I made of the door, that this is correct. *Secundo*: entry to and from that chamber was nigh impossible. *Tertio*: every scrap of evidence collected demonstrates that entry from the garden through the window must be ruled out for many sound reasons which I accept. *Quarto*: there are no other secret entrances. *Quinto*: we can account for the movements of all the possible suspects being outside that chamber when its door was broken down. *Sexto*: we have a man hanging by his neck. I suspect he was murdered, but how did he get himself placed on that stool with a noose around his throat? How did the assassin gain entry and, more importantly, leave as both door and window were clearly sealed, locked and barred? Oh, very, very clever,' Athelstan whispered. 'Sir John, we are confronting a most subtle assassin but . . .' He gathered up his chancery satchel. 'The day is drawing on, the hour passes. Soon, my large friend, we shall be for the dark.'

PART THREE

'Murdrum – *Murder.*'

Cranston and Athelstan exchanged the kiss of peace and the friar left Sir John to his reflections and his wine and made his way out into Cheapside. The crowds had now broken up as the sun began to set. The market horns were blowing and the stall-beadles insisting that the day's trading be completed. The denizens of the night were also slinking out: nightwalkers and shapeshifters in tattered clothes and cheap hoods with their harsh, pocked faces, glittering eyes and fingers which constantly hovered over the wooden hilts of stabbing daggers and dirks. Beggars whined for alms. Children, enjoying the last hours of daylight, screamed and chased each other, causing the skinny street dogs to yip and bark. Athelstan, his cowl covering both head and face, turned down an alleyway. He had to stand aside for a funeral party making its way down to one of the churches to conduct the death watch, the vigil of prayer before the requiem Mass was sung the following morning.

He retreated into a shabby tavern and was immediately accosted by the ale wife, an ugly-looking harridan with a hooked, dripping nose and skin rough as a sack. Bleary-eyed, she munched on her gums as she glared at Athelstan, one hand on her waist, the knuckles of her fingers glistening with grease. Beside her another woman, face wrinkled as a pig's ear, blowsy and hot-eyed: Athelstan pulled back his cowl, smiled and sketched a blessing in their direction. The ale wife nodded and pointed to a greasy stool where the friar could sit while the noisy funeral party, which had stopped to drink, and already had done so deeply, organized itself to continue. Athelstan took his seat and stared round the dingy taproom. Hens roosted on the open ale-tubs; his stomach pitched as he saw droppings from the birds fall into the drink, but this did not concern the ale wife, who began to strain the dung through a hair net.

Customers came and went. Many had no money but brought a rabbit, a pot of honey, a spoon or a skillet in lieu of payment. One woman carried a jug but she first sat down to cut a piece of leather off the sole of her tallow-smeared shoe to stop a hole in the jug. Athelstan watched all this with deepening unease. Just a walk away rose the stately mansions of Cheapside hung with silks and brightly coloured cloths, chambers crammed with precious objects. Outside of these stood stalls heaped with goods imported from abroad: oranges, barrels of fruit, glass goblets, rolls of damask and satin, pipes of wine, ornamental needles, mantles of leopard skin. Yet here thrived a different world, one which plotted the bloody destruction of everything Cheapside represented. Athelstan pulled his cowl back over his head as he swiftly scrutinized the other customers grouped around the overturned ale casks and wine tuns, shadowy figures in the poor light from the smelly tallow candles. Here undoubtedly thronged the Upright Men of the ward with their foot soldiers the Earthworms. Here, once the hush of evening descended and the dark gathered, so would the plotters. When the day of the Great Slaughter dawned and the strongholds began to fall, the flame of rebellion would burst out in places such as this. Hidden caches of bows, arrows, spears, clubs and swords would be opened and the inhabitants of this narrow lane would burst out to plunder the wealth of Cheapside.

'In the name of the King and the esteemed council of this city,' a voice roared from outside, 'move on and move away.'

'Meryen the bailiff!' one of the customers cried. 'He's warning that drunken funeral cortege. I'd recognize his trumpet voice across the city.'

Athelstan glanced sharply at the door as Meryen the bailiff swaggered into the alehouse. 'All clear now,' he roared.

Athelstan grabbed his chancery satchel and made his way out. He hurried along the streets, past the stocks crammed with miscreants fastened by the neck, wrist and ankle, and the moveable gibbets with their grisly burden of tarred corpses. He reached London Bridge and whispered a prayer as he made his way along the thoroughfare which cut between the lines of houses on each side. He always found the giddying height disconcerting, the rattle of nearby watermills, the roar of the water through the starlings, but he was determined to conquer such fears as he did when he climbed to the top of St Erconwald's tower to view the stars at night. He thought of the mummer's play his parish council was rehearsing and their use of the tower as well as Crispin the Carpenter's repairs. He paused, fingers to his lips; he also recalled the bell clerk of St Mary Le Bow. Athelstan blinked furiously. Wasn't St Mary one of the saints in that strange litany written out by Whitfield? What was that a reference to?

'Saints and bell towers,' he murmured, 'I must remember that.'

'Brother, are you moonstruck?'

Athelstan turned and smiled at the young courtesan whom he'd glimpsed earlier sidling along beside him.

'No,' he grinned, 'just struck by your beauty.' The young woman simpered. Athelstan blessed her and hurried on. He had almost reached the end of the bridge when he heard his name called. He recognized the voice and quietly groaned but turned to stare up at Master Robert Burdon, Custos of the Bridge and Keeper of the Heads. A true mannikin scarcely five feet tall, Burdon was a diminutive, barrel-bellied man who gloried in always being garbed in blood-red taffeta, the colour of the Fraternity of the Shearing Knife, the Worshipful Guild of Executioners and Hangmen. Burdon was standing on the top step of the side gatehouse, the iron-studded door behind him half open. He gestured at Athelstan to join him.

The friar forced a smile and, hiding his weariness, climbed the steep steps into a gloomy, narrow chamber lit only by a few candles. The floor was scrubbed clean, as was the long table running down the centre of the room. On shelves against the wall were ranged rows of recently severed heads, each washed in brine and tarred at the neck. A truly macabre scene, their glassy eyes staring blindly from beneath half-closed lids; blood-crusted mouths gaping as if about to speak. Athelstan tried to ignore the gruesome sight as he was ushered to a stool. From the chamber above he could hear Burdon's brood of children readying themselves for bed.

'What is it, Robert?'

'Brother, I am terrified.' Burdon gave vent to his fear in a rush of words. 'Rebels from the southern shires will seize the approaches to the bridge. They will storm this gatehouse, they will put me and mine to the sword, they will . . .'

'Hush now.' Athelstan seized the mannikin's small, gloved hand. 'Robert, you are the King's officer, you must do your duty, but the rebels mean you no harm.' He fought to keep the doubt from his voice.

'Yes, they do,' Burdon replied mournfully. He rose, crossed to a shelf and brought back a cracked beaker brimming with blood; it also contained a number of sharpened sticks, each with an onion on the end, two large, the rest small. The message was blunt and stark.

'The Herald of Hell?' Athelstan asked.

Burdon closed his eyes. 'He left a warning.' The mannikin lisped:

> *'Brother Burdon be not so bold,*
> *For Gaunt your master has been both bought and sold.*
> *Listen now and listen well*
> *To this final warning from the Herald of Hell.'*

'Quite the poet,' Athelstan retorted but softened as the panic flared in Burdon's eyes. 'Now, Robert, peace, when did this happen?'

'A few nights ago, in the early hours, before the bell for matins tolled.'

'The Herald talked of a final warning?'

'Oh, yes. The Upright Men have asked me before where my allegiances lie, but nothing so threatening as this.'

'In the early hours, you said?'

'Yes, Brother, and I know what you are going to say! The bridge is sealed after the curfew bell so, whoever the Herald was, he must have swum the river, climbed the starlings and left the same way.'

'Or he lives on the bridge,' Athelstan made a face, 'but, there again, that would create other problems. How does he get off the bridge at night to appear elsewhere in the city?'

Athelstan recalled Meryen the bailiff roaring outside that alehouse near Cheapside. He lifted his head and his gaze caught the sightless glare of one of the severed heads. The friar swiftly glanced away. He fully understood Burdon's panic and fear and how this was being exploited by the likes of the Herald of Hell.

The dark was truly rising. Time was flittering on. The harrowing of Hell was fast approaching. The chalice was cracked, the wine of life draining into the soil. Athelstan grew even more aware of impending disaster, conscious of a creeping, crawling malevolence seeping out to envelop the city. He had recently visited his mother house at Blackfriars and listened to the brothers who had been out amongst the villages in the surrounding shires. According to them, an eerie restlessness could be felt. 'Nature's struck and Earth is quaking,' was how Brother Cedric described it, quoting a line from the 'Dies Irae'. Owl hoots, prophecies of imminent disaster, haunted the night whilst during the day, birds of such ill-omen clattered around the high-branched trees before swirling darkly over sun-washed fields. The rebels were massing, gathering like some malevolent fruit coming to fullness. They kept well away from the main highways but slipped like ghosts along the coffin lanes, pilgrim paths and other ancient byways. Burdon was right to be fearful, Athelstan conceded to himself. When the rebels reached London their very first task would be to seize the bridge.

'Brother?'

Athelstan smiled even as his heart sank at the sheer fear in Burdon's face.

'Robert, as I said, you are the King's officer.'

'My wife isn't, or the beloveds. They are not the King's officers.'

Athelstan sighed and opened his chancery satchel. Taking out a piece of parchment, he set up his writing tray and carefully wrote his message to Prior Anselm of Blackfriars. He then signed and sealed the piece of vellum and handed it to Burdon, who read it slowly, lips mouthing the words. The mannikin's face became transformed, all anxiety draining from it.

'*Pax et bonum*,' Athelstan whispered. 'Be at peace, my friend. If the terrors . . .' He shrugged. '*When* they come, do your duty, Robert. However, at the first sign of real trouble, send your family to Blackfriars. Prior Anselm will provide them and you, once you have done what your conscience dictates, with safe and holy sanctuary. No one will dare touch you there.'

Athelstan gathered his writing material back into his chancery satchel. 'Now I must go . . .'

He made his way down the alleyway leading to the concourse which fronted St Erconwald's. He passed Merrylegs' cook shop but the pastry maker and his many sons had apparently locked up for the day and adjourned to the Piebald Tavern, to sample the ale of its one-armed owner Joscelyn. The tavern door hung open, its shutters flung back. As he hastily walked by, sniffing the ale-fumed air, Athelstan heard the laughter and the doggerel chants of the Upright Men. Something had happened but he did not stay to find out what. He reached the precincts of his parish church, skirting the cemetery wall, then stopped and groaned. Godbless the beggar, together with his omnivorous goat Thaddeus, stood lurking in the shade of the lychgate. The only consolation Athelstan could thank heaven for was that neither Godbless nor Thaddeus appeared drunk; moreover, the goat was still firmly tethered, even though it still managed to lunge at Athelstan's chancery bag.

'*Pax tecum*,' Athelstan murmured. 'Peace be with you.'

'God bless you too, Father,' the beggar man replied, pulling on the goat's rope. 'Rest assured, Father: Philomel your horse sleeps safely in the stable and Hubert the Hedgehog rests in the hermitage.'

'And all is well here?' Athelstan pointed across the cemetery at the old death house converted to a comfortable cottage for Godbless and his equally smelly companion.

'Invaded, Brother! Invaded by nuns and felons, all followed by dark shapes from Hell.'

'Godbless,' Athelstan soothed, 'now is not the time.' He stared beseechingly at the beggar man, who the friar secretly considered to be as mad as a box of drunken frogs.

'Brother Athelstan, Brother Athelstan!'

The friar turned away in relief. Benedicta stood on the top of the church steps beckoning furiously at him. He hurried across and she led him into the shadowy porch.

'Brother, there has been great excitement whilst you have been gone.'

'There usually is.' Athelstan smiled at the widow woman's pretty face framed by a white, starched, nun-like wimple. He was glad that it didn't hide all her lustrous night-black hair. He gently tugged a loose lock lying against her sweaty brow. 'What is it, Benedicta?'

'Rather what *was* it, Brother. You informed me that Pike the Ditcher was going to meet his cousin, Sister Matilda, a Poor Clare nun, here in our sacristy?'

'Yes, I gave him permission to do so. He claimed he wanted to meet her in some private place, well away from the usual parish gossips. Apart from quietly thanking heaven that Pike's family has some semblance of religion, I did wonder at the truth of it. She was to meet him about mid-afternoon. So, what happened?'

'Sister Matilda,' Benedicta grinned, 'was portly, red-faced and rather stout. I glimpsed her going up the sanctuary steps. Anyway, she and Pike apparently met, then Thibault's men turned up.'

'What?'

'Led by Albinus. They entered the concourse outside. Watkin and Ranulf, along with Moleskin and others from the parish council, thought they had come to seize Lebarge and refused them entry.'

'As they should have.'

'But it wasn't Lebarge they were after, Thibault would be too cunning for that.' Benedicta forced a smile. 'Brother, I know a little of him and what I've heard . . .'

Athelstan noticed her quick change of expression but was too intrigued by her message to reflect upon it.

'Apparently,' Benedicta continued, 'they intended to seize Pike and this nun. Albinus and his comitatus swept through God's Acre to the sacristy door. By then the whole parish was alerted and so was Pike. He used the ancient tunnel, the one beneath the parish chest. He and Sister Matilda escaped down that.' She smiled. 'The tunnel was narrow, the nun was plump enough, but they were safe. They reached Godbless' cottage. The Earthworms were lurking close by, and they hurried Pike and Sister Matilda across God's Acre, over the far wall and to safety.'

Athelstan shook his head in disbelief, staring at the fresh painting of St Christopher which the Hangman of Rochester had recently finished. He knew all about the trap door in the sacristy and the narrow passage beneath; the parish chest could be pulled away to reveal a shaft beyond it. He could picture Pike and the mysterious nun using it to escape. Sister Matilda, if that was who she really was, would have gone first, and Pike would have followed. Standing in the shaft, he would have pulled the chest back, then, on his hands and knees, followed the narrow tunnel to a trapdoor in the old death house. Once there, protected by the Earthworms, it would have been easy to use the broken ground, thick with sprouting gorse, not to mention the burial mounds, crosses and stones, to steal across the rest of God's Acre. The tunnel had been dug years ago, so Athelstan had learnt, in turbulent times when the priest of St Erconwald's had to hide and take with him all the precious and sacred objects. Now such turbulence was about to return.

'Brother?' Benedicta, hard-eyed, her pretty face all watchful, was staring quizzically at him.

'And where is Pike and his beloved cousin now?'

Benedicta just shrugged and raised her eyes heavenwards, a return to those pretty, feminine gestures which always intrigued Athelstan.

'I will deal with Pike later, but I wonder . . .' Athelstan murmured.

'What?'

'How on earth did Thibault know about Pike meeting his mysterious cousin in the sanctuary at that particular time?' He glanced at the widow woman. Benedicta lowered her head as if to hide her face. Athelstan felt a chill of fear as he recalled his meeting earlier that day with Thibault and his realization that Gaunt's Master of Secrets might have a spy deep in the parish of St Erconwald's.

'Benedicta?'

She lifted her head and he caught a wary look in those beautiful, dark eyes.

'Benedicta, what is happening?'

'Nothing, Brother.' She leaned forward to grasp his hands, but Athelstan turned and walked away to stare down the nave. The light coming through the roundel window above the sanctuary was fading to a dull grey.

'I wonder . . .' Athelstan murmured, distracted. 'It truly would be so beautiful if we had some painted glass here.' He knew his mind was wandering, eager to be diverted from his present troubles. The friar closed his eyes and murmured a prayer for help. Pike the Ditcher would have to wait. Lebarge was more important.

He opened his eyes, crossed himself and walked back to Benedicta, who stood in the shadows away from the light thrown by the candles before St Christopher's pillar.

'Our sanctuary man,' Athelstan indicated with his head, 'Oliver Lebarge?'

'Terrified, Brother, frightened out of his wits. He trusts you, me and Crim but no one else. Watkin tried to approach him and Lebarge protested loudly. He will only eat and drink what I bring him from your house. On the last occasion he asked me to taste both food and wine.'

'Has he said anything?'

'Nothing, Brother.'

'Very well.' Athelstan turned away and made his way up the dappled, dark nave through the heavy rood screen and into the sanctuary. He first visited the sacristy and, using all his strength, pulled away the parish chest, which revealed the shaft dropping into the tunnel beneath. He could see the shards of plaster knocked off when Pike and his so-called cousin had entered. Athelstan now entertained the greatest suspicions about that so-called worthy nun. He pushed the chest back and examined the outside of the sacristy door, battered and broken by the weapons of Thibault's men.

'Master of Secrets or not,' he whispered, 'Great Revolt or not, Master Thibault can pay for these repairs.' He strode back into the sanctuary and across the enclave where Lebarge sat huddled on the mercy stool, lost in his own thoughts. Athelstan fetched the footrest from the celebrant's chair and sat down opposite him.

'Oliver?'

Lebarge looked up.

'I've recently come from the Golden Oliphant. Whitfield is truly dead; his corpse now lies at St Bartholomew's . . .'

The scrivener put his face in his hands and glanced up. 'I will not say anything,' he hissed. 'I will say nothing unless I receive a royal pardon for all offences I may have committed or be accused of. If not, I demand that the law of sanctuary be enacted, and that after forty days I be escorted to the nearest port.'

'In other words, Queenshithe and Odo Gray's *Leaping Horse*, as you and Whitfield were plotting to do, yes? I have been to your chambers in Fairlop Lane,' Athelstan continued. 'You stripped them of all valuables and moveables. You arranged to pawn or sell these to Mephistopheles at the Tavern of Lost Souls. You were both preparing to flee. You wanted to be out of England for a while to escape the coming fury. You aimed to confuse Thibault. Whitfield even separated articles of clothing which would be found along the Thames with some other items, all pointers to an accident or possible suicide. I have also read Whitfield's death note and discovered that he was to meet young Camoys and help him with those enigmatic carvings left by his late uncle Reginald, which may or may not indicate the true whereabouts of the Cross of Lothar. And finally,' Athelstan edged closer on the footrest, 'I truly believe Whitfield did not commit suicide. He was murdered, wasn't he?' Lebarge, now all narrow-eyed with shock, stared in surprise.

'Well?' Athelstan insisted. 'I am correct? You do not contradict me . . .'

'I will not speak, Brother, until I receive a full pardon.'

'For what?'

'Then I will tell you a secret, a great secret.'

Athelstan stared up at the window. Darkness was thickening; night would soon fall. He felt tired. It was time to sleep. But first he must have some answers to his questions.

'Then at least tell me,' he spread his hands, 'why you also – and I wager you do – believe Whitfield was murdered?' He paused. 'What happened yesterday evening?'

Lebarge pulled a face and stared across the sanctuary. 'Whitfield drank his wine and retired to bed.'

'Joycelina went with him?'

'Yes, but she came down shortly afterwards saying Whitfield had drunk enough. I finished mine and went upstairs. Amaury's door was locked and bolted. I called goodnight and he answered, said he was ready for bed. I was desperate for rest. I fell asleep. I heard or saw nothing untoward. I was roused just after dawn. I remembered that Mistress Cheyne was to prepare my favourite spicy simnel cakes, best served hot. I was very hungry. I heard Master Griffin trying to raise Whitfield but I thought nothing of it.' Lebarge was talking in a monotone as if he had carefully prepared what he was saying. 'I went down to the refectory, my simnel cakes were ready.' He paused at the squealing from the far side of the sanctuary and flinched as a dark shape shot past, claws scrabbling at the floor. 'Rats!' he exclaimed. 'I hate them.'

'As does Bonaventure,' Athelstan retorted. 'Now, this morning,' he insisted, 'what happened in the refectory?'

'Joycelina announced Whitfield could not be raised. I became alarmed but Mistress Elizabeth said she did not want people charging through her tavern. She despatched Foxley to fetch the labourers and the battering ram. She also sent Joycelina out to keep the maids quiet once the hammering began. I knew what was going to happen. I stayed for a while. I heard people clattering on the stairs but the tension proved too much. I ignored Master Griffin and stole up to the third storey, hiding in a recess near the steps leading to the top gallery.'

'Why did Whitfield rent a narrow chamber at the top of the house?'

'I don't know,' Lebarge mumbled.

'In other words, you do, but you won't tell me?'

'I stayed there,' Lebarge replied. 'I heard the battering against the chamber door. Foxley was directing them, Mistress Cheyne shouting for Joycelina. I was all a-tremble. I heard the door crash open and the exclamations. I went back downstairs to the refectory – by then everyone was alarmed. The labourers came down to announce what had happened. I stole back up to Whitfield's chamber. I could not believe what I saw – Whitfield just hanging there. I panicked. I hurried back to my room, collected certain items and fled.'

'But you came here with virtually nothing.'

'True, Brother. Empty-handed except for the clothes I stand in.'

'Did you hide the rest with Hawisa?'

'Oh, that little mouse,' Lebarge scoffed, 'good to romp with on a bed but nothing else. They're all whores; they'll sell you for a penny. I hid certain items – I don't trust anyone. I will say nothing more until I receive a full pardon.'

'For what offences?' Athelstan demanded. Lebarge just stared dully back.

'I am safe here.' He gestured airily. 'I'm glad Radegund the Relic Seller has left.'

'Why?'

'Full of questions, he was. Anyway,' Lebarge shrugged, 'I know about Thibault's men arriving. I thought they had come for me but it was one of your parishioners, Pike, and the nun he met over there in the sacristy.' He sniffed noisily. 'I am sorry, Brother, I will not say anything else. I am tired, I should sleep . . .'

Lebarge's voice trailed away. Athelstan realized he would learn nothing further from the scrivener, so he blessed him and left.

The friar walked down the nave, lost in thought. Lebarge was virtually conceding he had done something highly illegal as well as being the keeper of great secrets. Whitfield must have been in the same situation. Yet what did Lebarge mean? Athelstan stood still and stared around. People were still drifting in and out of the church, pausing to light candles before this statue or that, moving shadows in the poor light.

'Ah, well,' Athelstan murmured. 'Sufficient for the day is the evil thereof; time for bed and board. Tomorrow will come soon enough.'

He made himself comfortable in the priest's house. A small fire, banked with the coal still crackling red, heated the pottage in a fat-bellied cauldron hanging from its hook above the fire. Recently baked bread lay stacked in the small, iron-gated oven beside the hearth whilst fresh ale, butter and cheese had been left in the narrow buttery. The flagstone kitchen, which served as Athelstan's solar, hall, dining chamber and chancery office, had been scrubbed, the table too with its leather-backed chair and cushioned stools. Bonaventure came scratching at the door. Athelstan admitted him and served the tomcat some pottage then broke his own fast with a steaming bowl, all the time being scrutinized by the unblinking stare of his one-eyed, constant dining companion.

Once finished, Athelstan cleared the dining table. He took out his writing tray, a sheet of scrubbed vellum and began to form columns under different headings: the customers of the Golden Oliphant, Whitfield's plans, Lebarge's flight, the death scene. Under each heading Athelstan tried to list everything he and Cranston had learnt, all the scraps of information, although they could not be formed into any logical coherence. He also listed his suspicions, the words he had heard and the scenes he had glimpsed. He finished his ale and had just begun to nod off to sleep when a pounding on the door roused him.

'Who is it?' he called.

Mauger the bell clerk cried that it was he. He had gone to lock the church for the night and found the sanctuary man, Oliver Lebarge, dead on the floor, foully slain . . .

Cornelius the corpse collector tugged at Pegasus, his huge dray horse which pulled the high-sided death cart around the filth-strewn lanes of Southwark. The curfew bells had tolled and the beacons been lit in different steeples. Cornelius, eyes down, trudged on. Hood pulled over his face, he was a shambling figure, yet he was keen-eyed for any corpse pushed under a mound of refuse, a midden heap, some filthy laystall or even in the crevices hollowed out of the walls of the ancient, leaning houses which towered above the tangle of alleyways running through Southwark. Nobody bothered Cornelius, the black-garbed figure of death who trundled his cart searching for cadavers. He would collect the mortal remains of some hapless unfortunate and take them to the Keeper of the Dead who presided over Heaven's Gate, a makeshift mortuary kept on a lonely, moon-washed coffin path leading out of Southwark. If there was anything suspicious about the corpse, the keeper would expose the cadaver for public view on the steps of Heaven's Gate where, if it was recognized, the relatives of the dead could redeem their kin for proper burial. The others, who the keeper called the '*Perditi* – the lost', would be soaked in a bath of lavender and stitched into a linen shroud by the Harpies, the Keeper's nickname for the gaggle of old women he hired for that work. Once ready, the corpse would be given swift burial in the great pit, the common grave which stretched behind Heaven's Gate . . .

Cornelius turned a corner and paused, pulling at Pegasus' halter as he stared down the narrow lane. He was now close to St Erconwald's, which over the last few days had been a hubbub of excitement. Cornelius always stayed well away from that particular parish. Watkin the dung collector claimed St Erconwald's as his domain: he was the one who would collect refuse and anything else hidden beneath it. Cornelius was highly wary of

Watkin, an Upright Man, a captain of the dreaded Earthworms. The dung collector could, if he wished, whistle up his legions of the dark, and Cornelius wanted no trouble with him. Indeed, the Keeper of the Dead believed the Earthworms would soon rise and the likes of Cornelius would be busy enough harvesting the corpses, but until then . . . This, however, was different. Cornelius stared down the alleyway. He could make out a figure lying on the ground and another above it pounding the prostrate person with a club or some other weapon. Time and again the blows fell, a sickening thud which prickled Cornelius' sweaty body with shivers of cold. Pegasus, also alarmed, whinnied and blew noisily, head shaking as the great dray horse caught his master's fear. Cornelius calmed Pegasus and stared back down the alleyway. All he could see now was the dim outline of the prostrate body. The attacker had disappeared.

Cornelius stared around. This was a deserted area. Certainly no one else had witnessed the incident. Intrigued and smelling profit, Cornelius pulled on Pegasus' halter and, with wheels rumbling, the death cart and its custodian rattled along the alleyway. The corpse collector stopped just before the mouth of the alleyway. He pulled a spindle-like dagger from its ring on his leather belt and hurried forward to kneel by the young woman's corpse. He could tell she was young from the texture and colour of her hair, her rounded, silky soft arms and what was left of her face. She had been killed instantly with a dagger thrust to the heart, the bodice of her dress heavily soaked in bubbling blood. Afterwards, the young woman's assassin had pounded her face with a rock taken from a nearby crumbling wall. Cornelius' quick, darting gaze took in the bracelets and rings on the young woman's fingers and wrists; the gold chain around her swan-like neck, the brooch pinned to the neck of her gown; her clothes and leather boots looked costly enough, too.

'Some pretty little whore,' Cornelius murmured to himself. 'No need to display her.'

The corpse collector swiftly stripped the corpse of its gown, petticoat, linen underclothes and boots, the tawdry jewellery disappearing into his cavernous belt wallet. Cornelius then lifted the young woman's corpse, marvelling that her smooth, marble-like skin was still warm from life and, despite the ragged, bloody mess to her chest and face, exuded a faint perfumed fragrance. Standing on tiptoe, Cornelius tipped the cadaver, her long blonde hair now free of its clasp floating down her back, into the death cart to join the remains of a drunk found drowned in a horse trough and those of a beggar man, crushed by a fall of masonry whilst sheltering in a derelict, rotting tenement. Cornelius wiped his hands on his leather jerkin and froze. Whoever had killed that young woman could well be lurking nearby watching him. The corpse collector breathed out slowly.

'All in all,' he whispered reassuringly to himself, 'a good night's work.'

He tapped his now heavy wallet and wondered what he should do. If the assassin was still close by and watching, he would surely not object to what Cornelius had done. Nevertheless the corpse collector realized he was vulnerable. He could not run away, leave Pegasus, the cart and its grisly load. He licked dry, cracked lips and made his decision.

'To you who dwell cloaked in the darkness.' Cornelius paused; he liked that, recalling his early days as a stroller, a mummer who played his part in the miracle plays. 'What you have done,' Cornelius continued, 'is a matter between you and God. Your victim lies dead, her face unrecognisable, and now she lies stripped of all raiment.' He patted the sacks hanging from the slats along the side of the cart. 'Her corpse will be taken to the Gate of Heaven, soaked in lavender, sheathed in linen and buried in the common grave unclaimed and unnamed.' Cornelius paused, eyes and ears straining into the dark. Satisfied, he grasped Pegasus' halter and slowly moved on, shoulders hunched, belly pitching. Nothing occurred. Cornelius relaxed. He stopped and looked over his shoulder at the dark mass of St Erconwald's rising against the night sky. Did the killing he'd witnessed have anything to do with what was happening there? he wondered. Had not a royal scrivener called Lebarge taken sanctuary in St Erconwald's? Murder and mystery were certainly active in that parish. After all, why should someone kill a young woman, pound her face into an unrecognizable, blood-splattered mess, but not filch her trinkets? Cornelius pulled a face. In the end that was not his business, and the corpse cart, carrying the naked cadaver of the young whore Hawisa, trundled into the gathering night.

Sir John Cranston was thinking about Oliver Lebarge as he strode, and now again stumbled, down the street leading to his house. Cranston had stayed at the Lamb of God to be entertained by Mine Hostess with more wine and the most succulent strips of pheasant meat. Now he intended a good night's sleep, even though after the events of the day his mind continued to tumble like dice in a hazard cup. He reached the door of his house. He was fumbling for the key on his belt when he heard the hiss of steel and, quick as a twirling coin, he brought sword and dagger slithering from their sheaths to confront the mailed men who emerged out of the blackness. Two of them carried torches. Cranston glimpsed the White Hart, the King's personal emblem, the insignia of the Cheshire archers.

'Peace, Sir John.' A figure strode through the mailed men and took off his helmet, pushing back the mailed coif beneath to reveal the sallow, lined face of Sir Simon Burley, the King's personal tutor and close advisor. Others also stepped forward to be recognized, including Walworth, Mayor of London. Cranston resheathed his weapons.

'Simon, gentlemen, this is no way to call on a comrade in the dead of night.'

'Jack, my old friend,' Burley replied, 'this truly is the very dead of a night that stretches out before us all. Great danger lurks in the darkness! Treachery, betrayal, the breaking of oaths and the deadliest treason. You must come with us.'

'Must!' Cranston exclaimed. 'Must? I am the King's own officer. I have knelt, placed my hands between his and sworn a personal oath of fealty to King Richard.'

'Sir John, it is the King and his mother, the Princess Joan, who demand to see you . . .'

Within the hour, Cranston and the rest disembarked at King's Steps and made their way up the narrow lanes which brought them under the magnificent, soaring turrets and towers of Westminster Abbey. They entered by the south door close to the cavernous crypt. The abbey, despite the late hour, was lit with torches, creating a shimmer of light and dancing flame against the great drum-like pillars that guarded the resplendent sanctuary, which also served as the royal mausoleum, housing the tombs of the Plantagenet kings. At the centre of this mass of carved stone rose the gloriously decorated shrine of Edward the Confessor, erected above and around the magnificent marble sarcophagus of the saintly king whom the Plantagenets regarded as the ancestor and patron of their royal house. Nearby stood the Confessor's throne and beneath it the Stone of Scone, once used to hail the kings of Scotland, until it was seized by Edward I and hurried south to become part of the coronation regalia of the kings of England. In the fluttering candle-flame the great wooden throne with its elaborately carved jewelled back and armrests seemed to dwarf the young boy sitting on the purple-cushioned, gold tasselled seat.

Cranston and his party immediately went down on their knees, daggers drawn, points turned towards their hearts, in an act of complete obeisance. The young boy chuckled and in a ringing voice, light and carrying as any chorister, ordered them to resheath their daggers. He added that they were his loyal friends, accepted into the love and protection of Richard, King of England, France and Scotland, Lord of Ireland . . . The titles echoed through the shrine. Once finished, Richard leaned forward, bidding them to look upon his face. Cranston did and returned the boy-king's infectious smile even as he secretly wondered at this angel-faced lad with his golden hair, snow-white skin and the strangest light-blue eyes.

Delicately featured, exquisite in all his gestures, Richard of Bordeaux was almost a fairy-tale prince. Cranston found it difficult to believe that this highly intelligent, intense and sensitive young man was the son of the ruthless warrior, Edward the Black Prince, a chevalier so fierce and fiery, so determined in battle to kill everything and everyone who passed across the eye slits of his war helmet, he had even killed his own destrier when its nodding head caught his gaze in the red mist of battle. Cranston and the other knights of the body who had fought alongside the Black Prince soon learnt never to go before him. Now the Black Prince was dead of some loathsome, rotting disease contracted in Spain, leaving this young boy as England's future king. As he

knelt there listening to Burley's declaration of loyalty on behalf
of them all, Cranston speculated on what would become of this
boy-king, so poised in his golden gown with the Lions of England
emblazoned across his chest, fingers and wrists shimmering with
jewellery, a silver circlet around the gold-spun hair. Sometimes,
and Cranston had only confided this to Athelstan, he worried
about the stability of this young king's mind, so taken up with
the sacredness of his office and the rights due to him from all
his subjects. The coroner shifted his gaze to the woman clothed
in dark-blue damask fringed with ermine, sitting on the King's
immediate right. If anyone was responsible for Richard's sensi-
tivity about his royal office, she was. Joan of Kent, mother of
the King, once considered the greatest beauty in all of Europe.

Joan caught Cranston's gaze, winked and smiled, pulling back
her head to reveal her not so golden hair and a face dissipated
by wine, luxurious living and the cares of high office. The lioness
and her cub, Cranston thought. So what lay behind this extraordinary meeting at the dead of night, here, close to the Confessor's
tomb? He stared around. Like Cranston, these men were the
King's personal bodyguard who had sworn to be Richard's men,
body and soul, in peace and war. Once Burley's declaration was
finished, Richard delivered a pithy reply and bade them sit on
the stools his retainers hastily set out. Cranston looked over his
shoulder to see that the lights were being extinguished, candles
capped, sconce torches doused, leaving only a shimmering glow
around the ghostly tombs.

'Gentlemen,' the Queen Mother's voice rang out. 'You have
been brought here to renew your oaths of loyalty and be advised
of a most sinister conspiracy against your king.' She paused for
effect, before lifting a gloved hand to caress her son's arm, a
gesture which only emphasised his youth and vulnerability. Once
again Cranston recalled those sombre words: 'Woe to the kingdom
whose ruler is a child.'

'Listen now,' the Queen Mother continued, 'we all know unrest
seethes both here and in the surrounding shires, in particular
Kent and Essex. Oh, we know the storm will come and, to quote
the great Augustine, "We shall bend lest we break." Now, Sir
John, my old friend,' she smiled dazzlingly, 'confidant of my
late beloved husband, comrade in arms to many assembled here,

you are investigating the mysterious death of Amaury Whitfield, creature of Thibault, the so-called Master of Secrets, henchman of His Grace, the King's beloved uncle, John of Gaunt.' Despite the smile and the courtly titles, the Queen Mother could hardly conceal her well-known loathing for her brother-in-law. 'His Grace, the King's uncle,' Joan continued, her false smile now fading, 'has left this sea of troubles to defend our northern march against the Scots. Anyway,' she pointed at Cranston, 'have you discovered the truth about Whitfield's death or the secrets he may have carried?'

'Your Grace,' Cranston stood up, 'my secretarius, my friend Brother Athelstan, has not yet resolved it, though he believes Whitfield did not kill himself. As for any secrets he may have held, we have a cipher which at this moment we cannot break. Your Grace, why . . .?'

'You are here,' the Queen Mother declared, rising to her feet and pulling back the sleeves of her voluminous gown, 'because we have received dreadful news. You know the rebel leaders have always proclaimed, sworn and solemnly protested that they have no quarrel with their king, our beloved son, but only with those who try and control him.' She let her words hang in the air. Everyone knew she was referring to Gaunt and his henchmen, Sudbury of Canterbury, John Hales, Master Thibault and others of their ilk.

'Now, however,' the Queen Mother's voice shrilled, 'matters have changed. We have received information from the very heart of the Great Community of the Realm that some of the Upright Men plot the greatest blasphemy, regicide! The murder of your God-given king and our most beloved son!' Her words created uproar. Shouts and cries of protest filled the hallowed precincts. Swords were drawn and raised as individuals shouted their defiance against such an outrageous act, even though some like Cranston wondered how true the threat was. The clamour was silenced by the King rising to his feet. Immediately swords were sheathed and the assembled council retook their seats. Cranston remained standing.

'Sir John,' the Queen Mother declared, 'you have a question, though I can anticipate it. What source informed us of this? Suffice to say,' she continued with one hand on her son's shoulder, 'that we accept this information unreservedly, as well as the warning of how it will be done.'

Cranston sat down.

'On no account when the troubles come,' the Queen Mother continued, 'and they surely will, must our soveriegn lord agree in any form or guise to meet the rebel leaders. If he does, if he is forced to, if he has no choice, remember this. Your king's very survival, your survival, our survival, will depend on one thing and one thing only.' She paused for effect, lifting her right hand as if taking a great oath. 'You must go armed. You must kill every single rebel leader present at that meeting because if you do not, they will undoubtedly slay your king, God's Chosen, Christ's Anointed, as well as anyone else who accompanies him. So swear.' The Queen's voice echoed like a trumpet. 'Here in this hallowed place that what I said tonight will be obeyed. On your souls' eternal fate . . .'

'*Absolvo te a peccatis tuis* – I absolve you from your sins.' Athelstan crouched by the corpse of Oliver Lebarge sprawled on the sacristy floor. He tried to avoid looking at the dead man's liverish face all twisted in the agonized contortion of a painful death. Lebarge had been poisoned, Athelstan was certain of that. The dead man's face was more than proof, especially the dirty white foam drying on his mouth, the bulging eyes, his slightly swollen tongue thrust through half-open lips; his limbs were rigid, head thrust forward as the dying man had fought for his last breath. The friar finished the absolution and hastily anointed the hands, chest and feet of the corpse, aware of his parishioners thronging at the half-open door leading to God's Acre. Apparently Lebarge had taken the poison, God knows what, how or when, and, realising he was in mortal agony, staggered out of the sanctuary only to collapse here in the sacristy where Mauger had found him.

'How, Brother?' Benedicta came across and crouched beside him. He turned and stared at her smooth, olive-skinned face. 'How?' she repeated. 'Brother Athelstan, this was a man terrified out of his wits. The only food he would eat was what I brought from your house; nothing was added whilst I fetched him his supper some hours ago.' She gestured at the door. 'He distrusted the doxies at the Golden Oliphant, he confessed as much, none of them came here. Moreover, why should he take anything from those he fled from?'

Athelstan agreed. He clasped shut the phial of anointing oil and rose to his feet. He took a lighted candle and walked slowly back out into the sanctuary, across to the mercy enclave, studying the floor at every step. He could detect nothing except dried drops of thick saliva which must have come from Lebarge as he staggered across to die. Once in the sanctuary recess, Athelstan put the candle down. Crouching on all fours, he carefully scrutinized the floor but, apart from dried mud, candle grease and some rat droppings, he could discover nothing unusual. How then had Lebarge been poisoned: by food or by some cut or wound? Benedicta and Mauger, having ordered the others to stay back, came across to join him.

'Where's Pike, Watkin, Ranulf and the rest of their merry crew?' Athelstan demanded.

'Celebrating in the Piebald.' Bladdersmith the bailiff, reeking of ale and unsteady on his feet, entered the sanctuary. 'Now what do we have here, a corpse?'

'Most perceptive,' Athelstan murmured. 'Master Bladdersmith, have the body shrouded and carted. It is to be taken to Brother Philippe at St Bartholomew's hospital. Ask him, for my sake, to scrutinize the corpse most carefully. Go on, go on,' Athelstan urged, waving his hands. 'There are enough of the curious outside to assist you, but first . . .' He knelt and went through the dead man's pockets and belt wallet. He was surprised to find a small, dark green velvet purse fastened with twine containing a number of silver coins. 'I will give these to Cranston,' he murmured, 'with a plea to return them to me for funeral expenses and what's left for the poor.' The friar continued his search and discovered a stiletto-like dagger pushed into a concealed sheath on the dead man's belt. 'Strange and stranger still,' he murmured.

'What is?' Benedicta asked.

'Here was I thinking Lebarge had fled here with only the clothes on his back, yet I now find him armed and monied. Benedicta, Mauger, are you sure no one else approached our sanctuary man?'

'Brother,' Mauger protested, 'true, we did not mount close

guard on the entrance to the rood screen or the sacristy door, but
I'm sure no one met Lebarge.'

'I agree,' Benedicta added. 'Master Bladdersmith,' the widow
woman turned to the bailiff, 'you were sleeping in God's Acre.
You and Godbless were sharing a tankard . . .?'

'I saw nothing,' the bailiff slurred.

Athelstan stared down at the corpse and blessed it one final
time. 'What is strangest of all,' he declared, 'is that Lebarge
would have nothing to do with anyone except us, yet he dies
of poison . . .' He thanked them all, walked quickly out of
the sanctuary and down the gloomy nave. Benedicta called
his name but he walked faster. He needed to think, to be alone.
He paused by the entrance to the church tower and glimpsed
Crispin's work-bench and tools. He smiled to himself and
slipped through the main door back up to the priest's house.
Athelstan believed he had done enough and fully agreed with
the verse from scripture which advised that one should not
worry about the morrow as each day had troubles of its own.
It certainly had! The friar sat for a while at the table quietly
reciting the office of compline from his psalter. He finished,
tended the dying coals in the hearth, then started at a rap on
the door.

'Who is it?'

'Brother, it's Pike the Ditcher. I need to speak to you!'

'And I want to speak to you,' Athelstan shouted back and,
without a second's thought, he unbolted the door and flung it
open. The grotesques who pushed him back into the kitchen were
frightening to look at: Earthworms, the Upright Men's street
warriors, garbed in cow-skin dyed and daubed in an array of
garish colours, their faces blackened, hair tied up in greasy tufts
like the horns on some demon goat. They were all armed with
oxhide shields, swords, daggers and maces. They crowded in
around Athelstan before parting to let a shame-faced Pike and
Watkin through.

'I could excommunicate you for this.' Athelstan tried to hide
his fear. 'Cursing you with bell, book and candle. Denying you
the church and all its sacraments. There is no need to come for
me like this in the dead of night as if I was some felon.'

'You have been summoned.' The Captain of the Earthworms,

his face hidden behind a grotesque raven's mask, beckoned. 'You must come. You have no choice.'

'Please?' Pike pleaded.

Athelstan put on his sandals and cloak and stormed out of the house. Immediately the Earthworms surrounded him and he was gently guided down the lane. Athelstan wondered if they were going to some desolate place along the river and hid his surprise when they stopped at the Piebald Tavern. He looked up and down the narrow lane: silence. No foraging cats or swarming rats, no dogs prowled or howled against the sky, nothing but moving shadows. The Piebald, and all approaches to it, would be closely guarded.

Pike rapped on the tavern door, bolts were pulled, locks turned and Athelstan was ushered in to the tangy warmth of the taproom. This had been transformed into a council chamber with men ranging either side of the long common table. A monstrously fat figure, head and face covered by hood and veil, sat enthroned at the far end. Athelstan glanced at the men. Most were his parishioners: Ranulf, the Hangman, Crispin, Hig the Pig Man, Moleskin and the usual motley crew. He glared at them as he sat down on the chair placed at the near end of the table. Pike and Watkin also took their seats. The Earthworms gathered near the door or fanned out behind those sitting there. The Raven walked to the top of the table and whispered to the veiled figure, who removed the heavy headdress to reveal a fleshy, sweaty face under a balding pate, hungry eyes and a strong mouth over a jutting chin.

'I am Simon Grindcobbe, Brother.'

'Of course you are.'

'I am a lord, a master on the Council of the Upright Men.'

'So you have lords already.' Athelstan's response provoked grunts of approval and even snorts of laughter from others around the table.

'The Great Community of the Realm demands leadership.'

'And naturally you regard yourself as the logical choice, hence your self-election?'

Grindcobbe leaned forward, lacing stubby fingers together. 'In the end, Brother, all my titles mean – and you know this – is that I will die a slower, more painful death than our comrades here.'

'Our comrades?'

'You are with us, Brother Athelstan, or so they say.'

'Those who say so can go hang, Master Grindcobbe. I have chosen my vocation. I am a Dominican priest.'

'And the Lord High Coroner's Secretarius?'

'He chose me for a task, necessary for good order in our violent community.'

'You have no solidarity with the poor?'

'If I didn't, what would I be doing here? Master Grindcobbe, I am tired and weary. You have brought me to you at the dead of night, for what reason?'

'To determine if you are a traitor.'

'My allegiance is to Christ and the Church, my Order and the King.'

'And to your parishioners?'

'I have never betrayed them.' Athelstan stared around at the men gathered there. None dared meet his gaze except Radegund the Relic Seller, who glared sullenly at him.

'You know,' Grindcobbe pointed at Athelstan, 'I was to meet Pike the Ditcher in the sacristy three hours after midday.'

'I did not know that. I was informed by Pike that he was meeting a cousin, Sister Matilda of the Poor Clares. He asked for somewhere quiet and reclusive, and suggested our sacristy. I agreed. I had my doubts then; now I realize how true my feelings were.'

'And you told no one else?'

Athelstan closed his eyes. He recalled meeting Benedicta in the sacristy. He repressed a chill and stared down at the table top. He had told her, he was sure he had.

'Brother, if you told no else – and I certainly didn't, and Pike the Ditcher wouldn't – who informed Thibault's men of the day, the hour and the place?'

Athelstan closed his eyes. 'I . . .'

'He told me.' Athelstan started in surprise. Benedicta came out of the kitchen at the far end of the taproom. She was shrouded in her cloak, wiping her hands on a napkin. Athelstan stared at her as he realized he did not truly know this woman, not really. He had judged her to be a pious widow, lovely in all aspects, dedicated to good work, the care of the church and the priest's house. He crossed himself as he secretly confessed to his own arrogance. Benedicta was so different now: her walk, her poise, the simple gesture of carefully wiping her hands on a cloth, the way she was staring at him, the half-smile which faded as she stopped behind Radegund the Relic Seller.

'You told me, Brother, in the sacristy. Radegund here, a veritable bee of busy gossip, in hiding because of an alleged fraud against some lord of the soil, crept across the sanctuary and eavesdropped.'

'I did not.' Radegund half turned on his stool. 'I did not!' he spluttered.

'Oh, yes, you did.' Benedicta leaned down and whispered hoarsely in his ear. 'Master Lebarge, then in sanctuary, saw you. He commented on how much you questioned him about this and that, but he definitely saw you and told me so.' She glanced up. 'Brother, do you remember when we discussed Pike the Ditcher's meeting? I went to the sacristy door. I thought I'd heard something – I did. But by then Radegund had hastily withdrawn.'

Athelstan stared at the relic seller as he recalled how Thibault, that sinister Master of Secrets, had insinuated that he had a spy in the parish of St Erconwald's. Radegund would be ideal. A man who flitted here and there, a friend to all who could act the merry rogue, a true son of the soil.

'You claimed sanctuary, Radegund,' Benedicta continued, now addressing the entire company. 'You claimed that you had offended a great one and so fled for sanctuary . . .'

'You knew about Lebarge,' Athelstan interrupted. 'You entered St Erconwald's and gained his confidence to discover what had really happened at the Golden Oliphant. And when you failed, you decided to leave. You knew you would be closely protected by Watkin, Pike and the others.'

'But he also learnt,' Benedicta declared, 'about Pike the Ditcher's meeting with a mysterious cousin and passed that information on.'

'I had to come here,' Grindcobbe declared, 'as you will learn, Brother Athelstan. I need to have urgent and secret words with you, which is why I met Pike in the first place. Thibault's spies swarm like fleas over a turd. I thought,' he grinned, 'I could pass through here as a rotund but cheery-voiced Poor Clare sister.'

'And we would both have been taken,' Pike screeched, 'had it not been for that secret shaft. In the end,' he shrugged, 'Godbless did not know what to make of it all, especially when the Earthworms appeared.'

Benedicta patted Radegund on the shoulder. 'We suspected we had a spy and you, Radegund, are he. You act the roaring boy, but in truth you are a whore touting for custom, blithely betraying those you eat and drink with.'

'Did you poison Lebarge?' Athelstan demanded.

'Of course not! I have done nothing wrong!' Radegund protested. Grindcobbe ordered the relic seller to be searched, and his pockets and wallet, the lining of his jerkin as well as his sack of geegaws were all emptied on to the table. Even before they were seized, Athelstan noticed the freshly minted silver, new from the Tower, and the green-ribboned seal bearing a crown above a portcullis: Thibault's personal waxed insignia given to protect Radegund if he was ever taken up. All of these were inspected and gleefully passed around. Athelstan stared pityingly at the relic seller. He was already tried, judged and condemned. Behind him Benedicta, so poised and so silent, watched everything closely. Athelstan thought the relic seller would be hustled away, but now the rest of the company thronged about Radegund, punching and tearing at his clothes.

'Guilty!' a voice cried. 'Treason!' another shouted. 'Traitor!' The violence deepened. Athelstan tried to intervene but the Earthworms held him back. He watched in horror as the fighting men of the Great Community lifted the screaming Radegund on to his stool, a rope was produced, looped over the roof beam and a noose fastened tightly around Radegund's throat. The Raven kicked the stool away. Athelstan shouted and struggled to break free but there was nothing he could do. Radegund jerked and choked until the Hangman seized his legs and pulled him down. Radegund convulsed one final time and hung still. For a brief while silence reigned. Athelstan looked for Benedicta, but she was gone. The others, however, were elated, triumphant at the discovery and summary execution of a traitor.

'You may have him now, priest,' a voice shouted. Radegund was cut down and laid on the table whilst Joscelyn, the one-armed former river pirate, ordered jugs of ale and tankards to be brought.

Athelstan walked around the table. He closed his mind to the living bustling about him as, shaking and sweat-soaked, belly lurching, he administered the last rites and commended Radegund's soul to the mercy of God. Once finished, the friar slumped on a stool and, for a matter of heartbeats, cursed both his life and his calling. He would get out of here! He would plead with his superiors to send him elsewhere. He could not understand, he could not bear this sudden, horrid violence. He felt a hand on his shoulder. Pike pressed a goblet of wine into his hand.

'Drink, Father,' he urged. 'Do not judge us. We knew there was a traitor. Radegund would have hanged us all, destroyed our families. He came crying "All hail" when like Judas he meant all harm. But come, Master Grindcobbe needs urgent words with you.'

Athelstan finished the wine and allowed Pike to take him up to a chamber above stairs. Simon Grindcobbe was already there, hunched over a table with a platter of cheese, bread and dried meats. He waved Athelstan to the stool opposite and filled a tankard, toasting the friar with his own.

'Be at peace, Brother.'

'I am – I was at peace until I saw murder.' Athelstan swiftly blessed the food and stared around. They were alone. The window firmly barred. The heavy door shut. No fire burnt in the grate. Candle spigots and lanterns hooked to the wall provided light.

'It wasn't murder, you know that, Brother. Radegund could have had every man, woman and child in this tavern hanged for treason and myself quartered and filleted at Smithfield.'

'I could do the same.'

'But you won't. Radegund was worse than a common whore in Cock Lane, selling what he knew to anyone who would pay, and to the devil with the consequences. Now, Brother, why I am here?'

'A very good question.'

'To talk to you. I came in disguise to meet Pike to arrange this meeting.' Grindcobbe shrugged. 'My features and form are well known. A Poor Clare sister, burly and big, face hidden by a veil, one who came and went within the hour, was probably the safest way. A nun closeted in the sacristy would not provoke as much attention as Pike and I meeting in some market alehouse or tavern where the likes of Radegund swarm like lice.'

'You suspected him?'

'No, we did not. We knew that Thibault had spies but never guessed our notorious relic seller was one of them, except for . . .'

'Benedicta?'

'Yes, she did.'

'She also sits high in the Council of the Upright Men?'

'Yes, Brother, she does. A good woman trusted by all, including you.'

'Perhaps not now.'

'Don't judge her hastily, Athelstan. Sharp and swift as a hawk is Benedicta. She is no hypocrite. Has she hurt anyone in your parish? Does she not care for you and the brethren? Believe me, she has good cause to be one of ours. She hails from the Weald of Kent, where her father was executed for poaching, hunting meat for his starving family. Benedicta's brother was cut down in an affray over taxes. Her husband had his ship impounded by the crown for the King's war at sea and, when both he and ship were lost, she received a mere pittance in compensation.'

Athelstan sipped his drink as he mentally beat his breast. One of my many faults, he considered, I must remember: still waters run very, very deep and behind every soul stretches a life known only to God.

'Why did you want to see me?' he asked.

'To pass on a warning.'

'I have been warned often enough. I will not join your revolt.'

'Something more serious than that, but, to show you my good-will, let me help you . . .'

'And reveal the name of the Herald of Hell?'

'Brother, I will not betray our secrets. I refer to Whitfield's death.'

'And?'

Grindcobbe leaned over the table. 'If Radegund acted like a common whore, Whitfield and Lebarge were no better. Oh,' Grindcobbe sipped from his tankard, 'Whitfield was the most skilled of cipher clerks who worked at the very heart of Thibault's chancery. Heaven knows what secrets passed through his hands, but Whitfield was also very greedy and lecherous, even though he was impotent. We know that from the whores with whom he played so many games. Whitfield needed silver and gold to pay his way and satisfy his appetites. He also had an eye for the future. He feared the coming troubles, especially when he, like so many of Gaunt's minions, was visited by the Herald of Hell.'

'Whitfield had a great deal to fear.'

'Oh, too true, Brother. You see, Whitfield had sold himself to others, including the Upright Men.'

Athelstan just shook his head.

'It's the truth. Indeed we called him "Chanticlere", the cock which crows so shrilly for all to hear and tries to mount every hen in his filthy yard. In return for good coin, Whitfield, through his scrivener Lebarge, would send us warnings, give us sound advice, not too much to provoke suspicion but enough for us to take precautions when needed.'

'And the gold and silver?'

'It would join the rest of Whitfield's illicit income.'

'What do you mean?'

'You have met Adam Stretton, Fitzalan of Arundel's man, at the Golden Oliphant? A mailed clerk, a true assassin, a killer born and bred who has carried out all kinds of nefarious crimes secretly, subtly, at the dead of night for his master. Stretton is most adept at arranging accidents: a fall downstairs, a fire which abruptly breaks out, a horse which suddenly turns violent and bolts. Did you know he once trained as an apprentice with the Guild of Locksmiths? A crafty, cunning clerk who can work wonders on bolts, locks and hinges. Oh, by the way, Odo Gray, our jolly sea captain, is no better. Many is the passenger who has disappeared over the side. The member of crew who protested too much tumbling from the rigging or the unwanted guest supposedly falling ill on board and buried swiftly at sea before any physician could examine the corpse and shout poison.' Grindcobbe licked his lips. 'To return to Stretton. His master Arundel hates Gaunt, who replies in kind. To be brief, Arundel, through Stretton, was also paying Whitfield for whatever information he could glean about Gaunt, Thibault and the rest of their devilish coven. Stretton had to be careful, so he would come to the Cokayne festivals or any other revelry at the Golden Oliphant. Whitfield attended the last joyous meeting, he always did, and Stretton joined him to discover more, to put pressure on him or . . .' Grindcobbe paused. 'Did Stretton also suspect that

Whitfield and Lebarge were preparing to flee across the Narrow
Seas for pastures new? Was he there to draw Whitfield into
Arundel's coven? To offer him protection, to discover more
information, or, more likely, threaten Whitfield that the Earl of
Arundel wanted a richer return on his investment? We certainly
did.'

'You have Upright Men at the Golden Oliphant?'

'Of course, as we do in all the wards, streets, taverns, alehouses
and brothels of London. The Golden Oliphant is no different,
you know that. When Thibault arrived there, the Upright Men,
whoever or whatever he, she or they may be, seized the opportunity to loose those crossbow bolts.' Grindcobbe chuckled. 'Of
course we did little hurt or harm but it served a powerful warning
to our demon enemy.'

'And you intervened again outside St Mary Le Bow?' Athelstan
asked. His surprise had now faded, replaced by a deep curiosity.
He had served at St Erconwald's for many a day. The Upright
Men had become part of the fabric of his life and that of the
parish, but now he was being drawn into the very heart of their
machinations.

'Yes, it was us outside St Mary Le Bow. We intended you no
harm. We guessed that Thibault had handed you the cipher that
Whitfield held, the one seized, or at least part of it, when that
arrogant madcap Reynard allowed himself to be captured. We
only wanted to hold you as a threat against Cranston, whilst
we emptied or filched your chancery satchel. Of course we, or
rather they, made a stupid mistake. Cranston, despite his bulk,
is still as fast as a lunging viper.'

'Good Sir John.' Athelstan toasted Grindcobbe with his
tankard. The captain of the Upright Men stared back, smiled and
grudgingly responded to the toast.

'At least Cranston is not corrupt. He has not sold his soul,'
Grindcobbe murmured. 'Which is why I am here tonight, but I
will come to that by and by. Now, to return to the Golden Oliphant.
Naturally we were deeply concerned by Whitfield. He had taken
our money, we wanted more information and were not happy
about the prospect of him disappearing.'

'Especially with the cipher?'

'We needed that back. We certainly didn't want Whitfield to

translate it.' Grindcobbe turned and glanced at Athelstan out of the corner of his eye. 'They say Whitfield was found fully dressed as if about to leave?'

'Yes.'

'He was,' Grindcobbe grinned. 'He was supposed to leave the Golden Oliphant in the early hours and meet me.'

'Why? Oh, of course,' Athelstan answered his own question. 'To return the cipher.'

'Correct, but he failed to appear. We knew him to be a toper so we thought we would wait for another occasion.'

'One small mystery is solved,' the friar conceded. 'I wondered why Whitfield was dressed in the early hours. So, in the end, he agreed to hand the cipher over?'

'We threatened him. If he did, we would let him go, if he didn't we would take action.'

'So the cipher is important?'

'Have you translated it?'

'No, is that why you wanted this meeting?'

Grindcobbe shook his head, swilled the dregs of ale around his tankard, promptly drank them and refilled it. 'The cipher is obviously important,' he conceded. 'It is related to what is about to happen. Do not worry, we will not search you or your house. You have undoubtedly made copies of it. Another little task performed in the Lamb of God.' Grindcobbe leaned across the table and grasped Athelstan's hand. He squeezed and let it go. 'Brother, believe me, in a short while it will not matter. The day of wrath will soon be upon us.'

'How soon?'

'Within the week at the very most.'

Athelstan went cold. The room grew darker; even the candle-light seemed to dim at Grindcobbe's sombre tone.

You are not lying, Athelstan thought. You are warning me.

'Brother?'

'I recall the words of the prophet Amos, Master Grindcobbe: "Israel, prepare to meet your God." When, how will this all begin?'

'As scripture says, Brother, it will come like a thief in the night and ye know not the day nor the hour.'

Athelstan took a deep breath. 'So,' he declared, 'back to

Whitfield and the Golden Oliphant. Desperate, wanting to escape, fleeing from his own master, hounded by you and Stretton. Who knows, perhaps he did commit suicide?'

'No, no.' Grindcobbe shook his head. 'Whitfield was plotting to flee, but not only him – the villainous Odo Gray was also hired to take Mistress Elizabeth Cheyne, Joycelina and all their household out of London to the . . .'

'All of them?'

'Oh, yes. Think of the Golden Oliphant, Brother! You have only seen some of the chambers. Believe me, Mistress Cheyne has packed up her valuables and movables, or most of them. The Golden Oliphant was to be boarded up and left under the protection of hired ruffians. Mistress Elizabeth and her moppets would soon adjourn abroad. There is a profitable market for English flesh as well as English wool in Flemish towns, and, when the troubles were over, back she would return.'

'And Whitfield and Lebarge would go with her?'

'Yes. Secretly, though. The accepted wisdom is that Whitfield was probably planning some pretend accident along the Thames: a slip down the steps, a fall from the quayside, a tumble from a barge, which would be portrayed as a possible suicide of a man whose wits gave way, whose soul fractured due to all his worries.'

'And Lebarge?'

'No one really worried about Lebarge, a mere servant, although I know he was more than that to Whitfield. In the end, he was just another man frightened out of his wits. I understand he too has died, poisoned whilst hiding in sanctuary.'

Athelstan nodded.

'By whom?'

'Heaven knows,' Athelstan murmured, holding up a hand, 'and that is the truth.' The friar closed his eyes. Grindcobbe was being honest, at least about what concerned Whitfield, though he was being very cautious not to betray any secrets of the Upright Men. Athelstan opened his eyes. 'So, Whitfield was pestered from every side?'

'At first he told us not to bother him, that he was frightened; he had done enough for our cause. I am sure he made Stretton the same response. Don't forget, Whitfield was wary of

Arundel but he feared Thibault the most. He was terrified that
Gaunt's Master of Secrets would discover what he was going
to do.'

'You could have threatened to expose him.'

'We did. Whitfield threatened us back with the cipher he held,
not to mention other secrets. We compromised. We would let
him go unscathed, providing he returned the cipher. I suspect he
was planning to do this when death, in some form, brutally
intervened.' Grindcobbe leaned across the table.

'Brother, Whitfield was not just a frightened clerk with a boot
in either camp. I mentioned earlier about the flow of secret
information across his chancery desk. I am sure he responded in
kind to any threat from Stretton.'

'Like some chess game,' Athelstan murmured, 'pieces thrust
against each other.'

'Precisely, Brother, and all Whitfield had to do was wait a
short while, perhaps not more than a day. Mistress Elizabeth
Cheyne would finish moving whatever else she wanted to take
with her, and ensure all the moppets and the rest of her household
had their secret instructions on what to take – not that such ladies
have much to carry.'

'And the members of your coven, the Upright Men would have
gone with them?'

Grindcobbe just wagged a warning finger. 'That does not
concern you, Brother.'

'But then Whitfield dies. Lebarge flees, panic-stricken, and it
all comes to nothing. Mistress Elizabeth and everyone in the
Golden Oliphant is now under strict instruction by the Lord High
Coroner to remain where they are.'

'True,' Grindcobbe agreed, 'Mistress Cheyne is deeply furious.'

'Let her rage, Master Grindcobbe. Other matters do puzzle
me. First, here's Whitfield anxious, agitated, fearful, bound up
with himself, so why did he offer to help Matthias Camoys try
to discover the whereabouts of the Cross of Lothar?'

'I have heard of that,' Grindcobbe declared, 'and of the mysterious carvings at the Golden Oliphant, but I cannot help; such a
mummery does not concern me or mine.'

'I wonder . . .' Athelstan tapped on the table. 'Those inscriptions, "*Soli Invicto*" and "IHSV", are familiar. Yet, for the life

of me, I cannot specifically recall why or what they are. "IHSV" is a Greek abbreviation for Jesus Christ, Son of God and Saviour. But why should Sir Reginald . . .?'

'What else?' Grindcobbe broke in testily.

'Well, it's obvious. If you are correct, and I accept that you are, Amaury Whitfield must have earned a great deal of silver and gold from you, Stretton and whoever else he did business with. Yet we found nothing of that treasure either on him or in his room, which makes me reflect on another problem. Whitfield hired a bleak chamber at the top of the house. He could have housed himself in more comfortable quarters on one of the galleries below. I am sure Mistress Cheyne has more luxurious accommodation for select guests. Whitfield, however, chose to climb very steep stairs – the one to the top gallery is especially long and arduous – why? To protect himself? To conceal something against an intruder who might find a lower chamber easier to break into through door or window? Was Whitfield guarding his ill-gained wealth, and if so, where is it now?'

'Brother Athelstan, the hour is passing, I must be gone. I have demonstrated, as much as I can, my good faith. Now I must tell you the reason for this meeting.' Grindcobbe moved the ale jug and platters from between them. 'The Great Community of the Realm have decided they are ready. The chosen day is fast approaching. Once upon a time the leaders of the Upright Men were united. Now, as the stirring time approaches, sharp divisions have appeared. We have always protested our loyalty to the boy-king; it is his evil councillors we wish to remove and punish. I am personally loyal to Richard. I fought as a captain of hobelars for his father the Black Prince.' Grindcobbe drew breath. 'Cranston may already have some intelligence about what I am going to say; a similar warning has been despatched to the court party with one significant omission . . .'

'What is all this?'

'Brother Athelstan, may God be my witness, but I truly believe a most senior captain amongst the Upright Men intends to meet the young king and draw him into negotiation. This will only be a ploy to allay Richard's suspicions before the captain kills him and all members of the royal party.'

'Impossible!'

'No, listen,' Grindcobbe held up a hand, 'there are some amongst the Upright Men who want the entire court party, all the lords spiritual and temporal, slaughtered. I and the others have always regarded them as hotheads, who could be restrained on the day.'

'I am not too sure,' Athelstan whispered. 'Once the bloodletting begins, killing begets killing.'

'True, but there's more. This is my suspicion and mine only. I have very little proof; it is more conjecture than anything else. My Lord of Gaunt is quitting London for the northern march. He claims he must deal with Scottish incursions across the border. Nonsense! Why, I ask, is Gaunt leaving London and the southern shires when the young king and the royal family need both his protection and that of his troops?'

'I agree.'

'Hence my suspicion of a plot forged in Hell. One of our leading captains has been suborned by Gaunt with promises and assurances.' Grindcobbe paused. Athelstan felt a fear grip his belly; he half suspected what Grindcobbe was about to say.

'Gaunt wants the young king dead. He will then come hurrying south to crush the revolt. More importantly, if Richard dies he leaves no heir.'

'And the Confessor's crown,' Athelstan murmured, 'will go to the next in line, away from the Plantagenets, to John of Gaunt, uncle of the King, brother of the Black Prince, head of the House of Lancaster and next in line to the throne. Do you have proof of this?'

'None, just a deep, gnawing apprehension as well as the whisperings of my most skilled spies.'

'And so?'

'Sir John Cranston may well be alerted to the warning I have already sent to the Queen Mother, but I did not voice my full suspicions. After all, not everybody in the court party can be trusted. Tell Cranston the threat is even more dangerous than he thinks. Young Richard must not meet any of our leaders, for if he does, royal blood will be shed.'

'Why not accuse Gaunt publicly?' Athelstan paused and sighed. 'I can guess your response. If any specific allegation is laid, then where is the proof?'

Grindcobbe nodded in agreement.

'I suppose,' Athelstan continued, 'Gaunt will be forewarned about what you know, whilst your spies who helped you reach this conclusion would be left vulnerable. In the end Gaunt would brush it off as just another devious stratagem to blacken his name and reputation. He would protest his innocence, his years of service, and then wait for some other occasion.' Athelstan stared at the dancing candle-flame. Grindcobbe was telling the truth. The friar recalled Lebarge's demand for a pardon for any crimes he may have committed or be accused of. If Whitfield knew the truth behind Grindcobbe's allegation and shared it with Lebarge, little wonder both men were desperate and wished to flee for their lives: such knowledge was highly dangerous and could engulf them in the most heinous treason.

'Brother Athelstan?' Grindcobbe brought him back to the present.

'Do you think Whitfield knew such secrets?' Althelstan asked.

'There is a very good chance he did, Brother, but,' Grindcobbe pushed back his stool, 'the hour is passing. I must be gone. It's only a matter of time before Thibault's soldiers return. Benedicta will walk you back to your house.'

Athelstan rose and crossed to the door.

'Brother?'

The friar turned.

'Athelstan, I doubt if we will meet again this side of Hell. Pray for me and, if I fail, pray that my death be swift.'

Athelstan nodded, gave his blessing and left, going down the stairs to where Benedicta was waiting in a now deserted taproom. They left the Piebald, walking in silence for a while. Benedicta slipped her hand into his.

'I never lied, Athelstan. I am what I truly am. I do what my heart tells me is right. I have made my confession to you at the mercy pew. You have sat in the shriving chair and absolved my sins. I have dedicated myself to you and this community.' She stopped and faced him squarely now, grasping his other hand. 'Well,' she added impishly, 'what would the parish gossips say about us standing, hands clasped, in the moonlight?'

Athelstan stepped closer; her smile faded. 'You could have told me, Benedicta.'

'No.' She shook her head. 'I kept it hidden from you because, my dear friar, you would have worried, worried and worried yet again. I am telling you now as it is the truth, but tomorrow when I rise, I shall put on my mask to meet the others who hide behind their masks, though not from you, beloved Brother.' And, leaning forward, Benedicta kissed him on both cheeks, pressed his hands and disappeared into the night.

After a troubled night's sleep, Athelstan finished his dawn Mass attended by Benedicta, Mauger, Crim and the ever vigilant Bonaventure, who seemed very interested in what might be lurking in the sanctuary, though Crim kept shooing him away. Athelstan was divesting in the sacristy afterwards and wondering what to do when the green-garbed Tiptoft slipped like a moon-beam into the church to whisper that Sir John sent his greetings and would Athelstan meet him in the Lamb of God as a matter of great urgency.

'I surely will,' Athelstan replied. He collected his belongings and whatever else he needed and followed Tiptoft with a small escort of Flaxwith's bailiffs down to London Bridge. The day was mist-hung. The swirling white cloud masked both sight and sound, though as they approached the gallows and stocks near the entrance to the bridge, Athelstan glimpsed the pole set up with Radegund's head spiked on the top, and beneath it a colourful scrolled proclamation which publicized the stark, brutal message: 'Radegund the Relic Seller, adjudged a traitor, condemned to death', followed by the date and the phrase, 'by order of the Upright Men and the Great Community of the Realm'. Athelstan murmured a prayer, pulled his cowl closer over his head, took his beads out and began a decade of aves as his escort led him across the mist-strewn bridge and up into the city. Cries and shouts rang out. Figures passed like wraiths, except for one of the numerous preachers of doom, garbed in animal skins, walking up and down with a torch in each hand, quoting texts from the Apocalypse.

At last he reached the Lamb of God. Mine Hostess had opened specially for Sir John who, all trimmed and freshly garbed, was sitting in his favourite window seat eating newly baked bread and drinking a stoup of ale. Athelstan and Cranston exchanged the kiss of peace whilst a heavy-eyed servant brought more bread and ale. The friar had hardly blessed this when Cranston started to describe the previous night's meeting at St Edward's shrine. Athelstan did not interrupt but, once the coroner had finished, he gave an equally terse account of all that happened: the murder of Lebarge, the confrontation with Radegund, the relic seller's swift and brutal execution and the information Grindcobbe had shared with him.

'Satan's tits!' Cranston grumbled, staring quickly around. 'We know enough treason to really set the pot bubbling. We have been given halves of the same coin, Brother.'

'And we will put them together when the time comes, though that is not now, Sir John.' Athelstan bit into the bread, eager to break his fast, chewed quickly, then continued. 'When that hour does come, my Lord High Coroner, you will know it. God forgive me, I am supposed to be a man of peace, but we are talking about the Lord's anointed, our king, an innocent boy. So, when the danger threatens, Sir John, strike hard and may God's angel strengthen your arm.'

Cranston sipped at his ale. He and his colleague, Walworth the Mayor, had already decided what to do when what Athelstan called 'the hour' arrived. He put his cup down.

'Amen to that, Brother,' he declared. 'Interesting, though, how the Upright Men, at the very time they need unity, are beginning to divide into at least three factions. There are those who wish to pull up everything, root and branch, and destroy the present order. The second group, like Grindcobbe, simply want the present order purged of all sin and reformed. And now a sinister third group. One, possibly more, of the leaders amongst the Upright Men have been suborned by Gaunt with a dream of a new king, a new royal house and fresh beginnings.' Cranston shook his head. 'No wonder Whitfield was murdered. Perhaps Thibault despatched his own assassins into the Golden Oliphant and all that rage and temper was just a pretext, a cover for his deep relief at the death of a clerk who knew too much and could no longer be trusted. The fact remains: we do not know who killed him, why or how. The list of suspects seems to be growing all the time. Mistress Cheyne is ruthless enough to hire killers. Grindcobbe correctly described the rest and it agrees with what we already know. Stretton enjoys a most sinister reputation. Odo Gray is no better. Foxley, and I truly suspect this, is an Upright Man. Did you notice the wrist guard on his left arm? I am sure he is skilled at loosing a crossbow. And of course there is Thibault's assassin, Albinus. Did he, by himself or with others, slink back into that brothel at the dead of night and kill Whitfield?' Cranston sighed noisily. 'Nor must we forget young Camoys, who had enough sway with Whitfield to coax our hapless clerk, desperate to escape, into trying to resolve the riddles left by his uncle. Well, talking of riddles, Brother, what about the cipher?'

Athelstan pulled a face, 'I have hardly looked at it. I suspect the cipher itself cannot be unlocked. As for the triangles and the litany of saints, I suggest these are Whitfield's workings, as much as he could deduce from the cipher. Well, Sir John, now I am in the city, I think it's time I spent a period of reflection in our library at Blackfriars where I can pursue these matters a little further.'

'Away from your parish and the likes of the lovely Benedicta?'

Athelstan just smiled. He thought it best if he did not inform Cranston about Benedicta, or at least not for the time being.

'Sir John?' a voice interrupted them.

Athelstan glanced up. Osbert Oswald, Cranston's Guildhall clerk, had slipped into the tavern, two pieces of parchment clutched in his hands. The coroner took them and read them swiftly.

'Well, Brother, one trouble after another. Physician Philippe has replied; copies have been sent to you whilst I have received what is due to the coroner. Lebarge was definitely poisoned. Some herbal plant. Our beloved physician believes it could be deadly nightshade.'

'That's no surprise,' Athelstan declared. 'The real mystery is how it was administered to a man so terrified that he would only eat what Benedicta brought and tasted.'

'And more trouble!' Cranston had unrolled the other parchment. 'It's back to the Golden Oliphant. Joycelina, Mistress Cheyne's principal helpmate, has taken a tumble downstairs and lies dead of a broken neck.'

They found the Golden Oliphant strangely quiet. The violent deaths which had occurred there seemed to have turned the brothel, as Athelstan remarked, into a place of deep shadow. Mistress Cheyne, face cleaned of paint, and garbed in a simple, dark brown gown, a veil covering her hair, ushered them across the Golden Hall into the refectory where all the guests and household retainers were assembled.

'When can we leave?' Stretton immediately shouted.

'Keep quiet,' Cranston snarled. 'Another death has occurred. You, sir, are a suspect.'

'And where is Mistress Hawisa?' Athelstan looked round. 'Hawisa?' he repeated.

'She is gone.' Mistress Cheyne, red-eyed and wiping her hands on the apron she'd swiftly donned, gestured around. 'People are very afraid.'

'What about Hawisa's belongings?'

'Gone. I will show you her chamber.'

'And Lebarge's baggage? You know he is dead.'

'So we heard,' Foxley spoke up. 'Slain in sanctuary, they said.'

'And his baggage?' Athelstan insisted.

'Also gone,' Mistress Cheyne replied. 'Sir John, Brother Athelstan, I do not know why Lebarge fled and died, or where his baggage has been taken.'

Athelstan nodded as if in agreement. He gazed round. The guests, household moppets and servants sat on benches along each table littered with the remains of their morning meal. The friar sensed their deep anxiety. Outside one of the mastiffs howled, an eerie, blood-tingling sound on the early summer morning. Stretton sat head down, playing with the hilt of his dagger. Odo Gray was fashioning a knot with a piece of rope. Matthias Camoys doodled with his finger in the drops of ale on the table top. Foxley sat back, staring up at the roof beam in patent exasperation. Master Griffin slouched beside him, eyes closed as if catching up on lost sleep. Whatever you appear, Athelstan reflected, you are all frightened. You wish to be gone. But . . . He clapped his hands.

'I ask you to stay here a little longer.' Athelstan ignored their groans and grumbles. 'Sir John and I will soon finish our business. Mistress Cheyne, if you could show us Joycelina's corpse?'

She took them out across the stable yard, glistening after it had been sluiced clean by water from the great well, sunk in the middle of the yard beneath its tarred, red-tiled roof. She led them past the stable where Stretton's destrier lunged, head back, lips curled as it banged sharpened hooves against the door.

'Keep well clear of that one,' Mistress Cheyne murmured. 'A killer like its master.'

'You know Master Stretton?'

'I certainly know of him, Sir John.'

'As you do Master Odo Gray, who was preparing to spirit away you, your moppets and all you hold dear?'

Mistress Cheyne turned, her hand on the latch of the door to one of the outhouses. 'I wondered when you would learn that, but so what? Has not your own wife fled London?' She waved around. 'I have removed furniture and heavy goods to Master Mephistopheles' warehouses. Other movables are in the hold of the *Leaping Horse*.'

'But you won't be leaving now?'

'No, Sir John, as you say, not until this business is finished.'

'Why did Whitfield hire a chamber on the top gallery?'

'I don't know, Brother Athelstan, I asked him that myself. I believe I've told you, he just wanted it that way.'

'Was Whitfield wealthy?'

'He had coins. Whitfield was not the most generous of men.'

'And his favourite moppet?'

'Why, Joycelina. She had certain skills.'

'Did Whitfield need these?'

Mistress Cheyne smiled coldly. 'Most men do. Whitfield had problems with potency. He was fat and drank too much.'

'Were you party to his plot to fake his own death?'

'Sir John, all I know is that Odo Gray made a great deal of money. He offered to take us to foreign parts. Whitfield and Lebarge were part of that, but why they wanted to flee from London, where they were going and what they were planning to do is not my business. I had troubles of my own.'

'Did you know that Whitfield was a holder of great secrets?'

'You mean just like us whores?' Mistress Cheyne pulled a face. 'What was that to us?'

'And Lebarge?'

'Whitfield's shadow? Or so it seemed to young Hawisa. A greedy man. He had a passion for my simnel cakes.'

'What about Hawisa?'

'As I said, she has fled, taking her baggage and probably

Lebarge's with her. Now, gentlemen, Joycelina awaits you.'

They entered the outhouse. Joycelina's corpse lay on a battered table covered by a canvas cloth; candles glowed at head and foot. Out of fear of fire all straw had been cleared from the mud-packed floor and some heavy herbal concoction poured out to provide a pleasant odour. Mistress Cheyne pulled back the cloth. Joycelina lay head strangely askew, her face a mass of bruises. Athelstan blessed the corpse, took out his phial of anointing oil and administered the last rites with Cranston reciting the refrain. Once finished, Cranston and Athelstan inspected the corpse. The broken neck, the cause of death, was easily identified, as well as the mass of bruising from the fall down those very steep, sharp-edged stairs leading to the top gallery.

'What actually happened?' Athelstan asked.

'I was baking bread. I went out into the yard to collect some sheets left over the stand close to the well. One of the moppets, Anna, the one Thibault almost hanged, came with me. She went back into the kitchen to fetch something and noticed the bread was burning. She ran out and told me. I ordered her to fetch Joycelina. She went back inside and I could hear her calling. Joycelina was on the top gallery cleaning Whitfield's chamber. Anna went up and shouted for her. She was on the stairs leading to the third gallery when she heard Joycelina's answer followed by a scream, a yell and a hideous crash. Anna ran up and found Joycelina had tumbled down. She realized it was very serious and came calling for me. The rest of the household, together with the guests, were having their meal in the refectory. I ran.' She crossed herself. 'Joycelina was dead. That was obvious. Anna and I went to the top of the stairs but we could see no reason why Joycelina had slipped, except I noticed one of her sandals had become loose. Now,' she spread her hands, 'whether this was due to the fall or not . . .?'

Athelstan walked to the foot of the makeshift bier and picked up the sandals. Each was supposedly held in place by a thong which went around the ankle to be clasped in a strap on the other side. The right sandal strap was broken, pulled away from its stitching. The sandals jolted Athelstan's memory about something but, for the moment, he could not recall it.

'It looks an accident,' Cranston observed. 'The sandal could have snapped due to the fall.'

'I would agree,' Mistress Cheyne declared. 'Joycelina would never wear a broken sandal. It would be too uncomfortable.'

'True, true,' Athelstan murmured. 'Mistress Cheyne, when you and Anna were out in the yard, most of the household were supposedly dining in the refectory?'

'Yes, but before you ask, Brother, people would go to our taproom to fetch more food from the common table or fill their tankards at one of the butts.'

'Anyone in particular?'

'Brother, virtually everyone who was there; they all had to eat and drink.'

Athelstan blessed the corpse again, pulled back the sheet and returned to the main building. They climbed the staircase to the top gallery, Athelstan in the lead. He studied each step carefully. On some of the lower ones he detected flecks of blood, but nothing else. At the top he paused to examine the two newel posts, one at the end of a narrow balustrade running along the gallery, the other opposite, slightly jutting out from the wall. Both felt very secure, whilst the top of the staircase was clear and firm – nothing to explain why Joycelina had fallen.

'A simple accident,' Cranston murmured.

Athelstan stared down the staircase. It was truly dangerous. Anyone who missed their footing would sustain serious injury, yet Joycelina must have gone up and down those steps time and again. So why now? Athelstan walked into the death chamber. The bed was half stripped, the chest and coffer lids flung back. A broom and bucket rested against the wall.

'Joycelina was cleaning here,' Mistress Cheyne explained again. 'We wanted to put matters right.'

Athelstan went back up the staircase. Had Joycelina been up here alone, he wondered, or had someone else been waiting for her to leave? A sudden push, maybe? And could her death be connected to that of Whitfield? Perhaps Joycelina had seen something. If so, had she tried to blackmail someone here at the Golden Oliphant and been murdered to silence her threatening mouth?

'Brother, are you suspicious?' Cranston came up beside him.

'As ever, but let us return to the refectory.'

The people waiting there were now growing restless. Athelstan noticed how easy it was for someone to slip in and out of the taproom. He made sure they were all present and asked about Joycelina's death. Each protested how they had been here for the evening meal just after the vespers bell and knew nothing about the mishap. The only exception was Anna, a wiry young woman with a high-pitched voice and ever blinking eyes. She confirmed in ringing tones everything Mistress Cheyne had said.

'You reached the foot of the stairs?' Cranston asked her.

'Joycelina was just lying there,' Anna's voice was almost a screech, 'body all twisted.'

'Was her sandal broken?'

'I didn't notice, Sir John. It was her neck, the terrible marks on her face . . . I ran to the mistress; she came and . . .'

'And so did I.' Griffin spoke up. 'It was obvious Joycelina was dead. I arranged for the poor woman's corpse to be moved to the outhouse.'

'Remind me,' Cranston asked, 'when was this?'

'The vespers bell had sounded,' Mistress Cheyne declared wearily, 'the curfew was imposed. Anyway, I sent a message to the Guildhall but you were not there.'

Athelstan plucked at Cranston's sleeve. 'Sir John, I believe we can go no further on this, not now, not here.'

They made to leave when Athelstan felt a tug on his shoulder. He turned. Stretton, angry faced, jabbed a finger.

'Friar, I have to be gone.' Behind him stood Odo Gray and an equally truculent Matthias Camoys. Cranston stepped between Athelstan and Stretton, poking the mailed clerk in the chest.

'Stay, Master Stretton, stay, Master Gray, stay, Master Camoys. Stay with us all until this matter is resolved. Until then you have a choice: remain here or lie in Newgate. Rest assured, that is not a threat but a solemn promise.'

Cranston grasped Athelstan's arm and they left the Golden Oliphant. Outside, they stood beneath the ornate sign as the friar ensured his chancery satchel was properly buckled and the coroner, still huffing over the sudden confrontation, adjusted his warbelt.

'Sir John, you have other business,' Athelstan murmured. 'I know you must confer with those who protect our king. I also have matters to attend to. I need to reflect, to study, to pray. I will not return to St Erconwald's; you will find me at Blackfriars . . .'

PART FOUR

'Secreta Negotia: *Secret Business.*'

Athelstan loved the library and scriptorium at his mother house – two long chambers with a meeting hall in between – a world adorned with oaken tables, lecterns, chairs and shelves, all shimmered to a shine with beeswax. The delicious odours of leather, freshly scrubbed parchment, polish, pure candle smoke, incense and trails of sweet fragrances from the crushed herbs wafted everywhere. Chambers of delight where even the sunshine was transformed as it poured through the gorgeous stained-glass windows to illuminate the long walk between shelves piled high with manuscripts, calfskin-backed books, ledgers and leather-covered tomes, some of which, because of their rarity, were firmly chained to shelf or desk. Athelstan, walking up and down the library passageway, recalled his glorious days of study here. The Sentences of Abelard, the logic of Aquinas, the fiery spirit of Dominic's homilies, the poetry of Saint Bonaventure and the caustic sermons of Bernardine of Siena. Now he was here for a different purpose. London might be about to dissolve into murder and mayhem, but he had been summoned to resolve a problem, and he would do so faithfully until he reached a logical conclusion.

Athelstan returned to the table he'd sat at during his novitiate: a smooth topped, intricately carved reading table with a spigot of capped candles to hand when the light began to fade. For a while he sat in his favourite chair watching the dust motes dance in the beams streaming through the painted glass. He half listened to the sounds of Blackfriars as he summoned up the ghosts of yesteryear, scampering around this library eager to search for proof of some argument he was drawing up in philosophy, scripture or theology. He recalled the sheer exuberance of such days, his dedication to his studies, the intense conversations he had with his brethren. Now all was different. Even Blackfriars had been caught up in the coming storm. Prior Anselm was distracted, while the librarian and the master of this scriptorium were deeply concerned about any threat to their beloved repository of books. Athelstan crossed himself, sighed and returned to the problems which confronted him. He was in the best place to try and resolve the enigmas and puzzles left by Reginald Camoys. He needed to do this so he could confront Matthias with his gnawing suspicions as well as ensure that these riddles were not connected in any way with the mysterious deaths at the Golden Oliphant.

Athelstan was certain Whitfield had been murdered, and the same for Joycelina. He had no evidence regarding the young woman's deadly fall, just a suspicion that a very cunning murder had been committed. He stared up at the shelves of books and manuscripts. Where should he begin? He had questioned both librarian and the master of the scriptorium, yet both brothers had been unable to assist. Athelstan tapped his fingers on the table top. If this was a question of scripture, where would he begin? He rose and found the library's great lexicon, but though he easily discovered an explanation for 'IHS', the Greek title given to Jesus Christ, he could not explain the additional 'V'. He then turned to the many entries on 'sol, sun' and came to an extract from the history of Eusebius of Caesarea who wrote about the Emperor Constantine and the establishment of Christianity as the state religion of the Roman Empire. The library owned a copy of this. Athelstan found it and, as he turned the pages, felt a deep glow of satisfaction. The '*Soli Invicto*' was a paean to the sun which lay at the heart of the pagan religion of Mithras, popular with the Roman army and undoubtedly something that Reginald Camoys had discovered amongst those ruins in the crypt of St Mary Le Bow.

Athelstan reached one chapter of Eusebius' History and clapped his hands in joy. He had found it! The well-known story of a famous vision that the Emperor Constantine had experienced before his great victory at the Milvian Bridge in the year 312. The letters 'IHSV' were an abbreviation for '*In Hoc Signo Vinces* – In this sign you will conquer'. He then consulted a word book, wondering if Reginald had continued to hide behind a play on words. '*Vinces*' in Latin was 'you will conquer', but '*vinceris*' could be translated 'you will be released'. What did that refer to?

He sat and reflected on the clever word games that contrived to hide a treasure. In many ways they might have little relevance to the mysterious deaths at the Golden Oliphant, though they did prompt some interesting questions.

First, the Cross of Lothar was a great treasure, stolen from a powerful religious military order. Yet there was not a shred of evidence to show that the Teutonic Knights tried to secure its return. Why not? Secondly, Mistress Elizabeth Cheyne, God bless her, had a heart of steel, a grasping woman who would never allow profit to escape her, yet she seemed totally impervious to Lothar's Cross and its whereabouts. Surely she of all people knew the mind of her dead lover, yet she showed no interest in the riddles he had left or the possibility that a priceless treasure, hidden in her own house, might be seized by young Matthias. Or was she just waiting for him to complete the hunt and then claim the cross as rightfully hers? Thirdly, why had Amaury Whitfield, desperately trying to escape all the snares around him, offered to help Matthias resolve the enigmas bequeathed by his uncle? Finally, what did the letters 'IHSV' really refer to? Why was it linked to the rising sun? Athelstan recalled all he knew about Reginald Camoys as he watched a shaft of light pour through one of the stained-glass windows and shimmer on the great spread eagle, carved out of bronze, on a lectern further down the library. He stared, then started to laugh at the solution which now emerged. Elated, he rose to his feet and paced up and down the empty library, revelling in the sweet odours and the beautiful light, the companionship of written treasures piled high on the shelves around him.

'So,' he whispered, 'if what I think is true, and I am sure it is, why did Whitfield try and help Matthias Camoys; what is the connection?' He paused, recalling what Grindcobbe had told him, then thought of Whitfield's shabby, empty chambers: those small caskets and coffers, broken up and thrown on the rubbish heap in that derelict garden.

'I wonder . . .' he murmured. 'Matthias Camoys was determined to find the cross and Amuary Whitfield was equally determined to escape. What would unite them? What would motivate this feck-less clerk – gold, or threats?'

He decided to calm his mind by joining the brothers in the

friary church for divine office. He walked across and borrowed
a psalter, then took his place in a stall, leaning back against
the wood and gazing at the great cross above the high altar. The
cantor began the hymn of praise, 'He is happy, who is blessed
by Jacob's God.' The brothers in the stalls replied, 'My soul give
praise to the Lord.' Athelstan tried to concentrate on the responses,
but every time he lifted his head he glimpsed the contorted faces
of the babewyns and gargoyles carved on the rim of a nearby
pillar. Each carried a standard and a trumpet and reminded
Athelstan of the Herald of Hell. The identity of that miscreant,
the friar reflected, had nothing to do with the mysterious deaths
at the Golden Oliphant or St Erconwald's. Nevertheless, if he
could discover who the Herald was, it might make it easier to
persuade Sir Everard Camoys to cooperate over Athelstan's deepening suspicions about the goldsmith's son.

Once divine office was over Athelstan returned to the library.
He took a scrap of parchment and drew a rough sketch of London
Bridge.

'Herald of Hell,' he whispered, 'you appeared here at the dead
of night even though the bridge is sealed and closely guarded
after curfew. So how did you get on to the bridge then leave?'
He stared at his rough drawing. He could not imagine anyone
swimming the treacherous Thames in the dead of night, climbing
the slippery starlings and supports beneath the bridge and then,
marvellous to say, leaving the bridge in the same fashion. 'So,'
Athelstan murmured, 'perhaps you live on the bridge? However,
if you wish to appear in this ward and that long after the chimes
of midnight, the same problems have to be confronted.' He
paused, fingers to his lips as he recalled Sir Everard's assertion
that he had recognized the bawling voice, just as those men in
that alehouse had recognized the voice of Meryen the bailiff.
Athelstan tapped the parchment. There was only one logical
conclusion, surely? He reviewed his evidence. 'If there is only
one possible conclusion,' he whispered to himself, 'then that
conclusion must be the correct one.'

Chewing the corner of his lip, he reflected on the murders of
Whitfield, Lebarge and Joycelina. He was convinced all three
deaths were connected, and possibly the work of the same
assassin. However, he could not detect a pattern in anything he had

seen, heard or felt. Nevertheless, somewhere hidden in all of this there might be a mistake by the murderer which he could seize on. Athelstan returned, once more, to the laborious task of listing everything he could recall about Whitfield, Lebarge and Joycelina, though by the time the bells chimed for compline he had made little headway. At last he admitted defeat and left the library to its keeper, who was anxious to douse the lights and lock the doors. Athelstan crossed to the refectory for a bowl of hot stew and some bread. He decided he would need to rise early the next morning, so he visited the church, said a few prayers, then adjourned to the cloister cell assigned to him.

Athelstan reached the Golden Oliphant at least an hour before dawn and was admitted by a tousle-haired Foxley, who complained of the early hour. Athelstan simply smiled his thanks and said he wished to walk the tavern. Foxley, sighing with annoyance, said he would kennel the mastiffs in the garden and open doors for the friar so he could go where he wished. Athelstan accepted this as well as some bread, cheese and dried meat to break his fast. For a while he sat in the refectory facing the window, watching the darkness dissipate. He had celebrated an early mass at Blackfriars and despatched a courier with urgent messages for Sir John, though of course his enquiries also depended on what he discovered here. Time was passing! He went out of the main door and stared up at the sign. The insignia of the huge Golden Oliphant was reproduced on both sides, the curved drinking cup capped with a lid on which a silver-green cross stood. The sign itself was a perfect square, the casing on each side about four to five inches wide, though it was difficult to be accurate as the sign hung high from the projecting arm of a soaring post. Despite the poor light and height, Athelstan noticed that both the white background and the Oliphant were clear of dirt and dust, probably due to the costly sealing paint used. As he had suspected, he realized that for a brief moment the sign would hang directly in the path of the rising sun which, according to the fiery-red glow in the eastern sky, was imminent.

He returned to the brothel along the passageways, through the Golden Hall and the spread of chambers beyond: the refectory, buttery, kitchens, scullery, pantry and bakery. The household were now stirring. Mistress Elizabeth Cheyne and the moppets, together with slatterns, scullions and tapboys, all milled about preparing for a new day. Mistress Cheyne, supervising the firing of the ovens, smiled with her lips and half raised a hand. Others just scuttled away from this sharp-eyed friar who seemed to be hunting someone or something in their house. Athelstan reached the back door. Master Griffin was in the garden with a basket of herbs. He assured Athelstan that the dogs were kennelled and pointed to the wooden palisade jutting out from the rear of the building.

'They will be fed and then sleep there for the rest of the day,' Griffin muttered. 'Don't you worry, Father, I wouldn't be out here with those savage beasts on the loose.' Athelstan thanked him and walked across the garden to where the workmen had been setting up the trellis fencing. He was now moving to the front of the Golden Oliphant and he could see the sign clearly. He walked a little further and smiled at sight of the flower-covered arbour with its turfed seat. He sat down.

'Of course,' he breathed, 'Reginald Camoys used this arbour and I shall do the same.'

Athelstan watched the sun strengthen and rise. The Golden Oliphant sign was directly in its path and, for a short while, blocked the fiery circle. Athelstan smiled even as he marvelled at the golden glow which appeared through the cross-piece of the crucifix which decorated the lid of the Oliphant, piercing it clearly as it would translucent glass. Athelstan revelled in the sheer beauty of the sight, then the moment passed. Distracted by what he had seen and learnt, the friar rose to his feet, but then froze at a low, throaty growl. He turned slightly. The two hunting mastiffs stood staring at him, great beasts with their tawny, short-haired bodies, powerful legs, massive heads and ferocious jaws. They stood poised, then one of them edged forward, belly going slightly down, and the other followed suit. Athelstan retreated back into the arbour. Childhood terrors returned. Memories of a similar confrontation years ago on a neighbour's farm. The hounds were certainly edging forward. Athelstan kept still, trying hard not to stare at them, recalling his father's advice on how to deal with such animals.

'Gaudete! Laetare!' Athelstan glanced up. Foxley appeared along the path to the arbour.

'Gaudete! Laetare!' He repeated the dog's names. 'Come! Come!'

Athelstan breathed a sigh of relief. Both mastiffs relaxed, turning away, tails wagging, heads down as they trotted to meet Foxley. He shared some biscuit with them, then, whistling softly, led them away. Athelstan waited until Foxley returned, sauntering down the path, crossbow in one hand, a quiver of bolts hanging on the warbelt around his waist. Athelstan scrutinized the Master of Horse closely: the scuffed, black leather jerkin, leggings and boots, the dark brown shirt, open at the neck, the wrist guard on his left arm, the quizzical look on that sardonic face. Athelstan recalled Benedicta's remark about putting on a mask to meet other masks. Foxley's mask had slipped. You are a fighter, Athelstan reflected, a man of war, and, if Sir John is correct, an Upright Man.

'Well, Brother?'

'Well, Master Foxley. I thought the hounds were kennelled?'

'They were.'

'And?'

'Brother, anyone could have slipped out of the kitchen, drawn the bolts and lifted the latch. You were lucky. The mastiffs are tired after a night's prowling. They have also eaten.' He smiled. 'They probably recognized the smell of the Golden Oliphant on you. But,' he slipped the arbalest on to the hook on his belt, 'still very, very dangerous.'

'And you just happened to take a walk in the garden with a crossbow, a quiver of quarrels and some biscuit for your two friends?'

Foxley laughed and drew closer.

'You are the Upright Men's representative here, aren't you?' Athelstan demanded. Foxley just hunched his shoulders.

'I asked a question,' Athelstan insisted.

Foxley came and sat beside Athelstan. 'I am what you say I am. Yes, I followed you into the garden because I am under strict orders. My masters in the Great Community of the Realm want you kept safe in this place of sudden, mysterious death. I watched you go out. I was in a chamber on the third gallery; I saw Gaudete and Laetare slipping through the garden like demons on the hunt. And, before you ask, Brother, no, I do not know who released the mastiffs. It could be anybody here.'

'Did you question Whitfield?'

'Of course, the Upright Men gave Whitfield silver and gold. We suspected he was about to flee. We were keen to retrieve the cipher he carried and any other secret information.' Foxley eased off his warbelt and sat watching the first bees of the day cluster above a flower bed. He pointed up to the window of Whitfield's chamber. 'I know the clerk was supposed to leave in the early hours to meet a captain of the Upright Men, but I was ordered not to show my hand or interfere in any way, so I didn't. Once Whitfield left the Golden Hall that evening I lost interest in him and became deep in my cups. I tell you this, Brother: Whitfield was frightened as any coney being hunted in a wheat field. He refused to talk. The only people he really conversed with were the moppets, the ship's captain and Matthias Camoys. Why he paid attention to that dream-catcher, I do not know. I believe the Upright Men would have let him go provided he returned the secret manuscripts he carried.' Foxley rose, gripping the heavy warbelt. 'Now *my* questions, Brother. What were you doing in the garden – not just watching the sun rise, I assume?'

'Oh, very much so.' Athelstan gestured for Foxley to accompany him back into the Golden Oliphant. 'Indeed, I have a task for you, several in fact. First,' he pointed back at the sign, 'I want that taken down and brought to the court chamber of Sir John Cranston at the Guildhall.'

'Is that really necessary?'

'Yes, it's very necessary. Tell Mistress Cheyne to comply or I will return with bailiffs and a writ. She also must accompany her property to the Guildhall, where she will joined by other people.' Athelstan waved a hand. 'Of course she will object, but she either comes of her own accord or faces an official summons and all that entails. Do you understand?' Foxley grimaced but agreed. 'However,' Athelstan continued, 'do not say anything until I have gone. Now . . .' He turned to face the Master of Horse. 'I am truly grateful for what you did. If it had not been for you I might have been wounded or even killed.' He pointed towards the Golden Oliphant. 'Somebody there wants me silenced, which only deepens my suspicions about these horrid deaths.'

'Murders?' Foxley queried.

'Yes, my friend, heinous murder, which is why my last question to you is so important. Did you see, hear or learn anything suspicious on the evening before Whitfield died?'

'No, Brother, I did not. True, like many of the others I became drunk, but not blind to what was happening around me. I glimpsed and heard nothing untoward.'

'And the morning after?'

'It was as I described. Whitfield's chamber was bolted, barred and locked both door and window. When the chamber was forced it was as black as pitch inside, but I shall never forget that dangling corpse. If it wasn't suicide, how did the assassin enter and leave so easily? I know the Golden Oliphant. There are no secret entrances, the chamber doors hang heavy and sturdy. No one heard or saw anything amiss.'

'You did.'

'Brother?'

'You said Whitfield did not look so fat in death.'

'Yes, that's what I thought. Strange, especially as I've seen enough people hang – their bellies always swell out. Why do you ask me that?'

'Oh, the answer is quite simple, Master Foxley. Whitfield may have been wearing a money belt,' Athelstan tapped the warbelt Foxley carried, 'thick and heavy with small pouches or wallets along the side, each crammed with coins.

'Of course,' Foxley whispered, 'if he was fleeing abroad he would need every silver piece he could seize and he would carry it like that.'

'Which is why,' Athelstan pointed across at the brothel, 'he and Lebarge chose chambers on the top gallery, safer, more secure against any attempt to seize his ill-gotten wealth. Now, Master Foxley, I thank you again. I would like to continue my wandering. Once I leave, please carry out my instructions.'

Foxley promised he would and Athelstan watched him go. Much as he was grateful to the Master of Horse, Athelstan remained deeply suspicious. Was Foxley protecting him or just creating the opportunity to curry favour? The Master of Horse could still be involved in Whitfield's murder. After all, the Upright Men, like Stretton's master Arundel, had probably lavished Whitfield with bribes. Was the clerk's death an act of revenge,

or an attempt to reclaim money spent? How many people would
know that Whitfield would strap a veritable treasure about his
waist? Whitfield would surely hide this from any whore or the
likes of the pirate Odo Gray, so who else? The belt must have
been fastened tight, hence the marks Brother Philippe had found
on Whitfield's corpse.

Athelstan entered the kitchen, now a hive of activity, and heads
turned but little acknowledgement was made. He went down a
passageway and had to almost push past Odo Gray and Stretton,
who, surly faced and mice-eyed, were making their way along
to the refectory. Once he was free of them, Athelstan paused at
the foot of the staircase to recall everything he had been told
about what had happened the morning Whitfield's chamber was
forced. He imagined Mistress Cheyne, Foxley and the two
labourers going up to the gallery, Joycelina quietening the maids
and the rest supposedly kept in the refectory under the watchful
eye of Griffin. All except for Lebarge, who had apparently slipped
away and climbed to the third gallery to listen to the door being
forced. Athelstan concentrated on recalling everything Lebarge
had told him and felt a tingle of excitement at one fact which
did not fit in with the rest.

He climbed the staircase until he reached the third gallery,
then stood in the recess as Lebarge must have done and half-
cocked his head, as if listening to the sounds from the gallery
above. In his mind he listed all he had learnt, comparing and
contrasting accounts. He glanced at the sharp-edged, steep set of
stairs and imagined Joycelina at the top. Did she trip, was she
pushed, or rendered unconscious then thrown down to smash her
head and break her neck? He murmured a requiem, crossed
himself and made to leave, slipping out of the tavern as quietly
as he had arrived.

Athelstan walked quickly down to the riverside, moving into
the seedy world of Southwark's stews and brothels, serving every
kind of taste: shabby cook shops and even shabbier alehouses
lined the narrow, dark, evil-smelling alleyways. The sun had
risen, so the denizens of the mumpers' castles, the hideaways,
secret cellars and dank dungeons were hurrying home, all the
night walkers and dark dwellers fleeing from the light. Athelstan
glimpsed white, bony faces peering out of tattered cowls or

battered hoods. Strumpets of every variety, shaven heads hidden beneath colourful wigs, retreated back into shadow-filled door-ways. Traders and hucksters who sold rancid meat, green-tinged bread and rotting vegetables to the very poor, now emptied their slops on to the midden heaps. By nightfall they would have refilled them with whatever scraps they scrounged or stole from the stalls and shops in the city. Funeral processions formed to take their dead to the different requiem masses in this chantry chapel or that. Even in death money mattered. The poor had to club together to send a collection of corpses soaked in pine juice and sheathed in simple canvas or linen sheets on death carts pulled by a couple of old nags with black feathers nodding between their ears. Priests, clothed in purple and gold vestments, moved in clouds of incense whilst altar boys scurried either side ringing handbells as the celebrants intoned the dreadful words from the sequence of the requiem Mass:

'Oh day of wrath, oh day of mourning,
See fulfilled heaven's warning . . .'

This simple plea for heaven's favour was drowned by the cries and shouts of traders and tinkers, watermen and milkmaids. The screams of whores, the curses of bailiffs, the tramp of booted feet, the neighing of horses and the rattling of carts and barrows all filled the air. Southwark was coming to life. Justice was also making itself felt. The cages for drunkards, rifflers and sleep shatterers were filling rapidly under the strident orders of beadles. The stocks were already full of miscreants fastened tight to receive all the humiliation heaped on them by passers-by. Two hangings had already taken place. House breakers, caught red-handed, now dangled from a twisted tavern sign. Nearby the fraternity of corpse-collectors were busy cleaning up the grisly remains of the river thief, taken and summarily condemned to be decapitated on the corner of a cobbled lane leading down to the quayside.

Athelstan sidestepped the mob gathering around this gruesome sight and strode purposefully on to the wharf. At least here the air was fresher. He eagerly breathed in the salty, fishy tang of the riverside, then found a waiting barge, agreed a price and clambered in. The craft pulled away. Sweaty and still slightly shaken after his confrontation with the mastiffs, Athelstan settled in the hooded stern to recite his rosary. The barge pulled alongside others bobbing on the swell. One drew very close. Athelstan paused in his prayers as a voice intoned: 'St Dunstan,' to be answered by a chorus of, 'Pray for us,' 'St Bride,' 'Pray for us,' 'St Andrew,' the litany continued. Intrigued, Athelstan stared around the canopy at the barge riding alongside with its small, fluttering banners of St Thomas Becket. He realized the passengers were pilgrims making their way across the river to visit the shrine to Becket's parents.

'What are they reciting?' he asked an oarsman.

'Why, Brother, the litany of London churches, or rather their patrons.' He indicated with his grizzled head. 'They pray for protection from all the churches which line the banks of the Thames, from St Dunstan's in the west to All Hallows in the east. A common enough practice; the Thames is treacherous, even at the best of times.'

Athelstan sat back, closed his eyes and breathed his own prayer of thanks. He believed that he would never break the cipher but at least he now understood why the saints' names were listed on that second piece of parchment and the significance of those two triangles. By the time he reached the battlemented gateway leading into the great, cobbled bailey which stretched in front of the black and white timbered Guildhall, Athelstan's speculations were hardening into a certainty. He disembarked at Queenhithe and strolled like a dream-walker through the streets leading up to Cheapside, so engrossed in his most recent discovery he was only dimly aware of what was happening around him. At first glance it was the usual Cheapside morning: market bailiffs with their white wands of office; scholars, horn-book in hand, making their way to schools in the transepts of different churches. The mixture of fresh, sweet odours from the bakeries mingled with the more pungent ones from the heaped mounds of refuse. This morning, however, was different. The Earthworms had carried out an attack on one of the Barbican houses where weapons were stored, so archers and pikemen still thronged the busy streets, grouped around knights in half-armour on their restless horses. The same was true of the City Council: the mayor and aldermen had whistled up their bully boys, who, dressed in city livery, now thronged the courtyards and buildings of the Guildhall.

Athelstan pushed his way through until he found Cranston's judgement chamber and chancery office, where Osbert Oswald, his clerk, and Simon Scrivener were busy over an indictment roll. They greeted him warmly enough, offered refreshments which he refused and took him into a small, stark ante-chamber. They assured him that Sir John had received and acted on his messages, but, for the while, the coroner was absent on royal business at the Tower. They both confirmed that certain individuals had been summoned to the Guildhall by mid-afternoon when the market bell signalled the beginning of the final hours of trading.

Athelstan thanked them, content to be left to his own devices. He took out his writing materials and narrow sheets of good vellum, four in all, each with its title, 'The Herald of Hell', 'The Cipher', 'The Cross of Lothar' and one simply titled, 'Homicide'. He ignored the third: what he had seen, heard and felt at the Golden Oliphant would be left to mature. Instead he turned to the other three but he could make little progress. Athelstan decided he would go and pray. He would sit in the Guildhall chapel and intone the '*Veni Creator Spiritus*' and ask for divine guidance.

He took direction from a candle trimmer working on the wall spigots outside and climbed the staircase, along a narrow gallery where the dust motes danced in the air. He pushed open the chapel door and entered the warm, sweet-scented chamber. Sunlight lanced the casement windows on the far wall. Incense fragranced the air. Candles spluttered in front of a statue of the Virgin. Athelstan paused at the sound of voices. Two men crouched before the sanctuary rail working to replace floor tiles which had become loose. They paused and rose as Athelstan walked across to sit on a wall bench beneath one of the windows.

'Do you want us to leave, Father? We can,' the tiler called. Athelstan peered through the light. The man was oval-faced, beetle-browed with a noticeable harelip. His companion was almost girlish in appearance with long blonde hair, clean-shaven, though Athelstan noticed the sharp, sloe eyes; the young man carried a long stave, probably used for measuring, and on his left wrist a heavy archer's guard.

'We are just working on the floor.' The tiler tapped his boots noisily, then grinned. 'If you want, Brother, you can help us. Just tap your foot along the tiles and listen for an echo.'

Athelstan smiled and shook his head. He sketched a blessing in their direction, left the chapel and returned to the room close to the coroner's judgement chamber.

Cranston eventually arrived, smacking his lips after a delicious repast in the Lamb of God, full of news about what he had been doing. The young king was now safely ensconced in the Tower. Most of the servants there had been dismissed and replaced with Cheshire archers. Only royal knights would be allowed into the King's presence. War barges lay moored, guarding the river approaches to the Tower, whilst Cranston had despatched the best horsemen with fresh mounts to take up station at taverns along the main roads into Essex and Kent.

'More than that,' he declared, taking a generous mouthful from the miraculous wineskin, 'I cannot do. Now, Brother . . .'

Athelstan informed him of his conclusions on certain matters. Cranston listened carefully, wiping his moustache with his fingers.

'Satan's tits!' he crowed when the friar had finished. 'My little ferret, you have been busy.' His smile faded. 'Those war dogs at the Golden Oliphant . . .'

'They will wait,' Athelstan replied. 'The person who released them will be caught, indicted and suffer a hideous death. Now, Sir John, let us prepare for our visitors. I will need a carpenter, a good one. I know building work is going on here, though,' he stared around, 'your chambers are as bare as any hermit's.'

'Everything is packed away,' Cranston retorted, 'stored in the arca in the cellars, great iron and steel chests; they now hold cloths, writing materials, records, pictures, crucifixes, virtually anything which can be moved.' The coroner breathed in noisily. 'The Guildhall will come under attack; its gates have been fortified. You are correct. We have hired the best craftsmen.'

He left the room then returned with a quiet-faced, sandy-haired man, Guibert Tallifer, a carpenter and leading member of the city guild. Athelstan began to explain why he needed him when there was a knock at the door and Flaxwith entered to announce the first of their visitors had arrived, along with the sign from the Oliphant, which would be laid on the great bench in Cranston's judgement chamber. They promptly adjourned there, a bleak, stark room with its blank walls and heavy oaken furniture. The Golden Oliphant sign had been placed on the judgement bench and

Athelstan explained what he wanted. Tallifer, his leather apron bristling with pockets for tools, scrutinized the sign carefully.

'It's a box,' he declared, 'a shallow box with about six inches between front and back. And, what is this?' He placed his finger into a hole piercing the cross-piece of the crucifix which decorated the lid over the Oliphant's cup. The drinking horn was delicately and accurately depicted and Athelstan had to concede that its artist, Reginald Camoys, had a God-given talent. The carpenter explained that the sides of the sign were held together by a very powerful glue. Skilfully, using hammer, wedge and chisel, Tallifer began to loosen one side. He was almost finished when Athelstan told him to pause and asked Sir John to bring up Sir Everard and Matthias Camoys along with Mistress Cheyne.

All three visitors came into the chamber exclaiming with surprise when they saw the sign and Tallifer's tools lying on top of it. Cranston demanded silence. Athelstan nodded at the carpenter to finish his work and lift the loosened side. He did so and Matthias Camoys cried with delight at the green and gold cross fixed firmly within. The cameo of the Roman emperor was carefully positioned so it lay accurately against the hole piercing the cross-piece of the crucifix on the lid of the Oliphant's cup on both sides of the sign. Athelstan firmly knocked Matthias' hand away.

'The cross is glued,' Athelstan explained, 'positioned carefully within the sign, which, in turn, was hung so as to catch the first rays of the morning sun. I saw it this morning, a shaft of pure light as you find in certain churches where a lancet window is used to guide the sunlight on to the altar.' He gestured. 'Master carpenter, if you could loosen the cross.'

Tallifer did so, swiftly and expertly, then handed the relic to Athelstan.

'I never knew!' Mistress Cheyne exclaimed.

'I don't think you ever really cared,' Athelstan retorted, holding his hand up to still her protests.

'It's mine!' Matthias lunged forward; Athelstan thrust the cross into his hands.

'You may have it, for what it's worth; it's a fake, a replica.'

'No!' Matthias looked wide-eyed at his father, who grasped

the cross, holding it up to the light. He took out a thick piece of conclave glass from his wallet and used this to peer closely at the cross, concentrating especially on the gold fretting.

'Very good,' Sir Everard murmured. 'Very fine, crafty and subtle, but you are correct, Athelstan, a most cunning forgery.'

Matthias jumped to his feet, knocking over the stool on which he was sitting. For a while Athelstan let him pace backwards and forwards before nodding at Sir John, who ordered the young man to sit down.

'You are quiet, Mistress Cheyne?' Athelstan smiled. 'You always suspected it was a forgery, a replica, didn't you?'

'Yes, I did, but I didn't have the heart to tell anyone, least of all you.' She pointed at Matthias. Athelstan noticed that she and Sir Everard had barely acknowledged each other.

'Sir Everard? Did you suspect?'

'I did wonder.' The goldsmith drew a sharp breath. 'Why the Teutonic Knights, despite their difficulties against the Easterlings, never made any attempt to recover it.'

'I followed the same logic,' Athelstan agreed, 'as you did, Mistress Cheyne. Reginald Camoys was a very skilled artist and sign maker. Formerly he had been a soldier who had lost a beloved comrade in the fighting. He stole the Cross of Lothar as some form of compensation or recompense. He brought his comrade's corpse home for solemn entombment at St Mary Le Bow. Eventually he discovered, God knows how, that what he had stolen was a replica but he still persisted with the myth. He could not destroy the artefact which, in time, became the symbol of his love for Simon Penchen. He would not willingly let such an object go. As I said, Reginald was a cultivated, educated man. He chose St Mary Le Bow to house the shrine of his fallen comrade. He would wander round that church, especially the crypt, which contains the ruins of an ancient Roman temple dedicated to a god much beloved of Roman soldiers, Mithras, the Unconquerable Sun God. He also discovered one of the most commonly used dedications to that deity, "*Soli Invicto* – to the Unconquerable Sun". At the same time he read or recalled the famous story about the Emperor Constantine, the first Christian emperor who converted after he experienced a vision of the Cross with the message, "*In Hoc Signo Vinces* – In this Sign you will

conquer." Constantine did; he won the battle of the Milvian
Bridge and replaced Mithras with Christ. Reginald Camoys, a
former soldier, would relish such a story, yet he had also learned
that the cross he had stolen was a mere replica, so, instead of
publishing the truth and destroying the symbol,' Athelstan tapped
the brothel sign, 'he had this made and the replica placed carefully inside so that the cameo at the centre would catch the first
rays of the rising sun. Reginald, on a fine morning like this,
would love nothing better than to sit in the garden of the Golden
Oliphant and watch that flash of light, is that not so, Mistress
Cheyne?'

'True, true,' she murmured, not lifting her head. 'The sign was
fashioned a few years before Reginald's death. At the same time,
those carvings appeared in the Golden Oliphant and the chantry
chapel of St Mary Le Bow.' She sniffed. 'Always a dreamer,
always mischievous, Reginald loved his dead comrade Simon
Penchen more than me.' Athelstan caught her deep bitterness of
loss. 'Always,' she continued in a whisper, 'full of fanciful ideas.'

'One final twist,' Athelstan added. 'The original quotation uses
the word, "*Vinces* – you will conquer"; Reginald changed it
slightly using the word, "*Vinceris*", or at least that's my educated
guess, so the inscription reads, "In this sign you will be released."
Reginald was actually addressing Lothar's Cross, bidding it an
affectionate farewell as well as challenging those who knew him
to find the cross and release it from the sign. A much more
pleasing prospect than having to admit its true worth. Reginald
wove a complex tale to satisfy himself as well as leave secret
puzzles, riddles and enigmas behind him.' Athelstan pointed at
Matthias. 'He also wanted you to use your brain, your wits, on
something better than drinking and wenching.'

'Reginald should have been a minstrel, a troubadour,' Sir
Everard declared. 'I did have my suspicions for the very same
reasons you did, Brother Athelstan. So we have the truth. But
you have summoned me here for more than this, I suspect.'

Athelstan turned to the carpenter who had sat fascinated at
what was being discussed. 'Master Tallifer, I thank you. Submit
all reasonable expenses to Sir John at the Guildhall and he will
ensure you receive speedy reimbursement.'

The carpenter collected his tools and rose. 'I have heard similar tales,' he declared, 'about signs containing some secret.' He grinned. 'But not like this.'

'Mistress Cheyne,' Athelstan gestured at the sign, 'Master Tallifer can also claim for rehanging the sign.'

She nodded, licked thin, dry lips and rose to her feet. 'I can go now?'

'You certainly can,' Cranston declared. 'I will arrange for the sign to be returned to the waiting cart. Master Foxley, I understand, accompanied you here?'

Athelstan rose and crossed to the window, staring down into the cobbled bailey where Foxley stood next to a cart. He half listened as Tallifer, Mistress Cheyne and Guildhall servants removed the sign from the judgement chamber. Once the door had closed behind them, Cranston resumed his seat in the coroner's chair; Athelstan sat on a bench facing Sir Everard and Matthias.

'I asked a question, Brother,' Sir Everard demanded. 'Why have I been summoned here?'

'Why indeed?' Athelstan retorted. 'I shall be brief. To assist your liege lord the King and his ministers, such as Sir John here, to resolve certain murderous mysteries and so bring the perpetrators to justice.'

'I have nothing to do with the deaths at the Golden Oliphant.'

'Yes and no, Sir Everard. But first let me try and win your favour as well as alert you,' Athelstan glanced quickly at Matthias, 'to a possible danger you might face. Sir John, you have the bailiff from Sir Everard's ward ready for us?'

'Poulter?'

'Yes, Master Poulter, and a speaking horn.'

Cranston, whom Athelstan had carefully instructed, left the chamber. He returned shortly afterwards grasping a very frightened Poulter by the arm as well as carrying a hollow, metal tube similar to a tournament trumpet.

'Master Poulter,' Athelstan gestured at the stool facing the judgement table, 'sit down.' The friar took the speaking horn from Cranston and placed it between his feet. Poulter, all sweat-soaked and quivering, glanced at this and moaned quietly. 'Master Poulter,' Athelstan began, 'I do not wish to torture you or put you to the question, but that could be arranged in the dungeons below, is that not so, Sir John?' The coroner nodded. 'You have a family, Master Poulter?'

'A wife and five children.'

'You are a city official?'

'Yes.'

'You have heard of the Herald of Hell?'

'Of course,' Poulter stammered.

'You *are* the Herald of Hell,' Athelstan accused.

'I am not! I had no choice!' Poulter's head went down and he began to sob.

'What is this?' Sir Everard demanded. 'Poulter is loyal and true. He came to my . . .' His voice faded away.

'To be accurate and honest,' Athelstan continued, 'you, Master Poulter, are simply one of the many Heralds of Hell plaguing the good citizens of this city. Let me tell you about my friend Robert Burdon, keeper of London Bridge. He, too, was visited at the dead of night by the Herald of Hell. Now I reasoned that either the Herald had braved the waters of the Thames to arrive or depart, or that he actually lived on the bridge. However, I also discovered, thanks to the good offices of Sir John, that on the same night Burdon was visited, the Herald of Hell was active in Farringdon ward. Despite his title, I know that the Herald cannot fly. He certainly did not walk the waters of the Thames, so the only logical conclusion was that he lived and worked on the bridge, as he did in Farringdon, in Cheapside and elsewhere. In other words, the Herald of Hell was truly legion. So who could he be?

'The only individual who walks the streets of London in the dead of night is the ward bailiff. I suspect the Upright Men, to further and to deepen what I call "the Great Fear", suborned these city officials with dire threats against themselves and their families both now and when the Great Revolt occurs. The task assigned to them was simple. A named house would be given along with a doggerel verse, a beaker full of pig's blood and sharpened stalks bearing the same number of onions as there were individuals in that particular household. In Sir Everard's case, there were two. The bailiff concerned would also be given a simple speaking horn which, together with the other paraphernalia, would be carefully hidden away. At some godforsaken hour of the night, when doors and shutters betray no chink of light, the bailiff, suborned and terrified, would choose his time. The jar of blood with its grisly warning would be left outside the door of the chosen victim. The bailiff, hidden in the shadows and armed with a simple speaking horn, would bray a blast and deliver the warning learnt by rote. A horn like this,' Athelstan tapped the one resting between his feet, 'would disguise his voice. Once finished, taking advantage of the darkness and chaos caused, the speaking horn would be hidden away for collection and the bailiff could now act the conscientious, loyal city official. The damage is done. The fear deepens. Security is threatened. People panic. They will either flee or try to seek accommodation with the hidden power of the Upright Men.

'Sir Everard was different, a veteran soldier made of sterner stuff. More importantly, because of his acute sense of hearing, Sir Everard recognized the voice despite the speaking horn, but he could not place it. He would never dream it was the faithful, loyal wardsman, but it was you, Master Poulter. And the damage you and your kind have perpetrated cannot be undone.'

'So the Herald of Hell is like the hydra of antiquity, many-headed?'

'Yes, Sir Everard, but,' Athelstan shrugged, 'in origin, the Herald of Hell could be one person. Such an individual acts out his title: suborns the watchmen, instructs them on what to do and gives his victims the necessary means to carry it out. Yes, I believe that's a strong possibility.' Athelstan paused. He did not wish to reveal more than necessary, but he secretly wondered if Reynard, the Upright Men's courier, had been bringing that cipher to the real Herald of Hell here in London when he had been caught.

'Anyway, Master Poulter,' Athelstan continued briskly, 'I have spoken the truth. You agree?' The bailiff was now quivering like a child. Athelstan winked at Cranston, indicating with his hand that gentleness was the best way forward. 'I have spoken the truth, Master Poulter?'

'Yes.' The bailiff sighed. 'Yes, you have, but what now?'

'Nothing,' Cranston declared, glaring at Sir Everard. 'You were placed under powerful duress. You could have put more trust in the Crown, though,' the coroner added bitterly. 'That trust is becoming a rarer commodity by the day. So go, Master Poulter. Have nothing more to do with the Upright Men. Tomorrow, you and all the ward bailiffs from the city will be summoned here to listen to good counsel and practical advice: those who admit their guilt and purge themselves will be warned and let go. Any who resist must face the consequences. Now you can leave.'

Poulter scuttled from the room. Once the door had closed, Sir Everard clapped his hands slowly. 'Excellent, Brother Athelstan, Sir John, very clever! The Upright Men forced city officials to spread fear and foreboding.'

'Oh, we have more,' Athelstan declared. 'We questioned Poulter in front of you to show you our good will. To reassure you that, as with Poulter, we shall not issue any indictment against you.'

'For what? Sir John, what is this?'

The coroner slouched in his judgement chair and took a swig from his miraculous wineskin. 'Amaury Whitfield. He lodged money with you, did he not?'

'Many do.'

'Sir Everard,' Athelstan warned, 'do not play games. We have shown you our good will. Now you may answer to us or to the Barons of the Exchequer who, under orders from Master Thibault, may move to issue a summons for you to appear before the King's Bench.'

Sir Everard glanced quickly at his son, who sat cowed, then he shrugged.

'Good,' Athelstan declared, 'now let me tell you what happened. Whitfield was a high-ranking chancery clerk in the household of Gaunt's principal henchman. Every quarter he would receive monies, robes and whatever purveyance he needed, not enough to make him wealthy but certainly comfortable enough. Whitfield often visited you on his master's business. Then, sometime in the past, he began to deposit monies with you. At first there was no problem, until these deposits increased in both content and frequency. Whitfield was crafty. He knew that his monies would be lodged under a symbol rather than his own title, that is how you bankers and goldsmiths do business. Whitfield's entries could be filed under the name of a flower, a precious stone or place name. He also knew that, according to the laws of your own guild, copied from the great Italian bankers such as the Frescobaldi of Florence, complete confidentiality and trust are the order of the day, the cornerstone of good business. You, however, grew increasingly uncomfortable. Here is a very high-ranking clerk in the service of the sinister Thibault, depositing monies, the origins of which are highly suspect. Should Thibault suspect, should he investigate and discover the truth, you could be depicted as Whitfield's accomplice.'

Athelstan held the gaze of this powerful goldsmith caught in toils not of his making. 'You are an honourable man, Sir Everard. I feel truly sorry for you. To cut to the quick, you told Whitfield you could no longer be his banker, and that is your right. You filled money coffers and caskets with what was due to him and told him to protect these as best he could. Whitfield had no choice. I suspect he kept such caskets in a secure, secret place at his lodgings. A few days ago, Whitfield left for the Cokayne Festival which was, and I tell you this in confidence, only a ploy to hide the fact that he and Lebarge intended to flee the kingdom. He also intended to dirty the waters deeper by disguising his desertion under a fake death, possibly suicide somewhere along the Thames. In the meantime, Whitfield must conceal his ill-gotten gains. You, Sir Everard, suspected quite rightly that such monies were lavish bribes paid by different parties to learn Master Thibault's secrets.

'Anyway, bereft of a banker and getting ready to flee, Master Whitfield had a thick, heavy money belt strapped around his waist, its pouches crammed with silver and gold. Little wonder he and Lebarge hired a chamber on the fourth gallery. He wanted to make matters more secure. That heavy money belt also explains one witness's observation that Whitfield looked slimmer in death than in life. Of course the money belt had been removed, stolen. Nevertheless, it left its mark on Whitfield's belly and flanks. Brother Philippe at Smithfield observed these marks when he scrutinized the corpse. Now Whitfield's death does not concern you, but your son is a different matter.'

Athelstan turned to the sullen-looking Matthias. 'Blackmail,' Athelstan declared. Matthias sat unmoving, his arms folded, glaring at the floor. 'Blackmail,' Athelstan repeated. 'You, sir, were waiting for Whitfield at the Golden Oliphant. You may have suspected that he was about to flee. You'd certainly learnt about the monies deposited with your father. You gave Whitfield a choice. He was a trained clerk, skilled in ciphers. He would either help solve the riddles confronting you about Lothar's Cross or you would denounce him to Thibault.'

'Matthias!' his father exclaimed.

'Am I correct?' Athelstan demanded. 'Or must I have you arrested?'

'On what charge?'

'Quite a few,' Cranston interjected.

'What is it you want?'

'The truth, Matthias, or what you know of it.'

Matthias squirmed uneasily on the stool. 'Whitfield was set on disappearing; Lebarge, too. They'd both been terrified by the visit from the Herald of Hell.' He laughed sharply. 'If they had only known the truth. Anyway, Whitfield did have a treasure belt about him and he was fearful of being robbed.'

'By whom?'

'In God's name, Brother, anyone. He was apprehensive about Stretton, Foxley, who seemed to be bothering him, nor did he trust Odo Gray, but he believed once he was on board the *Leaping Horse* along with Mistress Cheyne and her household, all might be well. He was most cordial with the moppets as was Lebarge, who was much taken with the whore Hawisa. Of course Whitfield was terrified that Thibault would find out about his plans. He had not decided, so he confided in me, whether he should arrange an apparent suicide or an accident along the Thames.'

'Ah,' Athelstan intervened, 'that explains the contradiction and confusion I have noticed.'

'Whitfield had yet to commit himself; he changed like a weather vane.' Matthias shook his head. 'Suicide, accident? Suicide, accident? He couldn't decide, nor how he was to arrange it. Eventually he went to the Tavern of Lost Souls to continue pawning valuable objects he could not take with him. I understand he had begun that in the days before he arrived at the Golden Oliphant. However, Whitfield also wanted Mephistopheles' help in arranging his disappearance. He talked about taking a bundle of clothing down to the Thames on the evening of the very day he was found hanging. These were to be used in whatever death he staged. I also know that he had drawn up a note hinting at suicide. I don't think he had fully decided on what to do. He needed Mephistopheles' advice.' Matthias drew in a deep breath. 'I suspect he may have even been considering another plan.'

'Such as?'

'Oh, just to walk out of the Golden Oliphant and disappear of his own accord. Brother Athelstan, there are other cogs which would have taken him to different ports, not just Flanders but Castile, even the Middle Sea.'

'And Lebarge?'

'A rift had grown between them. Lebarge was much taken with Hawisa. I believe he wanted her to be with him whatever happened.'

'And the riddles about the Cross of Lothar?' Cranston demanded. 'Did he offer any solution?'

'He said he had certain ideas. Whether he did or not, I cannot say. He scrutinized the carvings both here and at St Mary Le Bow. Nothing remarkable, except he added something strange.'

'What?'

'He told me to be very careful of that church, not to be there by myself or be seen prying about it.'

'Yes,' Athelstan smiled, 'he would say that, wouldn't he? And you know what, Matthias? Because of the help you have given us, I am going to ask the Lord High Coroner here to overlook your indiscretions and those of your father.' He waved his hand. 'You may take the replica and leave. However,' Athelstan held up the cross as if taking an oath, 'I have no proof of this, no evidence, not a shred, but thank God you did not meet Whitfield together with Mephistopheles at the Tavern of Lost Souls.'

'Why?'

'Ask yourself,' Athelstan said quietly, 'why you had to meet him there. Why not somewhere in the Golden Oliphant or a place nearby?' Athelstan shrugged. 'You blackmailed Whitfield. You were one of the few people who knew all about his wealth and its highly illicit source. I often make a mistake. I believe people behave more logically than they actually do. Whitfield was agitated about how he should disappear, where, when and with whom. I do not know the truth of it. However, on one thing he was decided: he would vanish. Mephistopheles could certainly help him with this, make all the arrangements, including the mysterious disappearance of someone whom Whitfield regarded as dangerous. You, Matthias, with your threats of blackmail.'

'You are saying Whitfield would have killed me?'

'Oh no, Matthias. Whitfield was no dagger man, but Mephistopheles certainly is. Oh, he'd deny everything if confronted now. He would ask for evidence and proof and I cannot supply it, but rest assured, Whitfield's mysterious death definitely saved your life. Now you can go.'

Both father and son rose. Matthias snatched the replica and stumbled from the chamber, followed by his father. Athelstan and Cranston sat listening to their footsteps fade.

'Helpful, Brother?'

'Very. But I am still threading the maze, Sir John. What Matthias told us makes sense: it imposes a logic of sorts on some events and proves what I suspect regarding others.'

'Such as?'

'The cipher, Sir John.' Athelstan opened his chancery satchel, took out the two pieces of vellum and stretched them out. 'This,' he picked up the grease-stained parchment, 'is a most cryptic cipher fashioned out of strange, closely packed symbols. I could study this until the Second Coming and wouldn't make sense of it. Whitfield had made some headway or at least a beginning; this second piece of vellum is his commentary. Look, Sir John.' Athelstan pushed the second square of parchment across the table. 'Let's put the cipher aside and concentrate on what Whitfield's workings tell us. It shows two triangles, not isosceles, the base of each triangle being longer than the other two sides. In addition one triangle,' Athelstan tapped the parchment, 'is longer than the other. However, notice how the apexes of each meet in the one spot. Finally, we have these saints' names scrawled down one side of the parchment: St Andrew, St Dunstan, St Bride and so on.'

'And?'

'They are the names of London churches, all with soaring towers, belfries and spires.' Athelstan waved a hand. 'Sir John, in brief, the three sides of each of these triangles map out the churches of London. The base of the larger one marks all those along the north bank of the Thames. The side of that triangle running south to east includes churches to the west of the city such as St Augustine's and St Paul's Gate. The side of the same triangle running south to west includes churches such as St Michael in Crooked Lane. The smaller inverted triangle does the same. Its baseline includes churches north of the city such as St Giles Cripplegate. The other two sides include churches such as St Peter Westcheap to the west and St Margaret Lothbury to the east. The apex of each triangle meets at the one spot, the same church . . .'

'St Mary Le Bow!' Cranston exclaimed. 'The Upright Men intend to seize all these churches, don't they?'

'I suspect they do, Sir John, for a number of reasons. When the revolt comes, the rebels will hoist their banners from steeples all over London, which will create the impression that the city is already in the hands of the Upright Men. They will also be able to light beacon fires and, above all,' Athelstan emphasized the points on his fingers, 'they will be able to observe troop movements across the city and . . .'

'The same church towers could easily be fortified into strongholds where a few men can withstand attacks by the many. Lord save us!' Cranston sprang to his feet. 'If they seize twenty such towers, the city will have to divide their forces to deal with each fortification whilst, at the same time, having to confront peasant armies coming in from all directions.'

'St Mary Le Bow,' Athelstan explained, 'will be at the heart of this plan. It stands at the centre of the city; it dominates the great trading area of Cheapside with the mansions and the warehouses of all the great and good. It will be ideal for the deployment of archers, the setting up of barricades, the closing of streets.' Athelstan paused to sip at a beaker of water. 'Which brings us to Raoul Malfort, bell clerk with specific responsibility for the tower at St Mary Le Bow. Our tooth drawer uses the tower chamber to carry out his gruesome task. The cries and groans of his patients, indeed everything associated with drawing teeth, would certainly keep people away. Secretly Malfort's friends amongst the Upright Men are busy fortifying the upper chambers in the tower, bringing in supplies and storing weapons against the day of the Great Slaughter.'

Cranston walked up and down the room in his agitation. 'The

original bell clerk, Edmund Lacy, was murdered by Reynard, who has gone to judgement. Everything is connected,' he murmured, 'like beads on a chain. I suspect the original bell clerk was a man of integrity, so he was removed and Malfort usurps his office. He sets up his trade in the tower chamber ostensibly drawing teeth, in truth plotting insurrection and treason.'

'I agree,' Athelstan declared. 'We will find all the proof we need in St Mary Le Bow.' He smiled drily. 'I am also deeply suspicious about my own parish council's interests in closing St Erconwald's tower for so-called repairs.'

'But St Erconwald's is south of the Thames.' Cranston laughed and shook his head. 'Of course,' he declared, 'and from the top of St Erconwald's you can view all the southern approaches to the Thames as well as London Bridge.' He picked up his warbelt. 'Brother, I need to act quickly. Within the hour Malfort will be under arrest and his chamber searched, then we will move against the rest.'

'There's more,' Athelstan declared. 'I referred to it earlier, the true identity of our Herald of Hell. I suspect he is our wicked bell clerk at St Mary's. Malfort certainly fits the bill. He holds the most powerful church tower in the city. I suspect he's also responsible for suborning the ward bailiffs, Poulter and the rest. Reynard may have been on his way to meet our cunning bell clerk, but then Reynard fumbled the murder of Lacy and was arrested. We should put all this to him, Sir John.'

'We certainly shall.' Cranston tightened his warbelt. 'I look forward to questioning Malfort. He is surrounded by so much mischief and mystery he could well be the Herald of Hell. Do you think Whitfield knew?'

'Indeed I do. The triangles prove our murdered clerk was making progress, whilst his veiled warning to Matthias to stay away from St Mary's is proof enough. But still, there's something very wrong here.' Athelstan rose and walked to the window. He stared down at the soldiers and archers gathering there. 'Leave St Erconwald's alone, Sir John,' he murmured. 'I am going to send my parishioners a message, repairs or not. I want my church tower back – that will bring any mischief they are planning to nothing . . .' He rubbed his hands together. 'Then I must reflect.'

'In other words, plot, little friar?'

'Yes, Sir John, plot. We will be busy soon enough, mark my words. In view of what we have discovered, the Day of the Great Slaughter must be very, very close.'

'Athelstan, you claimed that, despite all this progress, something was very wrong?'

'Yes, my learned coroner, so bear with me. First, we know Reynard brought a very important message – that cipher – to Malfort, either to hand to him personally or to leave it somewhere safe in St Mary Le Bow Church. You would agree?' Cranston nodded. 'Secondly, Reynard was also tasked with the removal of Edmund Lacy, the bell clerk at St Mary Le Bow, in order to give Malfort a free hand. He does this clumsily and openly flees to Whitefriars, where he is captured along with that cipher which he failed to deliver. Thirdly, the message of that cipher is crucially important, and now we know why, so the Upright Men must have sent a second messenger. On this occasion he or she would carry nothing in writing as time is now of the essence, so secret verbal instructions would be delivered on what Malfort has to do.'

Cranston grunted his assent.

'Fourthly,' Athelstan continued, 'Malfort realizes the cipher has been seized by Thibault and that Whitfield would have been instructed to unlock it and the same for us. For all he knows, we may even have translated it in every detail instead of just discovering the sketchy outline of what is being plotted. In the end, we know what the Upright Men intend to do but not when and how.'

'And just in case we do,' Cranston added, 'I suggest the Great Community of the Realm and the Upright Men would have changed certain details. Brother, we must seize Malfort before the day is out.'

'I agree, Sir John, but finally there is one other matter. Whitfield was a clerk of the Secret Chancery. Why didn't he leave the cipher in a strong box at the Tower? Why have it with him when he moved to the Golden Oliphant for the Festival of Cokayne?'

'Because Thibault wanted him to unlock its secrets as swiftly as possible, even though he had been granted boon days . . .'

Athelstan smiled and held up a hand. 'Or Whitfield took it

with him so he could translate it and sell it back to the Upright Men, or . . .'

'Or what, Friar?'

'Whitfield was playing the two-backed beast, the duplicitous clerk. He would translate the cipher, win Thibault's approval and then secretly inform the Upright Men how their plot was now clearly known to Gaunt's Master of Secrets.'

'Of course,' Cranston breathed, 'and he might acquire more silver for his flight.'

'And Whitfield's so-called death, however it was depicted, could be laid at the door of the Upright Men, who punished Whitfield for discovering their secret. Whitfield would have emerged as the faithful clerk who pleased his master and was apparently murdered for doing so. Even if his flight was later discovered, Whitfield could pretend that, because of what he had done and the threats from the Herald of Hell, he had taken fright and fled. Thibault might not be so pleased but at least it's understandable. There are so many variations to what Whitfield plotted, we will never know the full truth. Suffice to say, Whitfield was going to use the cipher for his own nefarious reasons.'

'Do you think, despite his sketchy notes, Whitfield had broken the cipher in its entirety?'

Athelstan picked up his cloak. 'Perhaps, but now we must get going. Our bell clerk awaits us.'

Within the hour, Cranston and Athelstan, accompanied by Flaxwith's bailiffs and a cohort of Guildhall men-at-arms and archers, swept through Cheapside and up the steps of St Mary Le Bow. Their arrival was not unexpected. Reports of the coroner's dramatic departure from the Guildhall with a phalanx of heavily armed men had been noted, the news being carried by scampering urchins who leapt like fleas round the busy stalls and booths. At Athelstan's hushed and breathless instruction, the church was immediately ringed with guards, placed at the Corpse and Devil doors as well as all the narrow postern gates built into that ancient church.

Cranston and Athelstan led their main company up the steps. The beggars, counterfeit men, preachers, relic sellers and tale-tellers swiftly disappeared like snow under the sun. Some attempt was made to swing the huge main door shut, but Flaxwith's bailiffs thrust this aside. They poured up the nave, hastening towards the entrance to the bell tower. Its heavy oaken door, reinforced with iron bands and studs, had been thrown open. The Earthworms secretly working there had fled and, to judge by the clatter of weapons from outside, Athelstan realized they had encountered the men-at-arms being deployed across God's Acre, the broad cemetery around the church.

Flaxwith kicked open the door to the bell tower and, sword and dagger drawn, entered the cavernous stairwell which served as Master Malfort's tooth-drawing chamber. Athelstan glimpsed the heavy, blackened oaken chair which Malfort used for his patients. On a table beside it stood a bowl with broken, rotting teeth, pincers, small implements and pieces of blood-caked string. Athelstan noted the black heavy straps used to pinion patients as well as the pots of crushed herbs and other potions and powders. The dirty, cobwebbed chamber was empty. A noisy scuffling echoed further up the stone spiral staircase. Flaxwith and his men were about to go up, but Athelstan called them back.

'Master Malfort?' The friar stood on the bottom step. 'Master Malfort and those with you, come down or face summary execution. I speak for Sir John Cranston, Lord High Coroner of this city with the power and life and death over all found in arms against the King.'

'Immediate and without appeal!' Cranston bawled, joining Athelstan on the step.

'Athelstan,' the coroner whispered, 'what do you think . . .?'

'When news of our imminent arrival reached here,' Athelstan murmured, 'I am sure the Earthworms were busy further up the tower while Malfort was practising his grisly trade here in this chamber. The tooth-drawer and his patients fled in panic the only way they could, up those steps – listen.'

The sound of angry voices drifted down. Men's gruff tones and the shrill, strident scream of a woman.

'You have only the briefest of times,' Cranston bawled, 'or I send armed men up. They will take no prisoners.'

At Cranston's signal, Flaxwith and his men began to rattle their drawn weapons against the walls, an ominous clatter of steel which echoed up the steps.

'Come down!' Cranston roared. 'Come now! The only person

we want is Raoul Malfort, bell clerk of this church and alleged traitor. Anyone found aiding, abetting or assisting him . . .'

This was enough. More shouts and yells, followed by the patter of footsteps, and a veritable gaggle of individuals came clattering down the steps. Two men, a woman and Raoul Malfort, held at the scruff of the neck by one of the men, a burly individual with a thick, heavy apron wrapped about him. He identified himself as Henry Vattier, vintner, his wife Margot and apprentice Simeon who, by his blood-encrusted mouth, must have been the object of Malfort's recent ministrations before the unexpected arrival of Cranston and his escort.

'In constant pain,' the vintner boomed, shaking Malfort like a terrier would a rat, 'we brought Simeon here, Margot and I, because we could not take his moaning from matins to compline.' He shoved the terrified Malfort, his long, ugly face now strained with fear, into Flaxwith's custody. 'We heard noises from the stairs above, though he,' the vintner pointed at Malfort, 'told us it was workmen repairing the steps. Then you arrived. It was as if the very doors of Hell had been forced, Earthworms leaping about like Satan's imps as they fled. Malfort,' he jabbed with his thumb, 'well, we didn't know about his involvement. We thought we would all be safe further up.'

Athelstan asked a few questions, satisfying himself that the vintner was innocent. The friar thanked all three, gave them a special blessing that Simeon's mouth would heal well, then he dismissed them. In the meantime, Flaxwith had bound the now shaking Malfort, who crouched in a corner, shivering and jabbering a stream of nonsense. A serjeant came in to report that three Earthworms had been slain in God's Acre; the rest of their company had scaled the cemetery wall and fled into the maze of Cheapside. Cranston ordered the corpses of the dead be stripped and displayed on the church steps while Flaxwith and his bailiffs climbed the steep, spiral staircase to inspect the different stair-wells. They returned with water-skins and leather sacks bulging with dried food, as well as a variety of arbalests, quivers crammed full of quarrels, longbows and bundles of yard-long shafts, feathered flights bristling, their barbed points sharp as razors. They also reported that the amount of kindling and charcoal for the beacon light in the steeple seemed more than plentiful, 'As if to create a bonfire.' They'd also discovered kite shields which could be used to defend the tower staircase, along with barrels of oil which, once spilt and torched, would create a powerful barrier against troops trying to retake the tower.

'Like a castle preparing for a siege,' Cranston murmured. He ordered the tower to be stripped of all such armaments before kicking Malfort to his feet.

They left the church, the hapless bell clerk pinioned in the centre of a phalanx of men-at-arms, halberds and spears bristling. Only when the reinforced, towering gates of the Guildhall swung closed behind them did the phalanx break up. Along that short journey back, Athelstan sensed the deepening tension over Cheapside and, bearing in mind what he'd seen in St Mary's tower, believed the revolt must be imminent. Once back in the Guildhall, he urged Sir John that Malfort be immediately questioned. The coroner agreed.

Flaxwith hustled the cowed bell clerk down the dank, dark steps leading to the dungeons beneath the main hall. The passageway below was mildewed and crusted with dirt; pools of light flared from the sconce torches pushed into brackets on the walls. Rats scurried across shimmering puddles of slime. They made their way past the different cells into a circular space where braziers glowed, making the shadows dance against the wall festooned with clasps and chains. Cranston, winking at Athelstan, ordered Malfort to be stripped to his loincloth and stretched out on the flagstone floor, wrists and ankles secured in heavy gyves.

Athelstan stood chilled by this macabre, sombre sight. The torture room of the Guildhall bore witness to its gruesome history, a gloomy, menacing place lit by dancing flames which shimmered in the chains and fitfully illuminated the dark bloodstains on the plastered walls. The floor was covered with slime, the air a thick fug of stale smoke and foul odours. The oppressive silence was broken only by the drip, drip of water splashing into puddles and the constant moaning and cries trailing along the gloomy galleries which branched off from this chamber of terror. Athelstan gazed pitifully at Malfort, now spread out, his thin, ugly face framed by matted, sweaty hair, his bony body all a-tremble. Cranston placed two stools either side of the chained prisoner, gesturing that Athelstan should take one whilst he squatted on the other.

He took a generous gulp from the miraculous wineskin and poured a little between Malfort's dried lips before leaning down.

'Come, sir. Tell me everything.'

'They will kill me, execute me horribly,' Malfort pleaded.

'I will do the same.' Cranston indicated that Athelstan should remain seated as he rose and beckoned his chief bailiff. 'Remember France, Flaxwith? That mercenary company, the Flayers? We will do the same.'

The chief bailiff walked away and talked to the turnkeys. A short while later Flaxwith returned, stepping into the pool of light around Malfort to hand over a leather funnel with straps. Cranston took this and held it above the prisoner.

'Master Malfort, I could fasten this over your mouth and keep pouring water until you choke or,' the coroner crouched down beside Malfort, 'I could lash the funnel to your side.' The coroner did so deftly, fixing the funnel firmly to the prisoner's flank. 'Then,' Cranston continued conversationally, snapping his fingers, 'I could do this.' He stretched out and took from Flaxwith the long, wire-mesh cage containing a huge rat, ears back against its knobbly head, eyes gleaming, its hairy snout pushing against the mesh, jaws gaping to expose sharpened teeth. 'The rat is starving.' Cranston stared down at Malfort who was now blinking furiously, his sweat-soaked face all aghast, mouth gaping, opening and shutting as if desperate for air. 'We place the rat in the funnel,' Cranston continued, 'and light a fire at the open end. Rats hate fire. It will try and escape. The leather is as thick and sturdy as armour but your flesh, Master Malfort, is soft; it's also food, as well as the only way out.'

Athelstan steeled himself against the sheer terror in Malfort's eyes. The bell clerk, he reminded himself, was dangerous. He had plotted treason, rebellion and murder.

'Now,' Cranston patted the side of Malfort's face, 'you can tell me all you know and I might consider letting you get dressed, be given a coin and a parcel of food and be put on the next cog heading for foreign parts on the strict understanding that you never return to this kingdom under pain of being arrested for treason and torn apart at Tyburn. Do you understand?'

Malfort, eyes crazed with fear, nodded, banging his head against the floor. Cranston began his questions, and Malfort

replied as both the coroner and Athelstan expected. He had been
suborned by the Upright Men and given the task of preparing
the bell tower of St Mary's as a fortress. Edmund Lacy had
proved to be an obstacle, so the Upright Men had despatched
Reynard to remove him. Malfort confessed to this but added that
he did not know the names or the identities of the Upright Men
concerned, as they remained shadowy, midnight visitors who
hid under the names of birds, animals or exotic beasts. Cranston
nodded in agreement; he had discovered the same in other
investigations he'd carried out. Malfort, however, terrified by
the sound of the rat scrabbling and squeaking in the cage,
hastened on.

'Reynard was supposed to leave the cipher and its key in a
crevice in St Stephen's chantry chapel, the one housing Camoys'
corpse. He carried them separate on his person. One without the
other was useless; only a trained cipher clerk like Whitfield might
be skilled enough to break it.'

'The cipher,' Athelstan urged, 'contained instructions about
the seizing of church towers, belfries and steeples, did it not?'

'Yes.'

'But how do you know that?' Athelstan persisted. 'If both
cipher and key were taken? Master Malfort,' the friar leaned
closer, 'you are in *gravi periculo mortis* – in grave danger of
death. Tell the truth. Let me help you. The Upright Men were
furious at Reynard, weren't they? I suspect they only recently
retrieved the key to the cipher, but they sent you another message
through an envoy who gave you strict verbal instructions on what
to do, isn't that right? Answer me!'

Malfort nodded. 'I was informed of the plot to seize the Tower,'
he gasped, 'and ordered to wait for a sign.'

'What sign?'

'A tile, yes, a tile emblazoned with an all-seeing eye. Once I
had received that, I was to fire the beacon light in St Mary's
steeple, a veritable bonfire just as dawn broke: it would be seen
all over the city. The Earthworms would move in immediately
to seize the designated towers.'

'When?'

'I don't know. I was still waiting for a further message, though
I sense that the time is very close,' Malfort chatted on. 'In the

meantime, I was ordered to pass on what I had been told to the leaders of the Earthworms.'

'So you know who these are,' Cranston demanded. 'Give me their names.'

'I can't. Every so often one would appear and I'd deliver the message, which he would pass on. Who and how, I don't know. Sir John, Brother Athelstan, I beg you to believe me. I was only told what was necessary; that is how the Upright Men work – constantly in the shadows, ever vigilant against spies and traitors.' Malfort drew a deep breath. 'I was given further instruction, something only I could do.'

'What? Who was this messenger?'

'He sheltered in the gloom of the church porch. I was told to stand well away. I . . .' Malfort coughed and spluttered. Cranston ordered the gyves to be unlocked and the bell clerk sat up, rubbing his wrists and arms.

'Continue,' Cranston ordered.

'You know,' Malfort gabbled, 'how one of the duties of the bell clerk at St Mary's is to collect rents from certain tenements the parish owns along Cheapside up to Newgate and Smithfield.'

'Bequests,' Cranston agreed. 'Property left to the church by wealthy parishioners in return for chantry masses being sung for their souls.'

'I collect them,' Malfort declared. 'Some chambers are occupied, others, particularly with the coming troubles, lie empty. I was given money and ordered to place, in certain of these rooms, the finest warbows fashioned out of yew along with well-stocked quivers of arrows. When the revolt began and the Earthworms fortified the tower of St Mary le Bow, I was ordered to leave and go to the taproom of the Lamb of God . . .'

Cranston whistled under his breath. 'Is nothing sacred?' he murmured.

Athelstan held a hand up. Sir John's favourite hostelry commanded the sweep of Cheapside.

'St Mary's,' Malfort continued, 'owns tenements there, in the gallery above the taproom. But I was ordered to wait for a stranger. He would show me a tile, glazed white with the word "Actaeon" emblazoned on it. I was to provide him with a list of the tenements. The doors to such rooms would be left open; inside each

I was to hide a warbow and quiver of arrows.' Malfort rubbed dried, cracked lips. Cranston made him take a generous gulp from the wineskin. 'I was also to warn the ward bailiffs of Cheapside not to interfere with any man at night carrying a small, white tile emblazoned with the word, "Actaeon".'

'Of course you would,' Athelstan agreed. 'You are the Herald of Hell, aren't you?'

Malfort nodded. 'I, with an escort of Earthworms, would meet the bailiffs on their nightly tours and give them instructions on what to do. The same applied to this.'

Troubled, Athelstan rose to his feet. He gestured at Cranston to join him in the murky entrance to the torture chamber.

'Actaeon,' he whispered. 'The hunter from Greek mythology, an archer, a master bowman. Something jogs my memory, Sir John, but I can't place it.'

Cranston stood deep in thought, staring down at the brackish pools of water coagulating on the paving stones.

'Sir John?'

'Tyler,' the coroner whispered. 'We have reports, Brother, of a leading captain of the Upright Men, Kentish in origin, called Wat Tyler, a former soldier, a true agitator . . .'

'And?'

'The records are being searched. Tax lists, muster rolls, court proceedings, Commissions of Array, all the sheriff returns every quarter to the Exchequer. However, no trace can be found of a Wat Tyler. He mysteriously appeared about six months ago, very active amongst the Upright Men in Kent . . .'

'But no one knows who he is?'

'Very much so, Brother. But I have my suspicions.' Cranston spun on his heels and shouted at Flaxwith, 'Get him!' The coroner pointed to Malfort crouched crying on the ground. 'Get him dressed. He is going to take us to all the properties owned by St Mary Le Bow which stand along Cheapside.'

A short while later Cranston and Athelstan left the dungeons. Two of Flaxwith's bailiffs pushing the bent, bedraggled Malfort out across the great bailey. The bell clerk flinched at the bright sunlight, raising his bound wrists to protect his eyes. Athelstan was aware of shouts and cries, the neigh of horses from nearby stables, the pungent smell of dung, urine and sweat. Men-at-arms milled around. Cranston was shouting at a retainer to fetch his court clerk. Athelstan stared around; his feeling of unease had sharpened. Malfort's confession had stirred a memory of something he had glimpsed here at the Guildhall. The friar glanced up at the whirring sound like the fast beating wings of a hawk. The sound was repeated. Athelstan spun around. Malfort was choking, screaming. One shaft had struck him high in the shoulder; the second was embedded deep in the bell clerk's chest. Malfort's face was twisted in shock, blood already seeping between his gaping lips. A third shaft caught the clerk in the throat, flinging him back on to the cobbles. The brief, abrupt silence of the courtyard erupted into shouts and yells. Men fled for the protection of doorways and walls, as far as possible from that blood-soaked prisoner thrashing in his death throes on the cobbles. Cranston pulled at Athelstan's sleeve.

'Brother, come away!'

Athelstan tried to shake off the coroner's grip as he stared up at the Guildhall. He glimpsed a half-open casement window and remembered what he had seen.

'The chapel, Sir John. Quickly!'

The friar, followed by a bemused coroner, hastened across the bailey, pushing aside retainers, men-at-arms and servants, now milling frenetically about. Cranston bellowed at them all to stand aside as he followed the friar up the staircase along the narrow gallery leading to the chapel. Athelstan tentatively pushed open the door. Cranston drew his sword and ordered the two archers he had summoned to string their bows. The friar cautiously entered. The chapel was empty; the door-window in the far wall hung open. No sign of the tiler and his sharp-eyed, stave-holding apprentice. The floor tiles had been fitted. Athelstan crossed to the window and picked up the small white square emblazoned with a crudely scrawled 'Actaeon'. Athelstan sat down on a wall bench. Cranston dismissed the archers and joined him.

'I saw him,' Athelstan whispered, 'and his so-called apprentice. In truth, our bowman and his protector, Wat Tyler. They were here. They must have been alerted by your arrest of Malfort and hastened here, just two more master craftsmen hired by the Guildhall.'

Cranston rose and made to go out.

'Forget it, Sir John, they will be long gone.'

'And that,' Cranston crossed, closed the door and returned, 'truly disturbs me.'

'Sir John?'

Cranston made himself comfortable and took a generous slurp from the miraculous wineskin, then offered it to Athelstan, who drank a mouthful of the rich Bordeaux. 'Little friar, to copy you. Item. We have Malfort the Herald of Hell in more ways than one. He not only suborned ward bailiffs, he was also the herald of chaos. He was to give the signal for certain church towers in the city to be seized and fortified once the revolt had begun. We now know the reasons why.' Cranston hastened on. 'Item. Malfort had other secret instructions. As bell clerk he had access to certain properties; I will get a list of these and search them. In these tenements Malfort was ordered to hide a warbow and quivers of yard shafts; we have just witnessed how skilfully they can be used! Item, my dear friar: we know from Grindcobbe that one of the principal captains of the Upright Men plots the sudden murder of our young king and we suspect, with good reason, that this particular captain is an accomplice of Gaunt. The revolt will occur, the church towers be seized and so on. Our king will shelter in the Tower but eventually he will leave, either to meet the rebels, be it with their envoys at Westminster, or to process through the city with banners unfurled.'

'Victory or defeat?' Athelstan murmured. 'The young king, if he is still alive, must leave the Tower, and the broadest, swiftest route through the city is along Cheapside.'

'Where,' Cranston declared, 'one soul amongst many lurks. Imagine our bowman, Brother, standing at a casement window, bow notched, waiting for the King, one shaft, two, perhaps, then the warbow is dropped and the assassin flees, just another panic-struck man amongst many others.'

Athelstan rubbed his face. 'I cannot believe this is true. Gaunt is leaving for Scotland, his son Henry of Lancaster with him. The revolt will engulf the city and Gaunt's creature, who calls himself Wat Tyler, will do all within his power to kill our king, Gaunt's own blood?'

'Brother, Edward II was deposed and killed by his wife Isabella, betrayed by his own half-brother Edmund Earl of Kent, father of our present king's mother. The power of the Crown is price enough for someone's soul, and Gaunt is prepared to pay it. Tyler, along with Actaeon, is proof enough – they were here. Accordingly, Tyler must have some special pass which allows him entry not only to the Guildhall but, God save us, to Westminster or even to the Tower, and that is something to truly fear.' Cranston patted his jerkin. 'I must be busy.'

'Sir John, I want to stay here.'

'Of course, little friar of deep cunning! There is a bedchamber above my judgement room: it is stark enough for an anchorite but it does have a cotbed, table, writing stool and a crucifix . . .'

'Luxury indeed whilst I can celebrate mass here in the Guildhall chapel.'

'So you intend to stay for more than a day?'

'Oh yes, my Lord Coroner, for more than a day.'

PART FIVE

'Omnium Finis: *the end of all things.'*

Athelstan made his home in the little chamber beneath the Guildhall loft. The only things he asked for were clean sheets and a prie-dieu to be placed beneath the stark black crucifix nailed to the lime-washed wall. He sent Tiptoft, Cranston's messenger, to St Erconwald's to deliver certain messages and collect other items he needed. Athelstan celebrated his morning mass in the small, timber-beamed chapel and broke his fast in the refectory used by the Guildhall servants. Despite his absorption in drafting and redrafting all he had learnt about the deaths of Whitfield, Joycelina and Lebarge, Athelstan sensed how frightened people were becoming, especially the Crown officials, men whom the rebels had publicly marked down for judgement. Already news was seeping in that the clerks, scriveners and other officials at the centre of royal government at Westminster were beginning to flee. Officials of the Exchequer, Chancery and the different courts sitting in the great hall, be it King's Bench or the Court of Common Pleas, were sending in their excuses and refusing to attend. At the same time the Guildhall was being turned into a fortress; heavy shutters were fastened over windows; doors fortified against a siege; the well checked and cleaned; the barbican or weapon store placed under the command of city serjeants; the narrow postern doors closely guarded.

Cranston, however, refused to be cowed. Accompanied by troops from the Tower, the coroner swept the city streets, moving from church to church. Some of these, already alerted by the summary arrest of Malfort, were found deserted of both men and arms. At others Cranston found the same as they had at St Mary Le Bow. In many cases the priests had no knowledge of what was happening in their bell towers, though, as Cranston wryly observed, he had never come across so many church towers in the process of being repaired or refurbished. The plot to seize and fortify certain steeples became public knowledge. Many of the Upright Men fled, taking their weapons with them. A few were caught and faced summary justice. Thibault was very pleased and sent a letter of congratulation to both Athelstan and Cranston along with a pipe of the very best wine from Bordeaux, freshly slaughtered meat and other delicacies for the Guildhall kitchen. Cranston kept Athelstan informed, though he could not draw the friar into any meaningful discussion. Athelstan would beg for the coroner to be patient and return to the drafting and redrafting of his memoranda under each of their headings. Secretly, Athelstan believed he had trapped the assassin, though how he was to seal that trap was a different matter.

A few days after his arrival at the Guildhall, Athelstan joined Cranston for supper in the refectory. The friar ate little and drank even less but asked the coroner, along with Flaxwith and his bailiffs, to join him in the great bailey just after he celebrated his Jesus Mass. Athelstan refused to provide any details except that Sir John should also ensure that Tiptoft, his messenger, accompany them. Early the next morning they arrived at the Golden Oliphant. Athelstan strode through the great taproom, calling everybody to sit round the tables. Under the watchful eye of Flaxwith and his bailiffs, the entire household were guided in to take their seats. Athelstan glanced around; all were there: Stretton, Gray, Camoys, Griffin, Foxley, Mistress Cheyne and her moppets and servants. At Athelstan's request, the bailiffs made a sweep of the galleries and chambers. Only when Cranston declared himself satisfied did Athelstan climb on to the dais in the Golden Hall, hands outstretched.

'Beloved brethren,' he began, 'I thank you for your patience and cooperation. I ask you to sit here and reflect whilst I make certain preparations.' He climbed down and beckoned at Tiptoft to follow him out of the Golden Hall, then gave him precise details on what to do. Tiptoft expressed his surprise, but Athelstan repeated his instructions before taking the messenger back into the taproom, where he demanded and received from Mistress Cheyne a ring of keys to all the chambers. Athelstan then visited the murder room on the top gallery. He entered the chamber next to where Whitfield had been found hanging, closely shuttered the window, put a stool in the middle just beneath the lantern hook, then returned to the Golden Hall, Tiptoft accompanying him.

'Very well,' Athelstan declared, 'I shall now stage my masque based on the events of that morning when Amaury Whitfield was found hanged. Please, I beg you, correct me if I err in any way. Some of you are more knowledgeable than others. I would be grateful for your close attention to what I say. Now I appreciate the guests were in the refectory but for the present, that is too small to hold you all. This taproom will suffice well enough.' He pointed at Tiptoft, who had been closely advised on what to do. 'You, Sir, for the moment, will act the part of Master Griffin. You have been upstairs to rouse the guests, that's what happened, yes?' A murmur of agreement, led by Stretton and Gray, greeted his question. 'Simnel cakes had been baked,' Athelstan continued. 'Lebarge in particular was greedy for them. Whitfield's absence is eventually noticed, so Joycelina is sent up to rouse him. She returns claiming that she cannot and something must be wrong.'

'That is correct,' Griffin shouted to cries of approval.

Athelstan's 'congregation', as he now called them, watched fascinated as they realized that the truth may be about to unfold.

'Mistress Cheyne,' Athelstan continued, 'you then sent Master Foxley to fetch two of the labourers from the garden to bring in that battering ram. Joycelina had reported Whitfield's chamber to be locked and barred; she'd glanced through the eyelet but that too was closed. I understand this battering ram has been used before when a chamber is locked and the guest within refuses to respond. Very well, Master Foxley, please do what you did that morning. Sir John, I would ask you act the part of Lebarge and follow exactly what he did. Tiptoft, you are now Joycelina; go along the galleries, assure anyone you meet not to be disturbed about what they may hear.'

'But everyone is here,' Mistress Cheyne protested.

'Yes, yes, they are. But on that particular morning, apparently they were not, which is why you, Mistress Cheyne, despatched your helpmate!' Athelstan pointed at Foxley and Tiptoft. 'Do what I ask.'

Both men left on their separate tasks. Athelstan waited until Foxley had returned with the two bemused labourers. One of the men carried a small, stout battering ram. Athelstan ordered everyone to remain where they were and led Foxley and the two labourers up to the top gallery and the chamber next to Whitfield's. At Athelstan's behest, Foxley pressed against the door, peered through the eyelet and keyhole and pronounced both blocked. The door was clearly locked and bolted with the key still inserted. Athelstan gestured at the door. 'Break it down, as you did that morning. Do not worry, Master Foxley, the city will pay for any reasonable repairs. Now, where is Tiptoft? I need him here.' Athelstan gestured at the labourers to begin as he went back to the top of the stairs calling for Tiptoft, his voice echoing harshly along the gallery. The labourers pounded the door, Foxley shouted encouragement and instructions whilst Athelstan continued to summon Tiptoft. At last the door gave way, snapping at the lock, its thick leather hinges breaking from the lintel. The chamber beyond lay in pitch darkness. Athelstan immediately dismissed the labourers whilst instructing Foxley to go into the chamber to unshutter and open the window. Once this was done, Athelstan led Foxley and Tiptoft back out into the gallery and down the stairs to join the rest in the Golden Hall.

'All is set,' Athelstan whispered to Cranston. 'It is best if we do this in the presence of a host of witnesses whose memories are now being stirred. So . . .' Athelstan walked into the centre of the hall.

'What were you doing?' Mistress Cheyne, who had been whispering to Foxley, sprang to her feet. 'This is my house, my home.'

'And your place of murder,' Athelstan retorted, silencing her and the murmuring of the rest. 'Master Foxley,' Athelstan asked, 'who was in the gallery when the door was forced, I mean just now?'

'Why, you, me and the labourers; Master Tiptoft joined us later. You were calling for him.'

'And the door we forced was both bolted and locked?'

'Yes, of course, you could see that for yourself.'

'And when the door was forced, the window?'

'Firmly closed and shuttered until I opened it.'

'Master Tiptoft,' Athelstan put his hand on the messenger's arm, 'you heard me shouting. Where were you?'

'In the chamber which was forced.'

'Nonsense!' Fear thrilled Elizabeth Cheyne's face and voice. 'Impossible!' Foxley exclaimed.

'I was in the chamber,' Tiptoft insisted. 'Brother Athelstan gave me the key. As soon as I left here, I went upstairs. I locked and bolted the door, closed the eyelet and made sure that the window was firmly shuttered. The room was as dark as night. I stood, as Brother Athelstan advised, to the left of the door as it opens. When it was forced and flung back, I stayed. Athelstan dismissed the labourers then Master Foxley entered, crossing the chamber to pull back the shutters. I simply stepped round the door and joined Brother Athelstan on the threshold, a matter of heartbeats. I did as Brother Athelstan asked. Remember the chamber was as black as a moonless night. I counted how long it took to step around the door, I barely reached four.'

Athelstan glanced around. 'Remember that, because I was calling Tiptoft, Foxley thought, when he turned around after opening the windows, that Tiptoft had been with me all the time. When the chamber was being forced, Master Foxley, you were concentrating solely on the door and what might lie inside. True?' The Master of Horse agreed. 'I also noticed,' Athelstan continued, 'that on the day she was killed, Joycelina was wearing sandals. Did she always wear those?'

'Yes,' Anna the maid shouted.

'So why, on the morning Whitfield was found dead, was Joycelina wearing red-capped, thick, soft-soled buskins?'

'Nonsense!' Mistress Cheyne exclaimed.

'So how do I know she had a pair?' Athelstan turned to the rest. 'She did, didn't she?'

'Yes.' One of the maids lifted her hand. 'Mistress, after Joycelina died, you gave them to me.'

Cheyne's head went down.

'Joycelina,' Athelstan explained, 'wore those same buskins that morning to ensure that for a few heartbeats, in that pitch-black chamber with Foxley terrified and having eyes and mind only for that swinging corpse and opening the window, she could slip soundlessly forward and join you, Mistress Cheyne, her accomplice.'

The Mistress of the Moppets did not reply, though she turned slightly as members of her household murmured their agreement to Athelstan's statement.

'Sir John?' Athelstan turned to the coroner. 'You imitated Lebarge. You left here and went to the foot of the stairs leading to the top gallery. Did anyone pass you?'

'Oh, of course not.' The coroner grinned. 'I heard you calling Tiptoft but he never came by. He never passed me. I stayed in that recess until the labourers returned and I followed them down.'

Athelstan went and crouched before Mistress Cheyne. 'I have demonstrated,' he held her cold, angry gaze, 'how you and Joycelina murdered Amaury Whitfield.' He rose, gesturing at Flaxwith to come forward and restrain the murderess, sitting on a high-backed chair, fingers firmly clutching its arms.

'Search her,' Athelstan ordered. Flaxwith did so, ignoring her protests, and drew the needle-like dagger, more of a bodkin than a knife, out of a secret sheath on the belt around her waist. He threw this on the table as Athelstan took a stool to sit opposite the accused. He stared around. He would have preferred to first question Mistress Cheyne in some secure, isolated chamber, but those present, although they did not fully realize it, were in fact witnesses to her crimes.

'Amaury Whitfield,' Athelstan began, 'came here to join the Festival of Cokayne, to forget his terrors and, above all, to complete his plans to flee abroad. True, Master Gray?' He turned to where the sea captain slouched on a bench.

'Answer!' Cranston roared.

'Correct,' Gray replied. He gestured with his hands. 'Whitfield, Lebarge and Mistress Cheyne's household. You must know that by now?'

'Good.' Athelstan smiled at him. 'Whitfield's mind and soul does not concern us now. He was a terrified man with an unfinished, ever-changing plot about masking his disappearance behind an accident or suicide.' Athelstan shrugged. 'This does not matter any more. However, Whitfield was not only a frightened man but a very, very wealthy one with a heavy money belt crammed with good coins, strapped around his waist. He would have provoked your suspicions, Mistress Cheyne, by hiring a chamber on the top gallery: that was a way of protecting himself. Of course, during her ministrations to Whitfield, Joycelina must have learnt about this treasure trove. Somehow or other, you both discovered how wealthy Whitfield was and how accessible his riches were. You planned to kill him and seize that wealth. You probably plotted to do it once you reached foreign parts. However, that part of your plan you could not control. We all know Whitfield was disturbed, deeply agitated, fearful of his powerful master and,' Athelstan glanced quickly at Stretton, 'other equally sinister figures. No wonder Whitfield moved from plot to plot and plan to plan. We shall never know the truth of it, but in the end, I believe he was thinking of fleeing on his own, possibly with Lebarge, which is one of the reasons he went down to visit the Tavern of Lost Souls. However, Whitfield's visit to Mephistopheles does not concern us. All I can say is that he went there panic-struck, considering all the choices he could make. Indeed, in the end I would say Whitfield's wits were turned, he was not thinking clearly.'

'I would agree.' The usually taciturn Griffin spoke up. 'Let's admit it. We all saw him talking to himself and drinking deeply . . .'

'You, Mistress Cheyne,' Athelstan accused, 'suspected Whitfield's ultimate plan. He was going to disappear, escape your clutches, so you and Joycelina concocted your murderous design. On the night before he died, Whitfield and you others drank deeply, yes?' Athelstan did not wait for agreement. 'Afterwards Whitfield lurched upstairs, possibly planning to leave either during the night after he had met a certain stranger or immediately the following morning. You, Mistress Cheyne, together with Joycelina, slipped upstairs and inveigled yourself into his chamber. No one would notice. Lebarge, who occupied the only other chamber on the gallery, had also drunk deeply. For all I know, an opiate may have been slipped into his drink, I suspect it was. However, let's move on.

'In that chamber, locked and bolted, Whitfield would prove to be most malleable to you and Joycelina. Drunk and sottish, you enticed him into some sexual game to rouse his potency. I understand that strangulation can be used to excite a man like Whitfield. Whatever, the fire rope was taken and transformed into a hanging noose. Somehow or other you or Joycelina inveigled Whitfield to stand on that stool. Drunk and confused, he would not realize the trap until the noose around his neck swiftly tightened and the stool was kicked away. He struggled, you and Joycelina may have grabbed his legs and pulled him down to hasten death. In a very brief period, it was all over.'

'You have no proof of this, no evidence. I have always been honest . . .'

Mistress Cheyne glared around. Athelstan could detect little sympathy or support for this grasping woman.

'We will come to proof in a moment, won't we, Sir John?'

Cranston nodded approvingly even though he secretly wondered what real evidence the little friar could lay against this cunning killer.

'You knew about Whitfield's note of desperation,' Athelstan continued. 'You left that out. Above all, you removed his fat, bulging money belt. No wonder Master Foxley thought Whitfield looked slimmer in death than in life.' Athelstan paused. 'All is how you want it. You and Joycelina slip out, lock the door behind you and take the key. No one else has access to that chamber.'

'Whitfield would have struggled, surely?' Stretton asked.

'No,' Athelstan retorted, 'he was deep in his cups when he left here that night. We know from another source that he intended to go out in the early hours, but of course, he was never given that choice. He was drunk, wasn't he?' A murmur of agreement confirmed this. 'A potion or a powder may have been added, but above all, Master Stretton, Whitfield did not view Mistress Cheyne and Joycelina as dangerous – why should he? He had come here to be entertained, to be pampered and cosseted by them. I suspect he babbled like a babe about his fears, his madcap schemes to vanish, the letter he planned to leave. In Whitfield's eyes, Mistress Cheyne and Joycelina were his lovers, his friends and allies.' Athelstan smiled bleakly. 'As you know, as we all now know, he viewed others sitting here as the real threat.' Stretton glanced away. 'We now come to the events of the following morning. Most of this household, guests and servants, are in or around the refectory. Lebarge had woken all mawmsy and dry-mouthed after the previous night's drinking. He was roused by Griffin and hurried down to eat his favourite simnel cakes. Whitfield does not. So . . .'

'Strange.' Anna the maid sprang all hot-eyed to her feet.

'What is strange?'

'Well, Brother. Joycelina was all important here, high and mighty. I cannot recall her ever going up to the top gallery to rouse guests.'

'Shut up, you stupid bitch!' Mistress Cheyne exclaimed.

'Whitfield was most partial to Joycelina,' another called.

'And those simnel cakes!' Anna shouted. Athelstan could see there was little love lost between Mistress Cheyne and her servant. 'Whenever have you made simnel cakes so early in the morning?' she asked accusingly.

'I did it because Lebarge wanted them.'

'No matter,' Athelstan intervened. 'Lebarge was down here. You, Mistress Cheyne, decided to act. Joycelina, whether it was her duty or not, went up to that chamber and returned claiming Whitfield could not be roused. You, Mistress Cheyne, acted decisively and swiftly: those in the refectory are instructed to stay. Foxley is sent to bring the labourers and the battering ram. Joycelina is despatched, ostensibly to inform the other servants about what is about to happen. In truth, she climbs swiftly to Whitfield's chamber, unlocks the door and goes inside where she ensures the eyelet is blocked, the key turned and the bolts pulled across; she then locks herself in with that dangling corpse. Tell me,' Athelstan glanced around, 'does anyone here recall Joycelina seeking them out that morning?' Silence greeted his words. A thin-faced slattern, wiping greasy fingers on her grubby gown, got off the bench, hands fluttering.

'I passed her on the stairs. My task is to empty chamber pots . . .'

Her words were greeted with laughter which the slattern dismissed with a flick of her rat-tailed hair. 'She told me to go immediately down to the refectory. I . . .' She shrugged and sat down.

'Does anyone else?'

'We were all here,' Anna, who could sense blood, called out.

'Hawisa might have helped us about what happened but we will come to her by and by.' Athelstan cleared his throat. 'All is now set. Mistress Cheyne supervises the breakdown of the door whilst calling for Joycelina as if her accomplice is still below stairs. Of course she isn't. The door is forced. The labourers are immediately dismissed. Master Foxley is sent to open the window. You, Sir, are shocked by the sight of Whitfield's swaying corpse. The chamber is cloaked in darkness, even so you only have eyes for that ghastly sight. You have to pass it and reach the window to pull back the shutters. Your eyes, ears, all your senses are taken up with the terrible tragedy confronting you. You would never dream that someone else was in the room. When you turned from the window you saw two people who must have been with you on the gallery. What else would you think? Before you battered the door down, you knew it was locked and bolted, and remember, you were mawmsy with ale fumes after being deep in your cups the night before. I played the same trick just now with Tiptoft and I convinced you even though you are more sober and alert. Now, to go back to that morning. Joycelina simply moved ever so softly in her buskins, from one place to another, all in the space of a few breaths. So, Master Foxley, think! When you were out on the gallery, whilst the door to Whitfield's chamber was being broken down, can you recall actually seeing Joycelina?'

Athelstan walked over to where the Master of Horse lounged against a wooden pillar listening intently to what the friar had been saying.

'Brother,' Foxley looked past Athelstan at Mistress Cheyne, 'for the life of me . . .' Athelstan tensed. Foxley's testimony would be vital. 'I cannot recall precisely either way.'

'Would you go on oath and swear that?' Cranston demanded.

'Yes, I would. Indeed, the more I reflect, the more certain I become that I did not see Joycelina. I never considered her not being there, it would just never occur to me.'

'Nor to me,' Athelstan replied, taking his seat, 'until I spoke to Lebarge. He left the refectory, didn't he, Master Griffin?'

'Yes, I couldn't stop him.'

'He went up the stairs, but paused on the stairwell leading to the top gallery. He never mentioned anyone passing him, though he remembered the door being pounded and Mistress Cheyne calling for Joycelina. He stayed there until the chamber was forced, sheltering in that small recess or enclave. He heard the labourers going down and the clamour above about Whitfield being dead. Sir John took up the same position when Tiptoft was hiding in the chamber I forced. Of course, despite all my calling, he never saw Tiptoft pass him. Lebarge said the same, no one passed him on that staircase. He certainly never mentioned Joycelina running up. I am not too sure whether Lebarge realized the full implications of what he was saying. Perhaps in time he would have done, which could well be one of the reasons you decided to murder him, Mistress Cheyne.'

'Nonsense!' Elizabeth Cheyne leapt to her feet. 'This is all a lie. A farrago of lies. You have no . . .' Flaxwith, pressing on her shoulders, forced the woman to sit down.

'Lebarge,' Athelstan continued, 'was truly frightened and confused. His master was dead, he did not know who to trust except for one person, young Hawisa. He hid his relationship with her behind a mask of diffidence, publicly dismissing her as just another whore. But I know, as you do, Mistress Cheyne, that secretly he was much taken with her. Strange that you never provided such information to me when I first questioned you. Whitfield wanted to flee, Lebarge also, and the scrivener intended to take little Hawisa with him. The moppet may already have been hiding Lebarge's baggage; she had a chamber here, or certainly some place where she could stow away his possessions. I admit I have little proof for what I say, but, to continue. On that particular morning after Lebarge had visited the death chamber, he had a few swift words with his sweetheart then fled to St Erconwald's for sanctuary. He went there because he was confused and frightened. He'd committed no crime but at least he would be safe in sanctuary against Thibault and any other adversary. Eventually he would be granted permission to leave London by the nearest port, which is what he wanted in the first place. Above all, safe in my church, he could think, plan and plot. Hawisa would know where he was, a place nearby, and, in time, easily join him. Lebarge decided to shelter there, determined only to take sustenance from myself or the widow woman . . .'

'Benedicta?' Mistress Cheyne spat the name out. 'We know all about her, Brother Athelstan . . .'

'As God knows about you being so determined on Lebarge's death. You learnt from Griffin or others here that Lebarge had left the refectory . . .'

'She asked me and I told her,' the Master of the Hall interjected.

'You, Mistress Cheyne, must have wondered what Lebarge really knew, what he had seen, heard or felt. You would realize he was safe in sanctuary with time to reflect. Above all, Lebarge knew about that money belt. It would be only a matter of time before he began to cast the net of suspicion wider and wider. Lebarge had to die and, if it was going to be done, it was best done quickly. You would use the one person Lebarge trusted . . .'

'Hawisa!' Foxley shouted. 'I saw you on the day Lebarge fled conferring with her.'

'Of course you did. Is that not so, Mistress Cheyne? You consoled her, promised help, every assistance. To cut to the quick. You offered to take Hawisa to St Erconwald's in the evening of that same day when my church is fairly deserted and full of dancing shadows. Just a brief meeting. You would help both of them. You wrapped a simnel cake in some linen as a small token of friendship. Lebarge would like that. Cloaked and cowled, both of you slipped into St Erconwald's, two women who would not attract attention. You told Hawisa not to be long. You would keep watch and alert her to any danger. You insist that Lebarge eat the cake immediately and Hawisa bring the linen covering back with her so there'd be no trace of anyone from outside assisting him, one of the rules for all who seek sanctuary. At the time these would appear trivial matters. Hawisa and Lebarge would be eager to discuss a future which, little did they know, you intended to destroy. I can imagine Hawisa, that little mouse, slipping through the shadows whilst you kept watch near some pillar close by the Lady Altar, ready to cough or give some prearranged signal if danger approached. The short meeting took place. Hawisa met Lebarge not in the mercy enclave but in the shadow of the rood screen door. The cake is handed over and eaten but, unbeknown to you, or even despite your instructions, Hawisa also provided Lebarge with a knife and some coins, just in case he decides to flee sanctuary. She then rejoined you. You would make sure all was well, that the cake had been eaten and the linen cloth returned.

'Afterwards, you both slipped away into the gathering darkness back to the Golden Oliphant, though only one of you reached here. You are a killer, Mistress Cheyne, to the very sinews of your wicked heart. You are steeped in evil with no conscience.

On the way back to the Golden Oliphant you murdered Hawisa
along some filthy runnel or alleyway: a swift stab to the heart
in some dark-filled cranny where you could take care of anything
that might indicate who she was or where she came from. Hawisa
became just another corpse amongst those of so many poor
women, found with their throat slit or drenched in their heart's
blood, lying on a filth-filled laystall or in a dirt-smeared recess.'
Athelstan gestured around. 'Somewhere in this house you have
hidden the possessions of both Lebarge and Hawisa.'

'Hawisa ran away!' Mistress Cheyne exclaimed. 'She's fled.'

'Why would she?' Cranston retorted. 'She, like the rest of
you, was under strict orders not to leave the Golden Oliphant.
Why should a little moppet challenge that?' By the murmur of
protest this provoked, Cranston could see why Athelstan had
chosen to confront Mistress Cheyne in public: everything the
whore-mistress now said or did was being closely scrutinized.

'Hawisa has not fled.' Anna led the attack. 'Where would she
go? Now Lebarge is dead, she would be alone with no home,
hearth, kith or kin. She risked being put to the horn as an outlaw.'

'I spoke to her,' another cried, 'the last time I saw her. She
talked about wishing to go abroad or returning to Coggeshall
where she was born.'

Others shouted their comments. Mistress Cheyne just sat
seething with hate, fingers curling as she glared at Athelstan.

'And now,' Athelstan raised his voice to still the clamour, 'we
come to the murder of your accomplice, Joycelina . . .'

'She fell.'

'She tripped,' Athelstan countered. 'Once again, you assemble
the household in the refectory and hall. You are busy in the
kitchen baking bread as well as at the wash tub outside. You'd
sent Joycelina to sweep and clean Whitfield's chamber. A macabre
task, a killer cleaning the very chamber where she had committed
murder. Joycelina would, quite rightly, be highly nervous, deeply
apprehensive, wary of her victim's ghost hovering close about
her, fearful that she might be discovered. You told her to clean
the chamber just in case any trace of what you had both plotted
might be found. The gallery is deserted, everyone, including
yourself, is busy below. You had Anna close by,' Athelstan pointed
at the maid, 'quite deliberately so. Young lady,' Athelstan smiled

at Anna, 'you have a most carrying voice; do you remember what happened?'

'Mistress Cheyne had left bread baking in the oven while she and I went outside. I came in. No, she sent me in, that's right. I found the bread burning.' Anna grinned in a display of broken teeth. 'She then told me to go and fetch Joycelina.'

'Why?' Athelstan leaned forward. 'Why did you need Joycelina down here? You had Anna and others to help you. A minor, most insignificant matter, a passing moment of no importance whatsoever except for what you had secretly planned. Joycelina was busy in Whitfield's chamber. You left her there and went downstairs. You had, however, prepared a lure, a snare. On each side of those steep steps leading down from the top gallery stands a newel post. Around one of these you had fastened a piece of twine, just to hang there, unnoticed. Before you continued down, you turned, took this innocent looking piece of twine and fastened it tight around the opposite newel post. The snare is set: those stairs are dangerous enough but you have created a death trap. You return to the kitchen. There is little or no chance of anyone going up those stairs, why should they? The only person coming down would be Joycelina and you wanted her dead.'

'Why should I?'

'To be rid of an accomplice who one day might talk and who would certainly demand at least half of Whitfield's treasure. In the end, Mistress Cheyne, you are a killer, a murderess. You had everything to gain from Joycelina's death and nothing to lose. So,' Athelstan continued, 'we have all this mummery in the kitchen. You allow the bread to burn deliberately, creating a petty affray. You despatch Anna to call Joycelina down. Anna's strident voice probably did little to soothe Joycelina as she cleaned the chamber where she'd committed murder. Summoned to come down urgently, she may even have thought something had gone wrong. Anyway, she hurries from the chamber, catches her ankle on the snare and tumbles to her death. The chances of anyone surviving such a fall, albeit with very serious injuries, would be rare. Joycelina lies dead, murdered. She is no longer a threat to you in any way. During all the hustle and bustle of tending to her corpse, you hasten to the top of the stairs and, with a concealed knife, ensure no trace of that twine remained.'

Athelstan held up his hand. 'Three murders. You tried to make it four. I am sure it was you who watched me wander into the garden and slipped out to release those mastiffs. You will hang, Mistress Cheyne, and deservedly so.' Athelstan paused at the sound of horsemen arriving in the yard outside.

'You have no proof,' Mistress Cheyne taunted. 'No real evidence.'

'Oh, I will find it here and I have this.' Athelstan leaned down, opened his chancery satchel and delicately took out the linen parcel, specially prepared by a cook at the Guildhall. He opened the folds and held up a portion of simnel cake. 'Admittedly,' he moved the piece of food from hand to hand, 'it is now slightly hard, stale.' He half smiled. 'More like stone than food. But,' he sniffed at it, 'still full of poison. When we throw you in a dungeon, Mistress Cheyne, I will put this in the cell next to it and wait for the rats to eat it and die in swift agony. I will have that witnessed and sworn to. I will also arrange for the Golden Oliphant to be scoured. We will eventually find Whitfield's gold and the possessions of both Lebarge and Hawisa.' Athelstan held up the piece of simnel cake. 'Strange that Lebarge, in his excitement, put this down on the floor and forgot it.'

'No, he didn't!' Mistress Cheyne closed her eyes in desperation at her mistake.

'Why not eat some?' Athelstan offered. 'Go on,' he urged. 'You have nothing to fear, surely?'

'You said Lebarge died after eating it. He was poisoned. Hawisa could have done that.'

'So you admit that Hawisa did take a simnel cake to Lebarge at the sanctuary?' Athelstan was determined that the sheer logic of his argument would break this killer. He had trapped the murderer – now he would show her there was no escape. He went and stood over the accused, using his fingers as he emphasized the evidence against her. 'Item, Mistress Cheyne: through Joycelina you knew about the money belt and Whitfield's determination to flee, whatever convoluted plot he was weaving to cover it. Item: on the night before Whitfield died, he was deep in his cups. After all, he had come here to celebrate the Festival of Cokayne. Joycelina, by everyone's admission, cared for him. He would allow her and you into his chamber. Everyone else was sleeping, sottish with drink. The Cokayne Festival was over. The guests were tired and sated whilst you acted the busy hostess, hurrying here and there. Nothing untoward. You are so skilled at that, Mistress Cheyne, using everyday routines to mask murderous intent. Whitfield would let you both stay. After all, drunk as he was, he was only biding his time until he slipped out in the early hours to meet someone, though that does not concern us now.

'Once in that chamber, you had nothing to fear from anyone else, least of all Lebarge, deep in his cups and smitten with Hawisa. Item: by use of wine, potions or the prospect of some sexual game, you persuaded poor, drunken Whitfield to stand on that stool with a noose around his neck and watched him die. You undid his clothing, took the money belt and made ready to leave. Item: soft-footed, you slipped from that chamber taking the key. No one would notice. Who else, belly full of ale and wine, would climb these steep steps to the top gallery? The only person would be a drunken Lebarge, but he had sunk into a deep sleep in his own chamber. You both fled unobserved. Anyone who later approached and knocked on Whitfield's door would receive no answer and conclude the clerk had fallen into a drunken stupor.

'Item: you assumed Lebarge would wake all mawmsy after his drinking bout, eager for his simnel cakes. He and the rest assembled in the refectory. Item: under your direction, Joycelina raised the alarm and you took over. Who would gainsay you as mistress of this house? You have the authority to tell guests and servants what to do. Item: Joycelina, now armed with a key, was secretly despatched to Whitfield's chamber under the guise of some errand. Item: You again, as mistress of the house, take Foxley and the labourers to the top gallery. You make sure Foxley, still befuddled from the previous night's heavy drinking, confirms the door is barred and locked. The ram is used as you shout for Joycelina to join you. Of course, she is hiding inside having ensured that both the eyelet and lock are blocked and the bolts pulled across.

'Item: the door is eventually forced back, bolt and locks snapping; the door built slightly into the wall is pushed open; hanging off its leather hinges, it actually conceals Joycelina. Even if it had snapped off completely, your accomplice stands hidden to

the left in a chamber which is pitch black with no light. Item:
the top gallery is gloomy at the best of times. Foxley, the only
one who now remains with you, has eyes solely for the grim
spectacle of Whitfield's dangling corpse as well as opening that
shuttered window. Terrified, he stumbles across, his boots
creaking the floorboards. All this disguises Joycelina who, in her
soft buskins, slips around the door to stand by you. Let us say
Foxley turned, and why should he? He'd glimpse nothing amiss
except the shadowy outlines of Mistress Cheyne following him
into the chamber with Joycelina beside her. This was logical;
after all, hadn't she been calling for her? That Joycelina had been
in the chamber all the time would never occur to him and, even
if such a remote possibility did, it would be his word against
that of his mistress, not to mention Joycelina.'

Athelstan paused and pushed the piece of simnel cake closer
to her face. 'Of course, this was not enough. You and Joycelina
were determined to silence both Lebarge and Hawisa lest they
come to suspect. Item: you have virtually admitted that Hawisa
went to St Erconwald's with simnel cake. You knew Lebarge had
to eat it and leave no evidence that anyone had come to assist
him lest he forfeit the right to sanctuary. Hawisa would also be
aware of that. She and Lebarge would be most careful and prudent:
their meeting in my darkened church would be brief enough for
the two lovers to reassure each other. After which Lebarge slipped
back to the mercy enclave to die as the poison took effect whilst
Hawisa left the chapel with you, slipping into eternal night. Poor
Lebarge! Poor Hawisa! They truly trusted you. How long that
would have lasted is a matter of speculation. The same is true
of Joycelina. It's only a matter of time before thieves fall out,
assassins even more so. You control this house, Mistress, that is
more than obvious. People come and go when you tell them to.
Joycelina, all agitated, is sent to clean that chamber. You set up
your snare. Everyone else is where they should be. You brought
about Joycelina's extraordinary death by very ordinary, mundane
means: burning bread, the strident summons of a maid, Joycelina's
haste and a simple piece of twine. Well, Mistress?' Athelstan
leaned down. 'That's what the lawyers will argue. What do you
say?'

'I will say no more,' she shouted.

'You will,' Cranston intervened, 'when you are taken to the press yard in Newgate and forced to lie under a huge door. Great iron weights will be placed on top, one after the other, until you confess the truth. Flaxwith, take her out to one of the outhouses, keep her safe until we leave. For the rest,' Cranston drew himself up, hands extended, 'everyone stays here until the Golden Oliphant is searched and the stolen money found. And that,' Cranston gestured at Stretton, 'includes you. If anyone does try to leave they will be arrested or, if they flee, put to the horn as outlaws.'

Athelstan bent down to pick up his chancery satchel. When he felt himself being pushed, he glanced up. Mistress Cheyne, despite being held by two burly bailiffs, had flung herself against him. Now she pulled back, eyes hot with hatred, lips bared in a snarl.

'I have secrets,' she hissed. 'I will proclaim such secrets before the King's Bench, I will . . .'

'Take her away.' Athelstan turned his back on the prisoner. He walked over to Foxley, deep in conversation with one of the ostlers, Mistress Cheyne's curses echoing behind him. The friar plucked at the Master of Horse's sleeve and apologised to the ostler. 'Master Foxley, a word.' Athelstan took him away from the rest, opened his chancery satchel and thrust a small, red-ribboned scroll into Foxley's hand.

'I owe you my life, certainly my health,' the friar murmured. 'You protected a *Domini canis* – a Hound of the Lord,' he explained the Latin pun on the name of his order, 'from other, more dangerous hounds. Now,' Athelstan continued briskly, 'take this, Master Foxley. The day of tribulation will soon be upon us and, whatever you believe, the Lords of the Soil will crush you. No,' Athelstan stepped closer, 'just take the scroll. You saved my life and this will save yours when the Retribution comes and your comrades are fleeing for their lives only to find churches locked and sanctuaries closely guarded. Take this to Blackfriars, my brothers will shelter you. Now . . .' Athelstan turned as Cranston gripped his arm.

'The horsemen we heard earlier, Brother,' the coroner murmured, 'were outriders, Thibault and his henchmen have arrived.'

Foxley duly slipped away. The Golden Hall swiftly emptied as Thibault, slapping leather gauntlets against his thigh, swaggered into the great taproom, Albinus slinking in behind him.

'Spies at the Guildhall,' Cranston whispered, 'Thibault must have been aware that something was afoot.'

'Brother Athelstan! Sir John! So good to see you.' Thibault exchanged the kiss of peace with both, pulling back the quilted leather hood which hid his face. 'I gather a murderess has been caught and your work is done. So,' Thibault gestured to one of the tables, 'appraise me of what has happened. I thought you would have done so earlier, hence my eagerness.' He grinned falsely. 'But here we are and the truth will out.'

Once his soldiers had sealed the doorways, Thibault, with Albinus sitting beside him, listened as the friar tersely explained his conclusions. Thibault betrayed little emotion at Whitfield's intended desertion or Mistress Cheyne's murderous plot. He simply sat, close-faced, interrupting with the occasional question or staring round the Golden Hall as if he was already assessing the true value of this busy brothel.

'I congratulate you, Sir John, Brother Athelstan,' Thibault declared once the explanation had finished. 'And once again, I thank you for your discovery of the Upright Men's plot to seize the towers of certain churches. The arrest and conviction of Malfort and the unmasking of the self-proclaimed Herald of Hell is a magnificent achievement. As for Whitfield,' Thibault grimaced, 'I should have seen the signs. Everything is breaking down, old allegiances are dying, new loyalties being formed as people shift, twist and turn against the coming storm.' He gestured around. 'I will seize this place. Mistress Cheyne committed treason, slaying a royal clerk, so all her property is forfeit.' Thibault's soft, round face twisted into a smirk. 'My men will stay here until Whitfield's gold is found. I also claim that in the name of the Crown. As for the murderous bitch herself . . .' He glanced at Athelstan from the corner of his eye. 'Oh, by the way, I heard about Radegund, but he is no great loss.' The Master of Secrets rose to his feet, beckoning Albinus to join him. 'I will have words with Mistress Cheyne myself. My men will guard the outhouse and everything else here. Sir John, Brother Athelstan, you may stay a little longer. You have told me everything?'

'Everything you should know.' Athelstan smiled back. He'd say nothing about Grindcobbe or Sir John's dramatic meeting with the Queen Mother at Westminster. 'As you said, Master

Thibault, everything is in a state of flux. The killer may be caught but Mistress Cheyne looks for protection from you, claims she knows certain things.'

'Does she now?' Thibault jibed. 'But not as much as you, Athelstan, eh?'

Thibault and Albinus sauntered off, out into the stable yard. Athelstan opened his chancery satchel, took out the little parcel, opened it and offered Cranston some of the simnel cake. The coroner shook his head, produced his miraculous wineskin and took a generous mouthful; he offered it to Athelstan, now munching cheerfully on the simnel cake. For a while they sat in silence, half-listening to the sounds of the household.

'Clever little friar!'

'Not really, Sir John.' Athelstan took a swig from the wineskin and returned it. 'Mistress Cheyne convicted herself by her care and preparations for each murder. In themselves, her actions appeared to be of no importance whatsoever, the sheer humdrum routine of any household. When isolated and scrutinized, they merge into clever preparations for subtle murder: the burning of the bread, sending Anna to call Joycelina . . .' Athelstan broke off as Thibault and Albinus re-entered the hall.

'Mistress Cheyne,' Thibault took his seat patting his jerkin, 'will be committed for summary judgement before the Justices of Oyer and Terminer who now sit in a special commission at the Tower to deal with all attacks on the Crown, its property and servants. She has told me where the money lies hidden so I have commuted her punishment from being burnt alive at Smithfield to a swift hanging on the Tower scaffold. And that will happen before sunset. Throughout the process she will remain gagged and under close custody. So . . .' Thibault turned swiftly as a royal messenger, his scarlet and gold livery coated with dust, burst through the cordon of men-at-arms guarding the door, holding aloft two scrolls of parchment which Thibault seized and took over to the light from the nearest window. He read both and sat down on a stall, whispering a prayer. Athelstan caught the words of *'Jesu Miserere, Jesu Miserere*, Jesus have mercy' repeated a number of times. Intrigued, the friar rose and walked across, Cranston following behind.

'Master Thibault?' The Master of Secrets did not look up but handed both documents to Cranston, who read them swiftly and cursed beneath his breath.

'Sir John?' Athelstan asked.

'Reports from royal watchers,' the coroner murmured, 'at Wodeford in Essex, to the north of Mile End, and a similar one from Ospring on the Canterbury road. The revolt has begun. Two armies, hundreds, perhaps even thousands, of men marching on London. They've unfurled huge red and black banners and issued their proclamations. They intend to destroy the Babylon of Satan and set up the New Jerusalem. God, they say, will punish us for our sins.'

'God does not punish us,' Athelstan replied, staring down at Thibault. 'Our sins do. We have sown the tempest and now we are about to reap the whirlwind.'

The Master of Secrets glanced up. 'You will remember your promise, Brother? My daughter, my beloved Isabella . . .'

Athelstan caught the pleading in this ruthless man's voice.

'I will keep my promise,' the friar replied. 'She will be safe, but will you be?'

Thibault forced a smile. 'I will be in the Tower.'

'Even though your lord and master is moving slowly north?' Cranston leaned down, his face only a few inches from Thibault's. 'The storm is about to break.' Thibault just shrugged. 'You will be in the Tower, Thibault – you, Gaunt's Master of Secrets – but you will not be alone.' Cranston forced a smile. 'Royal serjeants bearing the King's own letter, sealed orders for my Lord of Gaunt. They are on the road now.' Thibault's face went slack. 'Sealed orders,' Cranston hissed, 'instructing Gaunt to hand over his eldest son, Henry of Lancaster. He is to be brought south. He will be lodged with the King, so where Richard goes, Henry goes with him, very, very close.' Cranston lifted his hand, fingers interlaced. 'Close as this, Master Thibault! Even the most skilled of archers could not put an arrow between them.'

'What do you mean?' Thibault's face was pallid, a sheen of sweat prickling his smooth forehead.

'He means,' Athelstan stepped closer, 'that when the storm breaks and the lightning flashes in one corner of heaven to light up the other, we shall all be sheltering under the same tree, Master Thibault.'

AUTHOR'S NOTE

The Herald of Hell is, of course, a work of fiction, but it reflects the conspiracies which engulfed London and the surrounding shires in that fateful summer of 1381. The peasants were well organized. Former veterans of the wars in France, skilled master bowmen flooded back to England eager for further mischief at home. Everyone who has studied the Peasant's Revolt of 1381 comes across the name of one of its principal leaders – Wat Tyler, who has been described by successive generations of history books as an identifiable individual, a captain of the Kentish men as well as those of Essex. In truth, we have virtually no evidence about who Wat Tyler really was, where he came from or what thrust him into leadership. In this *The Herald of Hell* is correct. Local and central records throw no light on this mysterious individual who emerged on the political scene and nearly tipped – and almost murdered – the young King Richard II. If that is the case, and it seems most likely, Tyler may have been secretly managed and supported by more sinister individuals. Certainly Tyler's brutal and sudden end prevented the authorities from finding out exactly who he was and where he came from. Nevertheless, Tyler made no secret of what he intended. The chronicle of Walsingham (and it is from the narrative accounts that we know what we do about Tyler) claimed that the rebel leader did plan the execution of Richard as well as his chief councillors, followed by the sacking and burning of London.

John of Gaunt's behaviour at this critical time is puzzling and highly suspicious. Gaunt, self-styled regent of the kingdom, would be closely appraised of the seething discontent in London and the south. Nevertheless he decided on a military campaign along the Scottish march. This was not necessary. At the time the Scots posed no real threat to England's border; indeed, any crisis could have easily been contained by the powerful Earl of Northumberland, Master of the North, who, as matters turned out, deeply resented Gaunt's interference in his sphere of influence.

The great conspiracy described in the workings of 'The Great Community of the Realm' and the 'Upright Men' represents a political reality. The revolt occurred, bursting out in different places virtually all at the same time, and the Crown was caught totally unprepared. Peasant armies marshalled, banners were raised, proclamations issued and manifestos published. Royal officials in Kent and Essex had little time for counter measures and, in many cases, paid for this mistake with their lives. However, that is another story to be described in the sequel, *The Great Revolt* . . .

Paul Doherty
www.paulcdoherty.com